STORMY COURTSHIP

"It's true, isn't it? Everything I have heard about the brutality of Highlanders is true." Elizabeth's chin raised intrepidly as her courage increased with every word she uttered. "How dare you, Robert Kirkland! How dare you enter my chamber in the middle of the night and terrorize me! The fearsome Highland Lion! What a farce! A blustering bully capable of nothing but brutalizing women!"

Before she could grasp his intent, Elizabeth was imprisoned in his arms. His lips captured hers in a hard, bruising kiss. She struggled to free herself but her efforts were useless against his superior strength and, as the warm pressure of his mouth deepened, she lost awareness of just when she ceased to struggle. She closed her eyes and surrendered to the heady excitement of the kiss. Her body trembled—whether from fear or excitement, she did not know. Her eyes were wide and frightened as she backed away from him.

"Dare I hope, my lady, that you require further persuasion to convince you?" he asked huskily and took a step toward her.

D0685370

These Hallowed Hills

ANA LEIGH

LEISURE BOOKS   ∞   NEW YORK CITY

To Betsy;
a beloved sister,
a cherished friend.

Acknowledgement:

I wish to acknowledge the contribution and help
of my sister, Liz Bacher, in the writing of this
novel. It was a labor of love for us both.

A LEISURE BOOK

Published by

Dorchester Publishing Co., Inc.
6 East 39th Street
New York, NY 10016

Printed in the United States of America

These Hallowed Hills

PREFACE

Thermopylae, Balaklava, Borodino, Gettysburg—names and battles that historians would pen into immortality. Military tacticians would restage again and again on paper these victories or defeats, depending on which side one's sentiments rested, to determine the scope of the battlesite, the daring of the attackers, or the courage of the defenders.

Writers of history would thrill to the defense of a mountain pass by three hundred courageous Spartans, mourn the tragic charge of six hundred doomed Light Brigaders on a Crimean battlefield, or ponder the resolution of the French or the tenaciousness of the Russians in their bloody struggle over a village near Moscow. Historians all over the world would weep as they resurrected the bloodbath of over forty thousand Americans in the foothills of Pennsylvania. Over and over these battles would be refought to try to determine how a relief column, a stray bullet, or a daring maneuver might have changed the outcome of the battles—thus altering the tide of history.

These same scribes of history, these guardians of truth who separate fact from fantasy, rank the battle of Dundee on an April day in 1645 as one of history's greatest military achievements.

In combat, where statistics are measured by a bloody and fallen body count, what made this campaign a remarkable military marvel is one simple fact. Due to the brilliant strategy and benign humanity of James Graham, an enemy force was engaged, a walled city was besieged and conquered, a superior reinforcement force was evaded—and *all* while successfully avoiding the loss of a single human life in either army.

Ana Leigh

PROLOGUE

February 1638

The tinkle of the bell above the door interrupted the concentration of the goldsmith who was busy at his task; with a disgruntled scowl, he furtively slipped the gem he was polishing beneath some heaped papers on his workbench. He swung around, and his irritation changed to a gleam of anticipation with the sight of the two men in the store.

There was not a man or boy in all of Edinburgh who did not recognize The Graham on sight. James Graham, the twenty-six year old Earl of Montrose, was chief of the prosperous Graham clan and one of the wealthiest men in Scotland.

The goldsmith smiled as he remembered the sizeable profit he had made the previous year, when The Graham had commissioned him to decorate his crossbow with mother-of-pearl inlay. Indeed! Maybe a similar task was needed, he thought hopefully, anticipating a fresh heap of gold coins in his coffer.

"Good day, my lord," he greeted, his eyes taking in the elegant and fastidious detail of

Graham's appearance, from the Meclin lace of his ruff to the skilled Italian craftsmanship of his sword and gilded spurs. Gilded spurs! he thought enviously. What a pretty pound they would have brought!

James Graham was aware of the goldsmith's close inspection. Easygoing and aesthetically sensitive by nature, he was unperturbed by the perusal and flashed a friendly grin at the shopkeeper.

"Good day, Ian Ogilvy. Lord Ashley has need of your very skillful services."

The young Lord Ashley, Robert Kirkland, stood silently in the darkened corner of the room listening to the verbal exchange between the two men. He saw the goldsmith begin to preen under Jamie's sincere flattery. This was not an unusual sight to Robert, for he had often watched Jamie weave his captivating spell.

A born leader, with the ability to make swift and sound judgments, James Graham inspired the confidence and loyalty of all those around him because of his genuine sincerity. None knew better than Robert that Jamie not only believed, but practiced the virtues he espoused—loyalty, truth, honor and generosity.

The shopkeeper's attention swung to Robert, whom he eyed with an avid curiosity, for the man's reputation had preceded him. Robert Kirkland was a renowned professional soldier. Dubbed "The Highland Lion" by his friends and foes, he was fearless in battle and his mastery of the broadsword was legendary.

Sent to the Grahams' at the age of ten for a five-year fosterage, Robert had immediately worshipped James Graham, who had been five years his senior and already an earl.

The two men's love and loyalty for each other made them as close as brothers, and everyone knew that who ever would attempt to harm one unavoidably would have to reckon with the other.

"How may I service you, Lord Ashley?" Ogilvy asked eagerly.

Robert Kirkland stepped out of the shadows and for the first time the goldsmith was able to observe the man completely. He had an essence that dominated the small room, even in the company of The Graham, whose own presence was usually quite intimidating. Unlike the fastidiously clad Graham, the goldsmith observed that the Highlander was dressed casually in breeks and a white shirt. Yet he wore them with such a detached elegance and moved with such lithesome grace, that they could have been the velvet robes of the king himself.

"I seek a gift for a young lady," Robert said. He cast a nervous sideward glance in the direction of Jamie, dreading his reaction.

Naturally it would be for a young lady, the goldsmith reasoned at the sight of the handsome figure. A bauble, no doubt, for favors rendered, he thought lewdly.

"Aha! I have the very thing you seek," Ian Ogilvy declared with a sly wink. He had in mind an unclaimed ring in his safe that had been commissioned by an old lord who had unfortunately died from heart failure before he could give it to his young mistress. He took a glittering ring of diamonds out of his safe.

Robert did not even pick up the jeweled ring to examine it. He shook his head, declining it. "I seek something less ostentatious."

"Emeralds would be lovely on Mademoiselle du Plessis," Jamie suggested.

Robert grimaced in disapproval. "It's not for Desireé. I seek a birthday gift for my betrothed, Lady Elizabeth."

Jamie chuckled in delight. "Of course! I forgot. How old is your future bride now, Robert?"

Robert sighed and braced himself for Jamie's teasing. His resentment of the marriage contract his father had made for him was common knowledge to all of Robert's friends. However, he would not disgrace his father's honor by not accepting it. He could only attempt to stay the miserable event as long as it was humanly possible.

"I think a small dirk would be appropriate for a twelve-year-old," Robert declared.

"Are you not afraid the poor child will slit her throat with it at the prospect of marrying you?" Jamie asked facetiously.

Robert's brow quirked in sufferance at Jamie's raillery. "If she doesn't do it, Desiree will probably do it for her," he intoned dryly.

Jamie laughed and swatted him on the back. "Then I would also suggest a small bauble for Desireé."

"No doubt. I suppose you would suggest I

buy a rare stone for every woman I bed," Robert grumbled.

"Not at all! If that were the cause, the demand would be greater than the supply," Jamie joshed.

The goldsmith returned with a small pouch of precious gems and Robert selected several for the shaft of the knife.

"I will have it completed two days hence," Ogilvy promised as Robert and Jamie turned to depart.

"Oh, hell!" Robert growled, turning back to the goldsmith. "I'll take the damned ring, too!" He threw a pouch of coins on the table and snatched up the shiny ring.

Jamie was laughing convulsively as they stepped out on the cobblestone wynd where their horses were tethered. He crossed to his stallion and began to idly pat its head.

"Charles has summoned me to court, Robbie. He fears the unrest among the Covenanters."

"He should," Robert scoffed. "The new Prayer Book he is forcing on Scotland is tyrannical."

"Come with me to Whitehall, Robbie. Let him hear how the Highlanders feel about it. You know, as well as I, that he is being ill-advised on this issue."

"Nae, Jamie, I have promised my father I would return to Ashkirk. You would be wise to come with me." He shook his head sadly. "Oh, Jamie, it is dangerous and foolhardy to get involved with the affairs of the Stuart crown."

"I would die to preserve the Stuart crown, Robbie," Graham answered earnestly, reaching into his saddlebag and extracting a handful of small pieces of bread. One by one he began to feed them to his horse.

Robert watched him with a smile of affection, before he finally swung his long body into his saddle. "When are you going to stop feeding that horse bread and ale?"

"Do not scoff, youngster, it works," James Graham declared with a tolerant grin as he mounted his steed. "He has never lost a race yet."

"Well, he's about to," Robert challenged. "The last man to the inn buys the ale."

With a flurry of flying hooves the two horses and their riders galloped down the road.

I

May 1644

It was not vanity that convinced the Lady Elizabeth Scott that she looked particularly fetching as she descended the stairway of Ballantine, her pink gown swirling in folds about her. Elizabeth was alive with an inner feeling of beauty that comes as a result of happiness and contentment.

The strains of the music reached her ears and her round brown eyes gleamed with a bright sparkle of excitement and anticipation. This same radiance gave an added luster to a face that nature had long before molded into perfection.

The dark hair piled high on her head had been painstakingly converted into a mass of tiny curls, which tended to bounce enticingly as she skipped gaily down the stairs.

Elizabeth paused in the entrance of the Grand Hall, her eyes sweeping the room full of people who had gathered to celebrate her eighteenth birthday. Her cousin, Anne Barday, noted her appearance and, arms outstretched, was the first to greet her.

"Happy Birthday, Beth," Anne enthused, hugging her warmly and placing a kiss on her cheek.

Elizabeth stepped back to admire her beloved cousin and companion since childhood. The blonde delicacy of Anne's lovely patrician beauty was enhanced by the pale green brocade of her gown.

"Thank you, Anne. You look lovely. I fear, after seeing you, none of these young men will even notice me—and this is supposed to be my evening," Elizabeth teased with feigned rancor.

Anne responded with a tinkle of soft laughter. "That will hardly be the case, cousin dear, because here comes one of your most ardent admirers right now." With a conspiratorial wink, Anne moved away.

Elizabeth turned her welcoming smile to the young man who approached her. Walter Campbell was the nephew of the politically powerful Duke of Argyll. For years, Campbell had been courting Elizabeth in the hopes of winning her hand in marriage.

"Lady Elizabeth, your beauty increases with each passing day," he declared with an elegant bow.

"Why Lord Craver, how gallant of you," Elizabeth replied, as she extended her hand.

Walter Campbell raised the offered hand to his lips, his eyes locked adoringly on her. "Your most obedient servant, my lady."

"How kind of you to help celebrate my birthday."

Reaching into the folds of his satin doublet, he extracted a narrow box of velvet.

"Happy birthday, Elizabeth. Will you accept this small token of my esteem?"

"Why, Walter, how thoughtful."

Elizabeth's eyes glowed with excitement as she opened the slim box. Tucked amidst the satin lining was a delicately carved fan with an ivory handle. With an adroit flick of her wrist, Elizabeth spread the pattern of pale pink roses that were painted on the white silken folds, bringing it to her face. Her long lashes fluttered coquettishly above it, her round brown eyes a warm and enticing invitation.

"What a shame, my lady, that such a lovely design must go for naught. For truly, there is no one that would not be blinded to everything except the mahogany depths of those velvet orbs."

His fervent declaration was followed by Elizabeth's titilating soft laughter. "I fear, Lord Craver, you have muddled my poor mind. For I know not if I appear as some celestial sphere in the heavens or the dependable solidity of an over-stuffed chair."

Campbell grasped her shoulders in annoyance. "Do not mock me, Elizabeth. Is it not enough that half of Scotland knows how I dangle at the end of your rope!"

Elizabeth pressed a kiss to his check. "Oh, Walter, I only jest with you. Your gift is lovely and I will cherish it always."

His vanity soothed, Walter Campbell took

her arm and they proceeded to walk among the guests. Elizabeth smiled and nodded graciously, acknowledging the many offers of well-wishings and congratulations, until their progress was halted by a thin, dark-headed young man.

"Happy Birthday, Lady Elizabeth," the young man proffered with a shy smile.

"Thank you, Sir William. I am so happy you came to share this evening with us."

"May I have the pleasure of this dance, my lady?"

"Can you not see that the Lady Elizabeth is already occupied?" Walter Campbell flared angrily.

The young man's eyes clouded in embarrassment. "I do apologize, my lady. You will excuse me." With that, he hurried off in nervous agitation.

Elizabeth found herself provoked to anger at Campbell's rudeness and jealous possessiveness.

"Walter, I tire of these incessant displays of petty jealousy. William Campbell is your own cousin, and he is a sensitive and shy young man. There was no excuse for your boorish conduct. I am not wed to you, therefore, I will decide whom I dance with."

"We will be wed one day, Elizabeth."

"You know I am betrothed to Lord Ashley."

"Ha! You put no more worth to that contract than I do. Has he even bothered to visit you through the years? Now, with Scotland divided by a civil war, the Highlands are nothing more than a bed of rebels and insurgents such as Montrose. Your father would never insist you honor such a contract."

"Whatever may be, the decision remains my father's—not yours, Walter."

With a swirl of skirt Elizabeth stormed angrily away, leaving the young man standing alone, his smoldering gaze following her.

Elizabeth's anger quickly dissipated at the sight of her father standing across the room. She frowned with anxiety. Could he be ailing? For over a week she had noticed a change in him. His step seemed slower, his smile never seeming to reach his eyes. Often she caught his gaze upon her, his expression one of sadness and wistfulness. Perhaps his worry was over her brother, Andrew, away at the war, she thought.

Elizabeth walked to his side and pressed a kiss to his cheek. The Earl of Ballantine put a protective arm around his daughter's shoulders and hugged her to his side.

"Are you enjoying your birthday party, my dear?"

With open adoration Elizabeth looked up into the still handsome face of her father. "Oh yes, Father, thank you so much. It is a lovely party, but I do wish Andrew were here to share it with me. It is the first time we have not celebrated our birthdays together."

The smile on the earl's face was replaced with a pensive frown. "I fear now that you two have reached adulthood, the journeys of your lives will begin to lead you both down many more separate paths."

"Nonsense, Father," Elizabeth admonished. "The three of us will always be together. Now you erase that gloom from your face or I fear you shall spoil my evening."

Alexander Scott smiled indulgently, unable to resist her captivating gaity. "Come with me, Beth, to the library."

Once removed from the revelry, in the austere setting of the library with its walls lined with heavy tomes, the earl crossed to unlock the drop-front of his desk. He quickly removed a package and handed it to her.

"For you, Beth, from Andrew. Before leaving he gave it to me to give to you this evening."

Her excitement mounting, Elizabeth opened the gift from her twin brother. The package contained a folded square of Spanish lace and a pearl pin to hold it to her hair.

"How lovely!" Elizabeth exclaimed, her eyes brimming. "I will wear it when I go to the Kirk."

Lord Scott extracted another box from the desk and hesitantly gave it to her. "From your betrothed, Lord Ashley."

Her anger began to rise at the mention of Robert Kirkland's name, and eyes that moments before had been overflowing with love and affection now narrowed to loathing and scorn.

"Oh, the annual token demonstration of the all-consuming regard of my elusive betrothed. What a mockery! I am certain it is not my future groom that sends these gifts, but his father. I venture to say Lord Ashley has no knowledge of my birth date and concerns himself less. He is much too occupied bestowing trinkets on his mistress."

"Elizabeth, such talk does not become you. I hoped I had raised you to practice gracious amenities. A gentle lady would not refer to her betrothed's mistress in public."

"Oh, excuse me, Father! Forgive my lack of refinement," Elizabeth flared sarcastically. "How indelicate of me to mention the fact that Lord Ashley blatantly flaunts his French whore publicly, while I, his future bride, must sit docilely by awaiting his summons."

As she spoke, Elizabeth angrily tore open the package. Her eyes widened and she gasped in surprise at the sight of the tiny brooch within.

An intricately carved cameo of creamy white ivory was set in a backing of pale green jade. Meticulous detail had been given to the dainty carving so that it now duplicated the delicate profile of her mother.

"What a thoughtful, exquisite gift," Elizabeth half-whispered with complete abashment. "I should return to our guests," she stammered, fighting for composure, and quickly turned and departed the room.

The Earl of Ballantine slowly reached into his desk and removed a letter that had accompanied the gift. Once again he read the missive from his old friend Michael Kirkland. Shoulders slumped in dejection, he walked to the fireplace and leaned his head against its marbled mantel. For a long time he stood pondering its message, the letter held absently in his hand.

"Robert, when are you ever going to cease this wandering and come home to remain?"

The Earl of Kirkwood, the sovereign leader of the Kirkland clan, frowned with frustration, then condemnation, as he studied the tall figure of his son.

"Father, I serve no purpose at Ashkirk. You tend to the needs of the clan, and David sees to our ships. I am a soldier—and a good one. James Graham is in need of such men."

"I do not deny your ability, Robert, but if Jamie needed you as a groom, you would leap to the task. I fear I made a grievous mistake when I sent you to the Grahams for fosterage. It appears they gained a son—while I lost one."

Robert's eyes mirrored his distress. He loved and respected his father, but this was an issue over which they had argued often in the last few years.

"It hurts me to hear you voice such thoughts," Robert protested. "I love Jamie, but my loyalty is to you first, above any other."

With a desolate sigh Lord Kirkland sank into a chair. "Aye, Robert, I know this is true. Forgive me, son, for I fear my ranting rests upon envious prattle." He sighed deeply. "But I fear for your life, Robert. Jamie is embarking on a dangerous and desperate venture in attempting to raise a Scottish army. I can only forsee a disastrous outcome."

"I almost agree with you, Father. Unfortunately, King Charles asked Jamie for his help, and James Graham is so dedicated to the King that he is willing to sacrifice everything he owns for him."

The Earl of Kirkwood swung a sharp glance upward at his son. "Is he willing to sacrifice his life? I am afraid he will be doing just that, Robert." His face deepened in sadness. "However, I fear it will be many more lives other than just his own. Yours will be one of them."

Robert tried to mask the frustration he was suffering. "Father, I respect your judgment. I have done so my whole life. Why are you so certain Jamie will lose this fight?"

"Because it is impossible for Charles to win it. The Royalist forces cannot defeat Cromwell. He is too powerful. The evils of the English crown have been mounting for years. There were enough civil injustices without raising the religious issues. Cromwell knew that by trying to implicate Charles in accusations of Papist conspiracies, that fool Argyll would raise an army of Scottish Covenanters against the King."

"Charles is King of Scotland," Robert protested. "He is a Stuart. He not only sits on the English throne, but wears a Scot crown as well. As Scots, Argyll and the Covenanters' loyalties should be to Charles. The loyalties of all the clans should be to the King. Jamie is attempting to unite all of us and aid Charles. If he must, he is willing to die in that attempt."

"That is why I fear for you, Robert. You are

my son and heir. One day the task of governing the clan will rest on your shoulders."

Robert listened grimly to his father, knowing that his responsibility to his clan would someday have to supplant his allegiance to James Graham.

"If Cromwell wins this war, Father, he will set up a puppet government under Argyll here in Scotland. It will mean the end of religious freedom to us Scots. Do you want to see that day? Good Lord, Father, some of our own Kirkland clansmen still cling to the old Roman faith. This is true of most of the Highland clans. Are we to just abandon them to the bigotry of Argyll and Cromwell? Nae, Father, I know you too well to believe you would sanction such an act. This argument has a false ring to it. I suspect another motive as well behind your objections."

The Earl of Kirkwood grimaced with defeat. "I am afraid the son's cleverness exceeds his sire's. I do have another motive—an entirely selfish one. It is time you were wed and settled down, Robert. Your betrothed, Lady Elizabeth, has just turned eighteen. The time has come to honor the marriage contract that was entered into at her birth."

"I have no desire to wed as yet. Particularly to some Lowland Sassenach!"

Lord Kirkland rose angrily to his feet. "I insist you wed now, Robert. I will not tolerate any further defiance on this issue. I have been patient with you, but your obstinacy tries my patience."

His dark eyes flashed angrily and the authoritive determination that had made him an undisputed chief of his clan was in evidence on the still-handsome face. Robert's own dark eyes did not waver but met his father's with the same steadfast tenacity.

"In what way, Father? How have I defied you? Because I choose to follow James Graham? Because I do not wish to leap into a marriage about which I had naught to say?"

"Lady Elizabeth has been of marriageable age for several years now. In that time you have been consorting openly with Mademoiselle du Plessis, even bringing her here with you at this time to Ashkirk. You are making that innocent child at Ballantine appear a simpleton."

"That innocent child at Ballantine?" Robert scoffed. "From what I remember from my one visit there, that 'innocent child' was a spoiled brat, who was doted upon by everyone. She should have been put across someone's lap and soundly thrashed."

"Robert, you shame me with such talk. I had hoped I had instilled some degree of gallantry in you, or perhaps through your close association with James Graham some of his gracious manner would have rubbed off on you. However, I can see this is not to be. To speak of your future wife in such a derogatory fashion dishonors you. Was she not just a lass of five when you visited Ballantine? How can you presume to judge her now? You disappoint me, son."

Lord Kirkland knew that his last statement

was in the nature of being quite hyperbolic. Were the truth known, Robert's spirit and independence were a source of parental pride to a father who had raised his two sons to think for themselves. As much as Lord Kirkland feared for his eldest son's safety, the tales of Robert's daring and courage on the battlefield caused him to swell with pride.

For the Earl of Kirkwood was a Highlander —and, as such, his heritage necessitated the need for a cunning mind, stout heart, swift foot, and, above all, *a strong arm with the broadsword!*

Robert sighed, shrugging his shoulders in resignation. Nothing would be gained by continuing to postpone the damned wedding. It certainly did not warrant a rift to develop between his father and himself.

"Very well, Father. I will no longer delay this marriage. Make the wedding arrangements. I certainly cannot show my face at Ballantine, since Argyll has put his personal bounty on the head of Jamie and myself. I will marry the Lady Elizabeth as soon as she arrives here."

Lord Kirkland could not conceal the self-complacent smile of pleasure that covered his distinguished face. "Then you will remain at Ashkirk awaiting her arrival?"

A grin tugged at the corner of Robert's mouth. "Oh, no, you wily old fox," he declared, as he hugged his father affectionately, "you do not win that argument, too. I promised Montrose I would return to him. Send me a missive when my bride-to-be arrives here. I will return home for the marriage."

A worried frown creased the brow of the Earl of Kirkwood as he took the hand of his son in a warm grasp.

"Take care, Robert. And God be with you and Jamie Graham."

II

The following week the Earl of Kirkwood's fears would have been well-founded had he witnessed the conversation at the castle of Montrose's cousin, Patrick Graham.

The swarthy countenance of Patrick Graham betrayed the anxiety he was suffering, while James Graham's remained calm and unperturbed. While silently listening to the two men, Robert Kirkland brought a hand to his mouth to stifle a yawn. He and Jamie had ridden all of the previous day and night to reach Inchbrakie. At the moment he was thinking of how comforting it would feel to sink into the softness of a feather mattress.

Pate Graham's voice rose in frustration as he tried to reason with Jamie that his fervid dedication to the King was blinding him to the hopelessness of trying to raise a Scottish army to aid Charles—particularly since the Duke of Argyll had pledged the Campbell clan to the support of Cromwell.

Montrose raised his hand in a restraining gesture to halt Pate's tirade. "We must not challenge our monarchs' motives, my friends. For hundreds of years they have governed us wisely and well. It is they who are the care-takers of our justice and freedom, and it is their banners and wisdom that have preserved our liberties from the many nations that have eyed our isles. They are born to govern. It is their legacy. A crown would not rest well on the vulturous head of an Argyll, nor wouldst the throne support the bearish weight of a Cromwell for too long without toppling. Can you not see that a kingdom gained by the spilling of Stuart blood would continue its seepage until we all are bled?" he declared fervently.

"I have dwelled on this matter for a lengthy time, Pate," Jamie argued. "If the Mac-Donalds from Ireland join us, you know that the Scot MacDonalds will soon follow. Their hatred of the Campbells runs deep. They will always fight to regain the land that Argyll and his Campbells have taken from them."

Patrick Graham threw his arms up in the air in utter frustration. "One clan, Jamie! One clan! And I doubt they will be willing to cross the English border even if you would succeed in driving Argyll out of Scotland. Though how you expect to accomplish that feat I'll never know," Pate fumed in exasperation. "The Campbells completely dominate the West. You will need all the clans to help you."

"Trust me, my friend," Jamie assured him confidently. He turned to Robert with a wide grin. "He underestimates my persuasive tongue, doesn't he, Robbie?"

Patrick Graham and Robert exchanged

understanding glances. Both of these men adored this young Marquis of Montrose and would have done anything for him.

"I certainly would be the last one to ever doubt your persuasiveness, Jamie," Robert laughed. "I have not quite determined what I am doing here myself."

"Nae, nor I," Montrose exclaimed, highly buoyed with enthusiasm. "How did an intelligent man like myself ever put himself into a position of depending upon a heathen Highlander!" Montrose became sober, the jocundity erased from his face, and he reached out to place a strong hand on Robert's shoulder. "I will always need your skilled arm and stout heart, Robbie. With you beside me I need never fear some errant sword will find my back."

"I would follow you into the fires of hell, Jamie, and you know it," Robert sighed, with a complacent shrug of his shoulders.

"And you may be sure, Robbie, that the devil, himself, will be wearing a Campbell plaid," Montrose said, grinning.

They were interrupted by one of the Graham servants announcing the arrival of a stranger seeking Patrick Graham. At the intimidating appearance of the man who strode boldly into the room, Robert rose to his feet, his hand instinctively sliding to the hilt of his sword. The young man easily stood nine or ten inches above six feet. A curly shock of red hair covered his head and a large moustache of the same hue drooped generously from his freckled face. His dress was simple. The long piece of woven plaid, that no Highlander ever traveled without, was belted at his waist and fell in folds to his knees, the end pinned across the broad shoulders that were covered by a white shirt with flowing sleeves. Laced sheepskin buskins reached the muscular calves of his long legs, and a claymore dangled from the scabbard at his side.

Pate Graham's expression was wary as he rose to his feet. "Patrick Graham, sir. How might I serve you?"

The young giant nodded his head in a slight gesture of acknowledgement. "Sir, I hae be' told ye cud direct me to the Marquis o' Montrose."

Robert and James exchanged startled glances, but Patrick Graham's unwavering gaze remained fixed on the stranger.

"You are not alone in that request, stranger. There are many who covet that knowledge. The price rests highly on the head of James Graham. Who are you? For what purpose do you seek him?"

"Sir, I be Alistair MacDonald. I canna tarry as I mus' return to my men. Will ye gie a missive to yer kinsman?"

With a whoop of delight Montrose jumped to his feet. Alistair MacDonald was a famous and immensely popular Irish chieftain. Though only twenty-five, he had already distinguished himself as a valiant and competent warrior. Montrose embraced the startled Irishman and identified himself. MacDonald broke into a smile of relief.

"At last you have arrived," Montrose sighed. "How big is your force?"

"We are eleven hundred, sir, plus our women and bairns."

"Eleven hundred!" Montrose exclaimed with undisguised disappointment. "Lord Antrim promised the King ten thousand men."

"Did you say you have brought camp followers?" Pate Graham asked in disgust.

The young MacDonald's eyes flared resentfully. "They are no' camp followers, gentlem'. They are ou' wives an' children. We hae also brough' ou' cattle and stock."

He turned to Montrose in a capricious change of mood. "We may be late in arrivin', General, bu' we hae come to stay. Dinna fret a' ou' number 'til ye see wha' eleven hundred MacDonalds ca' accomplish wi' claymore an' dirk."

"The claymore is also the weapon of we Highlanders," Robert intoned ominously, "and we pride ourselves on our usage of it."

For the first time since entering the room MacDonald turned to study Robert. His brow quirked in annoyance.

"This is Lord Ashley, one of my officers," Montrose said with a quick introduction.

The tension hung heavily in the room. The Irish commander had heard of the exploits of the famed "Highland Lion," and the two young men's eyes locked, as they appraised one another.

"Ye forget, Lord Ashley, we ar' Highlanders too," MacDonald said, and grudgingly the two young warriors exchanged understanding smiles of mutual respect and acceptance.

A map of Scotland made a hasty appearance and within minutes they stood pondering over it.

"We ar' camped a' Badenock," MacDonald said, pointing to a site on the map. "The' be Campbells a' ou' backs."

Montrose studied the terrain carefully. With his ability to make instant decisions, and displaying his gifted military genius, he ordered MacDonald to the hillside of Blair Atholl.

Two days later, if one were to believe in the efficacy of amulets and talismen, the dazzling brilliance of the morning sun on the Scottish hilltop appeared to be an embolden sign from God to Alistair MacDonald, known as Cokitto to most, as he stood on the slope of Blair Atholl awaiting the arrival of James Graham. He gazed with reverent pride at the pastoral beauty around him. The river Tilt rushed eagerly downward from the barren peaks of Atholl, merging with the river Garry, to flow gracefully through a resplendent valley of green meadow and purple heather. Though raised in Ireland, this was his homeland— the country his people had been driven from. His father, even now, was still a prisoner in a dungeon of one of Argyll's castles.

The valley had turned into a colorful array of Robertson and Stewart plaids, after Montrose had persuaded the eight hundred men of those two clans to join them.

Suddenly cheers and shouts rose from the ranks as Jamie rode into the valley. A guard of honor quickly formed to greet him. Those among his men who had muskets raised them in the air and fired a resounding volley that echoed through the valley in a thunderous salute for the King's General in Scotland.

"Hail Mary, Mother of God, pray for us sinners," MacDonald intoned making a quick sign of the cross, as he shook his head with affectionate indulgence. "The crazy bastards hae jus' used up the las' o' their ammunition!"

In a short time Montrose gathered all the chieftains together.

"I know these Highland hills like the halls of my own home. I have hunted in them since I was a child. There are dozens of places that can shroud and conceal an army. We will choose our target and strike their garrisons swiftly, when and where they least expect it. At this time I have nothing to offer those of you who have joined us. I have been stripped of my title and estates. I have no money or arms, but these hills are full of friends who will help us."

Jamie paused, studying the reaction on the faces surrounding him.

"What is here now is my army. My weapons are the enthusiasm, courage and stout hearts of the Highlanders who fight with me."

A seasoned soldier would probably have

scoffed at the bagatelle army that began its march toward Perth that day. Its only uniform was a cockade of yellow oats stuck in the Highland bonnets, its weaponry, merely the broadswords and dirks worn at the sides of its soldiers. And those fortunate among the Highland clans to have muskets had little ammunition with which to use them. The evident lack of cannon was superfluous, for there were no horses to pull them anyway.

And behind the army trailed the women and children—driving their cattle before them.

III

"Hurry up or Artle will be gone before we get there," Elizabeth urged her cousin as they moved deeper into the dark shadows of the forest.

For days Elizabeth had been watching Artle closely to make sure she would not miss the moment when the old crone slipped away from the castle. When that time had come, Elizabeth persuaded Anne to accompany her when she decided to follow the old woman.

Anne's courage, however, was beginning to falter with every step she took. "I don't think this is a very wise thing to do," her cousin said nervously. "We really shouldn't stray this far from the keep without some protection."

"There's nothing to be afraid of," Elizabeth reassured her. "Artle comes here all the time and nobody harms her."

"Who would harm that old witch?" Anne scoffed. "She would probably put a black spell upon anyone who would try."

"We have nothing to worry about. I have my dirk with me." Elizabeth's hand slid to the tiny scabbard attached to the waist of her gown.

"I don't think that would be very much protection," Anne countered. "If any robbers would see it, they would probably slit our throats just to get their hands on it. It must be worth a fortune!"

"Oh, twiddle," Elizabeth exclaimed, brushing aside the fears Anne had planted. "What would robbers be doing this deep in the forest?"

"Are you certain you know where we're going? What does Artle come here for, anyway?"

Elizabeth's round eyes flashed mischievously. "Andrew and I followed her once when we were younger. She comes here to collect the herbs she needs for her potions."

"Why do we have to come way out here? Couldn't she tell you what you want to know at the castle?"

"You know Father has forbidden her to practice her witchcraft at the castle. He told her he would burn her at the stake if he ever caught her at it."

"That's ridiculous!" Anne admonished. "Uncle Alexander would never do such a thing."

"I know that, and so do you," Elizabeth giggled, "but Artle doesn't." The two girls broke into maidenly laughter at the thought of anyone being foolish enough to harbor such an outrageous belief.

A few moments later Elizabeth halted them at the entrance of a small cave. It appeared eerie and sinister to the two girls as they tried to peer into the darkened interior.

"I don't think we should go in there," Anne declared, as she hung back at the entrance. "Please, Beth, let's go back to the keep."

Elizabeth was as frightened as her cousin, but she had come this far and was not about to turn back. "Oh, don't be such a coward," she scolded. She took Anne's hand and practically pulled the frightened girl into the grotto.

After a few scary seconds, the girls' eyes adjusted to the dim light. The walls were lined with bottles containing strange cultures growing inside of them. Lichen trailed in the cracks and crevices and along the floor of the cave. Wispy, gossamer webs were strung wherever possible and the powder from pulverized bones was heaped to overflowing in a glass vessel. Feathers from dozens of different species of birds were strung on the wall.

"She really is an old witch, isn't she?" Elizabeth whispered to Anne.

A shrill cackle came from the darkened corner of the cave, causing both women to jump in fright. Anne screamed and clutched Elizabeth's hand. Artle, an aged and withered hag, sat on the floor watching them.

"So! Ye two pesty twits hae follow'd ol' Artle," she screeched. She emitted another piercing cackle that was enough to freeze the blood in their veins. Anne clutched Elizabeth's hand tighter, her whole body trembling with fear.

Elizabeth wanted to bolt and run as fast as her legs would carry her, but she forced herself to face the old woman. This is ridiculous! she told herself. You see this old hag every day. There is nothing to be frightened about. The old crone is just making sport of us.

She stamped her foot angrily in a show of bravado. "You stop this foolish act at once, Artle. I have come seeking your services."

The aged face creased into a wily, toothless grin. "Aha! So ye hae need fo' ol' Artle."

The old woman got slowly to her feet and the girls watched in fascination to see what she intended to do next. In a short time she had lit some tow and had a fire started.

The cave appeared more sinister in the dim light cast by the fire and Elizabeth shuddered in revulsion as she peered around at the bizarre collection. "Do you actually use all of this?" she asked in disgust.

"Aye, lass. The' be much healin' in the bones an' innards of the forest's li'l critters. Ye nae hae me use the remains o' one of ou' own depart'd, wud ye?"

"Of course not," Elizabeth declared indignantly. "Though I would not doubt that you haven't tried it."

The accusation caused Artle to break into another one of her shrill shrieks of laughter, and Anne whispered, "For heaven's sake, Beth, get on with your business so we can get out of here."

"Ah' jus' wha' business migh' tha' be, mistress?" the old woman asked.

"I want you to conjure a vision of a man and tell me what lies ahead for me with him."

"Och! So 'tis a lad that brings th' young

mistress to this place!" She motioned for the two girls to join her at the fire.

"Wel' now, hae ye a lock o' the lad's hair?"

"No," Elizabeth replied.

"Wel', how abou' a shavin' of his nails?"

"I haven't that either," Elizabeth replied, distressed.

The old crone broke into a wicked grin and her eyes flashed lewdly. "Wud ye be havin' a drop o' his spilled seed, so's I ca' tell if ye be luck' enough to hae a lusty stallion mountin' ye?"

Elizabeth flamed with embarrassment from the hot flush that swept her body. "You know I don't, you dirty old woman!"

Artle leaned back in disgust. "Wel', jus' wha' do ye hae o' the lad's? It mus' be somethin' he hae worn or touched."

Elizabeth reached into a pouch she had attached to her clothing and took out the fan that Walter Campbell had given her for her birthday. She handed Artle the fan along with the dirk that had been sent to her by Robert Kirkland years before.

Artle closed her eyes, holding the two items in her hands. She sat before the fire swaying slowly back and forth chanting a mysterious incantation.

"Beasties and feinns, kelpies and trolls,
Brownies and glastigs, bogles and trows.
Fan of silk or knife of steel,
Be ye false, or be ye real?
Demon below, or saint above,
Which is the face of my lady's love?"

Elizabeth and Anne watched with rapt expressions as Artle was drawn deeper and deeper into a trance. Neither spoke, in fear of breaking the spell the old woman had woven. Several moments passed, and Elizabeth thought she would burst from suspense. Suddenly the chanting stopped and Artle opened her eyes. She handed the fan to Elizabeth as though it were burning her palm.

"Beware, me sweet, for I see this fannin' fires of treachery aroun' ye."

Elizabeth could barely free the words from her throat. "And the dirk?"

"Twill pierce yer hear', bu' ye willna bleed, fo' yer destiny lies wher' the heather grows white. Now off wit' ye, fo' I hae much to do an' I canna do it wit' the likes of two such squeamish lasses."

Elizabeth said little as they trudged homeward, her mind pondering Artle's perplexing message.

"Have you ever seen any white heather before, Anne?"

Anne smiled in understanding and shook her head. Before her cousin could say anything Elizabeth added, "And how can a knife piece your heart and not cause you to bleed? Oh, Anne," she sighed deeply, "I'm more confused now than I've ever been."

IV

"How can you, Father? How can you turn me over to a horde of barbarians?" Elizabeth raved with injured incredulity.

"Really, Elizabeth, Lord Kirkland is a close and dear friend. We attended school together and served at the court of James the Sixth. Your own mother was a distant cousin of his wife. You can hardly call them barbarians," the Earl of Ballantine defended, as his patience began to wane.

"They are Highlanders, are they not? That puts them midway between illiterate aborigines and tribal savages," Elizabeth raged contemptuously.

"The contract was signed at your birth. You are to wed Lord Ashley and that is final. His father has waited until your eighteenth birthday, and with Robert off fighting with Montrose, Lord Kirkland fears for his son's life. The sooner his heir weds, the better it will be."

"With Montrose! You would have me wed a man whose allegiance is to Montrose, when your own son has pledged his sword to Argyll?"

"I find that your brother's hasty actions, as

well as your objections to this marriage, reflect the same rash impetuosity. Neither of you has knowledge of the facts, responding instead to an emotional sentiment. I refuse to discuss this any further. You will leave within the week. Lord Kirkland has sent a party to escort you to Ashkirk Castle. I will miss you, my dear, but I have no other choice."

"Apparently, neither have I," Elizabeth cried. She knew by the resigned tone in her father's voice that nothing she could say or do at this time would alter his decision and, sobbing, she ran from the room.

Sadness filled the eyes of Alexander Scott as he watched the hasty exit of his daughter. How he would miss her! Her warmth and pleasant laughter filled the castle. She was the pride and joy of the clan. Slim and tall by customary standards, Elizabeth could ride a horse as well as any man. Her long auburn hair framed an exquisite face, and round, responsive brown eyes mirrored an intelligent and inquisitive mind. A venturesome spirit, which was such a source of consternation to her chaperones and groomsmen, was counterbalanced with a captivating charm and delightful sense of humor.

From the rumors Lord Scott had heard regarding the "Highland Lion," he knew Elizabeth's spirited nature would be an equal match for the daring and intense Robert Kirkland, and he regretted that the current political structure prevented him from accompanying her, thus missing the meeting between these volatile young people.

"Ah yes, my dear, you may hate me now," he murmured, "but someday you will know that I did a wise thing in getting you away from the Edinburgh Court—and from that treacherous and deceitful milksop puppet of Argyll's, Walter Campbell."

Elizabeth ran up the narrow stairs and flung open the door to her room. She halted in surprise at the sight of her cousin. Anne Barday swung around, startled by Elizabeth's sudden appearance. Tears stained her cheeks and she turned back to continue helping the abigail pack Elizabeth's clothes.

"So you know," Elizabeth declared angrily. "I am to be shipped out like some kind of chattel!"

With a sudden change of mood, she turned pleading eyes to her beloved companion. "You will come with me, Anne, won't you?"

"Oh, Beth," Anne cried with relief. "I was afraid you would not ask me."

Sobbing freely, the two young ladies flung themselves into one another's arms, as their sad tears at leaving their familiar home and loved ones blended with their anxious tears of what lay ahead.

A loud commotion from the outside penetrated the girls' misery. Struggling with a heavy trunk, they succeeded in maneuvering it to the window and quickly climbed upon it to study the courtyard below.

One of the Kirkland entourage lay on the ground, his shoulder bleeding profusely. The other members of the retinue, drawing their broadswords, quickly rallied to form a protective ring around their downed clansman.

Walter Campbell sat astride his horse, his sword bloodied from the fallen Highlander, issuing orders to his mounted horsemen.

"Slay them, slay them," he shouted in a frenzied command.

The small party on foot braced to receive the assault from the superior mounted force.

"Cease this immediately," Lord Scott ordered, as he rushed into the courtyard. He turned angry eyes to Walter Campbell.

"How dare you, sir! These men are under my protection and you dare raise arms against them! Explain this foul treachery, Campbell."

"You harbor this traitorous rabble when their clansman Ashley fights at the side of Montrose?"

"The Earl of Kirkwood has not committed his clan to Montrose, nor have I pledged mine to Argyll. These men are here on a peaceful mission. Sheath your weapon at once. Your armed attack on them has brought dishonor to this house."

"What peaceful mission could bring Highlanders this far from home?" Walter Campbell asked skeptically, as he reluctantly returned his sword to its scabbard and dismounted. His men drew back and proceeded to the stables, as the wary Highlanders lowered their swords.

"You men," Lord Scott commanded, "bring your clansman into the house and we will tend to his wound. Pray to God it will not be a serious one."

As the men disappeared inside, Elizabeth

and Anne climbed down from their perch and rushed down the stairs. Lord Scott was bent over the injured man.

"Great mercy of God, it is only a flesh wound," the Earl sighed.

Loud murmurs of relief could be heard from the assemblage. Lord Scott looked up with a relieved smile. "You men may leave. The wound is not a deep one. We will see to Lord Blakely's needs."

With lightened glances toward their leader, the men filed out, their tension eased by the assured manner of Lord Scott.

Artle, skilled in the art of healing and midwifery, was hastily summoned. As Elizabeth and Anne looked on intently, she quickly cleansed and bound the wound.

"The' ye be, m'lord. 'Tis good as new. By morn ye'll be wel' ken to crawl into th' bed o' some lucky lass," she said with a toothless smile, giving him a conspiratorial wink.

The young man sat up, a wide grin across his handsome face.

"Beware, old crone, leastwise it be your bed," he warned, his blue eyes alight with devilment.

Artle's cackling laughter filled the room as she gathered up her tray and shuffled out. He directed his attention to the two young women still standing aside, eyeing them with evident approval.

"The old hag has indeed hastened my demise, for the sight of two such celestial illusions can only mean I have expired and gone to heaven."

Anne giggled under this outrageous flattery while Elizabeth cast a disapproving frown in her direction.

"Sir David, it is my pleasure to introduce you to my daughter, Lady Elizabeth, and my niece and ward, Lady Anne Barday. Ladies, Lord Blakely, Sir David Kirkland."

With an attempt toward gallantry, the young man tried to rise, only to sink back on the settle.

"Oh please, Lord Blakely," Anne cautioned, "you must consider your condition."

David Kirkland gave her a grateful smile and turned back to his assession of Elizabeth.

"My brother is a most fortunate man. He will find no fault with the selection of his bride."

Seething under his appraisal, Elizabeth fumed, "Indeed, sir! How can you be sure? It will take a great deal of adjusting for me to learn to eat with my fingers and forsake wearing shoes. And certainly my prowess as a brood mare has yet to be tested. He may find me a great disappointment."

Anne gasped with shock at her cousin's unladylike outburst, as Lord Scott covered his mouth to stifle a smile. David Kirkland's reaction was just the opposite. He threw back his dark head and laughed uproariously, pounding the bench with his uninjured arm.

"Oh, I cannot wait until Robert meets you. What a tourney! He will have to declaw a vixen, as you strive to beard the lion! But disappointment, Lady Elizabeth, I think not—neither to my brother, nor to you."

Dinner that evening was a tension-filled affair with David Kirkland's and Walter Campbell's open hostility threatening to erupt at any moment. Later as they stood conversing, Campbell turned smugly to David.

"Your brother has made some dangerous enemies in Parliament by foolishly choosing to side with Montrose."

David Kirkland calmly studied his adversary. Bright yellow hair receded from a high brow that bore a small scar received in some earlier skirmish. Pale blue eyes were spaced narrowly apart in a face that tapered to a refined, almost delicate, jowl line. Walter Campbell stood just a few inches taller than Elizabeth, with an imposing pair of broad shoulders that made his appearance seem squatty, contradictory to his refined bearing. His height and breadth were deceiving, for he moved with an agile grace and was an expert with the rapier, as many of his unfortunate victims belatedly discovered.

"My brother has always prided himself not only on the choice of his friends—but on the selection of his enemies," David said with deliberation.

"Then you condone his teasonable alliance with Montrose?" Walter Campbell asked, sneering.

"Robert spent five years of fosterage with the Grahams. Why wouldn't he be loyal to

Montrose? As for treason, Lord Craver, the Grahams have always been loyal to the Scot crown. Just because Charles has broken with the parliament does not alter the fact that he wears the Scot crown. It might appear your uncle has lost sight of that fact."

"You would be wise, Blakely, to curb your tongue, or you may find you will lose it with such talk," Campbell warned.

"If you are threatening me, Craver, I should warn you that this time I will be expecting your thrust. You have taught me the folly of turning my back on a Campbell."

Walter Campbell's hand reached to pull his sword, as David's fingers curled around the hilt of his own weapon.

"May I remind you both that you are guests in my house—and in the presence of ladies," Lord Scott intervened angrily.

"My apologies to you, sir, and to the ladies," David said contritely. "I have no intent to affront your hospitality. However, Lord Craver blinds himself to the fact that General Montrose's exploits are spectacular."

"Humph," Campbell snorted scornfully, "an incompetent peacock leading some rabble in arms. When my uncle succeeds in catching him, he will soon wring the cock's neck."

"It would appear, Craver, that is precisely your uncle's problem—to succeed in catching him," David scoffed. "For the last month and a half that 'incompetent peacock' has led your illustrious uncle on a chase that has all of Europe laughing at Argyll. When he followed Montrose's army north into Gordon country, he discovered they had suddenly turned west and were already in the Spey valley. By the time Argyll reached Speyside, Montrose was at Badenoch. When your uncle stumbled into Badenoch, the 'peacock' was already back where he started from at Blair. Why, he sat and rested his men for a week at his own village of Montrose before your uncle even reached Brechlin!

"Montrose has already forced Argyll to chase him over two hundred and fifty miles through the roughest terrain in Scotland," David continued proudly. "That so-called rabble, traveling lightly and at the pace we Highlanders are famous for, has forced the Campbells, weighed down with their heavy uniforms and weapons, to cross every possible rocky cleft, scale every possible barren slope, and traverse every possible wooded forest in their path. There isn't a marshy bog, trailess moor or desolate waste that Montrose has not marched them across. There isn't a pebble, stone or rock he has not forced them to stumble over. Need I point out, Lord Craver, Montrose's army can keep moving for months. They have no supplies to carry, as they get their food from the land and their warmth from their plaids. How long before Argyll finds his army too exhausted and demoralized to continue, and they will simply disband and go back home? Then what force stands between Montrose and the English border?"

"His point is well taken," Lord Scott interjected. "Argyll appears to be unwisely playing right into James Graham's hands."

Walter Campbell appeared apoplectic in his rage at Lord Scott's accordance. Elizabeth, distressed by his state, turned angrily to David Kirkland.

"You bore us, sir, with your baseless braying of victory. What did I tell you, Father?" Elizabeth declared. "A Highlander has no gracious or social enlightments. Come, Sir Walter, a breath of night air will feel soothing to both of us."

They climbed the narrow stairway to the tower and stepped out onto the battlements. Elizabeth leaned against the parapet, as she breathed deeply of the crisp fall air. Would the Highlands smell as sweet to her? Suddenly Walter Campbell's arms were about her, and his lips closed over hers. She found herself unable to respond to the urgent pressure of his lips.

"Come away with me, Elizabeth. Defy your father. Argyll will intercede in my behalf, and your father will forgive you."

"I cannot disgrace my father," Elizabeth protested. "I could never purchase happiness at the price of his shame and dishonor."

"What of us, Elizabeth? What of our feelings for one another? I have waited years to wed you. I cannot let you go," he whined.

Once again he reached to take her in his arms. Elizabeth's hands pressed against his chest to hold him away.

"You jest, Sir Walter. Your many conquests are common talk in Edinburgh."

"And what of your betrothed?" he sneered. "Ashley consorts openly with Desiree du

Plessis, the niece of Cardinal Richelieu. She has been his mistress for years. Do you actually believe he will forsake her because of this arranged marriage! Nae, Elizabeth, you are naive if you believe so."

"All you men disgust me—young and old alike," Elizabeth declared hotly. "Women are nothing more than pieces of chattel to you. We are not supposed to have feelings or sensitivities. We must accept whomever is chosen for us. Are we ever consulted—ever consoled? What care I of Ashley's amours? Should my husband's betrayal be worse to bear than my father's?"

Angrily shrugging aside his hands, Elizabeth turned and stormed down the stairs.

V

Their farewells already said, Anne Barday and David Kirkland sat mounted on their horses, as the Earl of Ballantine took his daughter into his arms. Elizabeth, her deep brown eyes swollen from a tearful, sleepless night, looked up pleadingly at her father, hoping to the last that he would relent.

"Beth," he said sadly, as he hugged her tightly, "please do not hate me for this."

"Father, how can I hate someone I have loved my whole life? Wouldst that it were so, for then saying goodbye could be painless." Elizabeth struggled to contain her tears. "I know you love me. If only I could understand why you are doing this. You gain nothing with this union."

"Elizabeth, try to understand that a decision to live with honor can often cost a man the very thing he cherishes most. I pledge to you now, as I pledged you to the Earl of Kirkwood at your birth, if this marriage becomes intolerable, I will do everything in my power to dissolve it. I swear this." Then, enfolding her in his arms in a final embrace, he kissed his daughter and released her.

Lord Scott's resolve wavered as he watched the entourage move slowly through the portcullis, and for a brief moment he raised his hand to halt the procession. His arm lowered, and the uncertain frown that creased his brow changed to a smile of positive conviction—when he saw the plaids of the Kirklands' close protectively around his Beth.

As the days passed, Elizabeth watched the rolling hills of her beloved Lowlands gradually change into thickly wooded hillsides of pine and birch. Neat stone-hedged lanes were replaced by narrow, steep passages, gouged out of the rocky cliffs by the glaciers of the Ice Age. The lush green of the Lowland's farms was replaced by the deep purple of heathered moors, as though God, by painting the Highlands in the hue of royalty, proclaimed its majesty.

Swirling, foaming waters twisted and writhed like monstrous, turquoise serpents through the hollows of the glens. Narrow sea locks, weaving their way through the eroded vales, were spanned by ancient causeways of crumbling rock and stone, vivid reminders of the Picts and Romans who had traversed these same routes.

Elizabeth was awed by the crimson glory of rowan trees, springing from rocky pinnacles—trees that for years had been dampened by the chilling mists of the westerly breezes sweeping across the Hebrides from the Atlantic or buffeted and tortured by the prevailing icy winds of the North Sea, as they whistled across the majestic peaks of the Cairngorm and Grampian Mountains.

Was this tree the analogy of the Highlander —his very existence a testimony of fortitude, his survival rooted in the rock beneath him? Because of his perseverence, a barren boulder became a living rock! This glorious, unrelenting victory over a stern environment was as untamed and beautiful as the mountain from which it had sprung.

Despite her malcontent and apprehension, as each day brought her nearer to Ashkirk, Elizabeth could not deny the magnificent splendor of the beauty that surrounded her.

Elizabeth closed her eyes and leaned her head back against the smooth trunk of the birch tree. Her thoughts were racing. Tomorrow was journey's end—Ashkirk Castle, and the beginning of a new and frightening life as the wife of Robert Kirkland. Strange—how swiftly passed the events of the last few weeks! She had known of the marriage contract her whole life, but somehow it had always been a remote intangible. Suddenly, the reality of it was here and now. She still wrestled with her disbelief that her father would honor such a meaningless contract. Why must the bond of an old friendship exact the sacrifice of youth?

Oh, God, if only Sim had been there to speak in her behalf. Her eyes glistened at the thought of her brother. She knew he would have interceded to prevent the marriage.

A tear slid down her cheek as her thoughts

returned to the days of her adolescence. Losing their mother at their birth, she and her twin brother Andrew had grown up under the kindly guidance of their father and the protective eye of their older brother Simon. Elizabeth had been instructed by diligent tutors in all the gracious amenities expected of a lady of quality; however, her brothers had taught her all the ungracious ones. Riding was her passion, and her skill and daring equaled, and often excelled, that of her brothers. Her eye and hand were steady and sure in her usage of the bow, and she had often accompanied her brothers on hunting and fishing trips.

Elizabeth had taken pride in these abilities, as well as in her independence, not realizing she had grown up terribly spoiled by these three men who adored her. They had been a close and loving family, and the death of her brother Simon, the previous year, had been a staggering blow to all of them.

"M'lady, are ye ailin'?" a timid voice inquired worriedly.

Elizabeth opened her eyes and smiled fondly at the small figure kneeling before her.

"No, Tims, I am fine."

A big grin of relief split the freckled countenance of the nine-year-old lad. The son of one of the Kirkland soldiers, he had quickly attached himself to Elizabeth, and the sight of his boyish grin or carrot-topped head was always a welcome sight to the lonely woman. Whenever she was ready to mount or dismount, Tims was always waiting eagerly with a willing and helpful hand to assist her. Nights found him curled up outside her tent like a protective sentinel.

"And what of you, my young squire?" Elizabeth asked affectionately. "Are you glad to be home?"

Preening with pride, Tims blushed with pleasure at this flattering form of address, for he had tumbled hopelessly in love at first sight of this lovely lady who was soon to wed his adored idol, and he wished for nothing more than the opportunity of serving her.

"Aye, mum, I dinna know how much I cud miss me home."

"I know what you mean," Elizabeth intoned sadly, suffering with the same malady.

Intuitively, Tims' young heart commiserated with her unhappiness.

"Ah, M'lady, ye'll nae be grievin' once ye and Sir Robert hae wed. He's a braw mon, mum, and will luv ye and be good to ye."

"Oh, my young Tims, wouldst I had your confidence."

With a shy and hesitant gesture, he reached into the pocket of his breeks and with undisguised awe handed her a rowel that had been broken off from a spur.

" 'Tis his very own," Tims said reverently. "From his very own boot." He then wordlessly passed her a tiny, knotted cockade of black ribbon.

"And this, too, his very own?" Elizabeth asked softly, respecting the intimacy of the moment.

"Aye, mum. Fallen from the band of his tam o'shanter," Tims replied.

Elizabeth returned them to him, and for a few additional seconds the young lad fondled the cherished items before returning them to his pocket.

"Whe' I come of age, me father hae gie me ken to go wi' Sir Robert and General Montrose," he announced proudly, as though that day was about to dawn.

"But, Tims, I thought the Kirkland clan was not involved in this war."

"Aye, mum, but the auld Laird is ailin', and me father says once the auld Laird is gaine, Sir Robert will commit the clan to Montrose. Then I wil' be ken to ride wi' him."

"Then I will pray harder than ever for a swifter end to this horrible war," Elizabeth said, reaching out to tousle the thatch of red. "For a young lad's head should be full of the morrow's fishing and gaming, and not the thought of riding off to war."

Later, after Tims' departure, her thoughts returned to her personal plight and the frightening prospect of what tomorrow would bring, her anxiety clearly etched across the features of her face.

"Mistress Scott, such painful reflections will only cause that lovely face to wrinkle."

Elizabeth smiled, despite herself, glancing up into the friendly, warm eyes of David Kirkland. She had to admit that Lord Blakely had been a pleasant surprise. His conduct had been the epitome of manners and consideration in his efforts toward making the tedious journey as pleasant as possible.

"It has always distressed me to see a lovely maiden with a frown on her face," he said grinning engagingly.

She dropped her eyes sheepishly, knowing her attitude toward him had been unbearable, deliberately going out of her way to be as unpleasant as possible.

"I am afraid, Lord Blakely, I owe you an apology. In my agitation over this marriage, I have permitted myself to slip easily into the role of a shrew."

He reached for her hand and clasped it warmly.

"Do you really believe, Lady Elizabeth, that I was blind to the frightened little girl that tried to hide behind that shrewish facade?"

Elizabeth looked up surprised, grateful for his intuition. A tremulous smile crossed her lips. "It appears intuition is a Highlander's trait of which I was entirely unaware."

"We develop it by having to outguess our hordes of enemies," he teased lightly. David's expression sobered and the laughter left his dark eyes. "Beth, Robert is not the ogre you believe him to be. At times he can be headstrong and domineering, but these are just small parts of the whole man. I speak not from prejudice alone, but out of love and respect. Could I not call him brother, I would want to call him friend."

Pressing her hand to his lips, he left her as silently as he had arrived.

Elizabeth pondered David's words long

after he was gone. Who, really, was this Robert Kirkland? His exploits in the bedroom were as legendary as those on the battlefield. Was he too much the man's man, (or woman's man, she mused wryly), to want to accept this marriage any more than she did? Perhaps she and this Highland barbarian actually had something in common—a mutual objection to the union. For the first time in weeks, Elizabeth felt a faint vestige of hope in the overlooked possibility that Lord Ashley himself would refuse to marry. All at once her previous apprehension toward meeting him changed to curiosity, and she found herself intrigued by the prospect of their meeting.

"What say you of this marriage, Robert Kirkland?" Elizabeth asked softly to the prudent ears of the night.

At that very moment, the farthest thought from the mind of Robert Kirkland was his forthcoming marriage to Elizabeth Scott, for he was just sinking his tall frame into the welcome warmth of a hot bath. He luxuriated in the tub, allowing the water to soothe his aching body. He had taken a nasty tumble, bruising himself badly, in a hand-to-hand struggle earlier that day. Drying himself with a towel, he padded barefoot to the bed and climbed in gratefully between the sheets, falling instantly asleep.

Robert had no knowledge of how long he slept, but awoke to the pressure of familiar soothing fingers caressing his back. The darkened room was lit only by a few remaining embers that glowed in the fireplace. A pair of warm lips began to nibble at his ear, and with a stifled groan he rolled over, hungrily pulling down the tiny figure and passionately claiming the lips that awaited him.

"Oh, *Cheri*," Desireé du Plessis sighed when he released her, "I have missed you so much." She rose up and smiled down enticingly at him.

"What in hell are you doing here?" Robert asked groggily. "I left you in Oxford."

"I was here in Perth when you attacked. I was so frightened, *Bien-Ami*, until I found out it was Montrose. Then I knew you would be with him. Are you not glad to see me, Robert?"

"Do you have to ask!" he murmured hoarsely, then drew her down to him. Their kiss left them breathless and aroused, and he swiftly began to undress her. Within seconds she was naked and laying atop him, as his arms eagerly embraced her. Her hot little tongue sent shocks of erotic waves through his body, even before she began to nibble at his lips as her hands swiftly began to toy with his swollen member. With a smothered groan he rolled over and quickly entered her, climaxing immediately.

"Well, I suspected that after such a drought, your eagerness would be, shall we say, uncontrollable!" she said with a saucy smile.

"It hasn't been a total drought," he responded wickedly.

"Oh, you *Bete Sauvage*," she pouted, leaning over to viciously sink her teeth into his shoulder.

"Damn you, woman, that hurts!" he complained, as he pressed her beneath him. "Furthermore, my little French bitch, I know you are never too long with an empty bed. This is the beauty of our relationship—we never demand more of one another than we are willing to give."

"I would be faithful to you, Robert, if you would ask," she declared pouting.

"Desireé, my love, if one has to ask, where is the faith?"

His mouth began to coax the nipples of her breasts to hardened peaks. "You are wicked," she groaned, and began to squirm beneath him.

Late the following afternoon Robert woke abruptly to a loud banging at the door. Desireé stirred restlessly, where she lay in his arms, and rolled over to her side to curl up contentedly.

"Go away," he yelled irritably.

"Robert, I hae a message for ye," the voice of Alistair MacDonald shouted through the closed portal.

With disgruntled annoyance, Robert rose and reached for his breeks. He stumbled to the door and pulled it open, his irritation plainly etched on his face.

Alistair MacDonald grinned down at him from his towering height.

"This missive hae com' frae yer father. Aft' a conference wi' his officers, General Montrose said 'twas agreed, becaus' o' me size, I wuz the only mon wud be safe in disturbin' ye to deliver it."

"You may relate to General Montrose and my fellow officers that I find no wit in their attempt at humor," Robert grumbled and snatched the letter from MacDonald.

He began to shut the door and a powerful arm prevented its closure.

"The General is mos' anxious to know whe' ye inten' to come ou' o' this room."

"How long does he plan to remain in Perth?" Robert asked irritably.

"For another two days."

"Then I will be out in two days," Robert declared, slamming the door with a resounding crash.

Robert Kirkland's frown deepened as he read the letter from his father. Then tossing it aside, he returned to the bed. Desiree lay awake and, with a wickedly enticing giggle, opened her arms to receive him.

Later that evening, the gnawing pain of hunger succeeded in overcoming the insistent pangs of passion, and the pair ventured from the room to seek a meal. Robert and Desiree ate ravenously of a spitted grouse, before turning their attention to a heaping bowl of mutton and vegetables in a savory stew. Their hunger appeased, they sat side by side, Robert's arm around her, as they sipped from large earthenware mugs of steaming, dark coffee.

A shudder of desire gripped Desiree as Robert's warm lips found the sensitive hollow behind her ear, and his tongue began a teasing play with her tiny lobe.

"Oh, *mon cheri*," she sighed, her almond-shaped eyes glazed with passion. Her hand slid intimately between his legs, and her lips parted sensuouly, as she cupped the swelling hardness.

"*Bebe*," he whispered hoarsely, "how do you expect me to get up and walk out of here?"

Desiree smiled with malicious satisfaction, gloating at her ability to direct all his latent strength and might toward a driving need for her.

"I knew you would have to come out some-time," an amused voice declared, interrupting their intimacy.

Robert looked up, surprised to find a familiar face grinning down at him.

"Nat!" he exclaimed in delight. His pleasure increased at the sight of James Graham accompanying him. "When did you arrive?"

"I got in this morning, only you were too occupied to be disturbed," Nat Gordon said with a rakish smile. "Ah, the beautiful Mademoiselle du Plessis," he said with a gallant bow, as he pressed his lips to Desiree's hand. "*Je suis charme de vous voir.*"

"*Merci, Monsieur Gordon. Se joindre?*"

Without waiting for Robert to second the

invitation Nat slapped him on the back and plopped down in a seat, as Montrose slid into the chair opposite.

Robert could only grin with pleasure. He and Nat Gordon were close friends, having served together in the French army and later under Montrose with the Royalist forces. They had spent many evenings in camaraderie, wining and wenching. Robert knew that of the officers beginning to rally to Montrose's banner, Nat Gordon was probably the best professional among them.

"And, General, you are as handsome as ever," Desireé purred, as she turned her flirtatious attention to Montrose. "I do not know if I can resist such temptation. *Mes bons amis*, how fortunate the young ladies who are forced to yield to such conquerors!"

"Desireé, you are the ideal woman, the supreme courtesan," James Graham said, as he kissed her hand lingeringly. "Wouldst that I could conquer such loveliness and claim it as mine."

"Ah, my General," Desiree said, caressing his cheek, "it would be a facile victory for you, were it not that I know the army is your mistress."

Robert leaned back amused, as he watched Montrose glow under Desiree's glib flattery. In the years since his marriage, Robert knew James Graham had never looked at, or touched, any woman besides his wife Magdalen. Undetered, Desiree continued her coquetry. Her penchant for flirting never bothered Robert. He knew she had a lusty appetite and did not resent her amorous liaisons when away from him, knowing no man could threaten his position when they were together.

Nat slipped his arm around the waist of the barmaid, as she placed tankards of ale before them. She giggled nervously as he whispered in her ear.

"Oh, my lord," she admonished, "you turn a poor lass's head." Brushing aside the hand that had crept to her backside, she hurried off in a flurry of swinging hips and agitated twitters. Nat's eyes appreciatively followed the voluptuous bosom straining to spill forth any second from the thin garment that restrained it.

"I can see the Don Juan of the Gordon clan is still up to his usual habits," Robert chided lightly.

Nat grinned conspiratorially. "You must admit, Robbie, that is a bonny pair of . . ." He stopped, remembering Desiree's presence. Picking up his tankard, he raised it slightly. "To drink, deviltry, and debauchery," he toasted with a roguish grin. In comradely accord, Robert raised his drinking cup.

An hour later, after constant toasts and shared reminiscences, the two companions were visibly showing the effects of their reunion.

"To warm wine and wanton women!" Robert slurred, as the tankards were refilled and raised again in sentiment. The sloshing ale spilled over, as Nat's cup clinked its reply against Robert's.

Montrose grinned with amusement, like an indulgent parent viewing the actions of his mischievous children. He knew these two men fought as hard as they played—and for that reason did not begrudge them these moments of relaxation.

Desireé, having lost Robert's attention, found herself bored by his and Nat's involvement with one another. Montrose reached over and patted her hand understandingly.

"*Il faut que jeunesse se passe*—boys will be boys! You must not be angry with Robert. He and Nat have an old and cherished comradeship."

"I am not angry, General. I am envious," she said sadly. "From our first meeting ten years ago in France, I have been at Robert's beck and call. Yet, I know I do not have the hold on him that any of the rest of you claim. Pity the woman who is foolish to love him, for I do not believe he will ever commit himself to her."

"I have known Robert since he was a youth," Montrose said quietly. "We are like brothers. This I know, my petite Desireé, despite his worldliness and derring-do, the Highlands are his love. He is bound to them and their traditions. The woman who wins Robert Kirkland will have to love them as he does."

"Oh, la-la," Desireé moaned mournfully. "If only my rival were a woman, I could fight her."

"Lovely lady," Montrose said gallantly, "if that were true, you would have no rival."

"Ah, General," she sighed with a conquettish smile, "I repeat what I said earlier—what a shame your true love is your duty."

"And what of you?" Montrose asked. "We will be leaving Perth. Where will you go? Argyll will be here soon."

"Do not worry, General. The Duke of Argyll will not harm me. He knows I have too many influential friends in the French court, and he dare not endanger his position with them. If France were to ally herself with your king, Argyll's cause would be crushed. When Robert leaves, I think I shall return to France. But for now, I would appreciate your escort, as I am anxious to return to my room. I will leave Robert to the enjoyment of his cups."

Much later Robert staggered into the room and fell across the bed, only to pass out instantly. Desireé removed his boots and scabbard, and studied his handsome face, relaxed in slumber. She reached out to smooth the hair from his brow.

"*Mon Bien-Ami,*" she sighed wistfully, as she pressed a tender kiss to his lips, "if only my rival were a woman!"

The next day they took their meals in the room, and against Desireé's protests, Robert extracted her promise to go to his home and wait for him at Ashkirk.

Their love-making was frantic, as though each sensed these would be their final moments. And at dawn the following morning, Desireé stood at the window of the inn and sadly watched as Montrose's army departed from Perth.

VI

The battlements of Ashkirk Castle loomed above them—silent and ominous. The Kirkland banner, proclaiming the laird of the manor in residence, fluttered from the top of one of the four turrets that stood at each corner of the crenelated battlements.

Elizabeth reined in her horse before passing through the outer bailey to study the crest mounted over the archway. A lion, partially reared on his haunches, dominated the heraldic coat of arms. Early Roman or Viking influence was evident by the erect trident he held in his front paws. The word *Gallantry* formed the left prong, *Integrity* the middle prong, and *Loyalty* the right prong, the three words merging at the Y to form the shaft of the spear. Beneath the lion appeared the words *Obair Ro Neach Fein* and Elizabeth turned questioning eyes to Tims.

" 'Tis Gaelic, mum. It means 'Serve Others Before Self.' "

Once inside the courtyard, she noted that from the rear of the original structure extended an additional wing two stories in height. The whole castle was truly massive and impressive. Built for fortification, it appeared impregnable, emanating the strength of its inhabitants; while at the same time, its lancet arches and mullioned windows softened the severity of its stony facade.

The ground level consisted of several rooms quartering the guards, a kitchen, a large larder, and a mess hall, all opening onto a community hall with a wide stone stairway leading to the first floor. Any married guard and his family were housed in small apartments in the wing addition.

The kitchen on the ground level had narrow stairs leading to another kitchen on the first floor, where the food for the lord and his family was prepared. This level also held a dining room, a library and den, a chapel and a Grand Hall for entertaining. The domestic servants and their families were housed in the wing addition.

The second and third floors of the giant structure contained the private apartments and chambers of the Kirklands, with the wing addition of the second floor reserved for any guests.

Elizabeth and Anne knew from the size of the exterior that the castle was mammoth. However, they did not anticipate the interior to surpass the elegance of Ballantine. Expecting the austerity of a male-dominated household, they were surprised to see huge chandeliers and leaded-frame mirrors reflecting the light in the Grand Hall. That was where the frivolity ended, for the rest of the room was furnished in tasteful but functional furnishings.

Several large settles were spaced around the room, along with large wainscot paneled chairs, with cushions of crewel and needle-point covering the seats for comfort. Massive drawleaf tables and backless benches lined the walls. An awesome side table, twenty feet in length, dating back to the Fifteenth Century, stood against one wall, with its mosaic marble top supported by three legs of carved columns.

The stone floor was bare, but the walls were generously adorned with rich paintings and tapestries. Crossed broadswords and a large escutcheon with the Kirkland crest hung over a fireplace that occupied most of the far wall of the grand room.

It was evident that this room was used for formal occasions, for its size alone discouraged any family intimacy.

The dining room was spacious, with a long highly polished table. Carved wooden arm-chairs with twist-turnings surrounded the long table. The seats of the chairs were a silk-faced fabric of deep red and the high backs were embroidered in richly colored red and gold thread. An elevated sideboard lined one wall with a massive carved chest opposite.

Upon entering the combination library and den, it became evident to the girls where the family spent its leisure hours. Their eyes were immediately drawn to a huge writing cabinet with a fallfront desk, its front and sides of walnut veneer with a marquetry decoration in various woods. In one corner stood a small game table with a chessboard of inlaid ebony and pearl. Four side chairs framed the small table.

A beautiful high-backed Baroque settee stood on gold and ebony legs before the fireplace. This lovely piece was upholstered in sumptuous hues of wine-red, dark-blue, deep-gold and a rich purple.

Two walls of book shelves stretched from floor to ceiling. The remaining walls were entirely covered with molded paneling. Colorful rugs were scattered generously on the floor.

Several wide Baroque chairs testified to the manliness of the room, as its earthy tones robed it in an aura of warmth.

Elizabeth ran her fingers over an elegant harpsichord. The keyboard had a double row of ivory keys and the box was a rich wood with gold inlay.

"A gift from James Graham when he returned from the Continent," David offered, seeing her gesture. "Unfortunately, no one here can play it."

"Oh, Beth plays beautifully," Anne said breathlessly.

"As does my cousin," Elizabeth quickly intoned.

"Then we can soon hope for the gentle strains of music," David said pleasantly.

"Lord Blakely, it is all so lovely," Anne enthused as they returned to the majestic Grand Hall. "Don't you agree, Beth?"

Elizabeth could only nod in speechless accord.

"A few of us barbarians do appreciate refinements," David gibed with a jocular glance toward Elizabeth. "That is why we are often forced to purloin some gentle maiden from the Lowlands to temper our boorish inclinations."

Unamused, Elizabeth's reply was a raised, disdainful brow.

The entrance of a tall, gray-haired man commanded all their attention. The two men hugged each other warmly, before turning to the women.

"Father, it is my pleasure to introduce Lady Elizabeth Scott and her cousin, the Lady Anne Barday. His Lordship, the Earl of Kirkwood."

The two young ladies dipped in a curtsy, their heads bowed in respect.

"I am not the King, you know," an amused voice announced. "Do rise, dear ladies, for I fear I am physically unable to join you at that level."

Elizabeth rose to meet a pair of compelling, deep-blue eyes.

"Lady Elizabeth," the earl acknowledged, bringing her hand to his lips. He quickly paid the same courtesy to Anne.

"How lovely you are, my dear," Lord Kirkland said, directing his attention again to Elizabeth. "I last saw you when you were but a child of five. My family and I had spent a pleasurable week with your family at Ballantine Castle. Do you remember?"

"I am afraid not, Lord Kirkland," Elizabeth replied regretfully. Her regret was sincere, for she was surprised to hear she had ever met this man—or her future husband. Elizabeth's surprise increased at his next words.

"I am sorry that my son, Lord Ashley, is not here at this time. I have sent a missive calling him home. However, his absence will enable us to become acquainted."

"I cannot deny I would welcome the same advantage with my future husband, my lord."

Lord Kirkland cocked an appreciative brow. This woman, indeed, lived up to all his expectations. She had beauty, intelligence, wit and spirit—all the attributes necessary to attract and hold the attention of his errant son. *If I can only get the damn fool home,* he thought irritably.

The Earl of Kirkwood was unaware that Elizabeth was studying him just as earnestly. There was no question the man was ailing, his body already bearing signs of emaciation. He frequently coughed, necessitating the constant bringing of a handkerchief to his mouth. Despite his illness, he still retained an aura of command, and Elizabeth regretted not remembering meeting this vibrant man when he was healthy and hardy.

"My health is declining," he apologized, after a coughing spasm. "I am afraid I must rest, but I will look forward to your company at dinner. David, will you show the ladies to

78

their chambers? Lady Elizabeth is quartered next to Robert, and Lady Anne is in the room opposite."

Her bedroom offered Elizabeth the most pleasant surprise of the day. The canopied bed was entirely draped in pale green with a low banquette upholstered in light yellow silk at its foot. Beside the bed stood a joint stool with a pearl inlay top to hold her dressing accouterments.

Two farthingale chairs, with backs and seats cushioned in the same fabric, stood invitingly on either side of a white marble fireplace that had a thin golden vein streaked through its polished smoothness. In front of the fireplace a green rug with intricately woven rose-colored petals lay on the floor. A large armoire with elegantly carved linenfold panels dominated one wall.

Elizabeth's eyes were drawn to a small toilet chest. Its front was adorned with delicate flowers painted and lacquered in a rose hue.

The completely feminine character of the room combined soothing comfort with graceful luxury.

"My mother decorated this room before she died, hoping one day for a daughter," David volunteered in answer to Elizabeth's look of amazement.

Later, Elizabeth stood alone, gazing out of the window that commanded a magnificent view of the surrounding hills. The golds and reds of fall still lingered on the landscape, contrasting with the perpetual green of the towering pines. She could only gasp in awe at this breathtaking beauty.

Having luxuriated in a hot bath, she dressed carefully for dinner. For some inexplicable reason she wanted to please the aged man, whose dignity of bearing reminded her so much of her own father. Elizabeth realized instinctively why this Highland lord and her father had become such close friends.

A light tap at her door interrupted her thoughts and she turned to see Anne entering the room. David Kirkland had monopolized most of Anne's time on the trip to Ashkirk, and it had been a long time since the girls had shared their accustomed intimacy. Now studying her, she could see that Anne glowed again with the luster once lost when Simon died—for Anne had been in love with Simon since childhood. Elizabeth was not so naive that she did not attribute this new sparkle to the attention Anne was receiving from Lord Blakely.

"Are your chambers comfortable, cousin?" Elizabeth asked lightly, somehow sensing Anne would have been satisfied with a dungeon if it meant being near David Kirkland.

"Oh, yes, Beth, and what about you? It has been so long since we have talked. Are you more resigned to your forthcoming marriage?"

"I will never resign myself to accepting a marriage I am forced into," Elizabeth protested. "And do not lose sight of the fact that Lord Ashley is not like David Kirkland, or he would be home and not off fighting with Montrose."

"David told me he handles the family's finances. They are quite active in shipping. An uncle and cousin captain their ships."

"If their income is from the sea, I would think Lord Ashley's interests would lie in sailing, not soldiering."

"David said General Montrose and Robert are as close as brothers. That is why Robert has always leaned toward soldiering. As Robert's heir, David promised to remain at Ashkirk."

"David said this, David promised that," Elizabeth quoted. "I suspect *David* has grown to mean a great deal to you."

The blush that crept across Anne's face only heightened her delicate blonde beauty.

"I suspect he has," she sighed softly. "Oh, Beth, I really care for him. I haven't felt this way since Sim's death. David is so warm, and so witty, and . . ."

". . . so tall and so handsome," Elizabeth teased, a twinkle in her dark eyes.

"Tell me truthfully, Beth. Do you think he cares for me at all, or is it just his way? He is such an adorable tease!"

"Has he not already been pledged in marriage, the same as Lord Ashley?"

"He was, but the poor lass died in childhood. When Robert raised such a row about being forced into a marriage, David threatened to enter a monastery if the same thing was done to him."

The two girls giggled delightedly, envisioning Lord Kirkland's distress with his two rebellious sons.

"If that is the case, I think David Kirkland would be blind if he did not care for you," Elizabeth assured her, hugging Anne warmly. "And besides, if I am forced to wed a boorish Highlander, it is only fair that you join me in my misery."

"Misery!" Anne scoffed. "I think not, Beth. After all, Robert Kirkland is David's brother. They must have something in common, and I certainly cannot imagine marriage to David beind miserable. No, cousin dear, I am beginning to believe that your marriage to Robert Kirkland is not going to be quite as dismal as we thought."

"*Et tu, Brute?*" Elizabeth sighed, clutching her heart dramatically. Then hand in hand, giggling conspiratorially, the girls went down to dinner.

Both ladies were distressed by the sight of David engaged in conversation with a lovely, petite blonde woman. David's face lit up at their entrance.

"Ah, there they are now," he said to the young woman. "Lady Elizabeth and Lady Anne, may I introduce Mademoiselle Desireé du Plessis."

The woman smiled a welcome, her almond-shaped eyes lingering on Elizabeth. Elizabeth sensed her immediate hostility and did not know what she had done to warrant it.

Surely, if this woman were interested in David, Anne posed the threat, not she. Her mind groped for a hidden memory. Somehow the name had a familiar ring, yet she was certain she had never met her before.

Elizabeth instantly sympathized with Anne, knowing this sensuous, desirable female would present a prodigious threat to any woman. Her mind still wrestled with an irritating itch. Desireé du Plessis? Where had she heard that name?

Suddenly the recollection dawned on her, remembering Walter Campbell's declaring "Everyone knows Ashley openly consorts with Desireé du Plessis . . . she has been his mistress for years." Elizabeth's eyes widened with appalling disbelief. This woman was not a threat to Anne's future—but to her own! This was her future husband's mistress!

David Kirkland witnessed her change of expression and knew she had just realized who Desiree was. He saw Elizabeth quickly compose herself and mask her thoughts behind a serene expression. David raised his glass in tribute. "You have a lot of class, Elizabeth Scott," he thought as he silently toasted.

Elizabeth would have been comforted with the knowledge that Desireé du Plessis immediately sensed that Robert's future wife would be a force to be reckoned with.

The following day, Lord Kirkland was taken with a chill and confined to his bed. His condition began to deteriorate rapidly and David dispatched a courier to try to locate

Robert and inform him of their father's condition. Elizabeth spent several hours each day with the elderly man. They laughed together as he told her of the deeds and misdeeds he and his friend Alex committed when they were young men. She thrilled in seeing the beauty and charm of her mother through the eyes of this sensitive and expressive man.

As the days passed into weeks, Elizabeth grew to love him, her heart wrenching with the knowledge she would lose this new friend in a short time.

Elizabeth's anger mounted with Robert's continued absence. Her only satisfaction lay in knowing he was not with his mistress, who, unfortunately, was under her very own nose. Afternoons, she rode the rugged hills with David and Anne, or more often, just Tims, who still remained devoted to her.

Early in his confinement, after a perusal of the well-stocked library, Elizabeth had offered to read Lord Kirkland a book.

"What would you enjoy hearing?" she had asked the earl.

Aware of her mounting anger with Robert, he could not prevent replying, "I would suggest *The Taming of the Shrew*, but would hope it might be *All's Well That Ends Well.*"

"Were it not the fall season, my lord," Elizabeth quickly retorted, "I would fear you are suffering more with a strong overdose of *A Midsummer Night's Dream.*"

Lord Kirkland laughed, completely captivated by her wit.

"Actually, my dear Elizabeth, that melancholy Dane has always had a hold on me. Let it be *Hamlet*."

From that time on, each night after dinner, Elizabeth could be found at his bedside, reading from one of the thick volumes.

VII

The face of David Kirkland broke into a wide grin at the sight of the tall figure who entered the library. He jumped to his feet and the two men clasped hands. Then abandoning any attempt at reserve, they reached for one another in a heartfelt embrace, as they thumped one another affectionately on the back.

"God's truth, Robert, it is good to see you," David Kirkland exclaimed warmly, stepping back to study his brother, his face an emotional blend of relief and affection.

Robert Kirkland's eyes mirrored the same sentiments before sobering, and the happiness that had covered his face seconds before was erased by an anxious frown.

"What of Father, David?"

The young man shook his head. "The doctor has very little hope. It is just a matter of time. Thank God you are back. He wants to see you so badly. I think it is the only thing that has forced Father to hold on this long."

"I will go to him at once," Robert said, putting aside his plumed helmet. He removed his sword and scabbard and the bright plaid that draped his shoulder. With a solemn nod to his brother, Robert left the room.

Robert quickly entered his father's large chambers. He gestured to the abigail, and as she rose and left, he took her seat at the bedside.

The paleness of the aged face accented each line that creased it. Lord Kirkland's once dark hair, whitened by the years, lay thick and wavy against the pillow. Robert reached down and gingerly picked up a frail hand that rested on the counterpane.

At his touch the eyes opened slowly, and Robert found himself looking into the same dark eyes that stared back at him daily from his own mirror.

The sight of his eldest son brought a warm glow to the earl's eyes, and Robert, unable to disguise his own emotion, cupped the hand he held between his own strong hands and pressed it against his heart.

"So, the prodigal son has returned," his father said weakly, the pride and affection he held for Robert clearly apparent in his voice. "What a shame an old man must die in order to lure his son home again."

"And now that you have succeeded in winning your way, old man, what say you abandon this act and tomorrow we will roust the hounds for a lively hunt," Robert said with loving banter.

Lord Kirkland sighed, his eyes alight. "Ah, wouldst that it could be! The excitement of the hunt in pursuit of a stag. The sound of baying hounds in my ears. The strength of the steed beneath me splashing across an icy rill with the feel of the wind on my face as it whistles down from the peaks of Ben Nevis. Ah, Robert, how sweet to live again such a moment!"

"You will, Father. There will be many such moments again."

Lord Kirkland looked up into the anguished eyes of his son with an ambiguous stare.

"Will there, Robert, or is this the time when one relinquishes the future and begins to embrace the past?"

"No, Father, the future still holds much for you."

"Yet the past holds so much more," Lord Kirkland said, as he gazed pensively into space. "I can hear again the lilting laughter of my lovely Kathleen, as we walk hand in hand through the heather on a summer's morn. Once again I know that awesome feeling of holding my newly born son in my arms. How natural this transition to the past! Its delights are so rich and rewarding."

Lost in reverie, a contented smile crossed the aged countenance, and his eyes closed as he dropped back into slumber.

Robert sat back, still gripping his father's hand. His eyes clouded with pain at the sight of the once muscular body now emaciated by the consumption that ravished it. How dear this man was to him, he thought with pride. How worthy his inspiration and guidance had been through the years. Robert knew of no ignoble act ever committed by his father. In the fifty-eight years of Michael Kirkland's lifetime, he had always conducted his life with honor and dignity. Laird of his clan, widowed twenty years earlier, he had guided his clansmen with a loving and prudent hand, exhibiting the leadership he expected his sons to emulate.

His father's eyes opened as his thin frame was gripped with a spasm of wracking coughs, and Robert reached for him, propping up the frail body to ease it.

"We must talk, my son," Lord Kirkland said feebly, lying back when the seizure subsided. "There are many matters to resolve. Have you spoken with the Lady Elizabeth?"

"You mean she is here?" Robert asked, surprised.

"She has been waiting you for over a month."

Oh, Lord! thought Robert, and I had Desireé come here! What a hornet's nest!

At that moment, they were interrupted by the entrance of the doctor, and Robert rose to leave.

"I will return after the evening meal," he said with an assuring pat to his father's shoulder.

Lord Kirkland placed a restraining hand on Robert's arm.

"When you return later bring the Lady Elizabeth with you. I do so enjoy her company."

For a few seconds Robert stood staring down at his father, unable to conceal the frown of apprehension that crossed his brow.

Returning to the library, he dropped his long body despondently into a large Baroque chair. David took one look at his brother and quickly poured some brandy from a decanter on the desk. Robert quaffed it, as though it were ale, and extended the empty glass for refilling.

"How could he deteriorate so rapidly?" Robert moaned, burying his head in his hands. "If only I had come sooner. When I saw him last he was well and on his feet."

"The doctor said his body seems to be stricken with something other than just consumption," David said sadly. "He suffers with severe internal pain. I tried to locate you as soon as his condition became critical, but you were playing 'Fox and Hounds' with Argyll, and it was difficult to find you. By pure chance, my messenger reached you at Blair Castle."

"I blame you not, David," Robert assured him. "I am at fault. I received his message in Perth, but he said nothing of his illness. I was not about to rush home to a marriage I had no taste for." He glanced at his brother with a forced nonchalance. "I understand my future bride is awaiting me here."

"She is indeed!" David said with a much lighter tone. "And from the way you have kept her waiting, I would venture a guess that any battle in your past will pale in comparison to the one that now lies ahead."

"So, the wench is shrewish," Robert bemoaned, misinterpreting David's meaning.

"What am I do to with Mademoiselle du Plessis? She cannot remain here in the same house with my future bride."

David could not conceal a frown at the mention of Desiree. "Robert, you know I have never interfered nor moralized in your relationships. At times I have even envied some of them, but what are your true feelings for Mademoiselle du Plessis?"

Robert looked at him warily. "Why do you ask?"

"For the past few days she has been at Kindarin at the invitation of Lord Langely. She is to return in the morning." His brows raised skeptically. "She refers to Roger as 'an old and dear acquaintance.'"

"Well, that at least settles my problem for this evening." Robert sighed with relief. "Somehow I must get her to Fort Linnhie until we can make other arrangements. Unfortunately, at this time the city will be overflowing with Campbells."

"Perhaps, brother dear, after you meet the Lady Elizabeth you may find you do not have the inclination for other liaisons."

Robert's cynical laughter followed this declaration. "My young and naive brother, if I am forced to honor this ridiculous arrangement of Father's, do not doubt for a moment I would ever trade the exquisite delights of the bed of Desiree du Plessis for that of a shrewish, listless Sassenach!"

For the tenth time in the hour, Robert

picked up the delicate brass clock on the mantel, frowned, then slammed it back down. His booted toe toyed angrily with a burning log in the fireplace, before he turned away to refill the tankard he held in his hand.

Anne Barday glanced nervously toward David Kirkland, who simply shrugged his shoulders with perplexed innocence. "I imagine, despite the infelicitous circumstances that bring you home, it is at least a minor comfort to be free of the battlefield," Anne said in an effort toward conversation.

Her voice managed to penetrate the mounting anger that was engulfing him, and Robert Kirkland swung around to her.

"I beg your pardon, Lady Anne. I did not hear your question."

Anne cleared her throat nervously. "I imagine you welcome this temporary respite from the war," she repeated.

"Oh, yes," he replied in an abstract manner.

David jumped to his feet eagerly. "Why don't we play some cards?" he suggested.

Robert turned a piercing glance in the direction of his brother. "It is not my wont to indulge in card games when dinner has been held for over an hour. Tell me, Lady Anne, is this lack of promptness a customary habit of Mistress Scott's?"

"I cannot imagine what has kept her. Beth is usually so punctual," Anne defended.

"Then I can only assume it is intentional," Robert declared.

With a purposeful stride he stormed from the library. David followed him to the doorway and watched him angrily mounting the stairway, two astride. With a devilish grin of anticipation, he turned back to Anne and raised his tankard.

"My darling Anne, I think the first joust of the tournament is about to begin!"

Elizabeth Scott slowly brushed her long auburn tresses and they lay in a shimmering mantle across her shoulders. She deliberately lingered over the task, knowing she was over an hour late for dinner.

So the mighty "Highland Lion" has finally returned, she thought with spite. Well, fine! He has kept me waiting for a month, so it is small satisfaction to let him cool for an hour. Elizabeth leisurely dabbed a touch of perfume behind her ear lobe, before removing the white rayle that covered her shoulders. As she reached for her dress the door suddenly crashed open. Startled, she swung around and the dress slipped from her fingers.

There was no need for anyone to tell her that the tall stranger who stood before her was Robert Kirkland. His pure male presence dominated the room. Neither the white shirt, covering his wide shoulders and casually unlaced at the neckline, nor the black breeks encasing his long legs disguised the tempered blend of muscle and strength that lay beneath. He closed the door and leaned back, as his dark-blue eyes, hooded by long thick lashes, insolently measured her. Rumpled black hair covered a head held with an arrogance that proclaimed recognition of no man as his master—and defied any to try to prove otherwise. A slight hook in the bridge of the nose and the dark full moustache above the lips accentuated the masculinity of his deeply tanned face. He slowly brought his silver tankard of ale to his lips, as his eyes continued to ravish her.

With a blush born of anger, not embarrassment, Elizabeth reached for her rayle and covered herself.

"I believe, sir, you have the wrong room. Your whore is bedded in the wing."

Elizabeth wanted to reach out and claw away the scornful smirk that crossed the tanned face.

"We have been awaiting your presence, mistress, for over an hour." The warm timbre of his tone belied the controlled anger that hovered below the surface.

"And I, sir, have been awaiting your presence for over a month," she hotly declared.

"Had I known of your eagerness, mistress, I certainly would never had tarried," he mocked.

"Eagerness? Hardly, my lord. Are you not confusing apprehension for enthusiasm?"

"Whatever, my lady," Robert replied, his brazen eyes sweeping her body, "it would appear the folly was mine!"

He straightened up leisurely and opened the

door to depart, then turned back, his hand poised on the knob.

"You have five minutes to join us, mistress, with or without the dress. The choice is yours."

His command was distinct and portentous.

Precisely at the final alotted minute, Elizabeth Scott strolled into the dining hall. At her entrance, David, seated next to Anne, rose to his feet, but Robert made no attempt to rise, as she slipped into the chair beside him.

As with every night since his confinement, a setting lay at the head of the table, the empty chair reflecting the absence of the laird of the manor. Elizabeth smiled contritely at David and he gave her an amused conspiratorial wink.

Small steaming bowls of cock-a-leekie soup were immediately placed before them. Elizabeth tried to ignore the electrifying presence of the man seated beside her, as she sipped the savory warmth of the bree, but her eyes would steal surreptitious glances in his direction, at times meeting his inquisitive frown.

Despite her lack of appetite, Elizabeth took a piece of the smoked salmon that lay on a silver trencher, but declined a bowl of haggis offered her. Later, after consuming small sweetened buns covered with a sugary marmalade of orange, quince, and almonds, David Kirkland leaned back in his chair, his hunger sufficed.

"Ardyss outdid herself with that haggis. It was delicious," he enthused.

"There is no one who has her touch with haggis," Robert agreed.

"I loathe it. Only you Highlanders could find enjoyment in consuming the waste of slaughtered animals," Elizabeth declared in disdain.

"We cannot afford to squander anything, Lady Elizabeth," David answered, defensively.

"This castle does not cry of poverty," Elizabeth scoffed.

"Our wealth is from the sea, my lady, but we are fed from the land, and the Highlands are not as bountiful as the Lowlands. The offal of the sheep is as fundamental to our diet as our oats."

"It is a primitive fare that encourages you Highlanders to continue denying the advancement of civilization."

Robert turned to her, his gaze cold and hostile. "Perhaps, Mistress Scott, someone should remind you that the English have eaten haggis for centuries."

"Indeed, my lord! Certainly not among those with whom I am acquainted," Elizabeth retorted.

"Lord, deliver me from the pretentious snobbery of a Sassenach," Robert taunted in disgust.

"Or the barbarous vulgarity of a Highlander," Elizabeth fired back, her eyes clashing angrily with his.

"I have developed a taste for it in the time we have been here," Anne interjected, in an effort toward arbitration. "In truth, Beth, I have learned to really like it."

"I have less taste to be schooled in its merits than I have for the haggis itself," Elizabeth retorted, feeling betrayed by Anne's defection.

"Methinks, mistress, a little schooling in the merits of social amenities would be more in order," Robert imparted with unconcealed anger.

"I quite agree, my lord," Elizabeth said with a self-complacent smile. "I am sure that the churlish act of barging unannounced into a young maiden's chambers would certainly attest to the need for a lesson in social deportment."

Robert still bristled with irritation, but he was too much a sportsman not to recognize a *coup de grace*. Obviously the lady had more than just a shrewish tongue. There was a resourceful mind behind those gorgeous brown eyes. As he studied the very attractive but defiant young face glaring at him, he could not mask his glimmer of grudging admiration. With a slight nod of concession, acceding to her having bested him, Robert rose to his feet.

"*Touché*, mistress. My apologies for that boorish deed. I can only plead unpardonable ignominy." He grinned and assisted her with her chair.

David Kirkland, who was aiding Anne,

leaned down and whispered in her ear. "I think the tally has just been tied. One up for each of them!"

As they left the dining hall, Elizbeth felt a firm hand on her arm and Robert guided her to the stairway.

"Will you please accompany me to my father's chambers, Lady Elizabeth? He has asked that we join him."

"I can only hope it is due to a change of heart regarding this ludicrous match," she hopefully opined.

They paused at the bedroom door and Robert turned her to him, a firm hand on each of her shoulders.

"I do not understand your hostility. Is your objection to this union due to a personal aversion to me, or simply to marriage in general?" he asked, looking searchingly into her eyes.

Elizabeth's gaze remained steady, returning his probing stare. "What matters my reasons or objections? Could they change anything?" she asked, attempting to turn away from him.

Robert's hands continued to restrain her. "My lady, look at me," he commanded.

Elizabeth turned resentful, hurt-filled eyes to him.

"They matter to me," he said slowly and deliberately, his eyes again probing hers. "Elizabeth, can we not call a truce? My father's remaining days are few in number. Let us not cause them to be troubled ones."

Despite her resentment toward this Highlander, Elizabeth's compassion swelled at the sight of the naked pain in his eyes.

"You do me an injustice, my lord. I have developed a deep fondness for your father. You need not fear I would say or do anything to add to his affliction."

For a few remaining seconds they stood motionless, his dark eyes seeming to penetrate to her very soul. Finding the assurance he sought in the probity of the brown eyes that met his, Robert slowly released his hold on her and opened his father's chamber door. Then warmly grasping her hand in his, they entered the room.

VIII

The moment Elizabeth returned to her room that evening, after a short visit with Lord Kirkland, she knew she had to leave Ashkirk.

The insufferable demeanor of Robert Kirkland made it impossible for her to consider wedding him at this time.

His return apparently had a stabilizing effect on Lord Kirkland, for it appeared to her that the earl's condition had been slightly improved. So, perhaps, she thought to herself, if I can just get away for a few days until Robert returns to the war, I will be able to delay the marriage.

She hesitated to inform Anne of her intentions. Her cousin was so smitten with David Kirkland that she would close her eyes to Elizabeth's plight and try to convince her to remain, or perhaps, even tell David himself! Therefore, as much as she hated not confiding in Anne, she felt she had no alternative but to leave without her.

But where would she go?

If only she were home, she lamented, there would be a dozen places to go. But here in the

Highlands there was nowhere, or no one, to turn for help except Tims. She knew that any attempt to contact him would only divulge her plans.

In a sudden dawn of inspiration, Elizabeth remembered that Walter Campbell often visited his uncle's castle, Innay, which was somewhere in the vicinity of Fort Linnhie. If only she could reach it she knew she would be safe there.

Elizabeth went to the writing desk and quickly penned a note to Anne, informing her of her whereabouts, then found her cloak and opened her chamber door.

A quick perusal revealed that the hall was completely deserted. She made her way cautiously down the stairway. A light was shining from the library as Elizabeth stealthily crossed the Grand Hall. Obviously, either Robert or David Kirkland was still awake. She slipped out the door without being observed by anyone in the house.

Elizabeth knew that the real challenge would be her attempt to get a mount. If anyone was in the stable the task would be nigh to impossible. She made her way across the courtyard and stepped into the stable.

Will, the stable master, was busily sweeping out one of the stalls. Elizabeth stepped into the shadows waiting for him to finish the task, but every moment she waited she knew it increased the danger that someone else might enter and discover her.

Her worst fears were recognized when

Robert Kirkland himself strode boldly into the stable.

"Saddle Shalir, Will," Robert ordered. "I am feeling restless tonight and want to take a short ride."

"Aye, Sir Robert," the groom replied. He went to get Robert's huge chestnut stallion out of its stall. "Ho' be the auld laird, Sir Robert?" the man asked as he and Robert saddled and bridled the mount.

"I am afraid we are going to lose him, Will," Robert said sadly. For a few seconds Elizabeth felt sympathy for the arrogant clod at the sight of his genuine sorrow.

" 'Twill be a sad day for ou' clan when the auld laird passes on. He's a fine mon, Sir Robert."

Robert patted the groom on the shoulder. "Thank you, Will. He has always valued your friendship," he said kindly.

Elizabeth could not help but notice that Robert Kirkland appeared as overpowering in the shadowy stable as he had back in the castle, although the dim lighting in the barn added an exciting, even sinister quality to his dark handsomeness.

She waited impatiently with a wily smile for Robert to leave, realizing this offered the opportunity she was seeking.

A few moments after he departed she stepped into the light.

"Good evening, Will. I feel like a short ride. Will you get the mare Sheba?"

The stable keeper looked at her in surprise

and Elizabeth flashed a flirtatious, suggestive smile. "Has Sir Robert left as yet?"

Och! Will thought slyly. The young lord an' his lady ar' sneakin' off togethe' in the woods! Ah, tha' Sir Robert, he thought fondly, ther' be nae a woman ca' resis' him. Even as fine o' one as the Lady Elizabeth.

A few moments later Elizabeth rode boldly through the postern gate, blessing Robert Kirkland for the only beneficial thing he probably had ever done in his life.

She put her mount to a hard gallop, trying to put as much distance between her and Ash-kirk as quickly as possible. The mare moved smoothly and easily beneath her. She had ridden her often since arriving at the castle and knew exactly how the horse responded to the rein.

After a safe distance she slowed Sheba to a canter and continued on her way, content in the knowledge that all had gone well. Elizabeth had never been afraid of the dark, so she was undisturbed at being alone on the narrow, inky road.

Several hours later, as Elizabeth was congratulating herself on a successful escape, Sheba pulled up lame. It was too dark for her to determine what was causing the horse's problem. She only knew that the unfortunate circumstances would certainly slow up her plans. She patted the mare's neck affectionately.

"I'm sorry, old girl. I hope it's nothing too serious."

She proceeded to walk down the road, leading the limping horse behind her.

Toward dawn Elizabeth spied a light in the distance and knew she must have reached Fort Linnhie. The town could boast of nothing other than a few shops and an inn. Set on the banks of Loch Linnhe it offered access to the sea as a quick route by water out of the Highlands.

The town bordered between Kirkland and Campbell territory, pledging its loyalty to neither clan but choosing to remain neutral in that long-standing feud.

She found no one at the stable at such an hour, although she saw several horses in stalls. She led her mare to an empty stall, removed its saddle and bridle, and after covering it with a blanket, she entered the inn.

A quick glance revealed the sleeping forms of several Campbell soldiers stretched out on the floor snoring loudly, after having imbibed an over abundance of ale.

A sleepy innkeeper eyed her entrance.

"I am seeking a room," she announced with a hearty show of bravado.

The innkeeper raised a skeptical brow. Clearly this was one of the gentry, but what was she doing alone at this hour of the night? Elizabeth saw his confusion and raised her head haughtily.

"I am the Lady Elizabeth Scott. I have gotten separated from my retinue on my way to Castle Innay," she lied glibly. "My horse has gone lame and I have put it in your stable.

I wish a room for the remainder of the night and in the morning perhaps one of these Campbell soldiers will escort me to Innay."

The innkeeper nodded in understanding. " 'Tis a dark nicht, mum. I ca' well understan' ye pligh'. I hae a room ye ca' use."

In a few moments Elizabeth was closeted in a clean, though not elegant, chamber. She slid the bolt on the door and collapsed on the bed in relief without even removing her clothing, As a precautionary measure she slipped her dirk under the pillow.

Easy! It was so easy! she thought with satisfaction. Seconds later she was sound asleep.

Elizabeth was jolted out of her slumber when a strong hand suddenly clamped down over her mouth. She started to struggle but a voice declared in deadly command, "Don't make a sound. If you as much as utter a peep it will give me a great deal of pleasure to wring your neck."

She froze at the sound of the voice. Even in the pitch blackness of the room there was no mistaking it.

"I am going to remove my hand now," Robert Kirkland warned. "I don't want to hear a sound out of you. Is that clear?"

Elizabeth nodded, uncertain of whether or not he could see the gesture. What choice do I have anyway, she thought haplessly, with his big hand practically suffocating me?

Robert released her and she remained lying quietly, as she struggled to slow the pounding of her heart. He lit the candle at the bedside then sat down beside her on the bed. Elizabeth could see in the flickering light that his eyes were black with anger.

"Are you trying to get me killed?" he hissed through gritted teeth. "This inn is full of Campbell plaids."

"I've never had cause to fear any Campbell," Elizabeth retorted with a defiant glare. "I see no reason to begin now."

"Birds of a feather!" he snorted disdainfully.

"And what is that supposed to mean?" she asked, sitting up in the bed. She was trying not to let him intimidate her, but his nearness was having an electrifying effect.

Robert grasped her shoulders in his two hands, the pressure of his fingers biting into the soft flesh. "It means that you are a two-faced, traitorous little bitch, and I should follow my instincts and cut your treacherous throat like I would any other God damned Campbell lover."

For a few seconds they stared at one another, the silence between them as telling as any words of accusation. Elizabeth was the first to speak when Robert rose and turned away.

"It's true, isn't it? Everything I have heard about the brutality of Highlanders is true." Her chin raised intrepidly as her courage increased with every word she uttered. "How dare you, Robert Kirkland! How dare you enter my chamber in the middle of the night and terrorize me! The fearsome Highland Lion! What a farce! A blustering bully capable of nothing except brutalizing women!"

Robert swung around to face her, his eyes blazing with rage. "Don't push me too far, Elizabeth, or you will learn first hand the extent of my brutality. I'll . . ."

"You'll what?" she challenged contemptuously, her own anger causing her to lose all sense of precaution. "You are nothing but a loudmouthed scoundrel. I would die before I would cower beneath your threats. Get out of this room at once or I shall scream at the top of my voice!"

"Curb your shrill tongue, my lady. My threats are not to be taken lightly just because we are to be wed."

"I'll not wed you," she lashed out. "I wouldn't wed you now if you got down on your knees and pleaded."

"Then perhaps there is another way of persuading you," he said ominously.

Before she could grasp his intent, Elizabeth was imprisoned in his arms. His lips captured hers in a hard, bruising kiss. She struggled to free herself but her efforts were useless against his superior strength and, as the warm pressure of his mouth deepened, she lost awareness of just when she ceased to struggle. She closed her eyes and surrendered to the heady excitement of the kiss.

When he finally released her Elizabeth opened her eyes to find Robert staring down at her with a bemused frown. Breathless, she met his gaze with her own confused look. Her body trembled—whether from fear or excitement, she did not know. Her eyes were wide and frightened as she backed away from him.

"Dare I hope, my lady, that you require more persuasion to convince you?" he asked huskily and took a step toward her.

Elizabeth raised up a restraining hand. "I swear I will scream aloud if you take one more step in my direction," she cautioned.

She backed into the bed and, as she fell across it, her hand grazed the edge of cold steel and closed around the shaft of the dirk that had been concealed beneath the pillow.

With the confidence of a weapon in her hand, Elizabeth rose to her feet. Robert's brow frowned in surprise at the sight of her confronting him with the drawn blade.

"Now get out of here before I thrust this knife through your black Highland heart. Be glad I care enough about your father or I would have done so sooner," she warned.

Robert remained undaunted. "I'm fast losing my patience with you, mistress. I don't take too kindly to anyone drawing a dirk on me."

With the striking swiftness of a snake, his hand reached out and grabbed her wrist. Elizabeth grunted with pain as his fingers increased their pressure. She thought the bones in her wrist would crack.

They tumbled backwards and fell across the bed, the weight of his large body pinning her down.

"Release the knife," he ordered.

Tears stung her eyes as the pain in her wrist began to travel up her arm. She finally was forced to relax her grasp on the knife and drop it.

Robert did not rise but remained lying on top of her. He stared down at her intently, watching a single tear slide down her cheek. Her heart was pounding from the excitement of his nearness and she felt she was suffocating as her breath began to come in short ragged gasps.

Was this barbarian about to ravish her? Her body began to tremble when his head dipped in a slow, inexorable descent. Elizabeth closed her eyes in despair, awaiting the bruising crush of his mouth. Her eyes flew wide in surprise when he caught the single tear on the tip of his tongue.

"I'll hate you for this as long as I live, Robert Kirkland," she murmured in a choked whisper.

Robert rose slowly to his feet and reached out a hand to help her up. Hesitantly, she placed her hand in his and felt a tingling sensation of pleasure as its warmth closed around hers.

Before releasing it, his fingers gently tested the tender area of her wrist.

"I am sorry if I hurt you," he said tersely. "Never again attempt to draw a knife on me." As though to show his confidence in the explicitness of his command, Robert picked up the dirk lying on the bed and was about to hand it to her when he stopped in surprise to study it.

"Well, well!" he commented with a wry smile. "Jamie warned me you would put it to use protecting your honor. Though I didn't think at the time it would be turned on me."

He gave it to her and Elizabeth immediately sheathed it at her waist.

"Now I suggest we get out of here at once. We have tarried too long."

Robert went to the window and waited for her to join him.

"Surely, you don't expect me to leave by the window!" she asked increduously.

"We can hardly depart through the main hall, my lady, when it is full of Campbells. Perhaps you are not aware there's a war on," he said mockingly. "Either you climb out of this window willingly, my lady, or I will toss you out."

Elizabeth stormed over to the window and leaned out to study the drop. "It's impossible for me to climb down in this gown," she declared vehemently. "I'll fall and break my neck."

"How unfortunate that would be," he remarked drolly. "Very well. Put your arms around my neck and I will carry you down."

"Don't bother!" she snapped. "I'll take my chances on falling before I would rely on your help."

"Elizabeth," he declared through clenched teeth, "when I tell you to, clasp your arms around my neck and hold on."

Reluctantly she agreed and he eased himself out the window onto the sloped roof, then lifted her body out. "Now put your arms around me," he ordered.

Robert worked his way cautiously across

the sloping roof, carrying Elizabeth as effortlessly as though she were a sack of feathers
strung around his neck. He stopped when he
reached the limb of an overhanging tree.

Robert reached up, grabbed the limb and
hung by his hands, suspended above the roof.

"This would be a most opportune time for
using your dirk on me," he grunted as he
inched his way hand over hand along the
branch. "Of course, you face the danger of
falling with me."

"It would be worth the risk of falling just to
have the pleasure of sticking my knife into
you," she answered spiritedly.

"My, my! You are a bloodthirsty little
wench, aren't you?" Robert exclaimed.

"The better to please you, my lord," she
growled.

With a deft movement he swung them onto
a thick branch that was strong enough to
support his weight when he stood on it.

"You do this with a great deal of expertise,"
Elizabeth taunted. "No doubt you have had a
great deal of experience climbing in and out of
windows of ladies' chambers at night."

Robert responded with a warm chuckle and
Elizabeth could not help but smile in response
to the infectious sound.

He began to work his way down to the
lowest limb of the tree.

"You can release your stranglehold on me
now," he said sarcastically.

Elizabeth pulled away in embarrassment,
not realizing until then how tightly she had

been clinging to him. Robert dropped to the ground and reached out his arms for her.

"All right, my lady, now jump," he declared.

"It's too far," she protested.

"I said jump, Elizabeth!" he commanded.

Elizabeth closed her eyes and jumped. The strength of his arms closed around her before she hit the ground.

Robert led her to his large stallion hidden in the trees.

"What of my mare?" she asked.

"It's too risky to get her. Besides, she is lame. We will just have to leave her behind."

"I like Sheba. I won't leave without her," Elizabeth declared emphatically.

Robert realized the stubborn wench had made up her mind, and it would probably be less dangerous to try to get the horse than to argue with her about it.

"Can I trust you to remain here quietly, or must I truss and gag you until I return?" he grumbled.

"You have my word," she answered.

He snorted in contempt. "The word of a Campbell lover!"

Elizabeth fumed in irritation, but she did not want to rile him too much lest he force her to leave without Sheba.

"On my father's honor," she swore.

He disappeared into the darkness and Elizabeth waited anxiously for his return. As much as she detested the oaf, she did not wish to be responsible for anything happening to him. In a short while Robert reappeared, leading the lame mare.

He lifted Elizabeth upon his horse and climbed behind her. Elizabeth held herself stiffly in his encircling arms, as he held the reins. However, after a short while, it became impossible to continue doing so, and she was forced to lean back against him.

"How did you know Sheba was lame?" she asked.

"I have been following your trail," he replied succinctly. "It was easy to read when she started favoring the leg."

"I hope it isn't anything too serious. Do you have any idea what may be wrong with her?"

"She's a smart little filly. Perhaps it was the scent of Campbell in the air," he answered facetiously.

"Oh, you're an insufferable oaf!" she fumed.

Elizabeth vowed she would not say another word to him. The sun had risen and they had been riding for about an hour when Robert swung the horses off the road.

"This is not the way I came. Where are we going?" she questioned suspiciously.

"A shorter route, my lady," he replied.

They followed a narrow path until he halted in a small copse of trees. Robert climbed down and lifted her out of the saddle. "It's best we rest the horses."

Elizabeth did not realize how stiff she felt until she began to walk. She headed toward a rowan tree and sat down beneath it. It was peaceful and quiet in the secluded copse; not a person or creature appeared to be moving in the glen. Since she had no say in the matter, Elizabeth leaned back and closed her eyes.

When she awoke she had no idea how long she had been sleeping. Robert Kirkland was stretched out beside her, sound asleep. How can such a rogue look so innocent, she wondered, as she studied the rugged face relaxed in slumber.

Elizabeth got to her feet and moved to the bank of a running rill for a drink of water to quench her thirst. She lay down on her stomach and began to sip the cold mountain water. When she had drunk her fill, she got to her feet and drew back in surprise at the sight of Robert Kirkland standing behind her. He grinned sheepishly and held a hand behind his back, concealing something in his hand. Elizabeth eyed him warily and he reached out and handed her the flower he had been holding behind him.

"A peace offering, my lady."

Elizabeth's eyes widened in surprise at the sight of the spray of white heather he had given her.

"It's said to bring good luck," he added.

Numbed with shock, her head raced with the words of Artle's prophecy. Was it possible that it was all true? "Thank you," she replied, still in a state of confusion.

"Elizabeth, it would be wiser if you do not say anything to my father about last night. There is no sense in alarming him about events that have already passed."

"I understand, my lord. Believe me when I

tell you I intended to return to Ashkirk after your departure."

He frowned slightly, his dark eyes clouding with doubt. "For what, my lady? His funeral?"

Robert turned away and walked back to the horse. He mounted, sitting patiently as he watched her approach. Wordlessly he reached down and lifted her up in front of him.

The sun was high in the sky when they rode through the outer baily of Ashkirk.

IX

The Earl of Kirkwood sat propped in bed, a weak smile crossing his face at the sight of the couple who had entered hand-in-hand. Without hesitation, Elizabeth bent down and pressed a kiss on his cheek.

"I missed your daily visit, gentle lady, and this morning's chapter," he said, glancing toward the leather-bound volume that lay on a nearby table. "Corla is an efficient nursemaid, but unfortunately she cannot read. I fear I will reach my demise before knowing the tale's ending."

Robert's surprise was clearly evident upon hearing of this relationship that existed between his father and his betrothed.

"I am sorry, my lord," Elizabeth said gently. "I am afraid Lord Ashley has kept me occupied all this day." She smiled. "But I am free now." She reached for the book, but Lord Kirkland shook his head.

"Nae, Elizabeth, forget it for this night." His eyes twinkled merrily. "So you have cast me aside for a younger man. How fickle a young woman's heart."

"Nae, my lord." Elizabeth smiled tenderly.

"This maiden is not so foolish as to forsake a rare wine, aged to perfection, for the unfermented juice fresh from the vine."

A pleased smile was erased from the earl's face as his body was seized with a violent coughing convulsion. Elizabeth and Robert exchanged tormented glances as she sponged the perspiration from his forehead with a cloth from the table. Lord Kirkland lay back weakly, his feeble hand clutched against his heaving chest.

"Robert," he gasped, "I know I grow weaker by the hour. My time is nearing and I have two requests to make of you. You are my heir, and when I go you will be the head of the clan. It is a responsibility you can never take lightly. You must think of your clansmen as your children, and never deny them your guidance or counsel. When they are sick, you must nurse them; if they are hungry, you must see them fed; when they are cold, you must offer them warmth. The gates of Ashkirk must always be open to any Kirkland seeking asylum."

He slipped the ring, worn only by the chief of the clan, from his finger and pressed it into Robert's hand. "The responsibility of this ring rests heavily on the finger. Never dishonor or shame it."

"I understand, Father. You need have no fear. Though I will never be able to attain the nobility you brought to it, I will always aspire to achieve it."

The old man nodded his head at Robert's sincerity. "Now my first request is a painful one . . . I am asking you to think carefully before you commit our clan to Montrose. When you are laird, the decision will be yours. I know your devotion to James, and the temptation will be there, but weigh it carefully, son. We Kirklands have always avoided the intrigues of the court, and for that reason our clan has been able to prosper and grow unmolested. When I see a great clan like the MacGregors put to fire and sword . . . ah, Robert," he sighed sadly, his mind returning to a bygone day. "They were so mighty and great—the Highland's finest."

Shrugging aside the painful memory, he turned back to his son. "The same is happening to the MacDonalds, as it will to the Grahams. Nae, Robert . . . keep the Kirkland clan intact. Do not sacrifice our finest young men for a lost cause. King Charles will lose his battle with his parliament. Montrose will only delay it—but the outcome is still inevitable. Argyll, in his vengeance, may cause any clan who aided the king to be put to the horn."

"Such talk of defeat and concession, coming from the mouth of a descendent of Robert, 'The Bruce!' You are indeed feeling your ailment tonight," Robert said in gentle banter. He grasped his father's hand tightly. "I pledge to you, Father, I will weigh my responsibilities carefully, and not let my personal feelings confuse my judgment concerning the welfare of the clan. I will not take action without first asking myself 'Would my father have done the same?' "

"You ease an old man's passing," Lord

Kirkland said with pride, as he looked into his son's eyes. "And now my second request. I want to see you and the Lady Elizabeth married immediately—this evening. I want to die knowing you are wed."

Elizabeth gasped in shock at this sudden announcement. She could not believe her ears. This whole thing had to be a nightmare from which she would mercifully awake at any moment.

"But, Father, there is no minister, and Elizabeth must have time to prepare herself," Robert protested.

"There is not time. Summon your brother and the Lady Anne to witness a handfast ceremony. That form of marriage is legal and acceptable here. You may marry later in the Kirk, but tonight, for expediency and a dying man, you and Elizabeth can be joined together in handfast."

Robert turned apologetically to Elizabeth, knowing how this request would affect her. Elizabeth's eyes mirrored her shock and disbelief at this turn of events, and she turned away, trying to force back the tears that threatened to surface.

"Go, Robert, and bring David," Lord Kirkland commanded.

Robert took a conciliatory step toward Elizabeth, wanting to offer her some word of comfort. He knew she had to be staggering under this latest circumstance. Elizabeth did not see the hand that started to reach out to her in commiseration, but at the sight of the proud back, straight and unbowed, he turned and walked swiftly from the room.

"Elizabeth, come here and sit," Lord Kirkland asked quietly, patting his bedside. "Do not hate me, my dear, for I have grown to love you in the short time you have been among us. I regret you did not come to us sooner."

Had his tone remained commanding, Elizabeth could have kept her composure, but at his declaration of love and gentle plea of understanding, she could no longer check the flow of tears. Sobbing, she rushed to his bedside and buried her head against the frail chest. Lord Kirkland's arms embraced her with loving sympathy, allowing her to spend her tears.

In a short time she lifted her head but remained sitting at his side. The earl took her hand and held it warmly in his own.

"Ah, gentle child, I know you do not understand why I insist upon this marriage. Believe me, I am not an addlepated old man, indulging a selfish whim. Any reservations I had regarding the contract I made with your father were erased when I met you. You and Robert were rightfully destined for one another, and your union will be the tempered blending of the best of two worlds.

"At this time our country is torn by a civil war—Scot slaying Scot. The only hope for us as a nation is through the merging of our nation's finest. Your children and your children's children are our only hope. When

the refined heart of the Lowlands is blended
with the stout heart of the Highlands, when
my people's impetuousity is mixed with your
people's prudence, when a Highlander's
inflexible pride in his heritage is fused with a
Lowlander's resiliency to change—then, and
only then, will there be hope for our beloved
Scotland. For all these qualities must be
present in a man for survival. And until we
recognize this, our people will always be at
one another's throats—small factions destroying each other—MacLeans against Camerons,
Campbells against MacDonalds, Gordons
against Frasers—always at the mercy of
Stuart kings, or any others who choose to prey
on us," he said fervently.

"So Robert and I are simply pawns in your
vision of a unified Scotland. We are strangers
to one another, yet we are to wed. Love?
Honor? Respect? Where are those virtues in
our marriage? Should not these qualities also
be imbued into this paragon of the future that
you fancy?" Elizabeth asked cautiously.

"My dear Elizabeth, those qualities you
mention are already present in both of you. I
know my son well, as I have grown to know
you. The chemistry is there—and time will
soon arouse it. Of that I am certain!"

A few minutes later at his father's bedside,
with David Kirkland and Anne Barday
looking on, Robert Kirkland, the Sixth
Viscount of Kirwood took the cold, trembling
fingers of Lady Elizabeth Scott into his warm
grasp—and calling upon the presence of God,
proclaimed her his wife.

Confused and reserved congratulations followed as both David and Anne were overwhelmed at the swiftness of events. The newlyweds received the blessing of the laird of the manor before Robert asked to be excused, promising to return after he escorted Elizabeth to her chambers.

She had been silent since the ceremony and, once in the privacy of her room, she crossed to a chair and buried her head in her hands. Robert leaned back against the closed door, trying to gauge the depth of her despair, hesitating to speak. He had first met this woman the previous day, and now she was his wife. He failed to understand why she could not see that he too was as stupefied as she.

"I understand, my lady, why this evening should have a disturbing effect on you," he began inadequately.

Elizabeth swung around in pent-up frustration, the tears still on her cheeks.

"Do you really, my lord?" she snarled contemptuously. "Do you really have any idea how disturbing this evening is to me? Do you know how it feels for a young girl to have to forsake her home, the familiar pastures and hills she loves, and come to a land as wild and untamed as the men who roam it? Is not this barbarous wedding evidence of which I speak?

"Have you any idea how a maiden dreams and plans each detail of her wedding from the early days of her youth? How she envisions herself in a grand hall, dancing on the arm of the man she loves, a chaste young bride, with hair flowing freely down her back, wearing the lovely gown sewn especially for the occasion? In her fantasies, she sees herself surrounded by those she loves, as she sheds uncontrollable tears of happiness.

"Well, my lord, I had my wedding day. I was that chaste young bride I had always envisioned. But what of the groom? Was this the young romantic I saw in my dreams? Nae, my lord. The man who loved me, I was forced to leave—the man I married is a stranger to me, a notorious womanizer who cares for nothing except fighting and whoring.

"And what of that wedding gown made especially for the occasion? Need I remind you it still remains folded in my trunk! My wedding hall was the desolate chamber of a dying man. Where was the beloved figure of my father among the well-wishers? Why wasn't my brother in evidence? Where were the gentle folk who raised me and watched me grow to womanhood? There was not even a minister to sanctify the ceremony, but only a few words spoken in handfast! Nae, my lord." She turned away, completely immersed in her own self-pity.

Robert could easily have responded with his own disappointment in the evening, but felt at the moment it would serve no purpose.

"Elizabeth, I had no control over this night, nor would I have planned it thus. I accepted this arrangement out of love and respect for my father, as I am sure you did for yours. I deeply regret you were forced to leave this man you love. I was away at war and was not told of your sacrifice. Am I acquainted with him?" he asked solicitously.

"You are, sir, if you have the privilege of knowing Lord Craver," she announced.

Elizabeth was unprepared for Robert's reaction. Her eyes widened in surprise when he threw back his head and began to laugh uproariously.

"Walter Campbell!" he cried in amazement. "That posturing, mincing, foppish faggot! Why, madam, I did you a favor. If that is your idea of a man, I can only tell you that you are in for some unanticipated pleasures when you are bedded by a real one."

Elizabeth's lovely face curled into a disgusted snarl. "Is that the only way you can measure a man? His prowess in bed?"

"Madam, I have never positioned myself to judge a man's prowess in bed. My tastes do not run along those lines. I fathom Lord Craver would be in a position to answer your question more so than I."

"I find your insinuations, sir, as vile and debasing as the whole evening's events."

"Then I will leave you for this night, my lady, and return to my father. To ease the indelicacy of this situation, I will summon a minister in the morn to sanctify the marriage."

His words, spoken in concession, became the straw that broke the camel's back, and Elizabeth threw all caution to the wind.

"Do not bother. I want no words said over this marriage by a minister or in the Kirk. We have a handfast marriage and that is what it will remain. I am your wife, my lord, for a year. I believe that is the legal length of time I will be forced to endure this relationship. At that time I will return to my father's house."

Until that moment Robert's attitude had been one of patronizing tolerance. Now, after her latest outburst, his temper finally exploded and Elizabeth felt the full measure of his cold, controlled fury.

"That is fine, madam. I could ask for no better arrangement. However, let me remind you that I, and I alone, will make the decision whether you will return to your home or not. If I choose to dissolve this marriage at the year's end, I will do so. I was attempting to pacify your discomfort with the relationship, but frankly, madam, I have never needed any sanctimonious mewler from the Kirk to pardon or purify any of my actions. Inasmuch as you find this arrangement to your satisfaction, you may expect my return this evening. As my wife, sanctified or handfast, there are certain wifely obligations you are expected to fulfill. You have an hour, madam, to prepare yourself. Spare me the dramatics of threatening to slice your wrists or fling yourself from the battlements. Be in that bed when I return."

In her anger and frustration, Elizabeth reached for a hair brush that lay on the nearby stool and flung it at the portal through which he had departed. A soft chuckle escaped Robert at the sound of the thud, and he continued down the hall, a grin of satisfaction on his face.

The candles in the wall sconces had been extinguished and the huge chamber of his father's was now darkened, lit only by the fire that burned in the hearth. The room was again empty except for the still figure that lay in the bed and Corla asleep in a nearby chair. Lord Kirkland's eyes opened at Robert's approach and a sanguine smile crossed his countenance.

"Father, that smile is downright complacent," Robert teased. "You look well-pleased with yourself."

"Tonight's events have gladdened my heart. I feel a heavy weight has been lifted from my chest."

"Since this night is so much to your liking, perhaps you feel well enough to deal with the wrath of my disinclined bride?"

"Gentle her to your touch, my son, but do not break her," his father cautioned. "Now leave me. This is your wedding night and you linger doltishly in an old man's chambers when your bride is waiting."

"The night is still young, Father, and I enjoy this time with you."

The earl relented willingly and motioned for his son to draw a chair to the bedside. "Then sit, Robert, and tell me how things go with Jamie Graham and the war."

For the next hour, as Lord Kirkland grinned with pleasure, Robert described in detail the chase through the mountains that Montrose forced upon Argyll and the later victory at Fyvie Castle.

Lord Kirkland finally called a halt to the

tale and closed his eyes, seeking the soothing balm of slumber.

"I tire now, Robert. I must sleep. It is time you go to your bride."

He glanced up at his son, a twinkle in the dark eyes—still alert and lucid despite his illness. His voice was strong with assurance. "Do not fear, my time is not yet upon me. We will talk again in the morning."

X

Robert Kirkland stood deep in thought, staring into the snifter of brandy he idly held in his hand, as though searching for a solution in its shallow depths. What would be the wisest approach with Elizabeth? Should he respect her privacy for this evening, or follow through with his bold threat? Lord, she was desirable—beautiful and spirited! Since their kiss in the inn he had thought of nothing but bedding her. But what of her contempt for him, and for all Highlanders in general, he thought remorsefully. She certainly will expect me to burst in and take her forcibly. Perhaps a more gentle approach would disarm her?

"Hell," Robert sighed, "she is but a woman! You are not a green school lad, fumbling and inept. You can soon have her purring at your fingertips."

With a nod of his dark head he slammed down the glass and reaffirmed his decision. "The gentle approach it will be. After all, there is no reason why this evening cannot be a pleasurable one!"

Some of Robert's confidence might have

dwindled had he been aware that his wife had reached her own decision as to how the evening would transpire. Elizabeth had pondered her plight for a lengthy time after Robert's departure. There was nowhere she could flee to avoid him, and she had discovered what a useless struggle it was to attempt to withstand him physically. Though it entirely went against every rebellious instinct she possessed, she felt the wisest action would be to simply submit meekly to him and bring the unpleasantness to a quick end. Once having bedded her, his abominable ego would be appeased, and he would leave her alone to seek the more proficient responses of the Desireé du Plessises of the world.

Having arrived at this decision, Elizabeth set about to prepare herself for Robert's arrival and now stood gowned, her hair brushed and flowing across her shoulders.

Despite her intrepid resolve, Elizabeth's stomach tightened and her breath quickened when the chamber door opened and he strode casually into the room, as though it were a nightly custom. For a few seconds his eyes examined her clinically, relieved at seeing her at least prepared for bed. His attention then swung to the large tester bed that dominated the room.

"Madam, that bed looks quick deserted. I am disappointed not to find you in it awaiting me."

Elizabeth's reply was defiant. "I recommend, my lord, you fortify yourself for further disappointments, for I have no intention of entering that bed to await you, or any man, to whom I have been chatteled."

Undaunted by her rebuke, Robert crossed to the bed and removed his boots. Then rising without haste, he poured two glasses of wine from a delicate crystal decanter that sat on the chest. He walked to her side and stood staring down at her.

Elizabeth felt dwarfed as he towered above her, and she raised a trembling hand to take the glass he offered. He sipped his wine slowly, his eyes never leaving her face. Elizabeth felt the heat from the flush that crept across her face, and she could not force herself to raise her eyes to meet his.

"How is your father?" she managed to stammer nervously.

"He is resting comfortably," Robert said. He placed his glass on the mantel of the fireplace, and, with a leisurely, controlled gesture, released the tie of her rayle. He sensed her rigid tension as he slid the lacy cape from her shoulders.

"This night can be as pleasant or as unpleasant as you choose to make it," Robert said softly.

Elizabeth had cast aside the seductive gown of sheer silk previously selected for her wedding night for a simple nightdress of white lawn that fell in flowing folds to the floor. The full sleeves were fastened at each wrist with three tiny mother-of-pearl buttons. Two similar pearls closed the round neckline that covered the lush fullness of her lovely breasts. Unbeknownst to her, the simplicity of her gown, contrasting with her dark hair shimmering in the firelight, gave her an ethereal beauty that robbed him of his breath.

"Your beauty is quite staggering, madam," he said hoarsely.

Elizabeth's eyes sought his face, surprised by the sincere tone in his voice.

"This situation is not to my liking, my lord," she half-whispered.

"Then relax, Elizabeth, and let me make it to your liking."

Robert reached out and covered her hand with the warmth of his own, bringing her palm to his mouth. Her eyes widened at the pleasant tingle that swept through her from the warm pressure of his lips. Elizabeth tried to withdraw her hand, but he held it firmly, his lips and tongue teasing her fingertips. With adroit deliberation, Robert slowly released each button at her wrist.

"Your actions unnerve me, sir," she gasped.

The corners of his eyes crinkled with humor. "I mean to undress you, Elizabeth, not unnerve you. It is not my intent to frighten you."

He released her hand and she clenched it tightly to her mouth, as though to smother the searing heat still lingering from his burning touch.

"You have not tasted your wine, and it is a fine vintage," he scolded lightly, taking the glass from her hand to drink of it. "Just take a sip, my lady, for it will relax you."

Elizabeth's lips parted to accept the glass he held to her mouth and she felt its glowing warmth as she swallowed the amber liquid.

"That's a good lass," he said almost mockingly, as he placed the glass aside. His dark eyes held her wide and timorous ones as he lifted her other trembling hand and once again slowly opened each button before placing a lingering kiss on her wrist. Elizabeth's eyes closed as a tremor shook her body when his lips found the hollow of her throat.

"Please, my lord?" she pleaded with a choky sob.

Robert's lips slid to her ear, the warmth of his breath creating a tantalizing sensation as he whispered, "Please, what, Elizabeth? Is it a plea to cease—or to continue?"

She felt an agonizing excitement building within, as his hands caressed her shoulders, before one finger burned its searing path to the buttons at the bodice of her gown. His lips found the enticing cleavage of her breasts, as his fingers released the tiny pearls, and a warm hand reached in to gently cup the swelling fullness. Elizabeth arched back, trying to pull away, but only succeeding in pressing her hips against him. Startled, she felt the bulge that his breeks were restraining.

"Would you force yourself on a woman who is not willing?" she asked with a defiant breathlessness.

"I have never had a need to force myself on any woman," Robert said confidently. "They have all come willingly, as will you."

The arrogance of his tone at once erased all her fright and preconceived intentions—and with a powerful shove she thrust him away.

"You conceited Highland whoreson!" she raged, her eyes ablaze. "You dare boast of your previous conquests while forcing yourself on me!"

For a few startled seconds Robert's eyes mirrored his surprise, before he broke into warm, timbrous laughter.

"Thank God," he chortled. "It appeared I was going to have to bed a trembling chit who would lay cowering beneath me, but now I can see that this evening holds the promise of a delightful romp."

As easily as her vision of a meek and submissive maiden dissipated, so did his fancy of a gentle and patient lover—and without any tenderness, he reached out and pulled her to him. Elizabeth found herself imprisoned by the steel shackles of his arms. His blue eyes laughed down at her, knowing she was helpless in his embrace.

"We Highlanders like our women as spirited as our horses—and we ride one as masterfully as the other," he boasted.

"No," she cried, struggling helplessly in his arms, "you can take your vile thoughts, vile tongue, and vile actions elsewhere. I am not some mare you are going to mount."

Robert's hand firmly grasped the back of her neck, forcing her head up to meet the slow, inexorable descent of his mouth. Elizabeth whimpered under the pressure of his warm lips. Walter Campbell's moist, fervent kisses had never prepared her for the mastery of the mouth that now claimed hers. Elizabeth's head reeled under the maze of confusion and excitement mounting within her, as she struggled against the devastating attack. Then, with a gradual, uncontrollable relinquishing, her lips opened to his.

When at last his mouth released hers, surprise and wonderment was evident on both of their faces.

Confused and frightened by her own response, she looked up with pleading eyes. "Please, my lord, I beg of you to stop."

"At this moment, my lady, I would probably grant you anything but that one request," Robert said hoarsely, and, once again, his mouth captured hers.

His lips were surprisingly tender as they began to draw the sweet nectar from hers. Elizabeth's arms slid around his neck and she found herself clinging to him, responding to his sensual persuasion. For a few fleeting seconds she toyed with the idea of attempting to pull away, only to have the thought incinerated by the searing heat of his touch, as his hand slid her nightdress off her shoulders.

Elizabeth stood trembling before him, fighting for some vestige of strength to resist him, her nakedness adding to her feeling of absolute vulnerability.

His gaze devoured her in a ravishing sweep of her body.

"I repeat, my lady, your beauty is staggering," he said with a rapt whisper.

Had Elizabeth been more sophisticated in *affaires d' amour*, she would have realized he spoke with sincere reverence. In her inexperience, she could only feel mortified by his lingering appraisal.

"Must you tease me, my lord, like a cat playing with a mouse? I have not the strength to subdue you—therefore, take your will with me and so be it! Then leave me to my privacy."

"I told you earlier, Elizabeth, I have no taste for bedding some lifeless cadaver, nor the need to force myself on some inefficacious female."

"Inefficacious female!" Elizabeth's temper flared, modesty forsaken by her anger. "What effrontery! Did it ever occur to that arrogant, overbearing, doltish Highlander head of yours that there is the possibility that some women may be revolted by the prospect of sharing your bed?"

"The possibility of that theory has occured to me. However, to date, the practicality of it has yet to be proven," he said with a smug smirk.

Robert effortlessly swooped her up in his arms and carried her to the bed.

"I will be more than happy to discuss the mating habits of the human animal at great length, madam, but right now I find the sight of your naked loveliness disrupts my concentration, and I feel it is time we cease tarrying and get to the business at hand."

Forsaking any attempt toward seduction, Robert dumped her unceremoniously on the bed and quickly shed his own clothing. Elizabeth stared in astonishment at the sight of his nudity. She never had seen a naked male before. He seemed all muscle and hair, molded and sculptured in a powerful, proportionate symmetry.

As her eyes traveled over his body, Elizabeth gasped at the sight of his swollen organ. Her eyes widened with alarm, and she stared transfixed.

"Surely, you do not intend to put *that* into me?" she cried, appalled.

Robert burst into laughter at her candor, and her mouth gaped open in amazement as the tumescent organ suddenly deflated.

"God's truth, woman, you do turn an effort to seduce you into a real *tour de force*," he chuckled, covering her body with his own. "I have never known an evening with more strain on my virility—for less copulation!"

The laughter left his face and his eyes began to deepen to dark violet.

"I think there has been enough words."

Elizabeth closed her eyes as his mouth lowered to hers. She shivered as the same exciting tension knotted her stomach when he began to swell against her. For some reason, unknown to her, she wanted to feel that hardness within her. Robert rained quick kisses on her eyes and face, each one a spark that seemed to imbed in her skin and lie smoldering beneath the surface. Her body quivered beneath his fingers, as his hand caressed the lush roundness of her breasts. An ecstatic moan escaped her when his tongue began to tease a nipple of a breast. The other globe quivered in anxious anticipation, awaiting the feel of his mouth, and when he finally turned his attention to it, Elizabeth cried out with pleasure.

Elizabeth felt on fire, her body ablaze with a heat that kept raging and raging. She had no rein over this inner blaze and feared she would be unable to survive before it burned itself out. Her body writhed at each touch of his exploring hands, and she arched against him, hungrily desirous of more.

Her hands began to ravage the muscular length of him, toying, seeking, as her tongue instinctively returned his darted messages. When his lips left hers, she pressed his head to her thrusting breasts, eager for the return of his mouth. Each suckling seemed to draw from the very core of her womanhood, as she tossed her head helplessly from side to side.

"What are you doing to me?" she cried in fearful rapture. "What is happening to me. I fear I will perish!"

Robert looked deeply into her eyes, now glazed with passion, and smiled tenderly.

"The French call it *La Petite Morte,*" he said passionately—then with a driving thrust he entered her.

Elizabeth cried out as she felt the painful rupture, and Robert began to slowly move within her. In seconds, all memory of pain was erased, as the scalding heat again began building, and she moaned in ecstasy when it suddenly overflowed and her body began shaking spasmodically. Robert's mouth stifled her sounds as his own body began its shuddering response.

They lay silently, Robert's arm encircling her as she rested her head on his chest. The sound of his beating heart was like a drum pounding in her ear, and she knew her own heart beat an accompaniment. When finally they regained their breath, Robert rolled her on her back and rose on his side to study her. Even the disheveled state of her hair could not detract from the exquisite loveliness of her face. She was the most desirable creature he had ever seen. He knew he had never had a more sexually satisfying experience in his life, and as he gazed at her luscious sensuousness, the fire that only moments before had been reduced to smoldering embers ignited again in the depths of his loins.

Elizabeth opened her eyes sheepishly, and for the first time she looked at him without hatred or resentment. "I had no idea," she said with wonderment. "I had no previous knowledge of a man, or how to please him. I am unskilled in the ways of love."

How was he to convince her, in her innocent throes of physical awakening, what he had already grasped with his wordly experience? That those past rapturous moments had spoiled both of them for all others—and neither would ever again know such ecstasy in any arms but one anothers.

Robert's kiss was tender when he leaned down to capture her lips, his breath a hoarse whisper.

"Who taught Euterpe to compose a lyric song? Did Terpsichore have an instructor in dance? Nae, Elizabeth, like one of those

Greek Muses, you too are a goddess—inspired in the art of love."

With passion-filled eyes he gathered her to him, his body hungry for the taste of hers.

"So, come, my lady, and transport me again to those glorious heights of Olympus."

XI

Like probing fingers, the rays of the morning sun crept across the room, seeking the large bed and the young woman who lay in it. Elizabeth stretched lazily, as the sunny beams teased her eyelids open. For a few minutes she basked in a soporific state, warm and contented. Rolling over, her eyes focused groggily on the indented pillow beside her. Long, dark lashes swept her delicate cheeks, as her eyelids repeatedly drooped, only to be forced open again, as the urge to sink back into the mellow depths of slumber wrestled with a nagging uneasiness tugging at the recess of her consciousness.

At once the significance of the indentations in the pillow washed over her in a freezing shock and she bolted upright, as though thrust into an icy bath. The blanket fell away to expose the sensual symmetry of her naked breasts. Her nudity was a bodily reminder of the events of the previous night, and the chill that seconds before had held her in a frigid grasp now warmed to a flushing heat, as she remembered her passionate response to her husband's advances.

With a quick, furtive motion, Elizabeth pulled the counterpane over the bed, as if blanketing the evidence of her hours spent in erotic delight could shroud it from her memory. A maidenly blush colored her cheeks at the sight of the nightgown, heedlessly discarded the previous evening, now lying neatly across the foot of the bed, for she knew only Robert could have placed it there.

Elizabeth hastily pulled it over her head and crossed to the window. To her surprise the first figure she saw in the courtyard below was Robert Kirkland. There seemed to be a flurry of activity as a group of riders was preparing to mount. Elizabeth's eyes remained glued on the tall form, welcoming this opportunity to study him unobserved. With grudging esteem she had to concede he was a magnificent figure of a man; he swung his long, powerful body into the saddle with a lithe and effortless motion. Helmetless, his thick black hair was cut short to the neck in the style that was so prevalent among the Highlanders. Elizabeth had to admit this pleasing contrast from the long curls worn in the fashion set by the court only added to the rugged masculinity of these men of the Highlands.

She knew she was intimidated by his manliness, and this was a new experience for her. Raised among men, she had always accepted the presence of any man with ease and comfort. Now, suddenly, she found herself entirely at a disadvantage.

From her vantage point, Elizabeth viewed

Robert Kirkland's agitation and sensed something serious was amiss, as he issued crisp orders to his men. As though sensing her stare, for one fleeting moment he glanced upward toward her window, before turning his horse and riding off with a clatter of hooves.

It was hard for her to visualize this commander as the same man who had held her in his arms the previous night. Despite her inexperience, she knew Robert had been a tender and considerate lover, when he had been in a position to take her in any manner he chose. Could her preconceived opinion of him be erroneous? With a shrug of her shoulders, Elizabeth shook her head in admonishment.

"You are a foolish twit, Beth, to allow such mellow thoughts. The man was merely playing a game of which he has mastered the moves. You are but a pawn!"

The captivating grin, that through the years had succeeded in winning her own way, captured the corners of her mouth. "Beware, oh mighty Highland Lion, for you may find yourself in checkmate!"

Elizabeth donned a simple gown of rust-colored wool, with wide short sleeves ending right above the elbow. Selecting a ribbon of matching hue, she brushed out her long hair and tied it behind to hang loosely down her back. With almost a skip to her step, she entered the room of the Earl of Kirkwood. As usual, whenever she appeared, his pleasure was evident.

"Tell me who this youthful sprite is that has

entered my chambers?"

With a gay smile, Elizabeth pressed a kiss to his cheek. Strangely enough, she could not feel any animosity toward this man, despite the fact that he had been the driving force behind her forced marriage to Robert Kirkland.

"You look enchanting, my dear, and surely not old enough to be a bride already wedded and bedded," he teased.

Elizabeth's blush accented her youthful luster. "You Kirklands have a penchant for ingenuousness," she scolded. "I dread my next meeting with David."

For the first time in weeks, the frail figure on the bed shook with laughter at the thought of his youngest son's passion for affectionate raillery. He lay back, spent and weak from his effort.

"My simple laughter has exhausted me. I will have to rest. Come back soon," he asked.

"Of course, Father," Elizabeth assured him tenderly.

Elizabeth had just finished a hot bowl of oatmeal porridge when David and Anne entered the dining room hand in hand. Her expression was noncommittal as she watched their approach.

"I swear you two are a matched set. I never see one of you without the other."

David gave Anne a broad wink. "Ah ha, the blushing bride has finally arisen. Tell me, Anne, would you say from her appearance our lovely Elizabeth passed a pleasant evening?"

He grinned audaciously at her. "Poor Anne

was beside herself with distress, fearing my black-hearted brother had done you ill—while I, on the other hand, examined him closely for evidence of knife wounds."

"Perhaps my weapons are more subtle," Elizabeth grinned impishly.

"If so," David exclaimed, bending down to kiss her soundly on the cheek, "they are most effective, for Robert seemed downright gratified this morning, until summoned away."

"Yes, I saw him take leave. What is the problem?"

"A raid by some Campbells on one of the outlying farms. Robert has taken off in pursuit."

"Does this happen frequently?" Anne asked in surprise.

"It is a way of life here," David replied, "though the war has kept most of the Campbells occupied elsewhere."

"And of course, you Kirklands never raid!" Elizabeth teased.

"Did I imply that, dear sister? Half of our horses are of Campbell stock." He grinned devilishly.

At that moment Elizabeth's gay mood vanished when she looked up to gaze upon the petite figure of Desireé du Plessis. From the time of her arrival at Ashkirk, Elizabeth always had been vexed by the presence of Mademoiselle du Plessis. Now, as the official lady of the manor, she felt it time to remove this irritating burr prickling her skin.

"Mademoiselle, may I see you privately?" Elizabeth asked, rising to her appreciable

height above the French woman. Desiree,
unaware of the turn of events, followed her
into the library. Once alone, Elizabeth turned
cold eyes to her husband's mistress.

"I will offer you escort to Fort Linnhie.
From there you may seek passage on a ship to
carry you to the port of your choice. I must
insist you leave immediately."

"Perhaps, Mistress Scott, we should wait
for Robert to decide such arrangements,"
Desiree replied, unabashed.

"I think, as Lady of the Manor, I am quite
capable of such arrangements."

"Lady of the Manor? Are you not elevating
your position prematurely!" Desiree asked,
amused.

"Mademoiselle, Lord Ashley and I were
married yesterday."

For the first time in the conversation, the
young French woman appeared taken aback.
However, Desiree was never one to be
thwarted by the mere existence of a wife, for
she had realized early in life that she would
never be as attracted to her own husband as
much as to someone else's.

"Since I do not care for indelicate scenes,
Lady Ashley, I will respect your wishes. I
have no doubt Robert will contact me
shortly," she said, smirking confidently. "Our
friendship is an old and deep one. I pity you if
you have possibly permitted yourself to
believe otherwise."

"I suggest you save your pity, Mademoiselle, for one who seeks it. I have no
intention of discussing your relationship with

my husband—nor, for that matter, my own with him."

On that declaration Elizabeth spun on her heels and left the room.

Later in the day, as she sat over tea with Anne and David, the trio was interrupted by the awesome sight of Robert Kirkland striding into the room, his spurs clinking an angry staccato on the floor. Elizabeth had time only to place her cup on the table, before she was pulled unceremoniously from her chair.

"You will excuse the Lady Elizabeth," Robert snarled to a startled Anne and David. "We have matters to discuss."

Without any consideration for her dignity, he grabbed her arm in a painful grip and ushered her roughly from the room.

Anne's eyes clouded worriedly. "He would not harm her, would he?"

"Of course not, sweetheart," David said, patting her hand reassuringly. Anne's frown remained directed at him, reflecting whether he was trying to convince her or himself.

Once in the privacy of the library, where only hours before she had stood confronting Desiree, Elizabeth now faced the glaring wrath of her husband.

"It is my understanding you sent Mademoiselle du Plessis from this house and dispatched her with an escort to Fort Linnhie."

Elizabeth raised her small chin defiantly and replied, "That is correct, sir."

Robert's eyes blackened with fury, as his anger raged uncontrollably. Grasping her shoulders Robert shook her until Elizabeth felt her head spinning.

"You damned little fool! Do you realize you have sent six of my men to their possible deaths? Fort Linnhie is full of Campbells who are bitter over their recent defeat. My men won't have a chance!"

Elizabeth's head ached from its recent rattling, and she forced back the tears that threatened to surface.

"For your information, your mistress has not gone to Fort Linnhie. She accepted the escort to Langely Castle, where I am sure she will be more than happy to accommodate you —that is if you have no objection to waiting your place in line."

Despite Robert's relief that his men were not in peril, his anger still raged.

"I told you last night, madam, I have no need or inclination for waiting in line. Since you have taken it upon yourself to banish my mistress, be prepared to fulfill her functions. And in the future, my lady, have no question. I am master here—and I, and I alone, will decide who is an acceptable guest and who is not!"

"Then let me assure you, my lord, I care not how many whores you keep—but be certain it is not under any roof that is over my head!"

The two antagonists tensely faced each other, their eyes glaring defiantly.

"I am ordering your belongings moved to my chambers. From this day hence you will be at my immediate disposal. As I stated earlier, I have no patience with delay, nor any desire to have to pat barefoot down a corridor to claim what is already mine. I prefer the convenience of simply rolling over and finding it at my fingertips."

Elizabeth, who had always been able to seek the privacy of her own chamber, stood stunned by his announcement.

"That is a vulgar and inconsiderate arrangement," she gasped.

Once again she found herself in his painful grasp, as he towered menacingly above her, a satanic expression on his face.

"But, madam, as you have repeatedly reminded me, we Highlanders are vulgar and inconsiderate."

As though to drive home his point, Robert's lips plunged down on hers in a bruising, insulting kiss. His arms crushed her against him, and Elizabeth felt his full wrath as his lips forced hers open and his tongue savagely invaded her mouth. She whimpered under the onslaught and struggled uselessly as she felt his hand slide into the neckline of her gown—and too soon his probing fingers found the fullness of her breasts. Elizabeth knew he was treating her like a cheap whore and she fought to resist this defilement. To her horror, she began to feel the throbbing tightening in her loins, as his hand continued to tease and caress. With a will of their own, her arms slid around his neck, as the searing heat consumed her. Elizabeth's tongue sought his, and she closed her eyes, surrendering to the sensation building within her. Her body began to writhe under the increased tempo of his fingers, as the volcanic sensation built toward eruption.

At the soft sound of his laughter, her eyes flew wide, glazed with passion, to find him leering insultingly. Robert released her and she stood, trembling, unfulfilled and completely debased.

"A simple object lesson, Elizabeth, to let you know who will always have the last word between us."

With a mocking bow, he turned and left the room as she sank to the floor in a sobbing heap of humiliation and frustration.

It did not take Elizabeth long to exhaust her tears, and she quickly rose and crossed to a mirror to study her reflection. Expecting to find some branded evidence of her humiliation, she was surprised to find the only change from the young girl who had gazed back at her in the morning, was a slight redness around the wide, brown eyes.

Elizabeth stared long at her image, appraising the worth of the face before her. Surely she had to possess some weapon to fight the complacent arrogance of her husband. Someday, in some fashion, she vowed she would make him rue this day for his demeaning treatment of her.

Later that evening Elizabeth leaned back to rest her head on the rim of the large tub. Closing her eyes, she surrendered to the lulling of the water. Long auburn tresses, spilling over the side of the tub, were transformed to a blaze of crimson by the glow from the fireplace, as it played on each silken strand.

For a few wayward moments Elizabeth forced aside the bitter memories of the afternoon, permitting her mind to drift back to the previous evening and those incredible hours of rapture. Lost in her daydreams, she was unaware that Robert Kirkland had entered the darkened room. He stared, transfixed at the sight of the enigmatic enchantress before him—a blending of spiritual innocence and sensual seduction. Soundlessly he moved to the tub to closer savor her loveliness.

"Should my vision be stricken forever, this moment would offer the sweet solace of knowing I had gazed on perfection."

Elizabeth's eyes flew open to encounter the very object of her dreams. Completely flustered, she sat up to reveal a pair of creamy white shoulders. Robert's eyes were instantly diverted to the tantalizing sight of two glistening breasts partly exposed as the disturbed water's sloshing motion teased them into view. Her eyes flashed with irritation as she attempted to cover herself.

"Sir, since I have been denied the privacy of my own chamber, I would appreciate your announcing your presence when you enter this room."

"Do you wish a drum roll, my lady, or would a blast from the pipes be sufficient?" he asked facetiously.

"A simple knock would do," she said irritably.

An amused chuckle escaped Robert. "Since

this is my chamber, madam, I have no need to announce myself when entering. Inasmuch as you are my wife, why this attempt to shield yourself from me?"

"My lord, we just wed yesterday. I find it most disconcerting to be bathing before a stranger."

Robert leaned intimately on the tub, an errant finger reaching out to trace a pattern with the drops of water that clung to the heaving swell of her breasts.

"My lady," he intoned coaxingly, "how can you think of us as strangers, particularly considering what we shared last night?"

"I find it easy and preferable to do so, my lord, particularly considering what we shared this afternoon."

"Last night introduced me to every inch of that lush body of yours, my dear, and my intentions are to renew that acquaintance very shortly. In the meantime, perhaps I can be of service," Robert added, reaching for the soap.

Elizabeth pounced, spraying him with water as she lunged for the bar.

"I am quite capable of bathing myself, if you will please allow me to do so," she riled.

Robert rose reluctantly. "As you wish, madam." He turned away and began to remove his boots. Elizabeth eyed him warily.

"Why are you removing your boots when we have not yet supped?"

The silent answer was a raised brow and wolfish grin.

Elizabeth's suspicious glance continued

following his movements around the room, and within minutes he returned to the tub.

"Madam, is it your intention to spend the remainder of the evening in that tub?"

"I shall remain in here until you remove yourself from this room."

The second the words crossed her lips she realized her mistake. With a quick motion he bent and lifted her from the water. Elizabeth, naked and wet in his arms, made no attempt to struggle. Embarrassed and self-conscious, she could only stammer inanely, "You are going to get wet."

"That is soon remedied," he laughed, lowering her to pull off his sodden shirt. Elizabeth reached for a towel in an attempt to cover herself, but it was quickly snatched from her grasp.

"It will be my pleasure, my lady."

Enfolding her, he began to towel her with slow, sensuous motions, his eyes never leaving her face. Elizabeth's eyes remained downcast, feeling the intensity of his gaze on her.

"Did you not have your sport earlier this day?" she pleaded. "Was not this afternoon's debasement of me enough? Must you again humiliate me?"

Robert's attention was drawn to a large bruise that darkened her arm, where he had brutally grasped her earlier that day in anger. He gently reached out to touch it, before lowering his dark head and tenderly brushing his lips to it.

"In our attempts to shame others, we often shame ourselves," he said apologetically. He released his grip on the towel and it dropped to the floor, as his hands slid up her back to pull her close to him. Elizabeth stiffened in his arms, her distrust of him evident.

"It would appear, my lady, you need to relax," he whispered softly. His strong, supple fingers began to massage the tense nerves of her shoulders. When the provoking hands moved to caress her neck, Elizabeth could not contain the erotic shudder at the feel of his arousing touch.

Robert had been waiting for this slightest sign of surrender, and he drew her to him with a smothered plea. "Trust me, Elizabeth, I will not hurt you."

Elizabeth raised confused eyes to meet his passionate stare, as he quickly divested himself of his remaining clothing. Warm hands slid up the smooth satin of her body, as he lifted her against him. Her full breasts were flattened against the crisp hair of his chest, as her body molded along the steel sinew of his. Once again, the nearness of him and the touch of his hands rekindled the flame he had masterfully lit within her, and her silky arms slid around his neck as their lips met hungrily.

With a flexible effort of his powerful muscles, Robert slowly lowered himself to lay back on the bed, never relinquishing his hold on her. His lips roamed her face and neck, repeatedly sliding to the sensitive hollow of her ear, only to return to reclaim her sweet lips. Raising her slightly, his mouth opened to a thrusting globe and his tongue began to tease the sensitive nipple, as his hands caressed her firm buttocks.

Elizabeth groaned in ecstasy, as the sensation consuming her climbed toward a towering peak. With an uncontrollable shudder, she stretched out atop the length of him, and her legs parted at the feel of his extended phallus. A fevered hand slid down, directing the throbbing organ as she would a key to its unequivocal lock. With a stifled groan, Robert rolled over and entered her, covering her face and closed eyelids with repeated kisses, before his mouth again captured a trembling breast and his tongue inflicted exquisite torture on the sensitive, hardened tip.

Elizabeth whimpered as the tempo of his thrusts increased, her body arching to meet them, and she cried out in rapture when she reached the peak and plummeted from its height, as he spilled into her.

XII

"The whole bundle!" David Kirkland shouted triumphantly, as he whisked up the final trick with a dramatic flourish. Jumping to his feet, he rushed around the table to place an enthusiastic kiss on the surprised lips of his partner. At this outrageous demonstration, Anne Barday blushed shamefully, casting sheepish eyes in Elizabeth's direction.

"Really, David, you should reward the poor girl, not punish her," Robert Kirkland teased, and turned back to study his wife. All through dinner and the entire game of Whist, his eyes had continuously strayed to Elizabeth. Her face was radiant in the afterglow of their loving. Each simple gesture or titillating laugh would capture and hold his fancy. He hungered at the sight of her lovely lips, still slightly swollen from the pressure of his, remembering the taste of their sweetness.

"Come, another hand?" David enthused.

Robert held up a protesting hand. "Another time, David. My mind is not on the cards tonight."

"A likely excuse," his brother scoffed. "Now

it begins. The lame alibis for getting thoroughly trounced."

"Then I will spare you and simply bow to superior skill," Robert conceded.

"What of this morning's raid, Robert?" Anne asked. "Did you catch the culprits?"

A grimace of disgust crossed his face. "It turned out to be nothing more than two lads stealing a cow."

At his announcement Elizabeth erupted into laughter. "You mean the mighty despot of the Highlands risked life and limb in pursuit of such dangerous desperados!" she ridiculed.

Again her infectious laughter spilled forth and spread to David and Anne, and the three of them were soon enmeshed in a fit of hilarity.

Robert Kirkland, who earlier in the day had been so frustrated by the incident that he had gone to the extreme of overreacting to Elizabeth's banishment of Desireé, again began to become irritated at finding himself the brunt of their laughter.

"And tell me, my lord, did you string these dastardly scoundrels up by their thumbs, or simply smite them with a mighty swoop of your broadsword?" Elizabeth continued recklessly, unmindful of Robert's growing displeasure.

"*Bien au contraire, madame*," Robert growled, "I lowered their breeks and thoroughly spanked them. A chastising, which at this moment, I am most tempted to apply to my wife."

In her short, but intimate, acquaintance with Robert Kirkland, Elizabeth had learned the full impact of this tone, and her laughter died as quickly as it had begun.

"I think, my lady, it is time we say our good-nights. I feel receptive toward another lesson in Greek mythology, and we must yet visit with father."

"Greek mythology!" David exclaimed. "Since when are you interested in Greek mythology?"

"Oh, Elizabeth's knowledge of it has me completely captivated," Robert declared, his dark eyes alight with mischief. He took her hand and drew Elizabeth to her feet. "Particularly, her comprehension of Mount Olympus. It leaves me gasping and pleading to know more."

As they mounted the stairs Elizabeth threatened through clenched teeth. "Someday, my lord, I am going to cut out your black Highland heart."

"I have no doubt, my lady." He laughed unabashedly, as his arm slid around her waist. "Of that, I have no doubt."

As the rapping on the door awoke her, Elizabeth found herself curled against Robert's long frame, her hand resting casually across his hip. The fire had burned itself to a faint ember, but her sudden chill was not from the coldness of the room but rather from the urgency of the pounding on the door.

"Sir Robert, come quickly. It is the laird, sir," Corla pleaded through the closed portal.

Robert was on his feet instantly and quickly pulled on his breeks as he hurried from the room. Elizabeth put on her nightgown and found a warm robe. She picked up Robert's shirt and carried it with her to the earl's chamber.

David Kirkland had also been summoned and stood opposite Robert at their father's bedside. Elizabeth slipped the shirt over Robert's bare shoulders, as he stood in these final moments with his father. She felt a familiar hand, turned to meet Anne's compassionate nod, and squeezed the hand grasping hers in acknowledgement of her sympathy.

A few minutes later, holding a hand of each of his sons, a tranquil smile crossed the gentle countenance of the Earl of Kirkwood as he closed his eyes and peacefully surrendered to a lasting slumber.

Elizabeth went to the chapel to pray and shed her tears. She knew she would miss the warmth and quiet dignity of this man who had grown to mean so much to her in the short time she had been in this strange, frightening land. His passing left a feeling of emptiness that only the loss of a good friend can bring.

When she returned to their room, she found Robert slumped despondently in a chair. Elizabeth wanted to reach out to comfort him, to let him know he was not alone in his grief—that others suffered the same sense of bewildered despair—but, unfortunately, the pattern set between them prevented any gesture of empathy. She dressed quickly and quietly, then crossed to him and stood momentarily before his chair.

"I loved him too," she said, commiserating.

Robert looked up at her with the same vague, obtuse expression she often remembered seeing as a child in her father's eyes.

"He was not a difficult man to love," he murmured, quickly returning to his seclusion.

Without any further testimony of sympathy, Elizabeth quietly stole from the room, leaving him alone with his grief.

The following day, the Kirkland clan and close neighbors began to gather for the funeral of Michael Kirkland, the Sixth Earl of Kirkwood. From daylight the road was crowded with mourners, some in carriages and some on horseback, but most on foot, making their way to the gates of Ashkirk.

The castle had been a flurry of activity—rooms were readied, and the ovens of both kitchens were busy throughout the night.

Elizabeth stood at a window, watching the steady stream of people arriving to pay their last respects. Lord Kirkland's body had been prepared for burial and lay in state in the Grand Hall.

Turning sadly from the window, Elizabeth crossed to the mirror to finish her dressing. Pulling her hair off her face, she wound it into a loose bun and pinned it to the top of her head. The starkness of the hair style tended to emphasize the striking beauty of her high cheeks and wide brown eyes. She chose a

simple gown of black velvet, its roundly
scooped decolletage and fitted long sleeves
complimenting the delicate lines of her lovely
neck. Her only adornment was a narrow strip
of red and black Kirkland tartan draped
across her shoulder and bosom and pinned to
her waist, its ends falling loosely into the folds
of her gown.

The Grand Hall seemed filled almost to
capacity. Robert, engaged in conversation,
halted in mid-sentence when he looked up to
see Elizabeth descending the stairs. Mesmerized, he crossed to the foot of the stairway and
waited, his eyes never leaving her face. When
she reached the bottom step, they stood, their
eyes locked, for a few brief seconds.

"You are quite lovely, my lady."

Elizabeth's faint smile acknowledged his
compliment. Robert reached out a hand and
picked up the plaid that draped her bosom,
lightly toying with the material between his
fingers, a tender smile of approval on his face.

"Across your heart, my lady?" His tone
belied the skepticism of the question.

"I wear it only, my lord, in deference to
your father," she defended.

Robert's eyes held hers for an endless
moment, and she felt herself flush under the
intensity of his stare.

"He would have been pleased. The Kirkland colors become you, Elizabeth."

With a slight nod he placed her hand on his
arm and they joined the assemblage.

The slow beat of the drum accompanying

the low mournful wail of the pipes carried plaintively across the quiet hills, as Robert's uncles and cousins bore the casket holding the body of the earl to its final resting place. The solemn procession of mourners followed behind, the different colored plaids and tartans in colorful array. Elizabeth shivered and pulled her wrap tighter, as an icy blast swept around them. She could not help but admire the magnificent sight of these tall Highlanders, their kilts swirling around them in the wind. Her eyes were drawn to Robert, who also wore kilts in honor of the occasion. A short black velvet jacket covered his white shirt, ruffled at the wrists. The muscular symmetry of his long legs were displayed by tartan hose, which came only to his knees, and his boots had been forsaken for a pair of brogues. His dark hair was covered with a red tam, a knotted cockade of black in the band. He reached the grave site and paused, his brother beside him.

David's dress was similar, the main difference being Robert's gold chain and medallion, worn only by the chief of the clan. The two men, standing side by side, appeared impervious to the cold, and though weaponless, they emanated an aura of invincibility.

Robert's suffering was etched on his handsome face, but he stood composed through the ceremony—silent and unwavering.

Feeling Elizabeth's stare, he raised his eyes and met hers with an inscrutable expression, and she found herself puzzling over the thoughts passing through his head, for this man was still a stranger to her despite the long hours spent in his arms.

As the ceremony ended, she felt a hand slide into hers and looked down to see Tims' sad eyes. Elizabeth squeezed his hand warmly and smiled tenderly down at him.

The skirling pipes began their mournful dirge, and each and every mourner paused briefly at the grave to shovel or scoop some dirt over the coffin, until finally the last man had paid this final homage—and a mighty Highland chieftain had been laid to rest.

Once the burial rite was over, the atmosphere of pall that had hung over the mourners changed to a quiet celebration of Robert's and Elizabeth's marriage.

She marveled at how easily people adjusted to the death of a loved one, stoically accepting the course of life. Somehow they were sustained in knowing that a new life replaced the old one, comforted not in the evidence of one's own immortality but rather the immortality of humanity.

Elizabeth was a charming and gracious hostess as she struggled to catalog the numerous faces and names. Robert's sudden marriage had come as a surprise to those present, and their expressions of condolence over the loss of his father were soon counterbalanced with offers of congratulations over the beauty and charm of his new wife.

By early evening most of the people had departed except for a few men grouped around Robert in discussion of the war. The remaining women sat in small clusters studying and discussing the new earl's young bride.

Elizabeth was piqued at the sight of Desireé du Plessis clinging to the arm of Lord Langely. Strangely enough, during the day, she had felt a tugging at her heart whenever she had spied the dark head of her husband bent attentively over the French woman who was whispering in his ear.

To her relief, Lord Langely was departing and Elizabeth crossed the room to the stairway to say goodbye. David Kirkland and Roger Langely were occupied in plans for a future hunt, and Desireé and Robert were engrossed in conversation. Robert was unaware of her approach, but Desireé saw her coming and immediately slipped into French, unaware that Elizabeth understood it.

"Je vais quitter Langely Castle la semaine prochaine. Quand te reverrai-je?" (I will be leaving Langely Castle next week. When will I see you again?)

Robert, frowning, replied, *"J'ai beaucoup a faire avant de retourner a Montrose. Je me mettrai en rapport avec toi plus tard."* (I have much to put in order before I return to Montrose. I will contact you later.)

Elizabeth forced back her anger, and with a fetching smile, turned to the two.

"Se vous voulez, je peux sertir afin que vous puissiez regler vos affaires entre vous." (If you two would prefer, I will leave while you make your arrangements; I will be glad to accommodate you).

Before turning away, Elizabeth had the satisfaction of witnessing the shocked surprise on the woman's face. Robert regarded the departing figure of his wife with an expression of amused esteem.

XIII

The warming rays of the morning sun had just brightened the gray sky and a blanket of frost still covered the ground and trees with an icy mantle. Clouds of vapor streamed from the nostrils and mouths of the snorting horses, as they pawed nervously at the ground in the cold dawn. Their acrid, pungent smell hung offensively on the frigid air.

Elizabeth stood shivering in the early morning light, anxious to be underway. She turned impatiently toward her husband. Robert and David Kirkland, their heads together, were conferring quietly.

When Robert told Elizabeth he must traverse the clan, she felt it was merely a ploy to go off with Desireé du Plessis. She had been pleasantly surprised when he had announced he expected her, as his wife, to accompany him. Strangely enough, Elizabeth had welcomed the opportunity.

As their conversation ended, Robert affectionately slapped David on the shoulder and approached her.

"Are you ready, my lady?"

As he reached to assist her, Elizabeth raised

her skirt to expose a pair of bright colored trews in the Kirkland tartan. The new Earl of Kirkwood's mouth gaped in astonishment.

"What in the world?"

Elizabeth halted before swinging her leg over her mount. The fetching roundness of her *derriere*, a blazing plaid of red and black, was suspended only inches from his face. Her eyes looked down mockingly into his.

"Worn obviously in deference to you, my lord."

Elizabeth settled in her saddle as Robert swung into his, his dark eyes glowing with contained laughter.

"You told me you wore our colors over your heart for my father. Is there some significance I should place on your selection this time, my lady?"

"You are most perceptive, my lord. You see, your father could claim my heart. While you, sir, will never be able to claim anything other than what I am sitting on."

"Would you not say you are at least keeping up your 'end' of the bargain," he teased, a simpering grin on his face.

"Your crassness, sir, only confirms my belief that we share nothing in common other than a few forced moments in bed."

With puckish devilment Robert chanted, "Alas, my lass thinks I'm crass. Denies me her heart, but offers her ass. *Impasse!*"

"Sir, if your vulgarity continues, I will turn about and return to Ashkirk. Perhaps the women you associate with are not offended by such talk; however, I find it insulting. I will never be able to suffer your company."

Never one to ignore a tossed gauntlet, Robert challenged, "How can you be so certain, Elizabeth?"

Elizabeth turned to the tall figure riding beside her. Their eyes met and held in a long, probing search.

"My lord, never doubt for a moment my will is less than yours. Do not confuse physical submission for total subjugation. You must resort to a usage of might to win your arguments. I prefer more subtle methods. Frankly, I find most of you Highlanders vulgar barbarians. But you, my lord, are actually the worst, for you have the knowledge to be otherwise, but you choose to deny that knowledge. You people steep yourselves in family pride and heraldry but are content to watch your lands lie wasted, while you idle in drunkenness and indolence. Yet you are all willing to rush off to fight any bloody battle that presents itself, under your noble guise of honor and loyalty."

Robert's dark eyes flared angrily. "Madam, we are oft falsely accused by our critics. The fact that our land is steep and rocky makes it unconducive to farming, yet we waste not a measure of any part of our beloved Highlands. *Where* we can, we raise *what* we can. Most would consider that industrious, not indolent.

"As for those barbarians you speak of with contempt, they do not have to prove themselves to you in any way. They are both feared and respected by all of their enemies. I do not feel I have to defend or explain my complete dedication and loyalty to them. Because I am of their blood, you too have that same loyalty. The respect has yet to be earned."

Elizabeth drew herself up in disdainful hauteur.

"And why, pray thee, am I expected to have that same loyalty?"

Robert's reply was an absolute, unequivocal declaration.

"Because you are my wife, Elizabeth."

His unrelenting eyes locked with hers. Unwavering, she met their challenge.

"For a year, my lord." With a prod from her heels, Elizabeth's mare bolted forward.

For the next quarter hour they rode in silence, both enmeshed in the tangled, confused web of their own thoughts. Elizabeth was perplexed by her mixed feelings for Robert Kirkland. She could not deny the strong physical hold he had on her. Despite her attempts not to yield, he always exacted a physical response from her during their coupling. Elizabeth hated herself for this weakness, vowing it was merely due to the fire that Robert had ignited within her. Surely once lit, any man would be able to kindle the blaze!

They soon reached the tiny clachan of Kirkmuir. The village consisted of several cottages, a smithy and a church. The cottages were simple, rectangular two-room structures with walls of unmortared rubble stone and thatched roofs. Windowless, they offered a single doorway that opened into both rooms. The family lived in one, and the livestock was stabled in the other.

Though most of the Kirkland clan was Protestant, Elizabeth was surprised when she noticed a Catholic Church, for those who still clung to the old religion. The small barren building, windowless like the other cottages, had wattle sides and a thatched roof. Its only adornment was a birchen altar and a crucifix hanging from one wall.

Robert and Elizabeth halted outside the largest cottage in the village, and, after dismounting, he lifted her from her saddle. The man who came to the door filled the small threshold with his girth. At least eighty years of age, the old man had hair of pure white. He wore the typical Highland dress: a wiz, which was the plain white shirt of the Highlands, along with a belted plaid, a pair of brogues on the feet, and tartan hose to his knees. A sleeveless deerskin vest covered his chest.

The most fascinating feature of the man was the quiet dignity of his bearing, as he stood straight and completely unbowed.

At the sight of Robert, the lined face widened to a smile and he stepped out to embrace him.

" 'Tis the young laird, Mary," he called into the house in a booming, deep voice.

They were joined by a woman in her late sixties. She was dressed from neck to ankles in a plaid, pleated and tied around her waist. A small linen square, tied under her chin, covered the wound braids of the top of her head. Her plump arms opened to embrace Robert, and the two stood, hugging one another warmly, before Robert kissed her. The woman reached up and rested a hand lovingly on his cheek, tears glistened in her eyes.

"Ah, Robbie, we hae missed ye, lad."

Robert again hugged her, before kissing her wrinkled cheek.

" 'Tis sad, I am, to hear o' the laird's passin'. 'Twas a grievous day for all o' us. We loved him, Robbie."

"I know that, Mary, as did he. He died content with that knowledge."

The old woman peered around him to stare at Elizabeth standing quietly aside.

"An' wha' hae we here? Is this bonny chil' ye bride? Ye Lady?"

Robert reached out a hand to his wife.

"Elizabeth, I would like you to meet my cousins, John and Mary."

Elizabeth returned the friendly nods that greeted her.

"John is the Seannachie of the clan, the official record keeper. He records all the births, deaths, marriages, baptisms, or what have you. He even keeps track of who owns what cow."

"It sounds like a very important responsibility," Elizabeth said.

"One I can nae take lightly, lass," John said with a serious smile.

"Will ye come hae a taste o' tea?" Mary offered.

Elizabeth soon found herself seated at a plain trestle table. Mary quickly brewed a pot of tea and appeared with a small plate of oatmeal cakes. John laid a thick tome on the table, and with a steady hand carefully recorded the dates of the passing of the Earl of Kirkwood, the name of the new laird, and the marriage of Robert Kirkland of Ashkirk to Elizabeth Scott of Ballantine.

"Were ye wed in the Kirk by Reverend MacKinstry?" John asked.

"No, we had a handfast ceremony at Ashkirk," Robert replied.

John's brow lifted in surprise, his disapproval evident. The scratch of the quill broached the silence, as he continued his laborious entries.

"And yer witnesses, lad?"

"The marriage was witnessed by my father, the Earl of Kirkwood, my brother, Lord Blakely, and the Lady Anne Barday, a cousin of my wife," Robert answered.

The quill was passed to Robert, and then to Elizabeth, as they documented their signatures in the historic chronicle. Blotting the ink carefully, John closed the book and returned it to a metal box. His business completed, he joined them at the table.

"Now tell me, Robbie, will ye be callin' up the clan?"

"I have not made a decision as yet."

"Ye are the laird now, Robbie. 'Tis your choice. Wha' ye wish, we all wil' do."

"I have not reached a conclusion. It is an important decision and I must weigh it carefully."

"Aye, lad, tha' ye must," John agreed, with a nod of his silvered head. "Ye're too braw a lad for me to turn o'er me knee wi' a whack, should ye dinna use ye head."

Robert threw back his dark head and laughed with pleasure, as John turned to Elizabeth.

"Aye, m'lady, manys the time I hae to put this young mon, or tha' rascal David, o'er me knee and pull down their breeks. They were devils, they were!"

"I do not have the slighest doubt," Elizabeth agreed, sensing the warmth and love in the chastising.

Robert's eyes crinkled with mirth. "And everytime he did, Mary would slip David and me a sweet cake when he was through."

"Robbie," Mary scolded, " 'twas our secret."

John raised his bushy brows sternly. "I ca' see, woman, I to' the switch to the wrong one. 'Twasna the lads that needed the whippin'."

Feeling like an interloper, Elizabeth sat and listened to the byplay between the three people and witnessed their deep-rooted affection and love for one another.

In a very short time they were joined by the other villagers, and Elizabeth remembered many of the faces from the funeral. Before they departed the clachan, Robert and Elizabeth joined them all for an afternoon tea of cheese and dark bread, washed down with an ale brewed from the tops of heather.

Elizabeth learned much that day, as they

rode through the clan. Wherever they went they were met with warmth and affection. If these people were warlike, it did not surface in their relationships toward one another. She witnessed a people gifted with a spontaneous humor. She saw their sensitive and genuine appreciation for the beauty of not only their Highlands, but the sound of a lilting tune or the lines of a poetic verse. Most surprising to her was the fact that despite their lack of education, they had a devastating satirical wit that could surpass the most sophisticated scribes and poets of the Court.

Elizabeth had never been a person to attempt to fool herself too long, so to her astonishment she found herself grudgingly admitting she liked these Highlanders.

The very appealing Countess of Kirkwood later that evening sat with chin propped on knees, reflecting on that very fact, unaware of Robert Kirkland's eyes on her.

A snowfall had caught them on the road and Robert had to abandon his intention of reaching his hunting lodge before nightfall. Elizabeth had been appalled at his suggestion of spending the night in a cave, but he had assured her it was a long-cherished boyhood retreat. Now, with a warm fire blazing away, and having dined on cold grouse, bread, and a bottle of wine that had been packed that morning, Elizabeth at the moment was feeling quite mellow—and very reflective.

"What deep thoughts, my lady. Am I any part of them?" Robert asked, as he added wood to the fire. Having studied her while she sat engrossed in her thoughts, his whole body had begun to ignite with a heated desire for her.

"How many cousins do you have, my lord? It seemed everyone called one another 'cousin.' "

Robert chuckled lightly. "It is a form of address we use here in the Highlands. It makes everyone equal to his neighbor, none having a greater position than the other. The only rank recognized is that of the laird."

Elizabeth pondered this concept, recalling the pretentious formality at home. She knew none of their farmers at Ballantine would ever think of calling her or Andrew cousin.

"I must admit—the custom has merit."

Robert's brow wrinkled with feigned astonishment.

"You mean there is actually something about the Highlands that meets your approval!"

"Oh, there is much about the Highlands I enjoy," she countered defensively, her chin thrust out at an adorable angle. "I find them breathtakingly beautiful and have never seen anything quite like them. They are inspiring. I can understand why all of you are poets, since there is a spiritual essence about them."

"That is quite a confession, my lady."

"That is why I am confused how they can harbor such blackguards," she added capriciously.

Robert's desire for her now was uncontrollable. He took her in his arms and pressed her back to the floor of the cave. His length covered her as he stared down into her round, startled eyes, his own ablaze with passion. Robert's hand reached out and tenderly brushed some dark strands of hair that lay on her face, his fingers lingering to caress a delicate cheek.

"And I must be the worst blackguard of them all, Elizabeth—for no matter how you feel about me, I want you and I must have you. If I cannot claim any part of you but your body, then that is what I will settle for. But take you, I must, Elizabeth," he whispered hoarsely before his lips closed over hers.

XIV

As they approached the small sequestered hunting lodge of Kirkmuir, Elizabeth felt she was entering a primeval forest untouched by a human hand, untrodden by the footfalls of man—Eden revisited! But unlike Adam and Eve, she was awed not by the knowledge of their being the first man and woman—but more so at being the *only* man and woman.

The tiny cabin appeared like an intrinsic part of the spectacular terrain. Nature had miraculously planted and nurtured it to grow in the same way as the towering pines and birches that surrounded it.

The pine lodge contained only a single room. An alcove bed was built snugly into one wall, while a loft accommodated any additional guests. A pine table with benches stood in a corner and fur pelts and rugs adorned the pine walls and floor. A wall of rubble stone offered a fireplace and oven. As at Ashkirk, the Kirkland coat-of-arms hung over the fireplace, a visual proclamation of ownership.

Elizabeth stood in the center of the room and looked around appreciatively. She liked the intimacy of the lodge, as well as its mas-

culinity, sensing an aura of placid composure
—complete harmony between the room and
its inhabitant.

"Will you be able to suffer it for a few
days?" Robert asked, studying her reaction.

"A few days?" Elizabeth asked, surprised.

Robert appeared almost apologetic. "I
thought we needed this time to get to know
one another."

Elizabeth's eyes widened with initial
surprise. "Then you have brought me here for
a honeymoon?"

"Are you disappointed, Elizabeth?"

"No," she answered quickly and frankly.
"David said I would have to 'beard the lion,'
and this is the lion's den, isn't it?"

"How did you guess?"

"It has the feel of you. I sensed it the
moment we entered."

"You are very intuitive, Elizabeth. I built it
myself."

"I like it, my lord."

The air was becoming charged with the
feeling building between them, and Elizabeth
said nervously, "I do think, though, we could
use a fire."

"I think we have just built one, my lady,"
Robert said softly, and turned away to the
fireplace.

In the days that followed, Robert showed
Elizabeth how to make biscuits from the
supplies he had brought with them. They ate
oatmeal or cheese in the mornings, and in the
evenings, feasted on fish from the icy lake or

whatever fresh game he managed to stalk and capture.

Often Elizabeth hunted or fished with him, displaying the skills taught by her brothers. This enticing wood sprite was a different woman to him, and Robert delighted in her. She had long abandoned her cumbersome skirt and roamed freely about in the trews borrowed from the brother of Tims Kirkland. Robert marveled at her horsemanship, as she handled her mare masterfully and confidently on the rocky terrain.

The day arrived when Robert knew he had to return to Montrose. It had been several weeks since he had left, and he could not put it off any longer. Elizabeth was napping, and he left the cabin to find something special to celebrate this last evening together.

Elizabeth awoke, disgruntled to find him gone. She had looked forward to an outing and was annoyed with herself for falling asleep, thus missing the opportunity to go with him.

Elizabeth soon convinced herself to take a ride, and dressing in her sheepskin jacket and hood, she saddled her horse and rode off. The first half hour was spent searching for Robert, but, finding no sign of him, Elizabeth abandoned herself to the sheer enjoyment of the ride.

The white flakes began to fall softly, unobtrusively, deceivingly tranquil in the silent way they fell to the ground. Then without warning, a blustering wind swept down from the mountains, driving the snow with blizzard force. Elizabeth quickly turned her mare to return to the cabin.

The might of the wind was devastating, as it pelted the blinding snow against them. The ground was bcoming wet and treacherous, and Elizabeth prodded the horse cautiously along. The snow had already deepened, making it difficult for the mare to find footing. Suddenly the horse's front legs buckled as it struggled frantically on the slippery granite rock, and Elizabeth was tossed forward over the mare's head. She had been unaware that they had been close to the side of a precipice, and Elizabeth found herself tumbling down the side of the craggy hill.

At the bottom, she lay momentarily gasping for breath, an excruciating pain in her right knee. Regaining her breath, Elizabeth sat up and gingerly reached down to check the injured leg. With relief, she discovered that no bones were broken, but when she attempted to rise to her feet, the knee immediately buckled and she slid to the ground.

Elizabeth could see the mare still standing above, apparently having regained her footing without tumbling over the side. She began to crawl up the side of the hill, but for every inch she gained, she slid back two inches on the slippery slope.

She had no idea how long she continued to struggle, but after hopelessly spending all her energy, Elizabeth finally collapsed in frustration. The cold began to penetrate her dampened clothing, sending shivers through her body. She looked upward for some vestige of hope, only to discover the mare had disappeared.

Elizabeth prayed silently that the horse had wandered back to the cabin, and that somehow Robert would find her. In her desperation she began to call out to him, hoping he would hear her voice above the howling wind.

Robert had already saddled his horse and was ready to start his search when Elizabeth's mare limped in. One look at the animal was all he needed to tell him the story. After quickly removing the saddle, he covered the mare and swung onto his mount.

Robert had returned to the cabin as soon as the first flakes had started to fall, having long been familiar with the force of a snowfall in these mountains. When he discovered Elizabeth gone, he had not wasted any time in preparing to set out to find her. Now, with the return of her mare, his worst fears had been confirmed.

He followed the track of Elizabeth's mare, hoping it had taken a direct route back to the lodge. The snow was beginning to deepen, and, in a short time, the prints were almost obliterated. The problem was intensified by a bitter wind driving the snow into swirling drifts. His anxiety continued to mount, since he knew full well that Elizabeth could not possibly survive if she were hurt and exposed. His heart leapt with relief and he said a quick prayer of thanks for the trews of Randy Kirkland when he spied a patch of bright color halfway down a steep hillside. Dismounting, he flung caution aside and rushed, half-sliding, down the hill to the fallen heap in the snow.

Elizabeth was unconscious, and Robert cradled her against his chest, tenderly brushing aside the snow that lay on her face and lashes. For a few brief seconds, his fingers caressed the soft cheeks, before forcing some brandy down her throat from a silver flask. Choking on the burning liquid, Elizabeth opened her eyes. At the sight of the familiar face, she threw her arms around his neck in unrestrained relief. Robert hugged her tightly, bewildered by the depth of his own emotion, and, without conscious design, his lips closed over hers in a deep kiss.

"I never believed I would ever be this relieved to see you," she stammered, shaken more from the kiss than her physical plight.

Robert began to rub the circulation back into her hands, a bemused expression on his face. He, too, had been physically affected by the kiss. He had always enjoyed kissing Elizabeth in the foreplay of their coupling. Once he broke through the barrier of her resistance, her sweet lips always opened warmly and receptively, and kissing her was exciting and arousing. But that was in the heat of passion, when his mind was on seduction. Why should he be shaken by a kiss on a frozen hillside in the midst of a blizzard?

Elizabeth continued to watch him wordlessly, her eyes wide and trusting, as he began to chafe her legs and ankles. She cried out in pain when he reached for her right leg and began to rub it.

"I am afraid I wrenched it in the fall," she said, in answer to his concerned look.

"Elizabeth, I must get you back to the lodge."

Robert's expression was grim, and once again, he brought the flask to her mouth, as he forced her to swallow some more of the scalding liquid. Picking her up in his arms, he struggled to the top of the hill and lifted her onto his horse. Mounting behind her, Robert grasped her tightly against himself, covering them both with his plaid. Elizabeth snuggled against his chest, seeking the warmth of his body, as his arms tightened protectively around her. She was reminded of their night in the cave, when he had held her in the same fashion, as they had lain together under the warm folds of his plaid.

In a short time they reached the lodge and he carried her into the warm cabin and sat her before the fire.

"I must stable the horse. Do not move until I get back," he cautioned.

Elizabeth had no intention of moving. She remained curled before the fire. Its warmth began to penetrate the chill that had gripped her body. Within minutes Robert had returned, and her wide eyes followed his every step as he set about preparing a hot bath for her.

"Get those wet clothes off," he ordered, when he had the water heated to his satisfaction. Without further argument, Elizabeth complacently removed her clothing, and Robert lifted her into the tub. In a short time the water succeeded in relaxing her tensed muscles and a languor enveloped her, as she lolled in its warmth.

"How do you feel now?" Robert asked solicitously, bending over the tub.

Elizabeth smiled at him. "I feel just as I did when I was about to freeze to death. Does this mean I am about to drown?"

Laughter sparked his dark eyes. "I guess I had better get you out, then."

Robert lifted her from the tub and began to dry her with a large linen. Elizabeth watched him as though removed from her own body, as he knelt to towel the length of her. He had removed his shirt and the rippling motion of the muscles across his shoulders held her completely transfixed. In her hypnotic state she saw the muscled arms reach out to lift her effortlessly. Robert carried her to the fire and placed her on a large fur, quickly covering her with another warm pelt.

"Now, my little snowbird, drink this," he ordered.

Elizabeth sat up, pulling the fur around her breasts, and drank the liquid offered her.

"It is delicious! What is it?"

"It is just some brandy in hot milk," he said and sat down beside her.

Elizabeth lay back languidly. The warmth of the fire and the brandy she had consumed blended to create a feeling of complete mellowness, with the sensuousness of the fur against her naked body an added aphrodisiac.

Elizabeth studied Robert, as he gazed pensively into the fire, sipping from a tankard containing brandy. He sat casually, leaning back on one arm, his long legs stretched out before him. The fire played on the dark rumpled hair and cast a carmine glow on the strong, handsome profile. Her eyes strayed to his broad chest with the dark hair tapering down the lean stomach. Elizabeth forced herself not to reach out to run her fingers up the arm that rested only inches away on the floor.

"I think we had better check that leg," he announced suddenly, turning his attention to her.

Elizabeth slid her right leg from beneath the fur. Robert held it firmly in his strong grip and began to probe it gently with his other hand.

"It feels fine now," she said, shaken by the sensations his fingers were creating, as they moved up her leg toward her thigh. She reached for the tankard he had set aside and drank the remaining brandy.

"This is a bonny limb, Elizabeth Kirkland," Robert said, admiring the leg he held.

Elizabeth leaned over and placed a hand on his arm, an adorable look of intensity on her lovely face.

"I have another one just like it," she whispered, and slid her other leg out for his inspection.

Robert laughed in amused appreciation. "I am afraid, my lady, you have drunk too much brandy."

Unabashed and completely uninhibited, Elizabeth continued boldly, "Do they please you, my lord?"

"Oh, indeed, they do, my lady." Robert nodded assertively with a pleased grin.

An infectious smile was his reward, and once again Elizabeth leaned over to confide to him.

"Yours also please me, my lord."

"Mine? My what?" he asked perplexed.

"Your legs, my lord. You have a fine pair of legs," she sighed, lying back on the fur.

Robert could not contain his laughter. "I am afraid, my lovely, besotted young wife, you are really going to hate yourself in the morning for what you are saying tonight!"

Elizabeth giggled gaily, her eyes twin pools of deviltry. "Am I really, Robert?"

Robert's breath caught in his throat at the sound of his name on her lips. It was like music to his ears. This was the first time they had shared such a moment with each other. She had never laughed with him before—or called him by his name. Her laughter had always been directed *at* him. As he stared down at her, an irrepressible smile crossed her face; her thick auburn hair was a coppery opalescence against the fur. Robert felt she was the loveliest, most desirable woman he had ever seen.

Elizabeth reached up her arms and lightly encircled his neck, toying with his hair.

"I also have two arms. Do you find them bonny, too? As a matter of fact, I have two of almost everything," she said beguilingly.

"Elizabeth, love, if you are attempting to seduce me, you are going to succeed." He grinned and lowered himself to her. His lips claimed hers in a long and tender kiss.

"Yes, my love, I find your two bonny legs pleasing. I find the feel of your two silky arms around me exciting, and I can get lost in the depths of your two unforgettable eyes," he said hoarsely, as he pressed a kiss on each eyelid. His lips slid to an ear and his mouth began to nibble at the lobe.

"I could play with these two tiny ears all night, were it not for those two tempting lips that draw mine to them."

With that, his mouth again covered hers in a searing, deepening kiss. He did not have to force a response from her, as her lips opened eagerly and hungrily to his.

Robert's hand slid down and swept the fur aside as he rose to study her breasts, cupping a quivering globe in each hand.

"And these two luscious, luscious breasts," he whispered softly, "I could feast on them forever."

Lowering his head, Robert's tongue began to lazily tease the rosy peak of one and then the other, until Elizabeth was drowning in passion, as wave upon wave of rapture began to wash over her.

Robert's lips trailed a scorching path down her stomach to the sensitive junction of her legs. Elizabeth's response was uncontrollable.

She writhed in ecstasy, as his tongue probed, begging him to stop while at the same time pressing his head tighter to her.

Robert again found her mouth, his lips savoring hers and smothering her moans of pleasure. Reluctantly, he drew away and gazed into her passion-filled eyes.

"You are delicious, Elizabeth. Do you want me to continue?"

Elizabeth's reply was instinctive. She covered his face with quick, fervent kisses. Her mouth sought his in a sweet, lingering kiss before sliding to his chest, as her hands leisurely explored every inch of his body with fiery probes. The limit of his control was pierced when she fondled his manhood. With a smothered groan, Robert entered her, and they rolled entwined to a torrid, devastating climax.

Later, Robert lay relaxed as Elizabeth studied him, her head leaning on her raised arm, as her other hand played with the matted hair on his chest.

"Did you ever bring *her* here?" she asked softly.

Robert had been trying to ignore the exquisite torture of her breasts pressing against his bare chest.

"Did I ever bring whom?"

"Desireé. Did you ever bring Desireé here?"

"No," he grinned, "I have never brought any other woman here."

An unconcealed smile of pleasure escaped Elizabeth at this announcement.

"Do you love her, Robert?"

"Do I love whom?" he asked, facetiously.

"Oh, you know who I mean. Do you love Desireé?"

Robert turned to her and stared up at her for a few seconds.

"Now, I am certain you are going to hate yourself in the morning," he grinned, placing a kiss on the tip of her nose. He pulled her down to him, his arms tightening around her.

Elizabeth lay contented, her head on his chest, listening to the wind howl around the exterior of the lodge. She felt safe and secure in his arms, unmindful of the fact that Robert had failed to answer her question.

The sound of Robert crying out awoke Elizabeth from her slumber. She found herself in bed, but had no idea when Robert had carried her there. He lay beside her, tossing in the delirium of a nightmare. Elizabeth reached out to feel his head and discovered he was in a cold sweat. She shook him gently, trying to wake him. Without warning, her shoulders were seized in a strong grasp, and he bolted up, crying out, "For God's sake, you must stop them!"

Robert's eyes opened and for a few dazed seconds he stared in a horrified stupor.

"Robert, what is it?" Elizabeth asked, her concern clearly etched across her worried countenance.

He lay back, his body beginning to shake with tremors.

"For heaven's sake, Robert, what is it? Are you ill?" Elizabeth cried in alarm. She quickly got a towel and began to wipe away the perspiration that covered him. Fearing he was chilled, she pulled his shuddering body to the warmth of her own, cradling his head against her breasts. Robert's arms encircled her waist in a clinging, desperate grasp. Elizabeth felt the shaking gradually subside and she gingerly turned him over, leaning across him to wipe his brow.

"Robert, what is it?"

"I guess it was just a nightmare," he replied, shakily.

"Why don't you tell me about it?" Elizabeth asked, sensing a dark secret that needed to be brought out into the open.

"It is not a pleasant story," he said, grimly.

"I do not think it could be to have such an effect on you," she said, intuitively.

"It happened during the war," Robert began with a shuddering breath. "We had taken Perth and marched toward Aberdeen. Our spirits were high, and I guess we were feeling pretty cocky. There were about three thousand enemy soldiers garrisoned in the town to about fifteen hundred of ours. These were much better odds than we had at Perth, except that we knew the citizens were also armed and had been drilled, so it certainly was not going to be easy. We now had about fifty horses and some muskets against their cavalry of about six hundred men. Our scouts reported that Argyll was about a three day march away with a force of over six thousand men and some heavy cannons.

"When we reached the city," Robert continued hesitantly, "the General divided us the same way he had at Perth. We had the Highlanders on the flanks and the Irish in the middle. I was mounted on the right flank, and Nat Gordon had the left flank. Jamie sent a messenger under a flag of truce to the commander of the garrison, advising him it would be wisest to send to safety the women and children, along with any ill and infirm. Jamie assured him we would not harm anyone who chose to leave. A young lad, the son of one of the Irish, accompanied the messenger as a drummer boy."

At this point Robert halted and threw an arm over his eyes unable to continue.

"Go on, Robert," Elizabeth urged, gently.

"The offer was rejected, and as the two returned, the garrison opened fire on them and the child was killed."

Elizabeth gasped with shock, and a sob escaped her as Robert continued his agonizing account of the grisly events of that day.

"The Irish were outraged at this vile, senseless act, and there was no restraining them. Colkitto said they would make an example of the town for all to see. Balfour drew his troops out right before the town. The son of a bitch figured he could annihilate us without any effort. They set up some skirmishing on my flank, and Jamie figured that since they were strongly dug in at the center of their line, their serious attack would come from the left. He quickly reinforced Nat's position. Just as Jamie figured, Balfour threw his cavalry at our lines. Oh, Elizabeth, whatever those crazy Irish lack, it is not courage! They stood their ground and let the cavalry ride down on them, then opened their ranks to let it through, following Montrose's orders. We then turned and faced them, cutting them off entirely from their own infantry and the town. Meanwhile, the Irish charged and completely shattered the Convenanters' lines. They broke and ran back into the city, with the Irish in pursuit.

"It was a raging hell," Robert said in his torment. "The fighting was completely disordered. It was a bloody hand to hand combat, from one house to another. There was no distinguishing between citizen and soldier—they both fell under the claymores of the Irish. The rest of us didn't reach the city's gates until we had broken their cavalry. We tried to round up as many of the citizens as we could, attempting to protect them while the Irish plundered and sacked the city. Jamie had no control over them. Even their own officers, like Alistair MacDonald or Magnus O'Cahan, could not restrain them. Bodies were strewn everywhere. Blood was spattered on walls and streets. Houses and warehouses were sacked, many of them burned. By the time we left the city, over one hundred citizens had fallen, and there was not a house that remained unpillaged," Robert said in despair.

Elizabeth tenderly mopped the perspiration from his forehead.

"Did you really believe that war could be

an honorable thing, Robert?" she asked gently. "Did you think it just a game where no one really suffered or died? Nae, Robert, in any war the innocent must suffer along with the guilty. That is what makes war such a heinous crime against mankind. Wouldst that it could be just the transgressors who perish! There will always be good and bad on both side—the innocent falling and perishing with the guilty. Are their deaths simply a victory over an enemy? Were they not Scots, too, Robert?"

He turned agonized eyes to her. "I guess that is what is the hardest to bear. When I fought in France, or against the English, it was simple and uncomplicated. God, I can still see the look on Jamie's face! You have never seen such torment. What happened there was against every principle he stands for. The killing of Scots—our own country-men—preys deeply on both our consciences."

Elizabeth's hands cupped his face lovingly, her eyes twin pools of compassion. "War has no place for men of conscience, Robert. My brother fights with Argyll. What if he falls at the end of your sword?"

For a few seconds, their eyes met in anguished despair. Then, with an agonized plea, he buried his head in the velvety fullness of her breasts.

"Oh, God, Beth, love me? Please love me?"

Elizabeth fondled the dark head, pressing it against her bosom. In the torment of a woman torn between love and honor, she lowered her lips to meet his, as she whispered sadly, "You were right, my lord. I will hate myself in the morning."

XV

The light from the lone lantern hanging loosely in the stall projected eerie silhouettes against the wall of the barn, as the two figures crouched over the thrashing beast that lay in the straw.

Elizabeth Kirkland brushed aside an errant strand of hair that had fallen free of the ribbon that bound her dark auburn locks, her concentration centered on the terrified animal.

"Hold down her head, Tims," she cautioned, wiping away some of the perspiration from the black velvety coat of the mare, the trembling body already sleek with sweat.

The panting of the horse, its lungs heaving from the strain of exhaustion, pain, and fright, was somewhat muffled by the straw.

Elizabeth felt the contraction along the smooth side of the horse and flung herself across the animal to restrain it, as the mare attempted to struggle to its feet.

"Hold her down, Tims, don't let her stand up," Elizabeth cried in alarm.

The glazed eyes of the agonized mare rolled upward, as the painwracked body contracted with another spasm. In horror Elizabeth saw thin, flailing legs begin to emerge from the birth canal.

"Oh, God, the foal is turned wrong. Its legs are out!" Her eyes frantically swept the stall seeking something to aid the animal's plight.

"Tims, quickly. Get me those reins," she cried, pointing toward the narrow strap of leather hanging on the wall.

Again the horse heaved violently in an attempt to get to its feet, as Tims released his hold on the head. Elizabeth struggled with the frightened animal, straining to keep the panicky horse down.

Suddenly, miraculously, strong hands reached out to aid her. Surprised, her head swung up to meet the dark eyes of her husband. For a few seconds she stared with shocked pleasure, before Robert drew his dirk from the sheath of his waist. He quickly sliced the rein and with a tender smile of confidence handed Elizabeth the strip of leather.

She quickly bound the four legs that had slipped from the horse's cavity, then leaned back with an exhausted sigh. Her eyes mirrored her mounting apprehension.

"The foal has to be turned now. I do not know if I have the strength remaining to do it," she half-sobbed.

"Let me, Beth," he offered as he rolled up a sleeve.

Elizabeth did not need any further coaxing and immediately moved aside to hold the mare's head.

"Where the hell is Will?" Robert asked irritably.

"Will broke his leg, and David has gone to Langely Castle," Elizabeth replied defensively, as she watched Robert carefully fold the foal's legs and push them back up into the birth canal. His hands were gentle as he cautiously probed until he found the wedged form, then began to slowly rotate it. The frightened mare began to heave against his invasion and Elizabeth began to whisper soothing words into its ear.

"Quiet, Lysia. Hush, girl." Her hands began to gently stroke the mare's head.

In a few seconds, Robert turned the foal and began to ease it out. Tims Kirkland gaped in astonishment as the foal, released from its almost fatal restraint, slid out of its mother, shrouded in a shimmering mass of grayish membrane. The foal's legs were quickly unbound; then, with a nod from Robert, they left the stall, leaving the newborn to its mother's care.

Robert quickly washed his hands, then turned to Tims.

"Tims, lad, will you go and ask Ardyss to fix me a meal? I have ridden all day getting home and some hot food will be welcome."

"Aye, m'lord." Tims grimaced and quickly scampered from the barn.

Now alone together, Robert turned his attention to his wife. Elizabeth leaned against the outside of the stall, her eyes aglow as she gazed at the mare and its foal.

"If you want a real view, madam," he said,

grinning, "the best seat is above." Reaching for her hand, he led her up the ladder to the loft.

Elizabeth stretched out on her stomach to watch the tender scene being enacted below. Lysia was gently licking clean the newborn colt. The foal's coat, shiny with moisture, was plastered down and Lysia was patiently cleaning the entire tiny body.

"Isn't it beautiful, Robert?" Elizabeth marveled, her eyes misting.

Robert dropped down on his stomach to lay an arm across his wife's shoulders, drawing her to his side. He buried his chin in the perfumed softness of her hair, his breath warm against her cheek as the two lay contentedly watching the horses.

With a gentle nudge the mare nuzzled her colt, and the young foal attempted to rise. Elizabeth gasped and grabbed his hand as she held her breath, watching the colt struggle to its feet on trembling, wobbling legs.

She sighed her relief. "He did it! Isn't he precious? He looks all legs."

Robert's only reply was a soft chuckle. Rolling over, Elizabeth looked up into his dark eyes. "Isn't it the most beautiful sight you have ever seen, Robert?"

Robert Kirkland gazed down at a pair of deep, brown eyes. His body began to feel the telltale stirrings, aware of the softness that lay beneath him.

"Nae, love. I am looking at the most beautiful sight I have ever seen." His lips lowered and began to tenderly press kisses on her lips and eyes. With a soft sigh, Elizabeth's eyes closed languorously as Robert's lips slid to the hollow of her neck. His hand began to release the buttons of her dress as his lips continued to rain kisses on her face and eyes. A sob of ecstasy escaped her when his lips trailed a scorching path to her breast. Seconds became centuries of exquisite rapture as his mouth and tongue suckled and toyed.

Elizabeth's body, as denied and starved as his, erupted into a writhing explosion of passion beneath him. Her hands and fingers helped strip him of his clothes, as he did likewise to her, until the soft curves of her body were molded to the muscular hardness of his.

At times during their passionate coupling, expressions of love and desire were muttered by both—but mainly whatever they had to say to one another was being said by their straining bodies and fevered lips.

Legs entwined as they rolled together. Lips joined as they clung together. Hands roamed and sought as they merged together—each of them offering generously and accepting greedily.

Finally, their passion spent, Elizabeth lay beneath him, Robert's head buried in her hair. Both of them were exhausted and breathless, unwilling to move.

When Robert finally pulled away from her, Elizabeth could not contain the shiver that swept over her, as her body protested against the removal of that familiar mantle of strength and warmth.

Robert quickly donned his trousers, then

attempted to help Elizabeth with her dressing. For some inexplicable reason she herself did not understand, she flushed self-consciously.

"Please, Robert, I can dress myself," she stammered in embarrassment.

She could feel his eyes on her as she completed her dressing. Finally, unable to resist the magnetic pull of his gaze, she was forced to look at him. Wordlessly, he reached out and began to pick pieces of straw from her hair. He was aware of her change of mood and completely perplexed by it. His hand grasped some of the auburn locks and pulled her head back. Elizabeth's eyes widened in alarm at this unexpected savage gesture. Robert's long supple fingers reached out and gingerly caressed her face, like a sightless man seeking knowledge through touch.

"Who is the real Elizabeth? How many woman lie behind the depths of those incredible eyes?" he asked in torment.

"I am no mystery, Robert."

"You are mind-boggling, woman! One moment you are full of inflexible strength, fighting to save an animal from dying— seconds later you bcome a captivating sprite full of awesome wonderment at the sight of a mare and her colt. In my arms you become a writhing, uninhibited wanton—until released, when you turn into a blushing demure innocent. Circe or Caesar's wife? Aphrodite or Medusa? Are you my fundamental strength—or my greatest weakness?"

Elizabeth lay back and Robert followed her

down, his lips finding hers in a long, tormented kiss.

"Am I truly such an enigma, Robert? Or does your mind seek to tell you thus? What does your heart say?" she asked breathlessly.

Robert's smile was pensive as his hand caressed her cheek.

"My heart tells me that I love you. That I should trust you. But I have never known a woman like you before. I never realized that a man and woman can share what we have shared together. My only need for a woman has always been sexual. Now suddenly I find there can be an intimacy between a man and woman entirely unrelated to their shared moments in bed."

"Or haylofts," Elizabeth said with a captivating smile.

"Or haylofts," Robert agreed lovingly. "This is a new experience for me, Elizabeth. A frightening one. It will take time for me to learn to live with such a feeling. You will need patience."

"I am not certain I have the patience you ask! I will try, but I cannot promise. This, too, is a new experience for me. My mind tells me that I can only be hurt."

"And your heart?"

"My heart tells me to savor the moments I can—that you belong to me as much as you can belong to any woman. But, I don't know, Robert. I don't know if that is enough.

"Come, my lord," she said, attempting to rise. "We dally here and your food must be long ready."

A firm hand pressed her back and his dark eyes flashed devilishly. "Surely, my love, you cannot think I traveled all the way back here simply to eat some of Ardyss's haggis do you?"

Elizabeth's arm slipped around his neck and the giggle that followed was smothered as his warm lips closed over hers.

Elizabeth paused at the stall for a lingering look at the curled up little bundle lying between its mother's front legs. Lysia, standing protectively over her foal, cast a dubious glance in Elizabeth's direction before continuing to chew on some hay.

The sun was already high in the morning sky when Elizabeth emerged from the stable. Little more had been said between Robert and herself because sometime during the night they had both fallen exhaustedly into a sound sleep; upon waking this morning, she had slipped from his arms, pausing only long enough to re-cover him with his plaid before descending the ladder from the loft.

Several brows were raised in surprise at the sight of the lady of the manor slipping into the rear of the castle through the kitchen entrance. Pieces of straw embedded in her hair and her disheveled appearance added to their curiosity. Elizabeth had almost succeeded in reaching the privacy of her room when suddenly her chamber door opened and a confused Corla confronted her.

"My lady, I have been seeking you. Lord Craver is awaiting you in the library."

Elizabeth was flabbergasted. "Lord

Craver! Whatever is he doing here? Quick, Corla, help me change my dress."

Within minutes, Elizabeth, in a fresh gown, her long tresses hastily brushed, waltzed through the doorway of the study. At the sight of her, Walter Campbell jumped eagerly to his feet.

"Walter, what an unexpected pleasure." Elizabeth beamed, as she reached a slim hand out to him.

With an elegant bow, Walter Campbell brought her hand to his lips, his eyes blatant with his hunger for her.

"Ah, Elizabeth, still as beautiful as ever. How I have yearned for the sight of that lovely face."

"Walter, it is so good to see you again," Elizabeth enthused. "You must tell me the news from home. My father and brother— are they both well?"

"Everything is fine, my love. They send their regards. Your brother Andrew is serving in the English army now."

Elizabeth sighed, relieved to find out that the possibility of her husband and brother meeting in combat had become more remote.

"Then he is no longer part of Argyll's army?"

The delicate, smug features of Walter Campbell contorted in a grimace of disgust. "My uncle no longer leads the army. Because of a few fortunate victories by Montrose and his rabble, Edinburgh feels he is not qualified to command and has put General Baille in charge."

"Well, what brings you this far west, Walter?"

"I am housed at my uncle's nearby castle in Innay. I heard David Kirkland was visiting Langely Castle, so I thought it would be an advantageous time to visit you."

Elizabeth frowned, remembering Robert's presence at the castle, and clutched his arm.

"It is not wise for you to be here now. You must leave, Walter."

Misinterpreting her warning gesture for eagerness, Campbell pulled Elizabeth into his arms and began to press a fervent kiss on her lips. His familiar touch awakened memories of a home and loved ones she had missed for so many months, and without any conscious design Elizabeth's arms encircled his neck and she returned his kiss.

"I hate to disrupt this touching scene, but it appears, Lord Craver, your timing is remiss. My brother is not in residence; I, unfortunately, am—an unexpected setback to your little rendezvous."

Startled, Walter Campbell swung around, his arms releasing Elizabeth. Robert Kirkland, legs crossed before him, lounged in the doorway. His arms were folded casually across his chest. Elizabeth had seen that casual pose often enough to know it belied the controlled predation of a jungle cat ready to spring.

"Robert, you do not understand. Let me explain."

Her words froze in her throat when he

swung cold, accusing eyes at her, blackened with his contained fury.

"Madam, I suggest you return to your room. I will attend to you later."

Elizabeth's temper flared at the audacity of the threat. "Sir, how dare you! I refuse to stand by and let you insult me or my guest."

"Lady Elizabeth, with your permission I will curb his libelous tongue," Walter Campbell declared, his hand reaching toward the scabbard at his side.

Robert's eyes mocked him, as his lithe body straightened slowly. "The pleasure will be all mine, Craver. Inverlochy proved how easy it is to defeat Campbells."

"You can scoff after such a heinous act?"

"Nea, Craver, I do not scoff at the fallen. Your kinsmen were brave men who fought valiantly. I scoff at the ones who ran. Where were you and that craven coward Argyll while your clansmen were defending his home?"

"My uncle thought it wisest to disembark. Since I was with him I had no other choice."

"You and that whoreson bastard deserted your own clansmen. Fifteen hundred men spilled their blood on the snow that day."

Elizabeth's gasp attracted the attention of both of the angry men. Her eyes were wide with incredulous disbelief.

"Fifteen hundred men! Are you saying fifteen hundred Campbells were slain at Inverlochy?"

"The Campbell clan was destroyed at Inverlochy," Robert declared.

"I cannot believe it! My God, I cannot comprehend such devastation! How many dear friends fell that day? How many Scot mothers must bury their sons? How many wives must mourn their husbands? Must the hills of Scotland flow red with the blood of our own, while Argyll and Montrose carry on this senseless struggle over who is to sit on the English throne?"

Elizabeth sank into a chair, her head buried in her hands.

"Walter, please, leave now. I beg of you, please go, before there is more killing."

"As you wish, Elizabeth."

Robert hesitated, then stepped aside, as Walter Campbell brushed past him. For a few moments after his departure they both remained motionless, the air heavy with tension, until Robert finally broke the silence between them.

"I congratulate you, my lady. You have truly amazed me. A cuckhold husband is a role I am unfamiliar with."

"I will not listen to anymore of your baseless, insane accusations," Elizabeth declared, rising to her feet. As she attempted to pass him, her arm was caught in the bruising grasp of her husband.

"You will leave this room, madam, when I say you may. Until that time you will listen to what I have to say."

Elizabeth exploded with anger. "I have no intention of listening to anything more you have to say. You have already said too much.

You are an uncouth barbarian, Robert Kirkland. I do not know why I believed that there could ever be a relationship between us. We will never have anything in common. I was a fool to think otherwise."

"Then we are both fools, madam, but I the greater. Like a lovesick knave I left my comrades to come back just to see you. And what do I find but my whoring wife in the arms of her lover!"

Unable to contain her fury at this last jealous accusation, Elizabeth placed a stinging slap on his face.

"I hate you, Robert. I will never forgive you for those words."

"Forgive me? Madam, you have refused me your love and denied me your loyalty. What need have I for your forgiveness? I will leave you and return to the war. I will expect your presence at Ashkirk when I next return."

With a slight nod of his dark head Robert turned and departed without a backward glance.

Elizabeth's eyes were red and swollen from crying when Anne returned with David that afternoon. David Kirkland was intensely disappointed at missing Robert's brief visit. Anne immediately attributed Robert's hasty exit and Elizabeth's appearance to a misunderstanding between the couple. She was attempting to pry the truth from her cousin when a breathless rider appeared to tell David Kirkland that Robert had been waylaid by

Walter Campbell and his men—and was now
a prisoner at Innay.

"What will happen to him, David?" Elizabeth asked in alarm.

"I am not certain. Since Inverlochy, Edinburgh has condemned Montrose to hanging
and quartering. I hate to think of the fate they
have decreed for his officers. Somehow, we
must get him out of there. The castle has only
a small garrison, but we can not possibly
storm the walls."

David Kirkland's handsome face frowned
in worried consternation. "How in the name
of God am I going to get Robert out of there?"

XVI

The metal gate creaked in protest as the gatekeeper sleepily cranked the lever that put the cogs and wheels of the heavy pulley into motion.

"Wha' lady wud be ou' a' this time of nicht?" he grumbled to himself, as he strained with the effort of raising the heavy gate.

Elizabeth Kirkland, accompanied by a groom, stepped beneath the heavy structure of the postern gate as it swung upward.

"I am the Lady Elizabeth Kirkland," she announced haughtily to the yawning attendant. "I seek Lord Craver. Is he in residence?"

"Aye, mum, tha' he is," the man replied. "Is Lord Craver expectin' ye, mum?"

"Just take me to him. I am sure he will have no objection."

Turning to her groom, she ordered, "Jim, see to the care of our horses. We will spend the night here."

Since nearly all within the castle had retired for the night, a sleepy-eyed servant aroused from slumber led her to a room at the end of the corridor. When Elizabeth entered it she was shocked to see Robert Kirkland tied to a chair, his hands bound behind him. Walter Campbell and two men stood above him, and it was evident from Robert's tousled appearance and the blood trickling from the side of his mouth what her entrance had interrupted. Robert's dark eyes could not conceal his surprise at her appearance.

"Lady Elizabeth!" Walter Campbell said, startled to see her. "If you have come to plead for your husband, it is useless. He is a political prisoner."

"Plead for him!" she scoffed. "Surely you jest, Sir Walter! I have come seeking asylum."

"From whom do you flee?" he asked in surprise.

Elizabeth glanced nervously at the men guarding Robert. "If I may speak privately to you, my lord?"

With a nod of dismissal, the two men left the room.

"Now, how may I serve you, my lady?"

Elizabeth flung herself into his arms and began sobbing against his chest.

"Oh, Walter, if only I would have listened to you . . . I should have come with you today. In fact, I should have defied my father and gone away with you before ever coming to this desolate and horrible place."

Walter's arms closed protectively, a smile of self-satisfaction on his face. "Did he harm you, my dear?"

"We had a terrible scene after you left this morning." An enticing white shoulder was exposed as Elizabeth pulled down the sleeve of her gown to reveal an ugly bruise on her arm. "Look what he did to me, Walter. My life has been unbearable," she sobbed, as he pulled a lacy handkerchief from his cuff and offered it. "Daily I am surrounded by uncouth louts with no manners or refinements. When he is home it is even worse. Then I am forced to submit to . . ."

Elizabeth halted, unable to continue, and again buried her head against his chest. "I am fleeing Ashkirk, Walter. Nothing will ever force me to return there."

"What of your marital obligation?"

"We have a handfast marriage. There were no words spoken over us in the Kirk. When the year is over I will be free—but I cannot bear another moment in that horrible place."

She turned pleading, helpless eyes to him. "You must help me, Walter!"

"Of course, I will, Elizabeth," he said smugly.

Elizabeth flung her arms gratefully around his neck and his lips closed over hers in a fervent kiss.

Robert had listened to the whole conversation with abject contempt, stunned by Elizabeth's betrayal. Now at the sight of his wife in another's man's arms, he strained helplessly at his bonds in an effort to free himself.

Breathlessly the two pulled part and Campbell's lips found the smooth satin of her neck. Elizabeth's hands roamed freely over Campbell's body, and encircling his waist she drew him to her. Robert silently cursed his fate, praying for a few seconds of freedom to be able to strangle her with his own hands.

"How I have waited for this moment, my love," Campbell declared ardently. "Tonight you finally will be mine."

Elizabeth's eyes widened with surprise when his hand slid into the bodice of her gown and caressed her breasts.

"At last I will taste of this luscious fruit."

Elizabeth drew away. "You forget, Walter, I am still a married woman. The Kirk will not accept any adulterous actions. As the nephew of the Duke of Argyll, the Kirk's staunchest supporter, you could never be a party to adultery."

"Your husband will soon be dead, along with the rest of his rabble."

His eyes gleamed greedily at a sudden thought. "Would you not be wiser, Elizabeth, to return to Ashkirk. With your husband's execution in the immediate future, you stand to profit quite handsomely."

Elizabeth studied the lean scheming face and for the first time wondered what she had ever found attractive about it.

"Lord Blakely is my husband's heir."

"That is true, Elizabeth, but a grieving widow always gets a piece of the pie. Then when we marry, a pretty dowry will accompany your pretty face." Greedily he pulled her to him and kissed her hungrily.

Elizabeth crossed to her husband and stared down at his blazing eyes.

"What say you, Robert? You have been unnaturally silent? Do you approve of our scheme?"

"Release my hands, you scheming bitch, and I will show you what I think," he said through gritted teeth.

"You can see, dear Walter, how abusive he can be, both verbally and physically. You are certain he is securely bound?" she asked fearfully.

"Of course, madam. You need not have any fear."

Elizabeth turned back to Robert and taunted, "How does it feel, dear husband, to have the shoe on the other foot? All that mighty strength you used against me is now useless."

"You best hope, my lady, it remains so." His eyes blazed his contempt. "It would comfort me to squeeze the remaining breath out of that treacherous, double-crossing whore's body of yours."

Robert's head rolled to the side as Walter Campbell reached out and struck him viciously.

"The cock crows with brazen bravado," Campbell sneered. "You are safe with me. He can never harm you again. A quick trial by my uncle and his head will roll."

"What a shame," Elizabeth mocked as she tousled her husband's dark hair, ". . . and such a handsome head, too! I venture to say on that day half the whores and wenches in Scotland—and I should add part of France—will be in a state of mourning. Without the mighty 'Rutting Lion'—oh excuse me, I mean 'Highland Lion'—it will probably be safe again for a lady to travel these hills." She smirked viciously.

"What of your escort, Elizabeth? Do you travel with a guard from Ballantine?" Campbell asked, returning to the table to raise a tankard of wine to his mouth.

"No. My father has no knowledge of my leaving Ashkirk."

"Surely, my lady, you did not dare to travel alone! What escort have you?"

"Why, who better to encircle the Lady of Ashkirk then Kirklands." She smiled innocently. Then with a flourish of her hand, Elizabeth added, "As a matter of fact, Walter, I fear they now encircle you, also."

Robert Kirkland's astonishment was as great as Walter Campbell's, and Walter swung around in surprise when the red and black Kirkland tartans appeared in several passages and doors.

"My compliments, Lord Craver," David Kirkland announced, stepping forward with sword in hand. "We meet again."

Walter Campbell drew his weapon. "This will be an easy night's work. First you, Blakely, and then your treasonable brother."

David Kirkland smiled and gestured beckoningly with his sword.

"Let us see if your sword's thrust is as bold as your tongue's."

The two men began to circle cautiously, the clang of metal echoing through the great hall as they thrust and parried at one another.

Robert's surprise was evident when Elizabeth produced Campbell's dirk from the folds of her gown and quickly sliced his bonds.

He rubbed his wrists to drive away the numbness in his hands and arms. Rushing to the table, he grabbed his scabbard and unsheathed the sword.

"He belongs to me, David," Robert called out.

Campbell smirked contemptuously. "I have no preference which of you I kill first."

David nodded and lowered his weapon. Robert and Walter Campbell approached each other slowly, like stalking lions, their weapons in readiness. As adept a swordsman as he was, Campbell soon found that the excessive amount of wine he had consumed rendered him no match for Robert's strength and skill. No matter how swift his thrust, or how quick his step, Robert was able to parry with a strong backhand or adroit movement. When Robert's weapon grazed his cheek, Campbell lowered his sword in concession.

"We said nothing of first blood," Robert taunted. "I think our quarrel goes beyond that."

Elizabeth ran to Robert's side, her eyes pleading. "No, Robert, please do not continue. I cannot be a party to this. I could not stand by and let him destroy you, but I cannot let you do the same to him either. I beg you to lower your weapons."

Reluctantly Robert's arm lowered. "All right, Elizabeth, I guess I owe you that." Turning to Campbell he said, "It appears, Lord Craver, the lady has extended your existence, as miserable as it is! Perhaps some day we will meet in battle."

"Robert, we still must get out of here," David cautioned.

"Then bind him quickly," Robert ordered.

Within minutes, Walter Campbell was securely gagged and bound in their chair that had just recently held Robert. Elizabeth paused briefly before him, her eyes contrite as Campbell glared up at her.

"Forgive me, Walter. I am sorry to have deceived you, but I could not bear the thought of any more bloodshed. Try to understand that in all honor I had to try to save him. He is my husband."

There was no time for any further comment as Robert grasped her hand and pulled her along with him. Stealthily they crept down the hallway to the darkened kitchen, lit only by the fire in the hearth. The garrison slept in the room beyond. The party cautiously inched their way past the open doorway, hoping no soldier would choose that moment to arise to relieve himself.

Once out in the cold night, they sped to the postern gate. Elizabeth saw the body of the gatekeeper trussed and gagged on the ground. Outside the gate Jim stood concealed in the trees with the horses. Robert quickly lifted Elizabeth into her saddle before swinging onto his mount. Then swiftly the party galloped successfully away into the night toward the sheltered and secured walls of Ashkirk.

"Thank heavens!" Anne Barday exclaimed in relief as the tall figures of Robert and David

Kirkland strode through the door. Her look of anxiety returned when she saw her cousin being towed behind. Elizabeth's hand was firmly grasped in Robert's and she was forced to stumble and half-run in an effort to keep pace with his long strides.

"I was so worried," Anne continued, "how did you . . ."

"Goodnight, Anne. Goodnight, David," Robert declared abruptly, cutting off any further comment. His step continued unchecked toward the stairway.

Elizabeth grabbed the railing and hung on tenaciously.

"Good Lord! Isn't anyone going to deliver me from the clutches of this madman?" she pleaded desperately.

Anne stepped forward to come to her aid, but David Kirkland's restraining hand on her arm immediately halted her rescue attempt. Undaunted, Robert pried Elizabeth's fingers from the stair railing and, effortlessly flinging her over his shoulder, continued to his room where he dumped her unceremoniously on the bed.

Elizabeth rolled off the bed and, eyes blazing, jumped to her feet.

"You barbaric bully," she raged. "You have bruised and battered me for the last time. If you dare lay another hand on me, Robert Kirkland, so help me I will kill you."

"Oh, for heaven's sake, Elizabeth, I am not going to hurt you. I just want to talk to you."

"We have nothing more to say to one another. It has already been said."

"I cannot accept that," Robert declared, and reached out a hand in a supplicating motion.

Elizabeth flinched, drawing back in alarm. Robert's dark eyes clouded in torment. For a few seconds he stood stunned by her obvious fright of him. Slowly his hand reached to extract the dirk from the sheath at his waist.

"Here, Elizabeth, take this."

Her trembling fingers closed around the handle of the knife. Elizabeth's eyes were round and luminous in her confusion. "I do not understand."

Robert grasped her shoulders and drew her to him until the tip of the knife punctured his shirt and pricked the bronze skin beneath it. Mesmerized, Elizabeth saw the red stain appear on the white linen of his shirt.

"Go ahead, Beth, don't stop now. This is your opportunity," he urged softly.

With a shuddering sob Elizabeth released her grip on the knife and it fell to the floor. A hand reached out to caress the reddish-brown luster of her hair, before sliding down to let a finger trace the ivory smoothness of her delicate jaw. He tenderly cupped her face in his hands, his warm breath tantalizing as his lips hovered above hers.

"You can't, can you?" he whispered huskily, before his lips closed over hers in a long, intoxicating kiss.

Shaken, Elizabeth drew on her remaining vestige of strength to pull away. His arms held her firmly as she strained to release his hold on her.

"No. You must stop. Nothing has changed between us. I will never forgive you, Robert. I cannot forget your accusations."

"I am a senseless bastard, Beth," he intoned contritely, in way of an apology.

His mouth began to explore the curves and hollows of her throat before finding her ear. Robert breathed deeply of her scent, the sweet fragrance of lavender that had haunted him day and night from the time he had met her. His tongue began a toying tantalization with her ear, and Elizabeth could not restrain a slight shiver.

Robert's lips seared an erotic trail down her slim neck, and Elizabeth felt the dress slide from her shoulders as his hands began to caress her back and buttocks, forcing the dress off her hips. A rosy nipple, hardened by the shock of cold air, was instantly captured by a warm mouth, and her head fell back languorously in the throes of ecstasy.

"Do you have any idea what the hell it was for me to see you in that bastard's arms?" he groaned, as his hand captured her other thrusting globe.

Elizabeth began to whimper, trembling with exquisite torture as his hands and mouth continued their fiery exploration of her.

Robert pulled away to stare probingly down at her. Any trace of fright in her coffee-colored eyes had been consumed by the passion that now filled them. His hands slipped up to encircle her neck.

"I wanted to strangle this lovely neck—to squeeze the last remaining breath from your body. Oh God, Beth, when I think of it!"

His lips bore down in a bruising kiss. Every instinct he possessed warned him to be gentle, but he was powerless to control his driving need to absorb her. His hunger demanded he devour every part of her. He tasted the blood on her lips from his savage pressure, but it only heightened his desire. The pounding of their hearts was deafening when Robert finally freed her lips. Breathlessly, Elizabeth swayed against him. Robert lifted her into his arms and carried her to the bed. He gently lay her down before divesting himself of his own clothing, then covered her with his own warmth.

For a few seconds Robert's gaze worshipped her. He leaned down and ran his tongue soothingly over her swollen lips, before he continued his scrutiny of her.

Elizabeth met his stare openly and adoringly. Her hand reached up to lovingly stroke his cheek.

"This is not the answer, Robert. Can't you understand I am a woman with a woman's needs? They cannot all be met in your bed."

Robert reached out tenderly to brush aside some stray strands of hair from her face.

"You are my lass, love. We both know that." His voice was warm and loving as he murmured in Gaelic, *"Tha gaol agam ort, Ealasaid.* I love you, Elizabeth."

Elizabeth's lips met his hungrily, and their bodies fused as one.

Taking careful aim, Elizabeth slid her

granite stone across the icy surface of the frozen pond. David Kirkland knelt beside his brother as Robert took the horsehair broom and carefully measured the distance from the center of the tee to where the stone rested. Satisfied with the outcome, Robert looked up and grinned smugly at David, then gave him a shove that sent David sliding across the ice on his backside.

"We beat them, love," he cried, tossing the broom aside. Grabbing Elizabeth around the waist, he swung her around in victory before covering her lips with his. The kiss was broken abruptly when a snowball splattered against his back, and the curling game was quickly abandoned for a wild snowball fight.

Robert and Elizabeth definitely gained the advantage when Tims joined them in the melee against David and Anne. Before too long, the defeated couple, pelted from the rear by snowballs, was running toward the protection of the castle walls.

Laughing, Robert fell back exhausted onto the ground, only to become the recipient of a cold pile of snow dropped on his face. A dark brow rose menacingly as he brushed aside the snow to peer into a pair of mischievious brown eyes.

"That was a mistake, madam."

Robert lurched to grab Elizabeth's ankle in an attempt to pull her to the ground. With an enchanting squeal she evaded his grasp and the chase was on. Swift as a deer she sped across the snow, seeking the shelter of the trees. Robert quickly caught up with her but

Elizabeth avoided him by keeping a tree between herself and his grasp. The pair circled the tree like two stalking animals. Suddenly a long arm reached out, successfully capturing her, and Elizabeth found herself helplessly pushed to the ground. A large hand filled with snow hovered threateningly above her face.

"Help me, Tims," she cried with a merry laugh.

Robert threw a stern look in the lad's direction.

"Remember, Tims, I am the laird!"

The young boy hesitated, torn between rushing to his lady's aid and obeying the command of his adored laird.

"Di' ye nae say I mus' protec' m'lady, m'lord?"

A chuckle of delight escaped from Elizabeth. "What say you now, my lord? Which order would you have the lad obey?"

"Tell me you regret your rash action, madam."

"I regret my rash action, my lord," Elizabeth responded docilely, an impish sparkle in her eyes.

"Now declare that I am your lord and master, and you will never again attempt to mock my sovereignty with vagrant acts of disrespect."

"I declare you are my lord and master and I will never mock your sovereignty again."

"You are doing fine, my lady. Now repeat after me, 'I love you, Robert' "

"Do you derive some vicarious pleasure out of torturing me into admitting affection for you?"

Robert's hand lowered threateningly, allowing some snow to drop on her cheeks. Elizabeth cringed away from the cold moisture and relentingly declared, "I love you, Robert Kirkland."

"Now say, 'Kiss me, Robert.' "

Elizabeth's laughing face contorted in protest. "I won't!"

"No?" he challenged, and once again the snow-filled hand descended.

"Oh, all right! Kiss me, my lord and master."

With a satisfied chuckle Robert cast the snow aside and lowered his lips to hers. Elizabeth felt the heat of their familiar warmth and began to respond to their pressure.

Robert reluctantly pulled away to glance up at Tims standing above them with a confused look on his young face.

"What is it, Tims?" Robert asked indulgently, as he sat up and began to brush away the snow that covered them.

"Is kissin' so unpleasan' tha' it be punishment, m'lord?"

Robert grinned and reached out a hand to help Elizabeth to her feet.

"Nae, Tims . . . just kissing the Lady Elizabeth is unpleasant. I force myself to do so to keep her content and not have to bear the sting of her shrewish tongue."

"You conceited oaf," Elizabeth muttered

aside, as Robert brushed the snow from her.

"As you grow older, Tims, you will learn that a woman always demands a man's attention. No matter how pressing the burdens of his responsibilities, she will insist he devote his time to her with silly, useless gestures of affection."

"Like wha', m'lord?"

Robert turned to gaze at his wife. His eyes darkened as the fingers of his hand gently reached out to toy with the delicate line of her cheek.

"Well, for instance, in the case of the Lady Elizabeth, I am forced to waste idle time telling her that the beauty of her face can oft rob me of my breath . . . that the gaiety of her laughter can erase my most grievous woe . . . that the gentleness of her touch can heal my most longing ache. Her sweet scent transports me amidst a summer's garden, and her soft lips tempt mine to taste them again and again."

For a few seconds they stood motionless, their eyes locked, revealing all that still remained unspoken.

"An' the kissin' of her? 'Tis nae to yer likin', m'lord?"

Robert forced his eyes away from her head and turned back to Tims. His eyes lit with devilment.

"Well, lad, it is a mite more pleasant task than shoveling the manure from the horse stalls—but it certainly cannot match the taste of a cold draught of ale on a hot day. But once she learns the proper way of it, I suspect it will become a more tolerable task."

"You unbearable knave!" Elizabeth groaned, and with a hardy shove she sent him sprawling backwards into the show. "Do not listen to him, Tims, for the man is ill and raving."

Tims stared up in adoration at sparkling brown eyes. The cold air had only enhanced the beauty of her face with a healthy and bright luster. To the young lad in love, she was a complete vision of loveliness.

"Nae, mum, I dinna believe all th' laird said wa' ravin's."

With a saucy smile she took Tims hand and the two walked hand in hand back to the walls of the keep.

But her happiness was short-lived, for the following morning—with the warmth of Robert's kiss a poignant ache on her lips— Elizabeth forced back her tears as she watched her husband ride back to the war.

XVII

Elizabeth watched the large golden eagle form large, swirling, pirouettes in its solitary dance across the blue sky. In an effortless motion, the powerful bird suddenly plunged to the earth, only to soar majestically heavenward, a tiny rodent the hapless prisoner of its mighty talons.

Spring had come to the Highlands. The hills were arrayed in spectacular cloaks of green or smothered in gay blankets of white wildflowers. The fruit trees abounded with tiny pink and white blossoms, and the evergreen hue of the larch and pines was joined by the bushy leafiness of the birches and ashes. The Highland forests had become a rejuvenated wonderland.

In every direction rushing waterfalls, tumbling and cascading from the towering peaks above, wove intricate and elusive trails among the crags and crevices of the granite cliffs in their search for the lochs below.

Elizabeth found herself marveling at the awesome grandeur. How beautiful were these Highland hills! How subtly their aura wound itself around one's heart and senses!

As she had done so often since his absence, she addressed a spoken message to Robert. "Damn you, Robert Kirkland! I suppose you knew I would grow to love your Highlands. No matter how foolish my sputterings against them, you guessed I would fall prey to them. I can just see the arrogant, smug look on your . . ." Her tone softened and her eyes clouded with gentle wistfulness. ". . . incredibly handsome face."

Elizabeth's eyes shifted downward and she sadly ran a hand across the flat surface of her stomach. Her monthly flow had begun that morning, bearing the disappointing evidence that she still did not carry Robert's seed within her. How she yearned for a child—a tiny replica of a dark curly head and laughing eyes whom she could keep near her always.

She turned from the window at the sound of the tapping on her chamber door, and her expression brightened as Anne Barday entered through the portal.

"Corla tells me you are not feeling well, Beth." Anne's concern was clearly etched across her lovely features.

"Nothing serious, Anne. Just my monthly misery."

Her cousin smiled in womanly commiseration and took Elizabeth's hand. "Then this gives us a good opportunity to talk. I have some wonderful news to tell you."

Elizabeth permitted Anne to pull her to the upholstered banquette at the foot of the bed. Once seated, Anne squeezed Elizabeth's hand, her eyes aglow. "David has asked me to be his wife."

Elizabeth's smile was warm as she reached out to hug her. "Oh, Anne, that is wonderful! But really, sweet, it doesn't come as too much of a surprise."

A dimple was teased into evidence in each of Anne's flushed cheeks when her face broke into a happy smile. "Well, I admit David and I have discussed it before, but he felt there should be a respectful mourning time for his father."

"Knowing his father, I am sure Lord Kirkland would have been delighted if you two would have married immediately."

Anne frowned slightly. "Well, there is one other consideration. David was hoping Robert would return home. It is his intention for us to live at Blake Hall, the dower house his mother bequeathed him. However, we do not want to leave you alone."

"Shame on you and David," Elizabeth scolded. "I am a big girl now, and as much as I would love to have you stay at Ashkirk, I know you and David have a right to be the master and mistress of your own home. Besides," Elizabeth intoned flippantly, "if we wait for Robert to come home to stay, I am afraid we would all be gray and wrinkled."

Anne sensed the deep hurt and longing that lay under the flippancy, and she hugged Elizabeth, tears filling her eyes.

"Dear Beth, Robert will come home soon. The war is going very well for Montrose.

David says he has been victorious. The war will have to end soon."

"And then how long before the next one?" Elizabeth asked bitterly.

Seeing the stricken, sympathetic look on Anne's face, Elizabeth forced aside her gloom. "Well, come on, cousin dear, when is the wedding day? We must begin making the arrangements."

Arms entwined around one another's waist, the two girls hurried gaily from the room.

Tims Kirkland sat propped against a tree as he attempted to juggle the stones in the same deft manner he had seen the painted clown performing with four shining balls at the fair. Concentrating all his efforts on this feat of dexterity, Tims failed to see or hear the approach of the horseman, until the tall rider suddenly loomed before him.

The stones fell to the ground as Tims jumped to his feet, and his eyes blazed with eagerness at the sight of his adored laird. Robert Kirkland grinned affectionately down at the surprised young lad.

"Good day, Tims. How goes your day?"

"Fine, m'lord. An' a good day to ye. 'Tis glad I am to see ye home." A big smile covered his freckled face.

Robert glanced at the two horses tethered to some nearby shrubbery. "I seek the Lady Elizabeth, Tims."

The carrot-topped head nodded toward the thick grove. "Hersel's aswimmin' in the loch, m'lord. Sha' I gie her a shout?"

"No, Tims, you may take her horse and return to the keep. I will see my lady safely back."

"Aye, m'lord." Tims mounted his horse and gathered the reins of Elizabeth's mare. "M'lady wi' be mos' happy to see ye, Sir Robert."

"Well, I certainly hope so, Tims." Robert chuckled, as he dismounted.

For a few seconds Robert watched the departing boy, then followed a worn path to the concealed lake that lay amidst the dense growth. His pulse began racing with the knowledge that in a few short moments he would be with Elizabeth again—feel that softness in his arms, taste the sweetness of those lips. His heart took a sudden leap when he spied her in the water, and he crossed his arms and leaned his tall, lithe frame against a tree as he watched her. If possible, he had forgotten how beautiful she was. Her thick auburn hair was pinned carelessly to the top of her head, while errant wisps clung to her forehead and the nape of her neck.

Unaware of his presence, Elizabeth bobbled carefree in the lake, invigorated by the chill of the water. Striking for shore, she drew up and began to tread water, when she spied the figure at the tree. Her cry of alarm was stifled in her throat when Elizabeth recognized the tall figure of her husband. Their eyes locked in an ageless message. It had been several months since they had seen one another, and neither could disguise the pent-up hunger and yearning. Robert straightened and removed the plaid that draped his shoulder.

"Legend has it, my lady, that a horny denizen inhabits this water and preys upon beautiful young ladies. 'Tis said he drags them to his lair at the bottom of the lake—in his endless search for a perfect mate."

A lovely brow arched skeptically. "Then pray thee, my lord, what shall be my wont? For I am torn between risking my fate to the horny beast below, or the hornier one that awaits me on the shore."

Robert's laugh of delight floated across the glen as he threw back his dark head. He unwrapped his plaid and held it open with a challenge. "Come out, Elizabeth. This denizen has already found the perfect mate."

She could not conceal the blush that swept her as she stepped self-consciously from the water. For a few brief seconds, Robert's eyes ravished her hungrily, before he stepped forward to wrap her in the warmth of his plaid.

"Ye're a well-favored lass," he sighed appreciatively with a slight Scottish burr before he lifted her into his arms. Robert gazed down at her and Elizabeth found herself devastated by his look of tenderness.

"I have missed you, *ghaoil*," he said softly, as the Gaelic expression for "love" rolled lazily off his tongue.

Elizabeth's reply was a smothered sigh as she slipped her arms around his neck—and her lips parted to greet the warmth of his.

* * *

Descending the stairs to the Grand Hall, Anne Barday glowed with a radiance that caused her groom to clutch the arm of his brother. In the manner of a Highland bride, Anne's long blonde hair hung loosely down her back, held by two combs encrusted with pearls that had been given to her by Robert as a wedding gift.

Elizabeth's gift to Anne was the bridal gown intended for her own wedding. It was ivory satin with delicate Flemish lace decorating the long tapered sleeves and modified ruff of the neckline. Elizabeth's eyes had brimmed with unshed tears when her cousin appeared in it, the tragic circumstances of her own wedding brought painfully back to mind.

Robert's eyes rested momentarily on Anne, before they settled on the vision that followed behind. Each time he saw his wife, Elizabeth appeared lovelier to him. Now, dressed in a yellow gown of silk, the thick coils of her hair woven with tiny pearls, Robert was awed by her breathtaking beauty.

David took his bride's hand in his and proceeded toward the chapel. When Robert's hand closed over Elizabeth's, he was surprised to find her fingers rigid with cold, and unwittingly, he brought her hand to his chest, covering it with his own warm hand. Then, wordlessly, they followed the bridal couple.

Robert could not pull his eyes away from the loveliness of Elizabeth's face during the whole ceremony. She deliberately avoided looking at him, her gaze glued to the couple who stood before the minister. Her mind was still wrestling with the painful memories of her own wedding. Finally, unable to ignore the intensity of Robert's stare, Elizabeth turned her luminous eyes toward him, helpless to disguise her heartache.

David's voice was softly repeating his vows, and in a silent declaration, Robert's lips moved for her eyes alone to read.

"I, Robert of Ashkirk, take Elizabeth of Ballantine as my wedded wife, offering all my worldly goods to provide for her, and pledging my right arm to protect her."

Elizabeth's eyes clouded with anguish, as she attempted to contain the tears that threatened to surface. Mercifully, the ceremony ended and hugs and congratulations were exchanged, as the surging crowd filled the chapel and hall.

In no time at all the musicians began their tunes and the wedding celebration was under way.

Tables lined all the walls of the hall, filled to overflowing with different bowls and trays of delicious food. The tables were covered with platters of finnan haddie and salmon steaks that had been smoked over oakwood fires. Pasties filled with venison and mutton were in abundance, and juicy pieces of crab floated in steaming bowls of thick creamy wine sauce. Large silver trays could be found everywhere containing the always present haggis.

There were cakes and wafers covered with almonds, currants, and jellies of quince and rowan, and bowls of juicy strawberries as an added temptation.

One toast after another was raised to the bride and groom, and before long, the guests began swirling around the dance floor.

After several dances, Elizabeth found herself partnered in a reel with Tims Kirkland. The nine year old's hair had been plastered down with water and his young face was glowing with excitement.

"May I say, mum, ye be a mos' bonny sigh' tonicht."

"Why, thank you, Tims. That is the nicest compliment I have had all evening" She bent down and placed a light kiss on his cheek, causing the young lad's face to match the color of his hair.

" 'Tis not only I tha' thinks so, mum. I hae been watchin' the laird, an' he canna take his eyes frae ye."

"Really, Tims! Is that so?" Elizabeth asked, surprised. Her eyes swept the room seeking the tall figure of her husband. She spied him dancing with Anne.

"The laird looks mos' braw himsel', doesna he, mum?"

Elizabeth again turned to study Robert. His white teeth flashed in a grin as his head bent over Anne's. For the first time, Elizabeth realized how easily laughter came to this man. He wore a dark brown velvet doubtlet, the color only adding to his outrageous good looks. His black hair was slightly rumpled, giving him an irresistible, roguish appearance.

"Aye, Tims, he is indeed most braw," Elizabeth sighed, unable to ignore the painful tug at her heart.

The dance ended and the crowd began calling for the Laird of Clan Kirkland and his Lady. The dancers stepped aside as the musicians began the strains of a lively galliard.

Robert crossed to her, a devilish twinkle in his eyes.

"Are you game, my lady?"

"It is not proper, my lord," Elizabeth admonished, as she looked around at the crowd watching them eagerly.

"We do not stand on propriety here in the Highlands." Robert laughed and pulled her into his arms.

Their steps began to match the lively beat of the tune, and soon Elizabeth abandoned herself entirely to the tempo of the music. Robert's hands spanned her waist as he swung her above him, their laughter blending as her hands grasped his shoulders. Faster and faster they spun together, as the tempo increased, until the crashing end when Robert swung her from the floor.

As the music halted, he slowly lowered her and placed a kiss on her lips to the hooting and cheering approval of the spectators. Elizabeth, who had been swept up in the excitement of the dance, blushed in embarrassment, realizing she was the center of the crowd's attention.

The evening lengthened, and the bride and groom took to the floor for the wedding dance. Robert's arm rested casually around Elizabeth's shoulders, as they watched the bridal couple in this moving ritual.

A silver chalice of wine was held in David's hand. Their right arms entwined, he and Anne moved forward several steps to the slow tempo of the music, before turning back to back. Entwining their left arms, they swung toward one another and David raised the chalice to his own lips, then to Anne's; as each sipped from the cup, their eyes locked lovingly. The steps were repeated, and each time the couple sipped from the cup an unspoken message was transmitted. David gazed at his bride adoringly, his every movement, every look proclaiming his love. Anne's reply was the same. They danced on, lost to everything and everyone, communicating a message to one another—a promise of a future full of love and devotion.

Elizabeth was overwhelmed by the tender poignancy of the scene before her. Fighting for composure, she raised tear-filled eyes to Robert then turned and raced from the room, seeking a moment of privacy. She mounted the stairs to her room, then glanced behind and saw Robert following at the foot of the stairs. In desperation, Elizabeth turned to the tower stairs and climbed up the narrow, winding stairway leading to the battlements.

Robert overtook her midway and spun her around. His eyes were clouded in confusion.

"Tears, Elizabeth?"

"Tears are quite common at a wedding, my lord."

"I fear they are not tears shed in happiness for the bride, but rather tears of self-pity."

"Have I not cause to shed such tears?" Elizabeth flashed defensively.

Robert grasped her shoulders angrily. "Damn it, woman, are you so shallow that you still sorrow because you were denied the trappings of a fancy fete for a wedding?"

"Nae, my lord. I weep not for the past—my tears are for the future." She shrugged aside his hands and continued her climb to the top.

Robert followed as Elizabeth stepped out on the battlements. Once again her shoulders were seized in a strong grip as he turned her to him.

"I see no cause to lament your future."

Elizabeth raised her eyes to confront him. The tears streaked her cheeks as she forced herself to speak.

"What future have we?" Her scorn was undisguised.

"Is my pledge to you any less than that of David's to Anne?"

"Need you ask? Do you see David rushing off to fight some hopeless cause? Nae, Robert, Anne will always start her day with the sight of her husband's face before her and know the feel of him beside her nightly. Am I to stand docilely by until your head is returned to me in a basket, or your blood is drained on some cursed battlefield? I cannot bear that. I have not the strength. Better I suffer the pain of losing you now—then the despair of losing you later."

"Are you so certain I will perish in the war, Elizabeth?"

"If not this one, it will be the next one you commit yourself to. This is your way of life—you desire no other." She raised a delicate chin in determination. "I will not spend my life waiting for a few stolen moments a year to know the touch of my husband. Nor will I bear a child to emulate a father that advocates the sword as a way of life. I will find a man whose needs are sufficed by the warmth of the hearth and the arms of his wife."

Elizabeth's head was pulled back roughly as Robert clutched her hair. His eyes blazed down at her, darkened pools of fury.

"You would settle for such an arrangement? You would substitute what we share to simply seek security? You are mine, Elizabeth, and bode this warning—I will kill any man you seek, any man who touches you."

His lips plummeted down to claim hers in a searing kiss. Elizabeth struggled to resist, but, as in the past, her will was not strong enough to refute what her heart and body would not deny, and she responded passionately. "Do you really believe you will find that in another man's arms? Tell me how you will ever be able to settle for anything less!"

"If I must, I will," she said defiantly, "and I will curse you every remaining day of my life for forcing me to do so. I hate you for this, Robert. I hate you for what you are doing to us. We could have had so much together."

In her embittered frustration, Elizabeth began to pummel his chest with clenched fists. "Oh, damn you, Robert Kirkland! Damn you! Damn you! Damn you!" she cried, finally burying her head against his chest as her sobs wracked her body.

Loving arms enfolded her as Robert pressed her tightly against him. His cheek nuzzled the perfumed thickness of her hair, before his lips sought the hollow behind her ear.

"Do not curse me, love," he pleaded softly. "Is not having to leave you tomorrow damnation enough?"

Elizabeth turned stricken eyes to him, brimming with tears.

"Then make the most of this night, my lord, for it will be the last we will share. There will be no other."

With a stifled groan Robert picked her up in his arms and turned to the stairs.

Dawn came too swiftly to the young lovers as they savored every moment of their final hours together. Elizabeth now stood at the window, her thoughts and emotions racing, as Robert dressed. Do I know so little of this man I have been made to marry? Do not our shared moments mean anything to him? Am I a fool to believe I might have some say in this matter? Am I to be the meek and loving wife obediently awaiting my lord's return?

His dressing completed, Robert crossed hesitantly to her.

"I must leave now, Elizabeth."

"You go to fight a war without even a cause of your own," she erupted accusingly.

In her anger, Elizabeth spun around, losing her balance. She stiffened as Robert's strong arms reached out to prevent her fall. Elizabeth did not want to be held in his arms, knowing his strength only weakened her own. Robert turned her to him, his anger flaring.

"I weary of these constant explanations, my lady. What can I say to you? This marriage is new to me, also. I am not accustomed to asking permission or answering to anyone. I am my own person. My loyalty to James Graham is my cause for fighting this war. I am both friend and soldier to him."

"Wouldst I could exact such loyalty from you!"

His grip tightened as his anger increased.

"Damn you, woman! Why are you able to anger me so quickly?"

"It appears, my lord, you too have that same ability with me. Unfortunately, though, your strength wins you yet another battle, as your hands will surely crush my bones if you do not loosen your grip."

Robert relaxed his hold, but did not release her.

"Beth, I do not wish to part this way. Let not the memory of the past hours be clouded by these angry words. Think rather of what we have to look forward to upon my return."

Elizabeth shook her head, denying his plea.

"How can I send you away with promises of a life we will never have together. This way my anger will help me survive. I told you last night I will build a new life and put aside any memory of knowing or loving you."

"And I told you I will never let you go. You are mine, Elizabeth, and when I return—if you are not here—I will find you wherever you are."

Robert turned and strode from the room. Elizabeth stood numbly, listening to the sound of his spurs echoing through the quiet hall. She turned back to the window and gazed down at the courtyard, her heart aching as she fought the urge to rush down and fling herself into Robert's arms for a final tender embrace—and give him her assurance she would remain at Ashkirk until his return. Elizabeth saw his final handshake with David and watched the tall beloved figure stride to his horse. Tims Kirkland stood sleepy-eyed, holding the reins of his laird's steed. Robert placed an affectionate hand on the lad's shoulders.

"Take care of my lady, Tims."

"Aye, m'lord," Tims replied, his small chest swelling with pride at Robert's confidence in him. Mounted, Robert raised his eyes toward the window, sensing Elizabeth's gaze. For a few seconds he sat silently, returning her stare, then turned and rode away.

XVIII

Elizabeth Kirkland reined in her mare Sheba and looked up admiringly at the lofty peak of Ben Nevis with its commanding position above the surrounding Highlands. Above its snow-capped splendor the sun sparkled over the whole valley, where the foaming current of the Firth of Moray rushed to mingle with the turquoise waters of Lake Linnhe.

She wore the colorful trews that had become her riding habit, and her brown lustrous hair was braided and concealed beneath a black tam o'shanter. The lush rounded curves of her body were obscured by the bulky doublet that covered them. Clearly she could have passed for a lad not much older than Tims Kirkland, who was riding at her side.

Elizabeth gave the mare a light prod with her heels and it once again moved on. She was intently examining the many groves of trees that bordered the trail they were following.

Suddenly, her eyes lit up triumphantly. "I've found it, Tims!" she called out in delight, and turned the mare into the dense shrubbery.

"Ye take care there, m'lady," the lad warned, like a doting parent cautioning a venturesome child.

The narrow path through the brush that she had been seeking was barely discernible to the eye, but the horse had no problem moving along its hardened surface. After several yards the path opened into a wide copse, and Elizabeth dismounted. She felt confident that this was the same glen where Robert had once brought her.

"You are certain that I can make a wish, Tims, if we find some?" Elizabeth asked, as the young boy swung his leg over the pommel of his saddle and jumped to the ground.

"Aye, m'lady, bu' ye mus' be th' one to do th' pluckin' o' it, or yer wish willna come true," the boy warned in a serious manner.

"Well, at least you can help me find it, can't you?" Elizabeth asked excitedly, and began to search the ground eagerly.

The two of them began to crawl around on their hands and knees among the undergrowth. In a short matter of time they both bore the evidence of their effort, as their faces and hands became smudged with dirt and grime.

Finally, after a diligent search, Elizabeth spied a stalk of white heather nestled among the many purple plants that covered the ground in a colorful carpet.

The two adventurers kneeled over the stem, holding the tiny bell-shaped white flowers as if they had just discovered a cache of buried treasure.

"Ye pluck it now, m'lady, an' make yer wish," Tims instructed.

Elizabeth felt her hand tremble as she reached for the single stalk. If Artle's prophecy was true, then perhaps she would find the happiness she was seeking. She closed her eyes and clutched the tiny petals to her breast.

"Please, my Lord," she prayed silently, "let me carry Robert's seed within me."

By the time Elizabeth and Tims ate some cheese and dark bread, the better part of the day had passed, and Elizabeth realized they would have to hurry if they were to get back to the keep before nightfall. She goaded Sheba into a faster pace.

In her haste she failed to see the two approaching horsemen on the trail. She galloped out of the brush and crashed into one of the riders. The jolt knocked Elizabeth off her horse and she fell to the ground, landing in an upright position on her rear end.

Both men had already drawn their swords from the scabbards and were preparing to defend themselves from other attackers. When only Tims appeared out of the shrubbery, they relaxed their guard and sheathed their weapons.

One of the horsemen leaned over his saddle and grinned down at her. "Well, lad, haven't you learned how to properly sit a horse?" he taunted.

The gibe was adding insult to injury as far as Elizabeth was concerned and her anger mounted, her dignity having been abused as much as her aching posterior.

"Are you hurt, lad?" the other rider asked kindly.

Tims had dismounted and was about to come to her aid, but she waved him aside. It appeared that these strangers were mistaking her for a boy, and Elizabeth thought it the wisest to let them keep that impression.

She regarded them with a surreptitious glance, trying to keep her face as concealed as possible. Both strangers were dark-haired and wore red tams. They were clad in black breeks and a white wiz. Certainly not the finery of royalty, she reasoned critically.

Elizabeth observed that the man who had unseated her was roguishly handsome, with a dark mustache and black eyes that seemed to dance with deviltry. He was wearing a Gordon plaid draped over his shoulder.

She did not recognize the tartan of the other. He was not as blantantly handsome as his companion, although the rugged planes of his face appeared to be quite pleasant beneath the dark beard that covered them. His coffee-colored eyes were filled with concern as he stared down at her.

Despite the plain grooming of both of them, Elizabeth knew by their speech, and the ease with which they sat their saddles, that they were not simple croftsmen.

"Are you hurt, lad?" the man repeated.

"No thanks to the likes o' ye," Elizabeth snarled, dropping her voice as deeply as possible in the hopes that it would sound masculine.

The black-eyed stranger grinned at his companion. "Spirited little scamp, isn't he! Tell me, lad, do you know the way to Ashkirk Castle?"

"An' who wud nae be knowin' th' way?" she grumbled as she rose achingly to her feet.

"Well, I, for one," the stranger declared. "But I expect you to change that dilemma very soon, you ornery little knave, or I am going to take down your trews and whomp that skinny arse of yours." The threat was made in a light-hearted vein, and she saw him exchange a wink with his colleague.

Elizabeth realized that at this time discretion was the better part of valor. Besides, she thought with a sly smile, there was a much better way she could get even with this loud-mouthed clout. The two men's eyes followed her slow progress as she limped to her mare, rubbing her aching posterior.

"Ye mus' take th' lef' fork in th' road aft' ye cres' th' hill," she directed. "Hae a fine day, m'lords, an' tak' care ye dinna miss the turn," she invoked in a friendly tone.

Elizabeth and Tims watched the two strangers ride away. Tims Kirkland turned confused eyes to his mistress.

"I dinna understan' why ye tol' them th' left fork, an' nae the righ'. Tis sure to be addin' another hour tu th' ride?"

The round brown eyes of the Countess of Kirkwood glowed with an undisguised gleam of mischief. "How careless of me." She grinned wickedly.

Elizabeth had gowned herself and ministered, as best she could, to her bruised rear end by the time the two strangers finally arrived at Ashkirk. Robert was delighted to see them and proudly introduced her to his two comrades, Colonels Nathaniel Gordon and Magnus O'Cahan.

To her consternation, she discovered Nat Gordon and Magnus O'Cahan were delightful dinner companions, and Elizabeth soon began to suffer pangs of guilt because of her childish prank.

Colonel Gordon was leaving at dawn and it appeared the men had a great deal to discuss, so Elizabeth rose to excuse herself.

The two men insisted upon escorting her to the door and Nat was the epitome of courtliness as he brought her hand to his lips in a light kiss.

"I can only hope we will meet again, my lady." His dark mischievous eyes danced with warmth.

Elizabeth turned to leave and unwittingly raised a hand to rub her aching rear as she limped away. The unconscious gesture was not missed by either of the two men, and a glitter of suspicion flashed in Nat's eyes.

"No, it couldn't be," he said skeptically.

Magnus chuckled in amusement. "How much are you willing to wager?"

"Why that little minx!" Nat said, amazed. He threw a comradely arm around the shoulder of O'Cahan. "I think old Robbie has his hands full!"

The two men returned to the side of their host, laughing aloud at their shared joke.

XIX

The following evening Elizabeth was sitting in the Grand Hall looking around in complete disgust at the contingent of men that had arrived at Ashkirk and now filled the mammoth room.

Seated at the long trestle tables was an assemblage of the most barbarous, treacherous looking men in Scotland. Even though they were eating a meal, they still wore their feathered and horned helmets, with claymores and battle axes hanging from their hips and waists. They appeared to her like grim Viking specters ressurected from the grave.

These were massive, powerfully built men, many boasting a girth equal to a bear's. Their shaggy heads and scarred faces, bearing ungroomed beards and drooping mustaches, added to their fearsome appearance.

The many settles and chairs that had normally stood in the room had been removed, and now the walls were lined with their hide-covered shields, adorned with patterns of nails and spikes. The heraldry of the owner was painted upon the hides, for

their very manner, very stance, proclaimed
these men the uncrowned kings that they
were. Each clan chieftain was a proud, undisputed ruler of an ageless dynasty.

As Montrose had hoped, the Donald clans
of Scotland had joined their Irish clansmen
and had come in under his banner.

Now, united against a hereditary foe, the
Campbells, were the MacDonalds that had
come from Ireland with Colkitto, the Mac-
Donalds of Glengarry, the MacDonalds of
Clanranald, and the MacRanalds of Keppoch.
There were MacIans of Glencoe, MacIans of
Ardnamurchan, MacLeans of Durant and
MacLeans of Lochbuie—but MacDonalds all!

Here was a confederacy of the finest,
fiercest guerrilla fighters ever assembled. It
was an irregular, but awesome, military force
of mountain fighters whose very name struck
the same mesmerizing terror in the hearts of
their enemies as the early Vikings from whom
they descended.

And it was the rhetoric and diplomacy of
James Graham that held them together as a
unit.

Elizabeth Kirkland, for one, felt it was an
impossible task for anyone to accomplish. In
fact, she did not understand why anyone
would even want to associate with this group,
let alone attempt to lead them. She found
them totally vulgar and uncouth. She had
wisely ordered all the women to their
quarters, and the serving duties had fallen to
the male servants. She was not about to
permit any of the women of the household to

be ravaged or abused by any of these drunken barbarians!

Transfixed, she watched in revulsion as one of the lot stood up and leaned across the table. With his bare hands he effortlessly ripped off the entire shank of a roasted boar. The slick, greasy limb slipped out of his hands and fell to the floor, where it was immediately kicked and trod upon by several of the diners. Retreiving it, and without even bothering to wipe it clean, the man settled back in his chair and began to noisily chomp on it, the grease running into his beard and down his hands.

She turned her head aside to avoid such a disgusting sight and was rewarded with the sound of a loud belch from the shaggy behemoth seated next to her.

Elizabeth wanted to scream aloud and order the animals herded out of the castle. How could Robert expect her to continue to serve as his hostess and see to the needs of his guests? In her opinion, their needs would be best served by allowing them to wallow in the sty outside the keep.

For what seemed like the hundredth time that evening she raised her head and forced a gracious smile to her lips, as the assemblage lifted their tankards of ale in the air to toast her health, as well as that of her liege.

What was keeping Robert? she wondered with irritation. Why hadn't he returned from the time he had been called away from her side? If he did not appear soon, she was determined to desert the hall.

Robert Kirkland had just returned to the

Grand Hall after having dispatched a return missive to Montrose. Jamie had requested he attempt to retain the MacDonalds at Ashkirk until Nat Gordon's return.

He could not contain his grin of amusement when his eyes swept the room and found his wife. She looked like a rose among a thicket of thorns. Magnus O'Cahan, standing beside him, was baffled at the sight of the crooked grin on his comrade's face.

"What in the name of Mary can you find to laugh about, Robbie?"

"I was just imagining what Elizabeth will have to say about this group. They certainly live up to her convictions of Highlanders." His face grimaced with misgiving. "And wait until she hears the news I'm about to announce." He returned to Elizabeth's side with apprehension. She acknowledged his presence with a sideward glance of relief.

However, that relief was short-lived. She turned to him in surprise when he shouted loudly for attention. It took several seconds for the voices to become hushed in the grand hall to allow him to continue.

"I have just received a message from Montrose," Robert announced.

The mention of James Graham brought a round of cheers from the assemblage. When the clamor abated once again, Robert continued. "Jamie regrets he has been delayed in joining us and asks for your indulgence and patience. He asks that rather than disband and return to your homes, you wait here for his arrival."

Elizabeth forced herself not to cry out in despair at the thought of this despicable horde remaining another night at Ashkirk. She listened in horror as Robert continued addressing the crowd.

"I think I have thought of something to ease the boredom of the delay," he offered. "What say we put aside our weapons and relax for a few days? It's been too long since any of us has had the opportunity of putting the stone or tossing a caber." His face broke into a wide grin and he took Elizabeth's hand and drew her to his side. "My Lady and I would like you all to remain at Ashkirk for the Highland Games," he shouted.

The roar of approval was thunderous, and she covered her ears and burrowed against his chest. Robert's arm encircled her protectively as he stood laughing as the men began to demonstrate their acceptance by banging their claymores and battle axes against their shields.

The lengthy demonstration appeared as though it would go on for hours, so Robert began to ease them toward the door with Elizabeth still held protectively under his wing. He knew the time had come to get his wife out of the room. However, their progress was slow, as they were halted constantly by the revelers.

Magnus O'Cahan observed their plight and managed to work his way to their side. The combined effort of the two men finally forced a way through the mass of bodies.

Robert took one look at Elizabeth and was

convinced she was on the brink of losing her composure. He cupped her cheeks in his hands and smiled down tenderly into her wide anxious eyes.

"Elizabeth, love, I must return to the hall, but Magnus will see you safely to your room."

She nodded meekly, grateful for the opportunity to free herself from the noisy clamor. She climbed the stairway hurriedly, without even a backward glance toward the young man who followed behind. On impulse she continued up the stairs and stepped out on the battlements. For several moments she breathed deeply of the fresh night air, savoring the first relaxed moments she had known all evening.

"How long will it go on?" she asked finally, unaware of the despair in her voice.

"Most likely until sunrise." O'Cahan hesitated, uncertain whether he should continue. "You must forgive their actions, my lady. They are men returning from battle. It is just their way of unwinding."

"Forgive me, Colonel O'Cahan, but from the looks of them I would judge they are more comfortable *in* battle than away from it," she intoned bitterly.

He leaned back against the parapet with a rueful grin. "I suspect you are probably right."

His smile was as contagious as a yawn, and Elizabeth was helpless to resist it. His calm presence had completely eased her tension and her mouth curved to return his smile.

"I suppose I have been overly critical," she

sighed in concession. "Robert considers me a pretentious snob."

"Well, they do take a great deal of adjusting to," he conceded warmly.

O'Cahan's eyes deepened in seriousness. "There is one thing you must never lose sight of, Elizabeth. The fact that you are the lady of a Highland chief would cause any one of those men in that hall to unhesitantly lay down his life for you. That is what makes them the enigma they are. Despite their barbarism they are governed by a code of chivalry."

Elizabeth weighed his words thoughtfully. She was thankful for the darkness that prevented him from seeing her guilty blush.

"What you are saying in your tactful fashion, Colonel O'Cahan, is that my attitude has made me the one guilty of being offensive —not they."

"No, my lady. Your actions were above reproach," he said gallantly. "You were a beautiful and gracious hostess to these men. They will always carry that memory with them."

Elizabeth now understood why Robert regarded this young, soft-spoken Irishman with such high esteem. He had once told her that someday history would record how much Scotland owed his twenty-five-year-old Irish colonel.

"Where is your home, Colonel O'Cahan?"

"I come from Ulster," he responded with a warm smile.

"Then why don't you return there? What

are you doing in this accursed war?" she asked kindly.

"I am a soldier, my lady, and I believe in the same principals as James Graham," he declared. The Irish commander's admiration and respect was in glowing evidence as he spoke. "I do not have the hatred for the Campbells, or the dedication toward destroying them, that the MacDonalds do. My Ulster men and I have pledged our swords and loyalties to Jamie Graham—thus to your king."

"Robert told me that the victory at Fyvie Castle was due to the efforts of you and your men, as much as to the strategy of Montrose." She flashed a derisive smile. "Believe me, Colonel O'Cahan, that is quite a concession for Robert to make, because he is convinced that James Graham is omipotent."

"He said that, did he?" O'Cahan demurred. "Did he fail to mention that we would never have been able to defend ourselves at Fyvie if he and Nat Gordon had not crept into the Campbell camp that night before and stole some kegs of gunpowder? They are two of the most courageous fools I have ever had the honor of serving with."

Of course Robert had failed to mention to her his own contribution, and Elizabeth could not help but feel pride in hearing of Robert's gallantry. "I am afraid he deliberately neglected to mention his own contribution, Colonel O'Cahan," she said with dismay. "But, it's better I remain ignorant of his foolhardy acts, for I spend too many troubled nights, as it is, worrying about his safekeeping."

She felt this was the proper time to confess a guilt she was harboring, and her brow arched into an impish curve.

"It was I, you know."

He understood the cryptic message at once. "Nat and I suspected as much." There was no condemnation, only amusement in his voice.

"What gave me away?" she asked lightly. "Was it my feminine voice, or perhaps, 'twas me poor imitation o' a Hieland burr," she gibed, the trilling accent rolling off her tongue.

Magnus O'Cahan chuckled good-naturedly. "Actually, it was neither, my lady. It was more your decided limp."

They both shared a moment of laughter remembering the day.

"Why didn't you tell Robert?" Elizabeth asked.

"I will some night—when the humor is most needed," he answered somberly.

His words brought back the grim reminder of the war that was always lurking on the brink of her thoughts.

Her happiness faded instantly, replaced with solemnity, and she turned away from him to return to her chamber.

Elizabeth was awakened by the delightful sensation of Robert's lips at the nape of her neck. She opened her eyes as every nerve in her body became attuned to his overpowering male essence. His strong arm enfolded her and pulled her against his muscular body as his lips trailed moist kisses to her ear. His breath was warm and tantalizing as he whispered, "Are you asleep, love?"

She twisted her head to look up to meet his dark, smoldering gaze, and a warm hand slid up the slim column of her neck to bury itself in her thick hair.

Robert's lips were tender and warm as they covered hers in a devastating, seductive assault. Her lips parted to accept a deep, disturbing kiss that ignited the smoldering flames within her.

His lips mercifully left hers, only to blaze a scorching path to the hollow of her throat, while his hand slipped into her gown to cup the round swell of her breast.

A rapturous moan escaped her lips and Robert shifted to turn her on her back. The moan became a cry of pain and he reared his head to study her with alarm.

"What is it, Elizabeth?"

"I fear my bruised derriere did not take too favorably to the maneuver," she kidded lightly, squirming beneath him in an attempt to ease the pressure on her spine.

"Let me ease the pain with some salve," he offered.

Elizabeth watched him cross the room and marveled at his indifference to his own nudity. She still could not refrain from blushing every time her own nakedness was exposed to him.

Robert returned, carrying the small bowl of

unguent, and sat on the side of the bed. He helped her remove her gown and then tenderly turned her onto her stomach.

"How does it look?" she asked, the side of her face pressed against the pillow.

"As fetching as ever, my lady," he responded, relieved to see that her injury was not as severe as he feared. He bent down and placed a light kiss on each bruised cheek.

"I'm serious, Robert," she admonished. "Are the bruises beginning to fade?"

"They are practically gone. It is more sore than bruised." His firm hand began to gently work the soothing balm into the aching flesh.

"Robert, what are the Highland Games?" she asked drowsily, as the healing pressure of his fingers began to lull her to sleep.

However, the satiny feel of her skin at his fingertips was having just the opposite effect on him. He had wanted her earlier, and now the throbbing ache in his loins was becoming painful.

"It's a Highland custom that goes back to the tenth or eleventh century. There are several different events, and we compete against one another." He trailed a finger up to the sensitive nerve of her spine.

"You mean like jousting or archery?" Her hand reached up to stifle a yawn.

His head dipped and pressed a trail of light kisses up the delicate line of her spine as he murmured, "No—more like hammer throwing, tug-of-war, some horse racing."

Elizabeth's eyes flew open at the sound of his last words. "Did you say horse racing?" A scheme was beginning to formulate in her mind. Clearly, horse racing was an event at which she excelled.

"Are women permitted to participate?" she asked slyly.

"Of course not, Elizabeth." His lips had now reached the nape of her neck.

Elizabeth turned over and entwined her arms around his neck. She saw a smoldering passion in the depths of his eyes and thought that perhaps she could turn this moment to her advantage. After all, Robert never denied her anything she really wanted when they were not quarreling.

She raised her eyes to his, with a beguiling pout on her lips. "There is always a first time, isn't there, my lord?"

Their mouths opened to one another and her tongue began to electrify him with fiery probes. Her fingers dug into the skin of his smoothly muscled back as she pressed him tighter against her.

"Have I succeeded in easing your pain, my love?" he asked huskily, his hand sliding to a rounded breast and his thumb beginning to toy with the hardened peak.

"Oh, yes," she sighed, as the tingling sensation crept slowly toward the junction of her legs.

"Then ease mine, my lady," he pleaded with a hoarse groan.

Elizabeth awoke in the morning and found herself still curled in Robert's arms. She smiled lovingly at the sight of his face relaxed in slumber. How she loved this man!

She basked in the afterglow of their love-making, still feeling satiated from its intensity.

She had never before attempted to be the aggressor in their coupling. Strangely—how satisfying the role had been! She recalled the excitement of feeling Robert writhe and groan under the coaxing of her bold moves. Her purpose for this aggression had been completely forgotten in the pleasure it had brought to both of them.

Robert stirred and slowly opened his eyes to be greeted by a dazzling smile from Elizabeth.

"Good morn, my lord."

"What a way to begin a day." He grinned puckishly. "To hear the most feisty and voluptuous wench in Scotland call me 'my lord.'" He pulled her down and kissed her ardently. "Good morn, *my lady*." Elizabeth did not fail to notice the emphasis he placed on the last two words.

"I'm afraid I have tarried too long in bed." He got to his feet and began to hurriedly dress.

With the light of morning came the memory of her scheme and Elizabeth smiled bewitchingly at Robert. "You will let me ride in the Games?"

He looked up disgruntled as he pulled on a boot. "Of course not, Elizabeth. I told you last night that the Games are not for women."

She sat up on her knees, the sheet dropping away to reveal the naked lines of her body to his gaze.

"But last night I thought that . . ." She

stopped, realizing what she had almost admitted about her actions.

He pulled on his other boot and stood up and warily approached the bed. "Last night you what?" His eyes were cold and accusing.

Elizabeth refused to answer and Robert loomed above her, staring down at her with scorn.

"You thought if you made love to me, it would gain you your wont." His mouth curled into a mocking sneer. "Why would I bargain for something that is already mine for the taking! Only a whore uses the bed as a bartering block, dear wife."

He turned and stormed from the room.

XX

In the days that followed Elizabeth watched the Games with as much enjoyment as the others. She marveled during the stone putting, when stones weighing twenty pounds were tossed as lightly as pebbles.

Her cheers joined those of her clansmen when the Kirklands of Ashkirk competed against the MacLeans of Lochbuie in a tug of war, with both teams ending up in the mud.

The most astonishing event was the tossing of the caber, as robust Highlanders picked up tall pine logs and tossed them end over end.

She became so engrossed watching a young man, his feet moving agilely and gracefully between crossed swords, dance the difficult *ghillie calum*, that she had to hurry to watch Robert participate in the archery competition.

He was wearing his kilts and his long muscular legs were encased in Highland hose to his knees. Because of the heat he had removed his shirt. Fascinated, Elizabeth watched his corded muscles ripple across his sinewy shoulders, as he drew back the string of the bow.

Robert had maintained a cool facade with

her in front of guests, but at night he lingered in the Grand Hall drinking himself besotted rather than join her in their chambers. When he finally would stagger upstairs, it was to collapse in bed in the adjoining room.

On the last day of the events, Elizabeth's competitive spirit could not be denied. When she was certain Robert was occupied elsewhere, she slipped back into her room and donned her trews. Satisfied that she could once again pass as a boy, she brazenly entered the horse race.

The course was grueling, requiring several jumps and the crossing of many deep rills. The pace was fast and steady from the second the race began. Elizabeth was riding comfortably in the second position, while the leader was a man from Clanranald, who handled his mount skillfully. There was no question in Elizabeth's mind that these Highlanders were born horsemen, but her lighter weight was giving her a slight advantage over some of the heavier riders.

As they approached the final jump, the leader's horse balked and he had to pull up. Elizabeth's mount went flying across the obstacle and raced to the finish line a full head in front of the next rider.

Elizabeth gloried in the roar of the crowd when the Kirkland's were declared the winner. She couldn't remember when she had felt so exhilarated. The smile on her face vanished when Robert furiously confronted her at the stable.

"Get to your room immediately." His voice

held the threat of violence. It was not difficult to sense the fury raging in him and Elizabeth turned and ran from the stable.

She listened to the sound of Robert's footsteps from the moment she heard the massive door slam below, hearing the staccato clatter of his spurs as he strode angrily across the floor and up the stairway to their chamber door.

It opened behind her and then was slammed with a fury that seemed to leap across the room and envelop her. She could feel the impact of his turbulent glare on the back of her neck.

Finally, with controlled anger, Robert addressed her. "Tell me, madam, is it your intent to bring about the destruction of my clan, or is it the aspirations of James Graham you seek to crush?"

"I don't understand what you're talking about," Elizabeth responded defiantly.

Her defiance incensed him more, and he grabbed her shoulders in a crushing grasp and spun her around to face the full fury of his wrath. "Do you have any idea what will happen if any of those men discover that my wife won that race?"

"I fail to see what is so staggering about a woman winning a horse race?" She refused to cower beneath him.

Robert wanted to shake her violently for her lack of compassion. "Don't you understand that the one essential for a man's dignity is pride in himself. If he loses his self-respect, he has lost everything. Those men will be made the brunt of mockery and ridicule if it becomes known they have been bested by a woman.

"Do you hate us that much, Elizabeth?" he asked incredulously. "Is your contempt for us so great that you are driven to humiliate us? My God, woman, some of those men are chieftans! Who knows what their shame will incite! Feuds have erupted for much less.

"These hills could run red with blood," he prophesied with strangled intensity as he pushed her aside and walked over to stare out of the window in frustration.

"Robert, I don't hate your people. I didn't realize I would hurt anyone by riding," she said contritely.

"We will be leaving tomorrow. Until then, I pray, madam, that no ill will come from the deed. When I return, we will settle the matter further."

"I think we should settle it now, Robert. There have been too many doubts and accusations between us."

He swung around, his voice wrought with torment. "Again you challenge my authority! Why do you persist in defying me? Must I beat you to gain your obedience?" He feared he would do just that if he remained—so he turned and left her, hoping that time would erode the wall that had risen between them.

The skirl of pipes shattered the morning's stillness and jolted Elizabeth awake. She jumped to her feet and pulled a heavy wrap over her gown just as Robert burst through the door of the adjoining room, still pulling on his breeks.

"Glory be to God!" he murmured as he stared out the window.

"What is it, Robert? Are we under siege?" She hurried to his side.

"It's Nat. He's returned with the Gordon cavalry."

He grabbed her hand and bolted to the door. Elizabeth could barely keep up with his long strides as he rushed up the stairway, pulling her behind him.

The castle's ramparts were already filled with cheering men, wildly waving their plaids and banners in the air.

Elizabeth's breath was trapped in her throat at the sight of the awesome and colorful spectacle. Approaching the castle, their red tartans blazing riotously in the sun, rode nine hundred Gordon cavalrymen, the most skilled and disciplined horsemen in Scotland. As the spectators watched, they fanned their mounts into columns of eight and rode across the glen in perfect precision.

Robert was ecstatic with happiness, their quarrel forgotten in his excitement. Elizabeth thought he would crush her ribs as he repeatedly hugged and kissed her.

"Do you know what this means, Elizabeth?" he shouted excitedly. "It will speed the end of the war. With the Gordon cavalry and the MacDonalds infantry behind him, Jamie will be invincible."

Nat Gordon brought word that Jamie

would not be joining them at Ashkirk, then let forth his anger over missing the Games.

"Damnation!" he muttered irascibly. "I would have been back sooner if that whoreson Argyll had not been with my uncle. I thought he would never leave!"

"I don't understand why the damn fool didn't arrest you on sight," O'Cahan declared laughing.

"He did worse! The merciless bastard made me do pennance." Nat grinned rakishly. "Of course I convinced him of my deep remorse for having been foolish enough to join you treasonable rabble. So you know what that spawn-of-a-whore made me do? I had to go to the Kirk every day and declare my shame and promise to change my sinful ways."

Even Elizabeth had to join in the laughter at the thought of this audacious rogue sitting in church.

"Lord, I had to swear to everything from not cursing to never considering adulterous actions. By the time they were through with me I was so sanctimonious it is a wonder I wasn't canonized!"

"Canonized!" Robert chortled. "If anyone is doomed to Hell, it's you, Nat Gordon."

"Aye, Rob . . ." Nat grinned, raising his tankard in tribute. "But you can be sure I'll have your flagon poured, awaiting your arrival."

Robert's expression sobered. "Argyll will never forgive you for making a fool of him. He will not rest until he sees you dead, Nat."

"Nobody lives forever, Robbie." Elizabeth

blushed as Nat Gordon stole a devilish wink. "Besides, it matters not when you die, just as long as you left a contented smile on the face of the last wench you bedded."

A short while later Elizabeth stood on the ramparts and watched the last column of soldiers disappear over the hill.

She pressed her hand to her mouth, still feeling the pressure of Robert's lips. Their parting had been guarded, almost hostile. A great deal remained unsaid between them.

"We have much to resolve on my return, Elizabeth," he had told her stiffly. She had been at a loss to respond.

Robert had stared at her for several seconds. Then, helpless in his need to touch her, his lips had come down on hers in a long, bruising kiss that had left her breathless and shaken.

XXI

By midsummer Elizabeth knew she was carrying Robert's child. The knowledge kept her aglow and helped her to overcome the loneliness that had come into her life since Anne and David's departure. She waited anxiously for word from Robert, knowing that David had sent him a letter informing him of his impending parenthood. Elizabeth hoped the news would cause him to set aside his warring ways and return to Ashkirk permanently. Was this too much to ask or expect of him?

Often Elizabeth rode the small distance to Kirkmuir. She enjoyed passing her time visiting with Mary and John. Their tales of the past, of the young and growing Robert and David, always held her rapt attention, somehow helping her to believe that her husband was nearby rather than on some distant battlefield.

More and more Elizabeth permitted herself to slip into a world of fantasy where a tall, laughing Robert Kirkland resided daily over Ashkirk. In her daydreams she saw herself waking each morning with him beside her, and she relived the rapture of each passionate moment spent in his arms.

Her mind was on such thoughts as she paced impatiently outside the small church waiting for Tims, who was attending Mass with his mother. The tiny clachan of Kirkmuir was entirely deserted, except for the six people gathered inside the Catholic church, since John and Mary, accompanied by the other villagers, had journeyed to the keep for a Sunday Protestant service. When the Mass was through, she and Tims were going to go on a Sunday outing to Blake Hall.

With indifference Elizabeth watched the approach of four riders to the clachan. They appeared to be youths of seventeen or eighteen years of age, but none appeared familiar to her. She could not conceal a grimace of disgust when one of the boys carelessly tossed aside an empty whiskey bottle.

At the sight of Elizabeth they reined in their horses and the largest of the four leered down at her.

"Well, wha' hae we here? Look, lads, we hae found a Kirkland slut."

Elizabeth was quite unintimidated by their number, and her eyes blazed angrily.

"I should have you flogged for that remark, you vulgar snit. You would be wise to get out of here immediately."

The youth climbed down from his horse and sauntered over to her.

"Wil' ye listen to her fancy airs. An' who

may ye be, me fine damsel?" he asked mockingly.

"I am the Lady Elizabeth Kirkland, Countess of Kirkwood."

"Well, wha' hae ye! The Earl's whore hersel'!"

Elizabeth's hand swung out rendering a stinging slap to his face. The young man grabbed her arm in a painful grasp, twisting it behind Elizabeth's back.

"Come on, Will," one of the riders cautioned, "le' her be."

"Nae, I think we shud teach this whore a lesson she'll nae forget."

With that he struck Elizabeth in the face and she fell to the ground from the force of the blow. Elizabeth attempted to scream but a hand was instantly clamped over her mouth. She thrashed and kicked in an effort to free herself, as Will continued to hold her down.

"Ye bes' no' harm her, Will, or ye'll hae the whole bloody clan a' our door. Let's gie on wi' the business we ca' for."

With a snarl Will released his hold on her and Elizabeth sat up, still dazed from the blow, and began to wipe away the blood from her bruised lip.

"My lord will kill you for this," she threatened.

"The' tell the bastard he shud ca' alookin' for Will Campbell of Illnay."

Without comprehending their intent, Elizabeth saw them take some tow from their saddles and light the ends. Without hesitation the youths threw the burning fagots onto the thatch roof of the church.

" 'Tis time we Campbells finally rid Scotland o' these Papist shrines."

"Good Lord, there are people in there," Elizabeth cried in horror.

Will went to the door and latched the lock, imprisoning the people inside the windowless cottage.

"Then le' them die for their Pope." He laughed in his drunken mania.

With a cry of disbelief Elizabeth ran to the door in an attempt to release the latch. In wild fury the drunken boy lashed out and again knocked her to the ground, viciously kicking her. A spasm of excruciating pain gripped her and she clutched her stomach as she suddenly felt the gush of warm stickiness between her legs. Elizabeth lay helpless, groaning with agony and pain, as she listened to the cries of panic from the people trapped within.

"Let them out! In the name of God, let them out!" she begged, tears streaking her cheeks. "There are women and children inside."

Her pleas were ignored, and in the throes of horror Elizabeth heard the desperate pounding and screaming of the helpless victims. Then the dry wattle of the walls burst into flames and the building became a blazing inferno.

"Tims," Elizabeth screamed hysterically. "Oh, Tims. Oh, God, help him! Please God help him!" she cried, before a blanket of blackness mercifully enveloped her.

The smell of smoke still hung in the air from the smoldering charred remains when Elizabeth returned to consciousness to find the kindly eyes of Mary Kirkland hovering above her. She felt Mary's gentle hands apply a damp cloth to her head.

"She's wakin', John" the woman called out behind her.

John Kirkland's white head appeared above her and he smiled tenderly down at her.

"Jus' lie still, lass," he cautioned softly.

The nightmare of the day's events returned and Elizabeth's eyes swung frantically to the burned out remains where the tiny church had once stood. Her eyes blurred. "Did any of them get out?"

John's face was tortured. "By the time we sae the smoke, 'twas too late."

"And my baby?"

John shook his head sadly.

Elizabeth began shaking with sobs and she buried her head in the pillow. Mary looked helplessly toward John, seeking some way to comfort the grief-stricken young girl. He patted Elizabeth's hands gently, then motioning to his wife, they left her to her sorrow.

Elizabeth had no idea how long she lay sobbing, tortured with the memory of a little freckled face smiling eagerly up at her. She could not stem her tears remembering the countless times the tiny figure had ridden beside her. Adding to her grief was the loss of her own child and all her hopes and expectations.

The sun had settled when she finally staggered from the cottage and approached the charred rubble. In a trance-like stupor Elizabeth walked among the ashes. A shiny object caught her eye and she reached down and picked it up.

The sound of approaching horses caused her to turn and step to the road. David Kirkland and a retinue of twelve soldiers rode up to her. Elizabeth had never seen such a grim and unrelenting look on her brother-in-law's face. His usually warm eyes were cold and merciless.

"Beth, you should not be on your feet."

"Did you catch up with them?" Elizabeth demanded, ignoring his greeting.

David nodded. "Come, Beth, I must get you back to Ashkirk."

"But where are they?" she asked, looking around perplexed. "Surely you did not let them go."

David's eyes met hers with an unwavering stare. "We hung them," he replied dispassionately.

Elizabeth slumped against his mount, trying to steady her shaking legs. For a few seconds she fought the dizziness and nausea that swept over her. Fighting back her hysteria, she took a deep breath and sank slowly to the ground. When would this savagery end? After how many more deaths?

Her eyes dropped to her clenched fist and she slowly opened her hand. A single tear from each eye slid down her cheeks as she stared at the piece of metal clutched tenaciously in her palm—once the cherished keepsake of a young lad, now the blackened remains of a spur's rowel.

The early signs of fall were in evidence when Elizabeth stood at the graveside of Michael Kirkland.

"I am sorry, my lord, I could not live up to your expectations. Forgive me."

Her lovely face suddenly contorted with guilt and anger, and she lashed out.

"I tried, old man, I tried, but I cannot do it alone. I do not have the strength."

Contritely, Elizabeth sank to her knees and lovingly placed a small bouquet by the grave. "It seemed so simple and logical when you explained it to me, but I made one irrevocable mistake, my lord. I fell in love with your son. By so doing, I became vulnerable and weak. I am not the woman he needs. I have not the strength to be the supporting wife he must have."

Elizabeth traced her fingers slowly across the tombstone, fondling the smooth granite surface.

"I am leaving Ashkirk, my lord—and all her painful memories. But her faces will haunt me forever. Robert's. Yours. Tims'."

Her eyes filled with tears as she continued.

"Wouldst that the time had been right for

Robert and me. Perhaps then our union could have been all you desired. For indeed, I grew to love your Highlands and the people who walk them. I leave much of my heart behind me."

Rising to her feet she paused for one final lingering look.

"Goodbye, dear old man. I love you, as I love Robert."

Anne and David had remained a discreet distance away, allowing her the privacy of the moment. Finally, unable to watch her misery any longer, David approached and took her in his arms.

The comforting feel of his arms was all that was needed to release the torrent of tears she had been fighting to contain. She sobbed broken-heartedly as he embraced her with compassion.

"Don't act in haste, Beth," David pleaded. "Wait for Robert's return. Leaving Ashkirk at this time is too grave an action to take without discussing it with Robert."

"I warned him before he went away that I would leave. Can't you understand, David? I cannot bear anymore heartache."

"He'll only come after you and bring you back, Beth. I know Robert. He'll not stand for your leaving him." He lifted her chin to force her to meet his stare. "He loves you, Beth, despite what you think," he said with a tender smile.

"I don't have the strength for his kind of love. Robert and I have mixed opinions of where one's loyalties lie. It is best I leave him now, before we hurt one another anymore."

With that Elizabeth turned and walked over to where a mounted Kirkland retinue waited silently and patiently for her.

XXII

Elizabeth rounded the curve in the road and with an emotional gasp reined in her horse. Ahead stood the high walls of Ballantine, and her heart raced with joy at the familiar beloved sight. How often as a young girl had she beheld this same view, unmindful of the worthiness of those cherished walls.

A lone horseman raced from the massive entrance of the castle, and Elizabeth squealed gaily as she goaded her horse to a gallop. The road closed rapidly between them and they leapt from their saddles to rush into one another's arms.

"Oh, Beth," Andrew Scott sighed, as he hugged his sister, "I have really missed you."

The tears were streaking down Elizabeth's cheeks as she stepped back to study her twin brother. His face still glowed with a youthful boyishness, but his eyes reflected the grimness of the past year.

Andrew Scott was thinking the same thoughts of his adored sister as he studied her lovely face. Those brown eyes had lost a great deal of their previous sparkle and now seemed to harbor a concealed hurt. Apparently, they both had been forced toward painful maturity in the past year.

The Kirkland escort had halted, remaining at a discreet distance to allow them this private moment, though their waiting manner bode no doubt that they would not leave her until she was secure within the castle's walls.

Andrew grinned at her, his head beckoning toward the assemblage. "It would appear that your escort is most anxious to move on. Shall we not cause them further delay?"

He helped her to mount and then swung into his own saddle. His head tilted in a jaunty angle toward the tall gate in the distance, his eyes an unspoken challenge.

"I will be kind to you, little sister, and gave you a head."

"I have never needed a handicup to beat you, Andrew Scott," Elizabeth retorted, accepting the challenge—and with a flurry of hooves, they raced their mounts toward the massive gateway.

"He died peacefully, Father," Elizabeth later related to the Earl of Ballantine after a poignant reunion. "Lord Kirkland lived to see Robert and me wed and passed away a few days later." Her eyes clouded with anguish. "I am almost glad he did not live to see the outcome of his great expectations. It would probably have broken his heart."

Alexander Scott feared the ache in his daughter's heart was far deeper than she was admitting.

"Are you certain, Elizabeth, this is what you want? I know you, my dear, and I sense your grief."

"Father, I will tell you what I told Robert. I can handle my anguish now, but would I be able to suffer it later? I am afraid not. Yes, I grieve for Robert Kirkland, but with anger and frustration and not the hopeless despair that his death would bring to me. I will learn to live with this pain. My anger will give me the fortitude to bear it."

"And what if you would not have lost his child? Would you have remained at Ashkirk?"

Elizabeth's lovely face contorted into a bitter grimace.

"Under those circumstances, I am sure Robert would never have permitted me to leave."

"And what makes you think he will permit you now?"

"What can he do to stop me?" she flared defiantly. "Our handfast marriage is soon over. He has no authority to keep me."

"My dear Elizabeth, Robert Kirkland is a Highland chieftain. Are you not aware that makes him his own authority? I fear we have not seen or heard the last of the Earl of Kirkwood."

Seeing the look of foreboding in her father's face, for a few seconds Elizabeth's confidence wavered, but then, burying her head against his chest, she sighed with assurance.

"Let the mighty 'Highland Lion' roar as

loudly as he wishes. He cannot hurt me here. I am safe at Ballantine."

Lord Scott's arms enfolded her protectively, but a worried frown creased his brow. "Nevertheless, I fear we have not heard the last of Robert Kirkland."

Elizabeth was forced to forsake the security of her father's arms at the sound of a light tap on the door and the entrance of one of the servants.

"Lord Craver awaits you in the library, my lady."

"Oh, no," Elizabeth groaned, clearly perturbed. "I have no desire for a confrontation with him now."

"I will tell him you are indisposed, Elizabeth," the Earl of Ballantine offered.

"No," she said, reconsidering with a resigned sigh. "I may as well deal with him straight away."

Walter Campbell rose warily to his feet when Elizabeth entered the library. His manner was petulant and aloof, as he brought her hand to his lips.

Elizabeth's brown eyes were warm and inviting when she greeted him.

"I am sure, Walter, you would not have journeyed to Ballantine if you did not wish to see me. Your distant manner confuses me."

"And well it should, Elizabeth, after your betrayal when last we met."

Elizabeth's face turned up in a pugnacious grin. "And what would you have had me do, Walter? Sit docilely by and let you execute my husband?"

"Your husband is a rebellious insurgent who warrants execution. By aiding him you are as guilty as he."

"Oh, tut, Walter," Elizabeth protested lightly. "If you attempt to dole out punishment to every Scot who has helped Montrose and his men, you would be prosecuting practically every man and woman in Scotland."

Her lips pursed in an appealing pout. "Besides, my lord, did I not prevent Robert from killing you?"

Campbell studied the enchanting face and bright eyes that confronted him, his wounded vanity seeking mollification. At the sight of her bewitching smile, his resolutions crumpled and he sighed in resignation.

"Oh, Elizabeth, how easily you twist me around your finger."

Walter Campbell's reward for his capitulation was another captivating smile.

"Now tell me, Walter, are you not glad to see me back home at Ballantine?"

"I can only hope it is your intention to remain."

"I have left my husband."

He looked around suspiciously. "I suspect the room will suddenly abound with those accursed Highlanders."

Elizabeth chuckled in amusement. "I apologize for that act, Walter, but fear not— I am telling you the truth. I have left Robert Kirkland and returned to my home."

At this announcement Campbell grasped her to him ardently. "Then may I hope that I may press my cause?"

Elizabeth's hand restrained him. "Please, Walter, I beg of you—give me time to think of this matter. I seek seclusion and the peace of Ballantine at this time. I do not want to consider a commitment to anyone except myself. I have just suffered a painful experience and I must have time to heal."

Walter Campbell brought her hand to his lips in a lingering kiss. "Of course, Elizabeth, forgive my lack of sensitivity. I have waited so long for you that I have permitted my impatience to cloud my consideration."

Elizabeth sensed his apology was shallow and lacked sincerity, but she did not wish to pursue the matter any further. She was relieved just to be home again at Ballantine. She must now begin to obliterate all the painful memories of Ashkirk from her mind and try to forgert the existence of Robert Kirkland, or how much at the moment she yearned for the feel of those strong arms around her.

The next day Elizabeth stood on the battlements and, with an aching heart, watched the final red and black Kirkland plaid disappear around the bend in the road. Her thoughts were racing with the ignominy of her own self-doubt. Why should I suffer this emptiness? I, and I alone, made the decision to leave Ashkirk. Must I constantly have to wrestle with the wisdom of that act? Did I think I could ride away with nary a backward glance? Oh, damn you, Robert Kirkland, release me!

"It is not too late, Beth. We can send a rider to halt them."

Startled, Elizabeth swung around to find Andrew leaning against the parapet, studying her perceptively. She tried to mask her feelings with an indifferent shrug of her shoulders.

"As far as I am concerned, it is good riddance. I hope it will be the last we see of them."

"Beth, I am your twin. We have been too close through the years for me not to know when you are troubled. Perhaps, now is the time for you to be honest with me, as well as with yourself. You are in love with Robert Kirkland, aren't you?"

Elizabeth turned to him with a pensive smile. "I think I will always love him, Andrew."

Her brother's expression remained composed.

"Then why, in the name of heaven, did you leave him, Beth?"

"I could not live with the knowledge that someone else can claim his affection."

Anger flared in Andrew's eyes at the announcement that Robert Kirkland had toyed falsely with the love of his adored sister.

"You mean he spurned your affection for that of his mistress?"

"Nae, Andrew. My husband's devotion is to James Graham."

For the first time since Elizabeth's return to Ballantine, Andrew began to comprehend Elizabeth's marital problems.

"Beth, you cannot let a man's duty interfere with your personal relationship."

Elizabeth wanted to scream out in protest. She was so weary of that argument. Time and time again she had heard this same rebuttal from Robert, David, Anne, her father—and now even Andrew. Was no one sympathetic to her needs? Was there no one who could see her side? Did she not have a need for Robert also? Was Montrose the only one who could lay claim to his loyalty?

"And what of his duty to his clan, Andrew? Should that not precede any loyalty to Montrose?"

"His commitment to Montrose was made long before he even met you. My God, Beth, this does not mean he does not love you. A man's honor must supersede any other claim. I pity the man. He must be wracked with conflicting demands. His loyalty to Montrose! His love for you! His responsibility to his clan!"

"You make him sound very noble, Andrew. If you knew Robert Kirkland you would realize he is entirely self-determined."

"Perhaps, Elizabeth, you do not know him as well as you may think, for the motives of a man in war often can be seriously misconstrued."

In the weeks after Andrew's departure, Elizabeth spent many hours pondering his words. She rode the familiar grounds, but they now lacked the luster and majesty of those Highland hills. Somehow the once placid beauty of a quiet rill running beside a plowed field paled when compared to the dramatic splendor of a cataract leaping gloriously down granite steps to a rushing stream below.

More and more she wrestled with the desire to forget her pride and return to Ashkirk—and Robert Kirkland.

XXIII

Every morning for the past week the bells from the towering spire of the Medieval cathedral of Saint Mungo, many of its ancient walls and pillars dating back to the twelfth century, rang out a message of jubilation. The gates of Glasgow had been opened in welcome to the triumphant army of the Marquis of Montrose.

Stunning and brilliant victories at Dundee, Auldearn, Kilsyth, as well as Inverlochy, had ended any Scottish resistance to the victorious forces of the King.

Even the mighty city of Edinburgh unlocked the grisly doors of its dank prisons to release the contingent of political prisoners who had been ignominiously seized and imprisoned—distinguished statesmen such as Archibald Napier, the brother-in-law who had raised James Graham; the Reverend George Wishart, whose only crime was that he had been the chaplin and secretary of Montrose; Sir James Ogilvy, the eldest son of one of James Graham's most loyal officers. These were but a few. The list was a long and shameful one—men and women who were related to or simply had voiced their approval of Montrose.

Now James Graham had called forth a parliament, in the prosperous city of Glasgow, reigning over it in the name of his cherished soverign, Charles.

He hoped this particular evening would be a momentous one, for the clan chieftains of Scotland's Lowlands were assembling to pay homage to the King's Lieutenant Governor. Jamie knew if he could get a pledge of support from this group of men, he could cross the English border with an army that would guarantee the defeat of Cromwell.

However, the war and its outcome were far from the thoughts of Robert Kirkland as he entered the jeweler's shop. At the sight of the tall Highlander, the goldsmith's eyes gleamed brightly, and he went to his safe and removed a small velvet box.

"I have it ready, my lord," he announced proudly.

Like a wizard about to produce a rabbit from his sleeve, the jeweler raised the lid of the box for Robert's inspection. Within the satin folds lay two slim, almost thread-like bands of gold, linked together by dainty rows of gold filigree. In the center was an exquisite ruby set in an elegant blossom of four delicate petals of spun gold, each trimmed with tiny diamonds.

The intricate detail reflected a pride of workmanship, and the smile of pleasure that crossed Robert's face was as rewarding to the goldsmith as the pouch of gold Robert proffered to him.

"Is it to your liking, Lord Kirkland?"

"It is exactly what I envisioned," Robert responded obligingly. "My congratulations on a job well done."

Robert's heart was light as he rode the eight miles back to Bothwell Castle, where Montrose had taken residence. He planned, after his promised trip to Edinburgh on the morrow, to return to Ashkirk for a visit. He was eager to see Elizabeth again, and he felt that happiness over their impending parenthood would erase the memory of the painful words spoken at their last meeting. His cheerful mood continued into the evening, as he completed his dressing.

Robert attired himself in the same effortless manner he carried himself—without conscious thought or plan. He was never influenced by current fads, relying entirely upon his own selective instinct, which resulted in a natural elegance that was even the envy of the fastidious James Graham.

The urgent rapping at his chamber door failed to alter his mood, and Robert swung open the door, a wide grin covering his handsome face.

"Will!" he exclaimed in astonishment, at the sight of the Kirkland courier.

"My lord," the young man replied, "I bring a missive from Sir David." Hesitantly, he handed Robert the letter and backed away with a nervous step. "I will see to my mount, my lord."

The young man knew his laird would be upset with the message, and he regretted being the one to have carried it to him.

With an absent nod of dismissal from Robert, he hastily made his exit, and Robert broke the seal and began to read its contents.

Once again Robert read the letter from David before angrily crumbling it into a wad and tossing it into the fireplace.

He was torn between a mixture of grief and fury. When last he heard, he was to be a father; now, it appeared, he no longer had that prospect to anticipate. His disappointment was tremendous. How often he had thought of the joy that precious little one would bring into their lives. Elizabeth would have nurtured the life within her until it became the living expression of their love.

Robert sensed how she must have grieved. Could she not have shared it with him? Could they not have looked forward to the prospect of other children? But nae—rather than that, she had followed through with her threat to leave him and had returned to Ballantine. As disappointing as the loss of the little bairn was to him, Robert was more upset with the news of Elizabeth's defection. The more he thought of it, the angrier he became. He was furious with her for not personally contacting him to inform him of her actions.

Robert picked up the black velvet box.

With a grimace of disgust he opened it and his fingers toyed with the tiny gold band—the wedding ring he had never given Elizabeth. Ignoring his own propensity toward inflexibility, Robert cursed her stubborness.

"Damn the woman!" he ranted aloud. "What a fool I was to let her talk me away from having the marriage sanctified! Somehow I will have to get to Ballantine, and then I am going to kick her beautiful little arse all the way back to Ashkirk!

His decision made and resolutely nodding his head, Robert tucked the ring into his doublet.

The Grand Hall of Bothwell Castle began to take on the semblance of a royal court, for paying homage to James Graham was the majority of Scotland's most prestigious noblemen. For several days they had been arriving in Glasgow, many personally summoned by the Marquis of Montrose. In his official capacity as the King's Lieutenant Governor, such an invitation bode more like a royal command.

Many came out of old friendship, a few out of scorn, and some out of curiosity. But come they did, friend and foe alike, and James Graham reigned over them as skillfully and graciously as though he were the sovereign he was there to represent.

With a tap of his sword on each of the broad shoulders, James Graham declared, "With the authority of my King, and in the sight of God and all men present, I dub thee Knight of the Realm. Arise, Sir Alistair MacDonald."

With complete abashment the huge Irishman rose to his feet, stunned, as were many, by this unexpected act. The drab garb of the Irishman had been exchanged for more appropriate dress. The worn plaid that usually draped the mammoth frame, had been substituted by a blue satin doublet and breeches; the laced buskins were replaced by black shiny boots. A jeweled dirk was strapped to his waist, and an ornate Celtic necklace hung loosely around his neck. That glorious shock of red hair had been fashioned into long curls that hung to his shoulders, and the drooping moustache was now trimmed and neatly groomed.

Indeed, he appeared as impeccably clad as any of the King's cavaliers, but his awesome height still struck a note of terror into the hearts of those encountering the gigantic Highlander for the first time.

Robert Kirkland and Magnus O'Cahan stood aside, both men grinning at the sight of their usually confident and swaggering comrade in arms now reduced to shocked humility.

"Poor Colkitto," Robert intoned dryly. "In a couple of days, when the obligations befitting his noble status begin to sink in, he will probably never forgive Jamie."

Magnus chuckled in agreement as Nat Gordon walked up and draped a friendly arm around each of their shoulders.

"Just think, comrades, old Colkitto will now have to defend a maiden's honor instead of assaulting it."

"Don't laugh too hard, Nat," Magnus cautioned. "Remember, we are the ones he will probably have to defend it against."

The three of them immediately erupted into laughter at the humor of such a situation.

"Dare I interrupt such merriment?" a soft voice inquired.

Astonished, Robert spun around to see the petite figure of his former mistress. He had not seen Desireé since the day of his father's funeral, and for a few seconds, he struggled with the guilty knowledge that he had not made any effort to contact her in all that time.

"Desireé," he said tenderly, as he brought her hand to his lips.

"I have missed you, *mon cher*," Desireé whispered huskily.

Robert did not release her hand, but continued holding it in his own warm grasp. "And I have missed you too, my love. The demands of war have kept me so occupied, there has not been any time for other considerations."

"The General's victories are on all the tongues in France. His exploits have won him many more friends in the French court."

"Desireé, my love, have you not missed me, too?" Nat Gordon inquired, breaking the locked gaze of the two people.

"Of course, *Monsieur Gordon*," Desireé cooed, her green eyes flashing coquettishly. "The men of the French court pale, when compared to you Highlanders." She returned her attention to Robert and reached up to caress his cheek. "And you, *mon cher*, how have you been? It has been so long."

Robert bent down and pressed a light kiss on her cheek.

"Much too long, Desireé," he replied sincerely, remembering all this woman had once meant to him and all they had shared through the years. He knew he must tell her there could no longer be anything between them, that his passion for Elizabeth drove away any desire for other women. This startling realization was as incredulous to him as it would be to her. Robert Kirkland suddenly realized he was a man in the totally ludicrous, and unheard-of, position of having to tell an alluring and desirable mistress that he actually preferred his own wife!

Elizabeth paused in the entrance of the Grand Hall, her eyes anxiously scanning the room in search of the familiar dark head. She was unaware that her entrance had immediately attracted the attention of the Marquis of Montrose.

James Graham admired beauty in whatever form it presented itself, and he suddenly found himself envying the man whom this exquisite creature so eagerly sought. He witnessed the beautiful brown eyes suddenly light up, and his gaze swung to the figure that had caused this reaction. A fond smile crossed his face and he shook his head indulgently. I might have known—Robbie, he thought.

Even with a room full of Scotland's most handsome, it would have to be you the lady seeks!

With surprise he saw the young woman's eyes suddenly cloud with pain, and, bewildered, he turned his attention back to Robert, who had just leaned over and placed a kiss on the cheek of Desireé du Plessis. James Graham's compassionate eyes returned to the young woman, whose own eyes were effusive, revealing the ache and longing she was suffering. So you are foolish enough to be in love with him, little flower, he thought sadly. Ah, Robbie, you are a fool—such a damn fool!

Graham saw the young woman joined by Alexander Scott and the major domo's voice rang out loudly and officiously above the drone of voices that filled the hall.

"The Earl of Ballantine and the Countess of Kirkwood."

The announcement reached the ears of Robert Kirkland. Flabbergasted he swung around to see Elizabeth, on the arm of her father, approaching James Graham. For an instant he forgot his previous anger with her and wanted to rush over and swoop her into his arms. Transfixed, he stared at the flawless beauty he so long had been denied. Unaware of the hand that reached out to restrain him, he began to move, mesmerized, across the room.

Elizabeth found herself looking up into the face of one of the most handsome men she had ever seen. Up to this moment she never had thought to envision James Graham. To her amazement, he was not only incredibly good-looking but appeared to be only a few years older than Robert. Because of her resentment toward him, Elizabeth was prepared to immediately dislike him and was totally dismayed by the warm, compassionate eyes that met hers.

"So you are Robert's wife," he said with a husky timbre, as he brought her hand to his lips.

"My Lord Marquis," Elizabeth replied.

Under his close inspection, a slight blush began to creep across her face, but she met his scrutiny with wide, probing eyes. Reluctantly, he pulled his gaze from her to grasp the hand of Alexander Scott.

"Lord Scott," he enthused, "it has been too long."

Within moments James Graham was miraculously recollecting the events of their last meeting that had occured fifteen years earlier.

Elizabeth sensed Robert's presence before he spoke. Her pulse began to race, but she forced herself to slowly turn and confront him.

"This is an unexpected surprise, my lady."

"One over which I had no control," she retorted. "My father insisted I accompany him this evening."

"And why would you hesitate to do so, madam? Are you that averse to seeing your husband?"

"My aversion was not to seeing my husband, my lord, but rather who would be accompanying my husband. I was not eager to make myself a public spectacle."

"I think, madam, you are trying to cloud the issue of your guilt by speaking in riddles."

"My guilt! What guilt have I, my lord?" she protested angrily.

He gritted his teeth to keep his temper in check. "I thought we agreed to resolve our differences when I returned to Ashkirk, Elizabeth."

A pert brow arched into a sarcastic curve. "*We*, my lord? I don't recall your consulting me on the matter." Her eyes flashed their fury. "Perhaps you were too occupied issuing threats and orders to me."

"You don't believe that I had cause, after the near disaster that might have occured."

"Does it begin again?" she flared in exasperation. "I told you at the time that I regretted my act. It was not my intent to create any trouble. I simply wanted to ride in the race."

"And do you cry innocent for following it with another shallow deed, madam?"

"And what would that be, Robert? What crime do you accuse me of now?" she asked bitterly.

He grasped her shoulders in his own anger. "Did you not think I warranted my wife being the one to tell me she was leaving me? Did I not deserve to hear the news of the loss of my child from you? Was that so fatuous of me? I believed we at least owed that to one another."

"How dare you speak of what we owe one another, when I find you publicly consorting with your whore! Indeed, my lord, you have an ambiguous concept of the meaning of obligation!"

"Surely, you cannot believe that Desireé and I have . . ."

"Elizabeth, my love."

Before Robert could clarify any further misconceptions regarding Desireé, Elizabeth had been grabbed and hugged tightly by an elegantly clad, though maturely plump, individual.

"Uncle William!" Elizabeth exclaimed with pleasure.

James Graham and Alexander Scott had been tactfully avoiding the conversation between husband and wife. Now, at the sight of the new arrival, Jamie turned and clasped the hand of this old and dear friend.

"Ah, Willie, I haven't seen you since we made the Grand Tour together."

William Douglas, who also bore the distinction of being a Marquis, was the richest man in Scotland. He purposefully avoided entangling himself in any of the political and religious issues that plagued his homeland. By living abroad, he could ignore the appeals of his own brother-in-law, the Duke of Argyll, as well as those of cherished friends such as James Graham. For here was a man whose commitment of men and money would guarantee the success of either side.

"Damn it, Jamie Graham, you haven't aged a day!" he roared gregariously. "It's vulgar to look as virile as you do."

Though of the same age, the chubby, overweight Douglas could easily pass for at least ten years older than the lean, handsomely bronzed James Graham.

"Are you enjoying the comforts of my house?" Douglas inquired facetiously.

James Graham raised a diffident brow. For indeed, Bothwell Castle belonged to William Douglas, and in his absence Montrose had not hesitated to comandeer the castle when he arrived in Glasgow.

"And when has The Douglas ever denied the hospitality of his hearth to James Graham?" Jamie asked boldly.

With a loud guffaw, the affable Douglas embraced him. "Ah, Jamie, I love you! What great times we have shared together!"

Elizabeth stood aside and listened in amazement to this exchange. Her uncle's genuine affection for this man was obvious.

What quality did James Graham possess to be able to extract such extreme demonstrations of loyalty? She had attributed Robert's feeling toward him to cloddish hero worship, but here was the most sophisticated and wealthiest man in Scotland literally throwing himself at Graham's feet. And Elizabeth knew her uncle did not suffer with even the remotest iota of humility or reverence to anyone or anything, except the memory of Robert, 'The Bruce.'

"I had no idea you were even in Scotland, Willie. When last I heard you were dallying in France. Can I hope your presence tonight may mean an offer of Douglas horse? We have need of your cavalry."

William Douglas raised a protesting hand.

"Now, now, Jamie, the saints have blessed you with too much common sense to jump to any hasty conclusions. Besides, isn't the young Lord Aboyne your cavalry commander? I fear my Douglas horse would suffer in its effort to comply with his arrogance."

The statement drew a grimace of pain from Jamie Graham. He was too gracious to deny his loyalty to a young man who had repeatedly risked his life in the King's cause.

"Do not speak harshly of the young man, Willie. The Gordon horse often has meant the difference between victory or defeat in many of our skirmishes. Don't you agree, Robert?"

"There is certainly no denying its contribution," Robert replied, reluctantly stepping away from Elizabeth to join the conversation.

Elizabeth used the opportunity to move away. She had honored her father's demands to attend the affair. Now having made an appearance and having her worst suspicions confirmed, she was going to attempt to slip away from the whole unpleasant situation and return to her lodging.

"Of course," Jamie Graham added, "I do not want to diminish in the least the accomplishments of my infantry. They are my mainstay and strength. Alistair MacDonald is the bravest infantry commander I have ever seen in action, and Magnus O'Cahan is unquestionably the finest tactician with whom it has been my privilege to work."

"Tell me, Jamie, is it true you all stripped down to your shirts and breeks at the battle of Kilsyth?" Alexander Scott questioned.

Robert Kirkland and James Graham both erupted into laughter at his apparent disbelief.

"Many had less than that!" James Graham grinned. "We were terribly outnumbered and were forced to make the best of the terrain. Our whole strategy was to keep their cavalry useless by picking a site where it could not be effective. We knew we needed complete mobility to gain any advantage, because we had to deploy attacks from several directions."

The men stood engrossed as Jamie continued his story.

"The heat was unbearable. I saw those Irish putting aside their plaids, many of them stripping down to their bare chests. They obviously knew what they were doing, and I felt it only prudent to follow their example." He turned to Robert, his eyes flashing merrily. "So strip we did, my officers and I. The sun soon became our ally, because the heavy-laden Covenanter force, sweltering in their uniforms and armor, were sluggish and ineffective against MacDonald's infantry charges."

Jamie stopped to grin broadly. "Let me say, gentlemen, they were more disrupted than defeated. A good general could still have saved the day for them, but instead, hundreds of them perished."

"So now Scotland is yours, Jamie," William Douglas interjected.

"Nae, Willie. Scotland is the King's, as it always was, and always will be."

"I hear David Leslie has an English force at

Carlisle," Alexander Scott cautioned.

"Aye, Sir Alex, and I do not look at it lightly," James Graham intoned ominously. "David Leslie is the best soldier the enemy has. That includes Cromwell. I am flattered that they consider me a worthy enough opponent to warrant his attention. I will need all the help I can get if I am to succeed."

"I fear the King is losing his war in England," William Douglas declared. "I am sure the Roundheads deployed their best against you to make sure you cannot go to the King's aid."

Alexander Scott nodded in agreement. "There is certainly no doubt they will try to see that you do not reach Charles, Jamie. No matter what the cost! They cannot afford to do otherwise."

Robert's attention had strayed from the conversation and his eyes had been following Elizabeth trying to make her way unobtrusively through the room. He saw her progress halted by Lady Douglas, and the two women exchanged pleasantries before Elizabeth moved on.

Robert's eyes were not the only ones observing Elizabeth. Alistair MacDonald had watched the lovely vision cross the room unattended. Having imbibed too generously, he was now completely besotted, which only added recklessness to an already impetuous nature. Never a man who practiced restraint, he now decided to take what he wanted.

Elizabeth let out a slight scream when the two huge paws spanned her waist and lifted her from the floor. She found herself eye to eye with the gigantic Irishman. Her mouth gaped in astonishment as she dangled helplessly in his powerful grasp.

"Wha' a sigh' ye be to a warrior's eyes," he declared drunkenly. "If Glasgow be mine, tha' I claim ye as my bounty."

The words James Graham were about to speak remained frozen in his throat. Horrified, he stared, along with all the others in the room, at the scene unfolding before their eyes.

This was no strumpet being treated in such a fashion. This was one of their own—a countess, the daughter of an earl, the niece of a marquis, the wife of a Highland earl. There was no way such an insult could go unavenged!

With sickening apprehension, Graham saw that Robert had arleady reached the couple.

"Put her down, Colkitto," Robert ordered in a cold, deadly command.

A murmur swept the room. Tales of the atrocities at Aberdeen, as well as his relentless destructive raids against the Campbells, had made Alistair MacDonald the most feared man in Scotland. All now waited with baited breath to see how he would react to this command.

The huge giant's head was spinning with indignation. No one, not even The Graham himself, dared use that tone to him. He slowly lowered Elizabeth to the floor and turned threateningly toward his challenger.

Magnus O'Cahan and Nat Gordon had already moved to the scene. O'Cahan put a restraining hand on MacDonald's arm.

"Forget it, Colkitto, and we will have a drink. After all, you were out of line."

With an angry roar MacDonald shoved his hand away, never breaking his glare on Robert.

"You have just sealed your own tomb, Kirkland."

Completely unintimidated, Robert's gaze remained fixed on MacDonald. "What will it be, Colkitto? Claymores or dirks?"

Elizabeth gasped in shock with the realization that these two men were about to fight—and sensed it would be to the death. The overpowering size and strength of Alistair MacDonald made the outcome obvious.

Nat Gordon stepped to Robert's side, his hand on his scabbard.

"Stay out of this, Nat. It is not your fight," Robert declared.

"Let us say I am going to even the odds," Nat said lightly.

Suddenly a wisp of green chiffon stepped between the two antagonists.

"Shame, shame on you naughty, naughty boys."

Desireé du Plessis's lips were pursed in an adorable pout. "Two such handsome men threatening to harm one another." Her eyes looked enticingly up at MacDonald. "Shame on you, General. Such a marvelous figure of a man need never fight to claim a woman . . ." She slowly ran a hand suggestively across his chest. ". . . when there are so many others who are anxiously awaiting such an invitation."

Colkitto looked down at the voluptuous blonde, who was obviously offering to bed him. Sensuous green eyes were promising erotic delights that began to heat his loins, and the need to satisfy his lust became greater than any satisfaction he would derive from killing the Highlander.

"An' ye, me wee lass, wud ye be waitin' such an invitation?"

Desireé's long lashes fluttered flirtatiously.

"Oh, la, la, General, such a question! I would be too embarrassed to answer in front of all these people." Her mouth curved into an enticing smile as she tucked her arm into his. "Perhaps while we are dancing?" She left the sentence dangling, an unspoken promise.

Without a backward glance in Robert's direction, Colkitto turned toward the dance floor. Robert made a motion to follow, but Nat immediately pulled him back.

"Let it drop, Robbie. If not for your sake, think of Jamie. It would not do his cause any good to have two of his officers fighting one another."

"I do not relish having to hide behind a woman's skirt, Nat. You know why Desiree did it?"

"Oh, come on, Rob, she's not a blushing virgin! Suffering old Colkitto for a night is not going to ruin her. As a matter of fact," he grinned rakishly, "she probably will enjoy it."

"Aye, Robbie, he's never had any

complaints yet," Magnus grinned. "Now get your wife out of here. In the morning Colkitto will have forgotten the whole incident."

Reluctantly accepting the wisdom of their arguments, Robert turned to the source that had triggered the whole incident.

"Are you ready to leave, Elizabeth?"

"Well," Elizabeth flared in outraged indignation, "I am glad someone has finally decided I may have something to say in this matter. Thus far this evening I have been forced to honor my sire's demands and attend this function; I have been publicly shamed by my husband's adulterous liaisons; I have been physically mauled by a vulgar, uncouth barbarian . . ."

"An' jus' think, darlin', 'tis nae caused a flaw in that lovely face," Nat crooned, cutting off her tirade as he put a protective arm around her shoulders and forced her toward the door.

As Robert went for her wrap Nat brought her hand to his lips. His voice lowered, he said softly, "I have grown too fond of your husband, my lady, to see his blood spilled all over this floor. I cannot believe you would want it either, Elizabeth."

"You are right, Colonel Gordon. I would not want it either."

Nat's dark eyes flashed appreciatively down at her.

"But old Colkitto has a discerning eye."

He placed a light kiss on her cheek, as Robert returned with her wrap and placed it around her shoulders.

"Well, my lady, now that you have succeeded in making a fool of me in public—and probably branding me a coward—shall we leave? I am sure that by morning the knowledge that I am an unchivalrous cad will be on the tongues of everyone in Scotland."

Brown eyes snapping, Elizabeth raised her chin defiantly.

"And when, my lord, do you think it hasn't been!"

Shrugging aside his offer of help, she stormed away. In frustration Robert turned his head to find Magnus and Nat, their arms draped around one another, laughing uproariously.

XXIV

The stillness of the night was violated by the synchronized clip-clop of the matched set of bays, as they pulled the vehicle through the narrow cobblestoned wynds of Glasgow. The two occupants of the carriage maintained a portentous silence, each immersed in a caldron of anger.

Creaking axles ground to a halt in front of one of the stone domiciles that lined the road. This strip of houses was the Glasgow residence of many of the Lowland lords when business or pleasure brought them to the city.

Robert Kirkland stepped adroitly from the carriage and reached up to assist his wife. With a disdainful haughtiness Elizabeth ignored the proffered assistance and stepped ankle-deep into a pothole overflowing with muddy water.

Round brown eyes widened with initial shock as she stood stunned into immobility. Only the warm timbre of Robert's chuckle snapped her out of her benumbed state.

"May I again offer my assistance, my lady," Robert asked mockingly, as he extended his hand with an exaggerated bow. Had she been able to read his thoughts she would have been further incensed to find he was thinking she had received exactly what she deserved.

Reaching for his hand to aid her, Elizabeth attempted to step out of the hole, lost her balance and found herself sprawled in the water, with a mud-splattered gown and face.

"You stupid, clumsy Highland oaf," Elizabeth sputtered, directing the anger she felt with herself toward his smug countenance. Climbing unassisted to her feet she eyed him glaringly.

"I am sure you did that deliberately."

Seething with rage, she stormed off, her dripping skirt leaving a watery trail.

A sleepy-eyed servant opened the door to her urgent knocking, and Elizabeth pushed past him in a flurry of sodden skirts and shoes. Robert followed behind and the two men watched her ascend the stairway, her water-filled slippers making squashing telltale noises with each step she took. When she reached the top of the stairs, Elizabeth turned to cast a final scathing glare in the direction of her husband before entering a room at the right of the stairway.

Robert's eyes had followed her progress, and after a few curt orders to the perplexed and dumbfounded servant, he mounted the stairs and opened the door through which Elizabeth had entered. She spun around in surprise at his invasion.

An anger, that only seconds before had begun to subside, once again flared up at the sight of Robert slipping the bolt on the door.

"What do you think you are doing?" she blazed, arms akimbo, a sodden shoe clutched in each hand that rested on her hips.

"I am still waiting for answers to my questions," Robert declared, his irritation mounting with her continued shrewishness.

"I have nothing to discuss with an adulterous womanizer. Now leave my room immediately. I cannot stand the sight of you."

In the fury of indignation Elizabeth threw the shoes she held in her hands at his offending presence. Robert had not anticipated such an unexpected action on her part and therefore suffered the onslaught from both shoes, one bouncing off his shoulder and the other smacking soundly against his chest.

"Damn it, Elizabeth, if you are going to act like a fishwife then I am going to treat you like one."

He took a threatening step in her direction, and Elizabeth's eyes desperately sought a weapon with which to defend herself. Her eyes fell on a nearby bottle of perfume, and she picked up the crystal container and threw it at him. This time Robert was ready and succeeded in ducking, only to have the bottle crash against the wall, splashing its contents over him.

No longer able to contain his fury at this latest effrontery, Robert let out an indignant roar and rushed her, knocking over a chair in his haste.

Elizabeth's grasping hand encountered a box of dusting powder and she managed to fling it in his face only seconds before he grabbed her. His momentum carried him forward and he clutched her to him as they tumbled to the floor, with Robert twisting to absorb most of the shock from the fall. Rolling over he pressed her shoulders to the floor with the weight of his body. Elizabeth's shrieks were muffled against his chest and he fought to restrain her flailing arms.

"Damn it, woman, you are going to pay for this evening's foul work!" he threatened.

Robert finally succeeded in pinning her arms above her head in a steel grip, but Elizabeth continued squirming beneath him, refusing to yield as she mouthed threats and curses.

Robert let her continue her useless thrashing about until her strength was drained and she finally calmed down beneath the pressure of his weight. In her frustration she turned her head aside, refusing to look at him. He felt her yield and raised up his head to stare down at her. He was furious at her actions and determined to mete out some form of punishment to make her rue the night.

"So this is an example of the gracious Lowland refinements with which you have taunted me. I have seen more evidence of gracious conduct in the actions of the lowliest whore in the brothels of Edinburgh," he declared scornfully.

"I am certain, my lord, there is no greater authority on the whores of Edinburgh than yourself," she answered contemptuously.

Her taunts only angered him more, and he

brutally grasped her chin to force her head around.

"Look at me, my lady. I have no appetite for speaking to the floor."

Elizabeth opened her eyes in blazing contempt, her chin tilted defiantly. Now that he had succeeded in overpowering her, she was determined not to cower or show any sign of fear. Let him do his worst!

At the sight of him, her eyes suddenly filled with mirth, and she caught her lower lip between her teeth, trying to contain her laughter. Robert continued glaring down at her, bemused at this change of attitude.

"I am glad you can laugh in the face of jeopardy, madam, for I am about to beat the hell out of you."

Elizabeth could no longer contain herself, and her body began shaking with laughter. A pert nose wrinkled in protest as she began to sniff the air.

"I admire your selection of perfume, my lord. However, I fear you have a tendency to apply it too generously," she taunted. "I might add you do the same with your powder. May I add that the blend does nothing for your complexion."

Once again Elizabeth could not restrain herself and burst into uninhibited laughter. Unable to ignore a nagging curiosity Robert rose to his feet and lifted her up. Her legs dangled helplessly, as he flattened her arms against her sides, the soft contours of her backside clutched tightly to the hardened steel of his chest and stomach. Robert carried her to the mirror of her dressing table, and, leaning over to peer around her, studied his own reflection.

His surprise was as great as her amusement. Ebon colored hair had lightened to a snowy mane. Even the once darkly curved brows and long spikey eye lashes were now totally white. Robert studied his own reflection for a few minutes, before a grin began to twist the corners of his mouth. His eyes met hers in the mirror and he teased defensively.

"Well, you do not look too impressive yourself, my lady."

"What do you mean?" Elizabeth asked in surprise, for the first time her eyes swinging to study her own reflection.

What once had been a flawless creamy complexion was now spotted with blotches of hardened mud. Errant strands of hair hung in tangled disarray from what had been a lovely coiffure of auburn curls. Robert lowered her until her feet touched the floor, releasing his grasp on her.

"Oh, Robert, look at me," she wailed, stepping back in dismay at the sight of her resplendent gown hanging in sodden folds. For a few seconds she continued to study her reflection, until her eyes rose and met his in the mirror. Neither of them could contain their amusement, and all their anger completely dissolved as they both erupted into laughter.

Without conscious intent, Robert reached

out, his arms encircling her waist, and pulled her back against himself. They stood laughing uproariously at the sight of their own disheveled images, until a knock at the door interrupted their hilarity.

"Yes, what is it?" Elizabeth called out.

" 'Tis your bath, mum."

"I ordered no bath water," Elizabeth responded and slipped from Robert's arms.

"I ordered it for you," Robert declared, walking over to open the door. "I felt a clean hot bath would be welcomed after the muddy one you indulged in."

When the door of the chamber swung open, the poor manservant, accustomed to the tranquil privacy of a usually empty house, was once again taken aback at Robert's appearance.

Robert quickly helped him fill the huge tub and dismissed him for the evening. His task completed, the old man shuffled off, relieved to be rid of the idiosyncrasies of the rich for the remainder of the night.

Elizabeth had removed her wet gown and seated herself on the bed to roll down her soaking wet hose. Robert quickly knelt to assist her.

"Let me help you, my lady."

As he slowly peeled off each stocking, Elizabeth's pulse began racing at the feel of the warm hands on her thighs. Robert did not remain unaffected either, when he felt the silken flesh at his fingertips.

"I fear you may catch a chill, Elizabeth,"

he murmured hoarsely.

"Robert, you need the bath more than I." She smiled softly. "You really reek of perfume."

He looked up and Elizabeth's breath caught in her throat at the sight of the well-remembered endearing grin.

"It always smelled enticing on you, my love."

"Perhaps, my lord, because I apply it a bit more sparingly," she teased.

The corners of the dark eyes crinkled with a warm glow and he began to chafe her legs, trying to restore some warmth to them.

"I seem to remember doing this before."

Their eyes locked, their thoughts returning to the memory of a few stolen nights in a hunting lodge at Kirkmuir. Their latent desire became charged, an excitement building between them.

"You appeared much younger to me at the time, my lord," Elizabeth teased, reaching out a hand to brush the snowy curls. At the sight of the cloud of white dust falling from his hair Robert rose to his feet.

"That settles the issue of who gets the bath water," he announced. "We will bathe together."

"I could never!" Elizabeth exclaimed. "It would be improper."

A whitened brow was raised in derision. "I fear you would be quite scandalized to find out what occurs in the bed chambers and bath tubs of many of your closest friends."

As he talked Robert divested himself of his own garments and turning to her, began to remove her sodden underskirts. When he picked her up in his arms, Elizabeth could not restrain herself from curling against him with an erotic shudder, as she felt his hands on her nakedness.

Robert stepped into the tub and lowered them into the water, Elizabeth remaining on his lap in the narrow confines of the tub. Once in the soothing balm of the hot water, Elizabeth lost all reservations and, closing her eyes, leaned back, relaxing against the muscled hardness.

"Before the water cools too drastically, my lady, I hope you will rinse my hair."

With a resigned sigh, Elizabeth turned to face him and Robert spread his legs to allow her to kneel between them. She quickly soaped his hair and reached for a brush and began to briskly scrub the clinging powder from his hair and scalp.

"A gentle touch would be appreciated, my lady," Robert complained, cringing under her efforts.

"What a bairn!" she groaned, and shoved his head under the water.

After several rinsings Robert's dark curls had been restored to their natural hue. Elizabeth returned to her original position on his lap and began ministering to her own needs. In a short time she too felt cleansed and refreshed.

Robert had finished his own bathing and in

a playful mood began to press kisses behind her ear and on her white shoulders. Her breath caught in her throat when his hand grasped her chin and turned her face to his. For a few endless seconds dark blue eyes probed the twin pools of brown velvet, before his mouth slowly covered hers. The kiss was sensually provocative, the warmth of the water an added aphrodisiac. Elizabeth's arms slid around his neck and her lips began responding to his hungry request. His arms formed a cushion for her head and he leaned her back against the rim of the tub, the long reddish-brown locks spilling over the side. His lips began to nibble and tease the sensitive hollow of her neck and ears.

Elizabeth's head felt as light as her body as buoyancy forced her against him, and Robert groaned when he felt the sensuous thrust of her sleek, wet breasts against his chest. A hand swept the length of her, to cup her buttocks, pressing her to his hardened shaft. Robert's excitement heightened at her gasp of pleasure, her warm breath tantalizing against his mouth. He rose up and stepped from the tub, her arms still encircling his neck. In her ecstatic state she was vaguely conscious of him toweling the excessive moisture from their bodies, before carrying her to the bed.

Robert stretched out beside her and Elizabeth curled herself to him, reveling in the feel of the strength that enfolded her. The soft sound of her sigh heightened his passion, and Robert's lips claimed hers in a smoldering kiss, almost savage in its demand. Breathlessly, they pulled apart and he began to caress the familiar sensitive areas of her body, the smooth texture of her skin a silken stimulus against his fingertips.

Every nerve, every fiber in her body was responding to the probing fingers, and her whole being became a throbbing need for him. His mouth nibbled and toyed with hers, and her warm breath mingled tantalizingly with his, her hot tongue tracing the outline of his lips before covering his face and eyelids with quick, fervent kisses.

The moisture of their bodies became an adhesive that bound them together, and his tongue licked the salty rivulets as it trailed a searing path to the rosy buds of her breasts. She could no longer stifle her moans, as his tongue and mouth began a game of exquisite torture with her hardened nipples. She clung to him, as her body began an undulating rhythm, her hips responding to the fingers caressing her inner thighs.

Her sudden gasp of fulfillment when he entered her incited his passion to a frenzy. She sobbed his name with each of his driving thrusts, until her eyes widened with wondrous incredulity as the final shuddering cry of "Robert" was wrested from her throat, when the evidence of his love spilled into her.

For several minutes they lay quietly, their ragged breathing the only sound that penetrated the stillness of the room. Robert finally rested his head on a propped elbow, staring intently at Elizabeth's flushed face. Her eyes were closed, as she wrestled with emotions that were spinning wildly within her.

A feeling of bewilderment ran rampant through Robert as he too tried to cope with his own confusion. What power did this woman have over him to create such an overwhelming need and desire? How easily his previous anger had melted at the feel of her softness in his arms.

Recalling the incident with Colkittó, he remembered how he had felt when the Irishman had touched her; his reaction had not been out of chivalry, but simply jealous possessiveness. Granted, the insult to Elizabeth was grievous and demanding of an apology, but it was not worth a man's dying. Yet, in his rage at seeing Colkitto's hands on her, Robert knew he had been prepared to try to kill him, this same man with whom he had often fought side by side in battle—and he himself would probably have perished in the effort.

No woman had ever secured such a hold on him before, and he was torn by a conflict of emotions. Robert felt absolute awe that he and this superb creature were an integral part of one another, drawing strength from their mutual dependency—yet suffered abject distress that this dependency made him vulnerable, his strength now at the mercy of her most rudimentary weakness.

Robert reached out to brush some strands of hair from her face. At the feel of his touch Elizabeth opened her eyes, and for a few timeless seconds their eyes were locked, unable to disguise their love. Long, supple fingers, that could effortlessly wield a broadsword, now cupped her face in a tender caress.

"Why did you do it, Beth? How could you leave me?"

His voice was a husky rasp, vibrating with the naked anguish he was suffering.

Elizabeth's eyes brimmed with tears as she fought to retain her composure.

"I needed you, Robert. Where were you when I needed you so badly? The day I lost our baby and the horrendous circumstances of Tims' death were . . ."

"Tims' death? Oh, no," he groaned in startled despair, "you mean that precious lad was lost, too?"

Now, unable to check her tears, Elizabeth related the grisly events of that day, while Robert's arms enfolded her comfortingly.

Elizabeth clung to him desperately, her head buried against his chest while she sobbed out her pent-up grief, safe within the strength of his arms. These feelings of security and love were all she would have needed that horrible day to have given her the necessary fortitude. But whose arms could she seek, she wondered, to lessen the pain that his loss someday would bring to her? Nae, there were no such arms!

Elizabeth's voice was ringed with defensive guilt, as though she stood accused.

"I could have borne it, Robert, had you been there, but your absence was only the evidence of what I already knew—you would never be there when I needed you. Then someday, I would be confronted with the fact that an intended bullet or fatal thrust had found its mark, shattering all hope forever."

Robert's lips tenderly closed over hers, silencing the tormented accusations. Elizabeth's lips parted willingly, responding to his probing message for reassurance.

"How easy I am for you! How facile your victory! I am nothing other than a whore—with a whore's body responding to your slightest touch."

Robert again leaned his head against his propped arm to stare down at her. His voice was edged with a slight measure of irritation.

"You know what you mean to me, Elizabeth."

"I know what my body means to you, Robert," she quickly retorted.

"Aye, love, but therein lies the rub," he teased. "Do I love Elizabeth because her body pleasures me, or does her body pleasure me because it is Elizabeth's? Am I captivated by you because of a gentle voice and soft touch, or is the touch soft and the voice gentle because they are yours?"

Robert's eyes deepened with emotion and his face sobered as he continued. "What wondrous spectre has invaded my mind, driving all other thoughts before it? Its willowly arms reach out to stir and entwine my passions, and its mystic essence breathes life into my body, nurtures my hunger, and

quenches my thirst. Were I to call it by name
—would it not be Elizabeth?"

Her eyes misted at his fervent declaration.

"Oh, Robert, I need you. I love you so
much."

Robert's smile was tender as his eyes
admired her.

"Your dependency gives me strength, my
love. Your trust gives me virtue. Your love
gives me excellence," he whispered hoarsely.

"You are a persuasive devil, Robert Kirkland," she moaned as her arms slipped around
his neck. Her lips began to nibble and tease at
his. "And I am such a willing fool," she sighed
and pulled him to her.

Dawn had long passed when Elizabeth
opened her eyes. To her surprise Robert had
already arisen and was just finishing his dress.

"Good morn, my lord," she greeted him
warmly.

With a tender smile Robert leaned down
and placed a kiss on her lips.

"Good morn, my love."

"I will dress quickly and we can take our
morning tea together," Elizabeth offered gaily
and began to rise from the bed.

"I am late now, love. I should have been on
my way long ago."

"On your way! You mean you are leaving?"

Robert turned to her guiltily. "I promised
Jamie I would ride to Edinburgh."

"No, I don't believe it!" she cried incredulously. "I don't believe it! Are you telling me

you are leaving me again?"

"Beth, I promised Jamie," he protested contritely.

Elizabeth jumped to her feet and pulled the cover from the bed. She wrapped it around herself with an angry, hurried gesture.

"You have done it to me again! What kind of fool am I? Lies! My God, they are nothing but lies!"

"I did not lie to you, Elizabeth. Everything I said to you was the truth. What has that to do with my trip to Edinburgh?"

"It has everything to do with it. Didn't last night mean anything to you at all?"

"Beth, the Covenanters have Jamie's twelve-year-old-son imprisoned in Edinburgh Castle. When Johnnie Graham died, they immediately seized young James because he became Jamie's heir. Nat Gordon and I are riding to Edinburgh to try to seek his release."

"I cannot believe someone else cannot go in your stead?"

"I promised Jamie I would go. Do you think the imprisonment of his son is not important to him? Am I to treat it so lightly, as to beg off simply to stay behind and hold your hand?"

"Oh, why did I weaken?" Elizabeth ranted in torment. "Why was I foolish enough to listen to you? Get out of here, Robert. Get out of my sight. I hope I never see you again."

"Elizabeth, for God's sake, will you listen to me?"

Robert reached for her and she began to struggle against him. In her attempt to elude him, she tripped on the dragging blanket and they both tumbled to the floor. Elizabeth attempted to crawl away but Robert caught her and pulled her back. He lay across her as he pressed her shoulders to the floor.

"When I return, we will journey to Ashkirk," he declared.

"Do not bother to return, for I will not be here. Can you not understand I never want to see you again. Now get off me, you big oaf!"

Robert reached into his doublet and extracted the wedding ring. Elizabeth's eyes widened in surprise as he reached for her hand. Guessing his intent, she clenched her hand into a tight fist.

"No," she cried determindly. "I will not take it. I will not wear your ring."

"Damn it, Elizabeth, you are my wife, and you will wear my ring." His tone was emphatic.

Angrily Robert pulled her two arms above her head and grasped them in a steel grip. Elizabeth struggled uselessly as he forced her left hand open and slid the ring onto her finger. With a grunt of satisfaction he placed a solid kiss on her lips.

"There you are, you little termagant! Don't you dare take that ring off your finger. You are my wife—and don't you ever forget it!"

His dark eyes swept Elizabeth's sensual loveliness. Her chest was heaving from her efforts to free herself, a tempting breast exposed in the struggle. Her mass of dark hair was fanned against the floor in beguiling disarray, and her brown eyes, ablaze with anger, were flashing a threatening message.

"Lord, you are an enticing wench!" he sighed appreciatively, and lowered his head to place a light kiss on the peak of her breast. Once again his lips captured hers in a long, lazy kiss.

"I will be back, love," he declared, arising. "Wait for me."

"I won't be here," Elizabeth cried toward the door that had already closed behind him.

Tears began streaking her cheeks and she brought her hand to her lips.

"Damn you, Robert Kirkland, I won't be here," she sobbed, and lovingly pressed a kiss on the ring he had forced on her finger.

As the morning progressed, Elizabeth held out the remote whimsy that Robert would alter his plans to journey to Edinburgh and return to her. However, by midday she knew that her fanciful hopes were just foolish daydreams that would never materialize. Anxiously, she paced the floor before finally settling her self at the harpsichord to vent her frustration on the keyboard.

Elizabeth lost herself in the music until the sudden sound of soft applause jolted her out of her concentration.

James Graham stood relaxed against the door. His tall, lithe body was clad in deep blue velvet breeches fringed with gray ribbon loops along the sides of his long, muscular legs. The open front of the loose-fitting doublet exposed a white cambric shirt with a falling band of point lace. The cuffs of the full sleeves were drawn at the wrists and trimmed with the same point lace at the collar. A short cloak of blue satin was draped casually over his left shoulder and the same blue satin lined the bucket tops of his boots. Butterfly spurs were attached to the heel of each boot.

His moustache and short beard were as fastidious as the long auburn curls on his head. Once again Elizabeth found herself marveling at the incredible handsomeness of the man, who, despite his elegant grooming, still emanated a crushing presence of masculinity.

"Forgive me, my lord," Elizabeth said blushingly, as she rose from the bench. "I did not know you were here."

A warm smile covered his bronzed face as he crossed to her.

"Your most obedient servant, Countess," he said with a gracious bow as he brought her hand to his lips. His dark eyes caressed her with their warmth.

Elizabeth saw this man as the source of the problem between Robert and herself and was determined to remain entirely detached from his persuasive charm.

"You honor our house, my lord Marquis. To what do we owe the distinction of a visit from the King's General? If you have come seeking Lord Kirkland you are foolish to expect to find him with me. I have the least demands on his attentions." Elizabeth could not conceal the bitterness that crept into her voice.

"I have come seeking you, my lady. I am totally devoted to Robert and am sensitive to the fact that you have hurt him. I am not immune when he grieves. I cannot stand idly by and watch him bleed."

Elizabeth's eyes flashed angrily. "I must take offense to your reasoning, my lord. You are the bleeder of him, not I. It is you who is drawing the blood from him daily. If that seepage troubles you now, how will you suffer it when it is spilled on the accursed field where you choose to bury him?"

A sad smile creased his handsome face. "So that is the basis for your hostility. You see me as the determining factor of Robert's destiny. Do you not put your faith in the Almighty?"

"I do, my lord, but unfortunately Robert puts his in James Graham."

This declaration brought a slight frown to Montrose.

"So I am, indeed, directly the cause of the friction between you and Robert.

"Oh, my lady, can you not see that Robert is his own person? He is not a pawn that either you or I can manipulate. This very trait is what gives him his excellence. Scotland is in need of such men in these troubled times."

"My lord, I see these 'troubled times' created by you and the Duke of Argyll."

"Others have said the same, my lady. But as a Scot I cannot sit by and silently watch the persecution of my countrymen. I will not let Argyll jeopardize the peace and freedom of *one* Scot in his obsessive drive for power. Our heritage dictates that we are not meant to be oppressed and enslaved subjects. I beg you, my lady, to believe that despite my loyalty and love for our precious Sovereign, I would never have taken arms for Charles if I were not convinced he believed in defending the rights and religions of our people."

James Graham continued softly, each word a fervent declaration.

"Judge me not by the contemptible guise of justice that Argyll and his puppets have foisted on our people. Let me be judged by the laws of nations who believe that man has an inalienable right to freedom. Judge me by the laws of Nature. Just as the eagle must be free to soar and the river to ramble, so must man be free to enable him to reach the heights of his nobility. And let me be judged by the laws of God, the Supreme and Righteous Jurist of us all."

Elizabeth turned away, unable to meet the beseeching sincerity of his dark eyes.

"I fear I owe you an apology, my lord. I have no right to condemn you. What you do, you do in good conscience. But so many Scots have died because of it. Even my own unborn child has become a victim to this struggle."

"I, too, have lost a son, my lady. He died at Inverlochy. Argyll now has my heir imprisoned at Edinburgh."

Elizabeth turned back to him in commiseration, realizing for the first time how much this man had sacrificed in dedication to his king.

"Do you have other children, my lord?" she asked, tears misting her eyes.

"Aye," he said sadly. "A lad, Robert, and a lovely lass, Jeanie. Our son David died when just a wee one."

"And your wife, my lord?"

James Graham's eyes clouded with pain. "My wife, Magdalen, and our bairns are with her parents. My shame was too much for her to bear and she has left me." He shook his head in a self-debasement. "I can never stop blaming myself for the pain and suffering I have caused that poor soul. Our marriage was arranged and we were wed when we were still children. I was just a lad of seventeen."

James Graham grasped her shoulders, his sad eyes probing hers, seeking understanding.

"This war has destroyed my marriage, my lady. Do not let it destroy yours and Robert's!"

James Graham gently caressed her head, before he took her hand and brought it to his lips. He smiled tenderly down at her.

"Robert Kirkland is a man among men, Elizabeth, and he loves you. Do not try to deny that you do not love him also. Let that love surmount any obstacles the two of you must overcome." For a few seconds he held her in his arms. "Now, dear lady, I must say good day. The affairs of state demand my attention. Let us all pray for a swift end to this war."

James Graham kissed the top of her head

and Elizabeth's eyes followed his departure from the room. The man had deeply touched her, and, whatever the outcome between her and Robert Kirkland, Elizabeth knew from this moment on she could never again remain impervious to whatever fate had designed for James Graham.

XXV

"Jamie, it is folly to meet Leslie in the Lowlands. He is too strong. We must draw him into the mountains," Robert protested.

He and Nat Gordon had returned from Edinburgh after an unsuccessful attempt to get Montrose's son released from prison, only to find the army was already on the march.

Montrose turned sad eyes to Robert.

"His Majesty is desperate. A mountain campaign would take weeks, and Charles needs our help as quickly as possible. He has asked me to march South and engage Leslie close to the border."

"My God, he is sealing your doom," Nat Gordon ranted. "Huntly has called home his Gordons; Alistair MacDonald and the Irish troops have taken off on some senseless raid."

"Not all of the Irish troops," Magnus O'Cahan interrupted with a soft tone. "My Ulster men and I have remained."

James Graham flashed a grateful glance toward the young Irishman as Nat Gordon continued. "We have seven hundred men and about two hundred Douglas horses. Leslie has over six thousand! What does Charles think we can do against Leslie in the open? He may be a king, but obviously he is no military strategist!"

"I have promises of infantry from several of the border lords, and the Earl of Traquair has promised me some cavalry before we reach the border," James Graham replied calmly.

"The Earl of Traquair!" Robert echoed derisively. "He has no loyalty to you or the King."

"Jamie, why do you listen to your enemies more than your friends?" Nat interjected. "We all have warned you, but still you choose to risk your life on half promises. Haven't you learned from the past? At least wait until the Gordon clan or the MacDonalds return," he pleaded.

"The King's position is precarious, Nat. I cannot fail him. What value am I to him if I cannot render aid when he needs it the most?"

"Will you be of greater value to him with your head hanging from the walls of Edinburgh?" Robert asked in frustration.

James Graham faced the three commanders and smiled affectionately. "I know it is a very weak military maneuver, but I can do no other at this time to aid him." His smile deepened. "I know, too, that your concern is for my life. Why should a man be so blessed? Can anyone claim greater riches than the loyalty of such dear and trusted comrades? And tomorrow I am given the opportunity of returning Scotland to its rightful sovereign, Charles. No man would be privileged to die in greater company or for a finer cause."

With his disarming grin, he clasped their hands warmly and declared, "For God, Covenant, and Country!"

The next day a scout brought the word that an English army under General Leslie had crossed the border and reached Berwick. As they continued their march South to meet it, Montrose's army was joined by the Earl Of Traquair's son with nearly one hundred horsemen. Robert watched skeptically as the Traquair troop joined their ranks. When Nat Gordon rode up beside him, the two seasoned veterans exchanged knowing glances.

"Are you thinking the same thing I am?" Nat asked. "This whole thing has the foul smell of Argyll."

Robert Kirkland nodded his agreement. "I do not like the look of Traquair. I wish Jamie would not put so much trust in such people. Whatever happens, Nat, one of us must see to his safety."

Nat Gordon nodded his agreement, and the two friends clasped hands to seal their vow.

Montrose rode up to them, encouraged by Traquair's arrival.

"A hundred horse is better than none at all," he enthused, seeing their skeptical expressions.

"Hey, Jamie, perhaps you should mount the Irish on their cattle. That way Leslie might think you have a cavalry," Nat said sarcastically.

"We need no horse, Nat," Montrose declared zealously. "A Highlander's feet are as swift as his hands."

"They will have to be," Nat intoned dryly, "when Leslie's cavalry rides over them."

"Why, give me a hundred good Scots at my back, and I will storm the bloody Tolbooth itself!" Montrose exclaimed fervently.

"Can you be certain they are good Scots, Jamie?" Robert asked ominously.

"There are no bad Scots, Robbie—just misguided ones," James Graham declared sincerely, as he turned his horse and rode down the line.

"Why do I feel I am one of those misguided Scots to which he was referring?" Nat murmured wryly.

Robert scoffed, "Now just what would a rake like you have done in the Convenanting army anyway? You would never have been able to even take their oath of allegiance."

A serious frown creased the brow of Nat Gordon as he reflected on Robert's words.

"Well, I certainly could have taken their oath not to plunder. It would have been difficult, but I might have even been able to swear not to curse—but forbidding the keeping of whores? God's blood, Robert, that is asking too much of any man!" Nat declared with mock solemnity.

Robert leaned across his saddle laughing vociferously, the sound of his laughter carrying the length of the column to the ears of Montrose. James Graham turned back in his saddle and smiled fondly, knowing full well that Robert's amusement could only mean that Nat Gordon had launched one of his irreverent barbs at Argyll or the Covenanters.

The smile quickly left his face at the approach of a new rider. After a hasty consultation he immediately assembled his officers.

"I have just received grievous news. The men sent by Roxburgh and Home were met by Leslie's force. They had no choice but to join them. I feel the only prudent action would be to pull back to the mountains as quickly as possible. Do any of you feel otherwise?"

"How close is Leslie?" O'Cahan asked.

The young Traquair spoke up immediately. "I have it on very good authority he is still at Berwick."

"Nevertheless, I think we should make haste in getting the women and children out of here," O'Cahan declared. They all nodded in agreement with the young Irish colonel.

"We will strike toward Silkirk at once," Montrose declared, trying to cover up his mounting apprehension.

The army turned around, and after a fast forced march, the cavalry bedded down at Selkirk and the Irish and their families two miles farther up the Yarrow River at Philliphaugh.

That night, as Robert lay wary and fretful, his thoughts turned to Elizabeth. Just thinking of her began to arouse him. She had all the attributes he had ever hoped for in a woman —fabulous beauty, a witty and intelligent mind, and indomitable spirit and courage. Sexually, she was the most satisfying woman he had ever had, despite her initial reluctance. Once aroused, she became a woman made for loving—a natural outlet for her volatile nature. From their first explosive embrace they had molded together in perfect unison, each instinctively discovering the one natural mate above all others.

He grinned in amusement remembering their last encounter. Lord, what a spirited wench! He looked up at the stars above and his grin changed to longing. "And, Lord, do I miss her!" he murmured yearningly. He continued tossing restlessly for several hours until his eyes finally closed in slumber.

Robert was awakened a short time later by the sound of men and horses moving stealthily about him. Traquair and his cavalrymen were attempting to steal away silently in the night. Montrose also had been awakened and turned to him with a worried frown.

"What do you think it means, Robert?" he whispered. "Do you suspect a betrayal?"

"Definitely! I have never trusted Traquair," Robert said. "I think the wisest thing is for me to ride and inform O'Cahan of this latest development."

"I can send a courier, Robert. It is not necessary you go," Montrose offered.

"I feel restless, Jamie. The ride will do me good."

They were suddenly joined by the crouched form of Nat Gordon.

"I knew we should never have trusted those bastards," he hissed softly. "I wager they have already sent a rider to Leslie to inform him of our position."

"Robert is riding to warn O'Cahan," Montrose whispered.

"I will go with you, Robbie," Nat offered. "It might be wiser."

Montrose nodded his agreement. "Then take care, dear friends," he warned them, as he shook their hands with a warm clasp.

The first light of dawn was just beginning to streak the autumn sky when the two riders reached the Irish camp. Dense mist rising from the Yarrow River blanketed the ground with a damp and chilly veil.

O'Cahan's reaction to the news was identical to theirs. He immediately began to roust his camp to move out, and after a brief conference, Robert and Nat mounted to return to Montrose.

There is an almost eerie silence about the hour just before the sun's rising, as though the whole earth lay in a state of hushed suspension. As the two riders neared the outskirts of the campsite, the silence was shattered by the sound of a musket shot. Robert Kirkland, astride his horse, had been an easy target for the English marksman, whose bullet slammed into his chest, and he toppled to the ground.

At once, complete pandemonium broke loose. The Irish, alerted by the sound of the first shot, grabbed their weapons and attempted to take cover behind the stonewall enclosures. O'Cahan began waging a valiant but hopeless struggle, as he attempted to strategically deploy his meager force, unaware that over six thousand English soldiers completely surrounded the embattled Irish camp.

Nat Gordon successfully returned to O'Cahan's side.

"Let's regroup and try to smash through the line," he shouted. "Perhaps some of us will be able to make it to the mountains."

O'Cahan shook his head to imply the uselessness of that ploy.

"Where would we go, Nat? How far would we get on foot? We have our families with us."

Nat Gordon grabbed the reins of his horse and remounted.

"Then I am going to try to cut a hole in their North flank. Be prepared to try to get your people through it."

"It's useless, Nat. Tell Jamie we will try to hold their attention as long as we can," Magnus declared. "But get him out of here. That is all that matters."

"I'll be back, Magnus. I swear it," Nat declared fervently. Then with a sad smile the cynical and totally irreverent Nat Gordon clasped his comrade's hand. "God be with you, Irish."

The sound of battle carried down the strath to the neighboring camp. Grimly, Montrose mounted his cavalry hoping an advance patrol had simply stumbled on the Irish camp and that the full English force was still to come. They rushed along the river bank at full gallop, then reined up in horror at the sight that greeted them.

The English troops were five and six lines deep. Mounted cavalry was beginning to ride in to squelch the remaining resistance from the beleaguered infantry.

"Oh, dear Lord," Montrose cried in anguish. "They haven't a chance."

There was nothing that could be done for the doomed infantry. Despite this, Montrose was determined to go to their aid. With relief he saw Nat Gordon riding up, then sickened when he realized Robert was not with him.

"Robert?" Montrose asked hopefully, already knowing Nat's answer.

"He fell on the first shot, Jamie."

The abject pain on Montrose's face was more expressive than any words.

"The day cannot be saved, Jamie. You must get out of here," Nat yelled.

"Are you insane, man?" Montrose shouted in disbelief. "I cannot abandon them."

"I just came through those lines. O'Cahan has already lost over half his force. There is no way two hundred cavalrymen can get them out."

"I am still going to try. Those are my men down there. If you got through, why can't we?"

"I made it through by pure chance. Their lines have since closed up. It is solid man and horse now."

The horseman next to Montrose fell to the ground as the small force came under musket fire. Over a thousand cavalry had veered away from the main column and was now charging them. Nat grabbed the reins of Montrose's horse as he shouted to those nearest them.

"Scatter and fire. Every man for himself. Try for the mountains, lads. It is your only hope."

He handed the reins of Montrose's horse to two nearby Graham horsemen. "If you value his life, get him out of here," he shouted. "We will try to delay pursuers."

Nodding their understanding, they galloped away, towing a protesting Montrose, as Nat and a few of the others turned back in an attempt to repel the charging cavalry.

The two soldiers entrusted with Montrose managed to evade their pursuers, but many less fortunate were soon captured—among them Colonel Nathaniel Gordon.

Meanwhile the Irish infantry continued its courageous fight until O'Cahan finally was forced to raise a white flag.

General Leslie and Colonel Middleton, his second in command, both experienced and distinguished soldiers, agreed to spare the survivors, and the Irish came out and laid down their weapons.

As the victorious army moved in, one of the fallen bodies caught the attention of a young officer.

On several past occasions Lieutenant Andrew Scott had glimpsed the famed "Highland Lion," and he realized that before him lay the body of his sister's husband. As Andrew bent over the fallen form, a weak moan escaped Robert Kirkland's lips. Andrew quickly wadded a piece of his brother-in-law's plaid and shoved it between Robert's shirt and the bleeding wound.

No one had observed his actions, as the attention of those closest had been attracted to a heated argument between Leslie and the Council of Ministers, the current governing body of Scotland that was traveling with the army. An ashen Leslie left the group and turned to Middleton.

"I have been overruled by the Ministers. All Scot officers are to be taken for future execution, and there will be no quarter for any others."

Middleton blanched at this announcement. "Does that include the women and children?"

Leslie nodded. "They are to be the first ones put to the sword. Our compassionate ministry wishes the male prisoners to see their families destroyed."

Within minutes the unsuspecting women and children were turned over to their executioners. Andrew watched in horror as helpless women and children were run through with swords or held in the river and drowned. The weaponless male prisoners, crying with rage and grief at the sight of their families being brutally slaughtered, attempted to rush to their aid—but were chopped down or run through.

After a few minutes the scent of blood began to arouse the English soldiers like a frenzied school of sharks, and soon some of the young infants were being picked up, their heads bashed against rocks and trees.

Andrew sank to his knees, sickened by the carnage. He looked across at his brother-in-law, lying wounded and helpless, and knew it would only be a matter of time before Robert Kirkland's body would be discovered, only to meet the same fate. Unobserved, he dragged the unconscious body into some nearby trees, quickly concealing it with brush.

When he returned to camp they were stringing up some of the Irish officers from trees. General Leslie and Colonel Middleton were visibly ill. Andrew saw one of his fellow officers helping a prisoner to escape into the trees.

Magnus O'Cahan, bound and under armed guard, was openly crying as he watched the slaughter of his clansmen. Nat Gordon sat slumped against a tree, deliberately diverting his eyes from the scene.

The Ministers, seemingly the only ones unaffected by the brutality, calmly walked among the soldiers, piously declaring, "Jesus, and no quarter."

When at last the final act of bestiality was performed, Leslie ordered the troop to assemble and move on.

Lieutenant Andrew Scott approached his colonel, whose eyes remained downcast.

"Sir, may I assume the victory is ours?" Andrew asked contemptuously.

Middleton raised his tortured eyes to him.

"The battle has ended, Lieutenant."

"Then I wish to inform you I am resigning my commission immediately and returning to my home. I care not for the dishonor to my uniform, but I cannot dishonor my father's name by continuing to be a member of an army that would sanction this carnage."

The English officer's face conveyed his anguish.

"War is an antithetical mistress, Lieutenant," Middleton said sadly. "It can elevate a man to noblest heights, or lower him to base depravity. I accept your resignation and relieve you of your command. You are free to leave. Would that I, too, were as fortunate!"

With a slight salutary nod of his head he turned away.

The two bound prisoners, Nat Gordon and Magnus O'Cahan, were preparing to move out when Walter Campbell approached. At the sight of the Ulster plaid of O'Cahan's he turned to one of the guards.

"Why wasn't this man executed with the others?"

Nat Gordon immediately protested angrily. "This is an officer of the King. As such he is entitled to a military trial."

Campbell smiled his contempt. "An officer of the King! We do not look on these Irish invaders as anything other than what they are —felon rabble."

He turned to O'Cahan, his zealot's face sliced with an evil sneer.

"Can't you plead for your own self, Irishman?"

There was an incredible dignity and resignation to O'Cahan's bearing as he raised his head and looked at his tormentor.

Magnus's scorn for this fanatic was not reflected by a defiant or vindictive glare, but rather in the serenity and composure of his expression when he looked at the man. Then with a soft tone that was so germane to the gentleness of his nature, he replied, "Long live the King and Jamie Graham!"

In fury Walter Campbell turned to the guards that flanked the tall Irishman.

"Hang him!" he rasped with a malevolent snarl.

XXVI

Andrew Scott watched the last soldier disappear over the hilltop, then rushed to the concealed body in the brush. He struggled with Robert Kirkland's large frame and succeeded in pulling it out of the thick growth of the protection of a nearby tree. He placed his ear against the chest of the unconscious form and in relief heard the weakened heartbeat.

The wound was still bleeding lightly, and he knew he must somehow check the seepage before Robert bled to death. Covering the Highlander with his plaid, he made his way down to the river for water.

The young man glanced around him with revulsion, trying to force back his nausea. Wherever he looked lay evidence of the carnage. An infant, no more than three or four months, lay battered on nearby rocks. A few feet away were the bodies of several women lying on the riverbank, their heads still submerged in the swirling water.

Bodies were strewn everywhere. The air he breathed was permeated with the stench of blood. Flies glutted on the gore and swarmed over the bodies.

Stumbling to the riverbank, Andrew threw himself down and lay retching into the flowing waters.

Robert's eyes fluttered feebly as he slowly returned to consciousness. He fought through the mist that veiled his vision, aware of a burning pain in his right shoulder. Repeatedly he forced his eyelids open, only to have them immediately flicker closed. Struggling, he focused his eyes on a huge sack swaying gently back and forth from a nearby limb; his groggy mind was seeking an explanation why anyone would hang such a large bundle in a tree.

The pain in his shoulder was like an astringent acid that began to eat at the tissue of his stupor, and hazily Robert was able to distinguish what appeared to be a pair of legs. It slowly dawned on him that this was a body, and his eyes groggily traversed the length of the form until they reached the top. In appalling horror he recognized the dark head, the face already blackened and distorted.

"Oh, God, no," he pleaded in anguish. "Cut him down! In the name of God—somebody—cut him down!"

On trembling legs Robert rose to his feet. He drew his dirk from its sheath and, halfstumbling, staggered over to O'Cahan's lifeless form. He tugged at the body to lower the limb of the tree until he was able to reach up and saw off the rope with his dirk, then fell to the ground under the weight of the still form.

Robert's strength was waning rapidly, the blood now flowing profusely from his wound, his mind befuddled by pain. He rose on his knees and in a stupor, began scraping and digging at the dirt with his hands in an effort to bury his comrade. Weakened, he toppled over to sink into the merciful blackness of oblivion.

When Andrew returned from the river, a single glance told him the full story, and he broke into a chain of curses. What had once been a difficult task had quickly developed into an almost impossible one.

Robert Kirkland was still breathing, but now weakened to the point of not being able to mount a horse—let alone ride one! The additional loss of blood created another serious problem. How was he to get an unconscious man out of here! The hills abounded with English and Campbells—and only one horse! His one advantage was his English uniform. It might ward off some suspicion. He grinned wryly to himself. At least it was good for something!

Andrew set about tending to Robert. He stripped the shirt from him, the right side of it already soaked with blood, and tore it into strips. Andrew cleansed the wound as best he could and applied a compress to it. There was no way he could do anything more without Robert being conscious to aid him.

Slumping down, he leaned back against a tree. The all-night march and the events of the day overtook the young man, and within minutes his head nodded in slumber.

* * *

Andrew woke to rumbling sound in the distance that sounded like cannon fire. Bright flashes in the night sky revealed an approaching storm rather than a major battle. Brilliant jagged bolts of silver streaked the sky, accompanied by low rumbling crashes of thunder that reverberated across the valley.

He leaned over to check Robert's condition and was relieved to see that his chest was still rising and falling with shallow breaths. At least he was alive!

The whinny of a horse jolted his attention toward the road. Peering through the faint light offered by the moon, he was able to distinguish a small cart, being driven by what appeared to be an old man. His spirit soared at this stroke of good fortune. With sword in hand, he stepped out onto the road and grabbed the harness runner of the nag's head.

The already frightened driver pulled up, terrified. Word of the battle had spread to the neighboring farms, and the old crofter, in hopes of some favorable loot, had decided to risk the ghostly terrors of the night.

"Saints preserve us!" he cried, as an apparition suddenly appeared on the road before him and, unthinkingly, reverted back to his old religion and made the sign of the cross to ward off the evil.

"It would not be wise to go any farther, old man. There has been a massacre and it is not a pleasant sight to see," Andrew warned.

The old man sighed with relief and tried to control his trembling body.

"Aye, m'lord, I'll nae tarry."

"I need your cart, old man. I have a wounded comrade who cannot ride."

"Och, lad, be ye daft! I hae need o' me cart."

"I will pay you well for it," Andrew cried desperately. He pulled a pouch from his saddlebag and handed the man a 5 pound gold piece.

The old crofter's eyes gleamed greedily, for it was more money than he would see in a year. He could buy many wagons with such wealth. Andrew believed the man's hesitation was doubt as to the worth of the transaction.

"My horse, old man. It is a fine steed. I will give you my horse also."

At this announcement the old farmer's eyes fairly bulged in disbelief. His glance compared the proud head and sleek lines of the magnificent chestnut stallion with his sway-backed, worn-out dappled mare. Truly the lad must have been wounded in the head! For sure, there would be no convincing his wife of the night's trade!

" 'Tis a bargain met," he announced, stepping down from the cart as quickly as his aged legs allowed.

"I will need your help in getting my friend onto the cart," Andrew declared.

"The' let's be on wi' it. For I hae a long way home," the old man grumbled, anxious to be on his way before the muddled lad had a change of mind.

With much heaving and struggling, the two men succeeded in getting Robert's heavy frame on the tiny cart. Andrew turned him on his side, nestled in a bed of straw. He covered Robert with his own blanket and was folding the plaid—that blazing evidence of Robert's true identity—into his saddlebag, when he heard thundering hooves, as the old man galloped away into the darkness.

The chilling downpour reached them during the night and he was forced to pull into a copse of trees for protection and to rest the tired horse. After several hours it became apparent that the deluge was not going to slacken, and he had no alternative but to continue.

By midday the road had become a quagmire and progress was slower than ever. Andrew huddled on the small cart, now completely drenched. He had been forced to forsake caution and stretch Robert's plaid across the top of the wagon in the hope of keeping the unconscious body as dry as possible.

Finally at sunset he pulled off the road into the trees and unhitched the poor overburdened animal.

"You get us to Ballantine, old nag, and you will never have to do another day's work," he promised, with an affectionate pat on the tired flank.

Andrew knew that no Highlander ever traveled without oats for sustenance. A hurried search of Robert's body produced a small pouch, and combining the oats with some of the soaked straw from the cart, he was able to form a mulch for the poor nag to eat.

Andrew next turned his attention to his patient. He quickly started a fire in an effort to dry out the blanket and plaid.

Robert was tossing feverishly, and as Andrew leaned over to check the wound, Robert opened his eyes. The only thing Robert Kirkland was aware of in his dazed state was a pair of compassionate brown eyes staring down at him, those same velvet brown orbs that had haunted his dreams and fantasies.

"Beth, love, sweet, sweet Beth. Is it really you?" he mumbled hoarsely.

Andrew reached out a hand and placed it on Robert's heated brow.

"I am Andrew Scott, Lord Kirkland. Elizabeth's brother."

Robert fought to clear his muddled mind as he tried to focus on the male counterpart of his beloved Beth. The resemblance was uncanny —the incredible brown eyes and long thick lashes! However, a moustache above the generous mouth transformed the face into one of profound masculinity.

"You are Beth's twin?"

Andrew grinned, and Robert gasped at the startling similarity of their smiles.

"Then obviously, I am your prisoner, Sir Andrew."

"I resigned my commission," Andrew assured him. "You were badly wounded and I found you. I am attempting to get you to Ballantine."

"I cannot remember what occurred," Robert said in confusion.

"General Montrose was defeated at Philliphaugh," Andrew declared.

Afraid of the answer, Robert asked fretfully, "And what became of him?"

"To my knowledge he succeeded in avoiding capture."

At Robert's evident relief, Andrew added sadly, "However, the Irish army was entirely destroyed."

"To a man?" Robert asked in disbelief.

Andrew Scott could only nod mutely.

With mounting apprehension, the memory of what Robert had believed to be a tortured nightmare began a painful return to his already afflicted consciousness.

"Colonel O'Cahan? What became of Colonel O'Cahan?" he rasped desperately.

Andrew needed only to look at Robert's tortured eyes to recognize the depth of his torment.

"I am sorry, Robert. I think you already know the answer."

Robert's eyes closed in anguish. "And Colonel Gordon? Do you know what became of Colonel Gordon?"

"Captured," was Andrew's painful and reticent reply.

In the wrenching ache of intense emotional despair, Robert sank into unconsciousness, and within the hour his mind was racing with feverish incoherent mutterings, often crying out for Beth in pitiful, ragged pleas for help.

Later that evening, hungry and cold,

Andrew Scott huddled beneath the cart seeking protection from the downpour. His thoughts swirled with as many conflicts as the night around him.

So Robert Kirkland loved Beth, Andrew thought, as his mind reeled in confusion. The Highlander's feverish mutterings were repeatedly full of expressions of love for her. What fools the two of them! How much happiness had they denied themselves? Now if he dies, what is gained? Had Beth sacrificed what final moments they may have shared together for the sake of her pride?

Now, more than ever, Andrew was determined to get Robert Kirkland home to Ballantine.

XXVII

It was five days after the infamous battle at Philliphaugh when, with the candles glowing warmly in the comfortable dining hall at Ballantine Castle, Alexander Scott and his daughter sat down to their evening meal, unaware of the tiny cart that was creaking through the postern gate at that very moment.

Astonishment was evident on both their faces at the sight of the weary figure who entered the hall.

"Andrew," Lord Scott exclaimed pleasantly, rising to embrace his son. For a few brief seconds Andrew Scott lingered in the comfort of his father's arms, before raising anxious eyes.

"Father, I have brought Robert Kirkland with me."

"Robert! Here?" Elizabeth cried, jumping to her feet. Her pulse began racing in breathless anticipation. "Where is he?"

Andrew frowned gravely, and Elizabeth's eagerness immediately dissipated at the sight of the distress on her brother's face.

"Beth, he is badly wounded. In fact, his condition is very critical."

With a stricken cry Elizabeth rushed to the door. The two men exchanged portentous glances, then quickly followed.

A gasping sob escaped when Elizabeth saw Robert's condition. "Take him to my chamber," she ordered and sped up the stairway ahead of the two servants who were carrying him.

Elizabeth hurriedly pulled aside the yellow coverlet, and the men laid Robert's long frame on the bed.

"Summon Artle at once," she cried, as her hand pushed back the tousled hair from the fevered brow. The usually bronze face was now ashen and gaunt, shadowed by unshaven growth.

The words were no sooner uttered, then Artle shuffled through the door with her tray of herbs, having already been summoned upon Andrew's arrival.

" 'Twoud be wiser if ye all gi' ou' of here while I tend to the lad," she announced firmly.

"I am remaining. I can be of service," Elizabeth declared.

The old hag studied the determined tilt of the young girl's chin. She was well-acquainted with that look and knew the issue was already a closed one.

"Very well," she conceded, "bu' the res' of ye be off."

Reluctantly Andrew and Alexander Scott left the room, the two servants following.

"Now we mus' gie off the lad's clothin'."

With a nod of understanding Elizabeth

drew the tiny jeweled dirk from the sheath of her waist. Strangely enough, the knife had been a gift from Robert Kirkland while they were betrothed. She quickly slit the seams of Robert's breeks while Artle tugged at his boots in an effort to remove them. Elizabeth aided her in pulling them off, before sliding down the pants.

When all his clothing had been removed, they covered his nudity, and Artle began to cautiously peel away the bulging compress on his shoulder.

Elizabeth brought her hand to her mouth to prevent gagging. The stench from the festering wound was nauseating. The flesh, mottled with blood and yellowish-white pus, was swollen and inflamed. Moribund tissue lay whitened and ragged around the mouth of the injury. One did not have to touch the throbbing wound to feel the heat it generated, and vivid red lines streaked from its nucleus, carrying poisonous toxins towards the heart.

The old hag clucked grimly. "We hae our work cu' ou' for us. We wil' soon need water."

Within moments, two of the servants appeared carrying a large vat of hot water. They set about building a fire, before departing with a woeful look toward the direction of the bed.

Artle soaked several of the linen towels in the water, then gingerly lifted them out with the point of Elizabeth's dirk. Fascinated, Elizabeth watched her wring the dripping cloths with her withered hands, impervious to the scalding moisture. Soon Elizabeth was doing the same thing—over and over. The two women labored over the prone body, changing the hot compresses as quickly as they cooled. Elizabeth's hands became red and swollen from the scalding cloths, but she paid them no heed in her anxiety over Robert's needs.

Robert groaned and thrashed about—whether in protest to the latest assault, or simply in delirium, neither woman knew. The additional discomfort to an already tortured body was unavoidable at this time.

After several hours of constant soakings, much of the putrid pus had been drawn from the wound. Artle took a bodkin sterilized in the boiling water and began to dig several tiny white scraps from the wound.

"What are they?" Elizabeth asked her worriedly.

"The' be piece of his shir', lass," Artle said softly. "The bullet wen' through him, bu' it tore his shirt. We mus' gie them all ou' or the wound wil' keep festerin'. Here, lass," Artle declared handing Elizabeth the bodkin, "yer young eyes are more apt than mine."

Forcing back her revulsion, Elizabeth cautiously probed the inflamed flesh and was able to extract another tiny white scrap.

"I think that is all of them," she stammered as she stepped away.

Artle leaned over to give a final inspection to Elizabeth's ministerings, then with a nod of approval she placed a poultice of mold and herbs over the wound. Finally straightening up her frail old back, she looked at Elizabeth.

"We hae done all we ca' for the young laird. 'Tis up to his own body now. I mus' be off for I hae a birthin' o' a bairn this morn."

In astonishment Elizabeth saw that the morning light had begun to filter through the narrow slots of the dormer window.

"Whene're ye ca', gie him some water and keep him warm." Artle picked up a tiny vial from her tray. " 'Tis a potion for the fever. A cool cloth on his brow wi' also ease the discomfor'. Wud be wise to gie him a bath."

Her face contorted with a toothless leer. "He's a braw lad—'twill nae be an unpleasan' task for a young lass."

Elizabeth felt the hot flush that crept to the roots of her hairline.

"You're a dirty-minded old woman," she answered, defensively. "I was wed to him, you know."

"Then more's the pleasure." Artle grinned and, gathering up her tray, shuffled from the room.

Elizabeth returned to the bedside and for the first time since his arrival was able to spend a few moments alone with him. Her heart leapt at the sight of the beloved face now ashen and wan. Deep in the world of delirium he was mumbling wild, incoherent mutterings, many in Gaelic.

Her hand reached out to gently caress his

brow, and as though he knew her touch, his eyes flew open. Completely glazed with fever, he sat up grasping her shoulders in a savage grip.

"Cut him down, Beth," he cried out hoarsely, before releasing her and limply falling back on the bed to return to his muddled ravings.

She lovingly bathed his long frame. The lithe, muscular body, that had always been aroused by a simple touch or tender stroke from her, now lay impassive and unresponding to the fingers and hands that freely roamed across its most intimate areas as she cleansed them. Before covering him, with a gesture born of love rather than passion, Elizabeth ran a hand caressingly down the length of him, as though the feel of his throbbing warmth at her fingertips could give her the assurance of a pulsating life within.

She moistened his fever-cracked lips with a cloth and attempted to trickle a few drops of water down his parched throat. A light rap at the door announced the arrival of her father, who tiptoed to the bedside.

The twisting, thrashing form gave him the answer he sought. Robert's head rolled from side to side as he fought the violent fever raging within. There seemed nothing further to do to aid him in that tormented conflict.

Alexander Scott's eyes rested on the haggard face of his daughter and he pulled her into his arms. Elizabeth's head slumped against his shoulder and at the feel of his loving arms embracing her, her pent-up emotions erupted as she released her tears. He held her tightly, letting her exhaust her grief.

"He must live, Father. He must!"

"It is in God's hands now, Elizabeth," he soothed, running a hand over the dark head that rested on his shoulder. "You must rest now, my dearest. There is nothing more to be done for him now."

"I could never sleep. I am fine, Father."

"Artle said it may take days before we will know anything. You cannot do him any good if you become stricken yourself. I will sit by his bed and you can leave the chamber door open. I will call you, Elizabeth, at the slightest change in Robert's condition."

The auburn head immediately shook in protest. "Perhaps later, Father. I know I could not rest now."

Lord Scott frowned in annoyance at his daughter's stubbornness. "Very well, Elizabeth, but I will insist you rest later. I will not see *your* health ruined."

The days passed slowly for the household. Around the clock Elizabeth sat at the bedside, leaving it only for small naps. She agonized listening to the rantings of the poor tortured soul in the bed. Her eyes would brim when Robert called out her name in ragged sobs from the depth of his throat. She recognized his torment as he relived again and again the agonizing events of that long ago battle at Aberdeen. But through it all came the same repeated, racked plea—"Cut him down! For God's sake, somebody cut him down!"

Artle came often and they changed the poultice and dressing. The wound appeared to be improving, and, after the first week, Robert would have moments of consciousness when they were able to force Artle's potion down his throat.

By the end of the second week the fever broke, and Robert lapsed into a relatively untormented slumber. Elizabeth hugged Artle and kissed the withered cheek.

"Oh, thank you, you old witch," she cried out fondly. "I knew you could do it! God bless you, Artle."

The old crone beamed a toothless smile at this glowing beauty she had watched grow to womanhood, often having nursed her through the many illnesses that strike children. She had never seen the young mistress more radiant than she appeared at the moment.

"God blessed me whe' he brough' me to the house of Scott," she declared shyly.

"How can I ever reward you? Name it, Artle—anything you want is yours."

The old woman threw a sly look at Robert's sleeping form.

"Then I claim the privilege of birthin' the first bairn of ye an' the braw lad." She winked and, with her usual cackling laughter, departed the room.

The smile remained on Elizabeth's face as she set another log on the fire. For the first time in two weeks her shoulders were not slumped nor her eyes veiled with despair. She gave Robert a final inspection to assure herself he was resting comfortably, and then, leaving the door ajar, entered the adjoining room to quickly shed her clothing and climb into bed for a short nap.

Whatever her good intentions, the minute her head rested on the downy pillow, her eyes closed and she sank into an exhausted slumber.

Robert Kirkland slowly opened his eyes. He gazed about him in confusion. The dimly lit room was comfortable and clean, as was the canopy bed he lay in. The sound of the log crackling in the fireplace was a welcome sound and he enjoyed a feeling of warmth and security.

Robert had no idea where he was, or how he had come to be there. He only knew he felt an overpowering serenity. What was there about this room that emanated such an aura? Why should he waken in a strange bed and not know wariness? He struggled trying to determine his whereabouts. Then slowly his mind began to grasp that which his senses already knew—the faint, delicate aroma of lavender that hung lightly in the air. *Beth!*

Weakly he rose to his feet and on trembling legs staggered to the open door. He gasped at the sight of the lovely vision in the bed, convinced he was in the throes of a dream.

Elizabeth lay deep in sleep, her auburn hair fanned out on the pillow. The lovely face was serene in the depth of slumber. The cover on the bed had fallen aside, exposing the smooth satin of her shoulders. His eyes strayed to the even, rhythmic rise and fall of her breasts, covered only by a thin silken gown that clung to the rounded mounds. Unhesitantly, he climbed into the bed and drew her to his side, before slipping back into contented sleep. Unaware, Elizabeth slept on, snuggling against the familiar welcomed warmth.

Elizabeth felt the warmth beside her at about the same time Robert Kirkland became aware of the ache in his shoulder. Slowly they both opened their eyes, blinking against the morning's rays that had crept into the room.

"Robert, what are you doing here?" she exclaimed in astonishment.

"My very question!" He grinned weakly. "What am I doing here, and where am I? Though I am not complaining," he.added as an afterthought.

"Oh, Robert, what have you done?" she moaned. "We must get you back to bed before anyone sees you."

Elizabeth started to rise and Robert pulled her down to him.

"Not yet, Beth. Just lie here and let me hold you."

"Robert, you do not realize how grave your condition has been. You have been in a fever for weeks."

"Where am I? How did I get here?"

"You are at Ballantine. My brother Andrew brought you here. You were wounded at Philliphaugh."

"Oh, yes . . . I remember," Robert said slowly, as the grisly events began to return to him. "I remember your brother . . . and rain . . . and his telling me about the battle, the loss of my friends . . ."

His voice fell away as more and more of the painful memories began to grip him.

Elizabeth knew he was lost in grief and she rose from the bed. "Come, Robert, I will help you to your bed."

Unresisting, he let her put his arm around her shoulders as she propped his weight against herself. They soon had him back in his bed, and Elizabeth left him to dress herself.

By the time Artle arrived, Elizabeth was spooning broth into Robert's mouth. Robert lay patiently while Artle changed the dressing on his wound. The old woman was strangely silent, sensing the young man's grief. She quickly gathered up her tray and prepared to depart when Robert remembered his manners.

"I heard of my condition and what you have done for me. There is much I owe you, old woman. You are a remarkable and skilled healer."

The aged woman turned back to him, finding herself embarrassed by his thanks.

"*Chan eil euslainte gun ioc-shlainte,*" she said softly.

Robert looked up in wonderment, but the woman had already disappeared.

"I did not realize that anyone from this region could speak Gaelic," he said amazed.

"Artle is from everywhere," Elizabeth

declared. "I do not think there is anything she cannot do. What did she say to you?"

"She said, 'There is no disease without a remedy,' " he replied, still awed by the old woman.

Her tongue caught between the pearly tips of her teeth, Elizabeth carefully drew the sharpened edge of the razor across Robert's cheek. She felt his steady gaze on her, but she hesitated to meet his eyes, concentrating on the task of shaving him. Finally, after repeated strokes, the unnerving chore was completed, and with a sigh of relief she set aside the razor and basin of water.

"I must admit I am getting quite adept at shaving you," she boasted proudly, while Robert ran an examining hand across his face. "Now 'tis time to trim your moustache and hair."

"Perhaps it would ease your burden if I have you shave off the moustache," he offered.

"Oh nae, my lord, do not shave it off. You look so handsome in it," she quickly protested. Then, embarrassed by the revelation of her hasty outburst, she shifted her eyes downward and picked up the scissors and comb.

"Do you tire of nursing me, Elizabeth?" he asked guiltily.

"Of course not, Robert. I enjoy it," she assured him. How could she tell him of her delight at having him near, being able to do things for him?

Her fingers fondled the thick dark hair as

she clipped its strands. It fell easily into curls as the scissors and comb slipped through it. Her hand lingered at the nape of his neck as she brushed aside the loose hairs that clung to him. A nerve twitched nervously in his cheek, and fearing she had displeased him, Elizabeth hastily withdrew her hand.

It had been over a week since he had regained consciousness, and in that time a strange silence had sprung up between them. Robert seemed withdrawn and aloof, almost guilty for the trouble he was causing.

Even though he was on the road to recuperation, no effort had been made to move him and they still shared adjoining rooms. Despite this, Robert had never again entered her chamber but seemed content to remain where he was.

Elizabeth was aware of his eyes on her constantly. She knew they followed her every moment. So often she wanted to bend down and place a kiss on those tempting lips, but a sudden shyness and self-consciousness prevented her from doing so. She was entirely perplexed by this withdrawn and aloof man.

The day dawned when Robert felt strong enough to attempt the stairs to join the family for dinner. His boots had been cleaned, his breeks mended and laundered, and a shirt had been found to fit round his broad shoulders. Thankfully, some of the pallor had disappeared, but the face still lacked its customary bronzed ruggedness.

Shrugging aside any offer of help, with slow deliberation he descended the stairway. Elizabeth waited breathlessly, watching his cautious descent. There was no doubt he found the effort taxing, but clearly he was on the road to recovery.

The conversation between Robert and her father and brother was stilted in the beginning, but by the time the savory mutton was served, all of them seemed to relax, talk flowing freely.

"Has there been any word of Montrose or his whereabouts?" Robert asked.

"Rumor has it he is in the West. It is said he and Willie Douglas have gone to see Huntly,' Alexander Scott declared.

"Argyll and his Campbells are combing the countryside looking for him or any of his men. They are hanging them as quickly as they find them. The people are beginning to call the gallows 'Argyll's Altar.' It's said the same fate awaits anyone who tries to aid any of them," Andrew blurted out tactlessly.

Lord Scott cast a disapproving eye at his son and Elizabeth could only glare angrily. Robert Kirkland's eyes clouded with guilt.

"Then my being here is endangering this household," he said contritely.

"Have no fear, Robert. Argyll is afraid to anger any of the large clans. He only ruffles the feathers of the smaller birds. He is not about to risk angering any Lowland laird."

"Still, my lord, I have overly abused your hospitality."

"Say no more, Lord Kirkland. Need I remind you your father was my dearest friend. I would nae turn his son out to be left to the mercy of Archibald Campbell! My son's tongue has a tendency to flow as freely as the wine he is consuming."

Andrew lowered the flagon he was about to drink and cast sheepish eyes in Robert's direction. He had realized his tactlessness as soon as he had spoken.

"I owe much to Andrew, Lord Scott. He saved my life."

" 'Tis true," Scott relented, with a proud glance at his son. "He is still but a lad, and I fear I am too hard on him."

"Your son is a man, Lord Scott, and has proven himself to be so. I doubt many could have done what he did."

Andrew looked gratefully at Robert Kirkland, and the two men exchanged respectful glances. Elizabeth smiled lovingly at Robert for the gracious way he had eased her beloved brother's predicament.

"I leave you gentlemen to your brandies," she said, and the men rose to their feet as she departed. Robert's eyes hungrily lingered on her departing figure as she left the room.

Elizabeth climbed to the battlements and gazed up at the starry sky. The threat of snow hung in the air and she welcomed the invigoration of the cold night air. She sensed Robert's unrest and knew he soon would insist on leaving Ballantine. How sweet it was to waken each day with the knowledge that she would see him. She did not understand his aloofness. Whatever was bothering him would have to be aired. She would not let it fester any longer within him.

They were no longer man and wife. Their year of handfest had passed the previous week and the marriage had never been sanctified. Strangely, neither had mentioned this fact to the other. Though why they would, she did not know—for nothing on a personal level was ever discussed between them. Elizabeth could not believe Robert was unaware of their status. Apparently, it did not disturb him.

She studied the wedding band he had forced on her finger. Should she remove it? Should she offer it back to him? Her eyes shifted heavenward seeking an answer.

"Oh, Lord, what shall I do?" she prayed softly.

Robert lay in bed staring at the closed chamber door. He knew Elizabeth was behind it, lying in the next room. His hands broke into a cold sweat just thinking of her; he wanted her so badly.

How sweet it would be to hold her in his arms, to feel that softness, the sweet scent of her. He had made up his mind this was not to be.

Elizabeth had been right about his wanting the best of two worlds. He might have died and left her carrying his child—only to have it raised fatherless. Who knew what the next battle might bring? He must get away from her as quickly as possible. In a few days he would be well enough to travel. He resolved he would not render her any more harm. Up to now he had foolishly believed he was invulnerable—that James Graham was invincible. Philliphaugh had proven the fallacy of such beliefs. If he perished in this war, he was determined not to make Elizabeth, and possibly their child, unwilling victims also. He would give her up before he would heap anymore grief upon her.

Lost in his thoughts, he was unaware when the door opened and she stepped into the room. Suddenly she was there before him, her long hair flowing freely down her back and lying across her shoulders. A white flowing robe covered her slim form. She stood silently and their eyes met in dim light. Elizabeth could read the confusion and hurt in his dark eyes, and she was woman enough to recognize the raw hunger that also lurked there.

Mesmerized, Robert watched her hand slide to the tie of her gown and release it. Almost motionlessly she shrugged off the gown, allowing it to drop in a heap at her feet.

Robert grasped the covers, fighting for control. Before him stood the Goddess Aphrodite personified. He could not force his eyes away from the milky nakedness of her round curves and shadowed hollows. Hungrily his eyes traveled the slim column of her neck down to the full rounded breasts, whose ripened peaks were hardened with passion. The milkiness tapered to a narrow waist, before curving into the slim curve of her hips. His body trembled with desire as his gaze lingered on the darkened mound at the junction of her long, slim legs, and his tongue unconsciously snaked out to moisten his dry lips.

With a lithe, graceful movement, Elizabeth was on the bed, and with a stifled groan, Robert pulled her to him. His mouth devoured her as his hands ravished her body. His lips covered her eyes, her face, her neck. No curve, no hollow remained unexplored by his lips and hands. Elizabeth writhed under the assault of his lips on her breasts and her stomach. When his tongue began to probe the vulnerability at the junction of her legs, she could only cry out in agonized rapture.

Their love-making had never been so intense—tenderness would come at a later time. Now there was only passion—hungry, raw, searing passion! There was nothing they denied one another. When his tongue found her mouth with fiery probes, hers responded as boldly. If his mouth suckled the thrusting nipples of her breasts, her mouth teased and nibbled at his. With every hollow, intimate area his hand sought, her searching hands found a like one on him.

The two lovers lifted themselves higher and higher to a soaring peak, until he thrust into her, and, entwined, they plummeted over the brink.

They both lay gasping, their chests heaving in their need to breathe. Still he would not relinquish his hold on her. When their breathing had slowed, they then were able to whisper terms of endearment to one another. His hand tenderly cupped her cheek as he pressed light kisses on her mouth and eyes.

"Oh Lord, Beth, how I love you."

Robert fell back, his strength debilitated by the intense love-making. While Elizabeth leaned across him and returned his kisses.

"I love you, Robert. I love you so much I have become your whore. We are no longer man and wife and still I come to your bed."

"You are my wife, love. You will always be my wife." He sighed, and, his strength exhausted, dropped into peaceful slumber.

For a few minutes Elizabeth gazed tenderly at the sleeping face. Her hand caressed the cheek and she brushed back the tousled hair from his forehead. Then, rising from the bed, she covered him carefully and slipped on her robe.

Elizabeth paused again at his bedside and leaned down to press a final kiss on his lips.

"Nae, love. I fear I have become nothing but your whore. But I love you, Robert Kirkland, and I will be content to play that role if I must."

XXVIII

"Elizabeth, my pillow feels lumpy," Robert Kirkland complained.

For the fifth time that morning Elizabeth walked over and leaned across him to fluff up its feathers. In so doing her full breasts pressed against his bare chest and she felt his warm breath against her neck.

"There, my lord, are you comfortable now?" she asked him through gritted teeth.

Robert leaned back, a secret smile tugging at the corners of his mouth. "For the time being," he conceded.

"Do you think it wise to attempt a ride today?" Elizabeth asked, as she sat back down on the chair at his bedside, picking up her needlepoint.

"I will have to—if you cannot control yourself," he replied, his voice laden with self-sacrifice.

Elizabeth looked up in exasperation. "Robert, you know I was speaking of horses," she scolded.

"My apologies, my lady," he intoned with a licentious smirk.

Elizabeth returned to her tapesty, and Robert lay studying her. How beautiful she was! How quickly his noble intentions not to touch her had been consumed in the heat of their passion. How was he to resist her? Robert knew there was no way he ever could. Elizabeth was so entwined around his heart and thoughts that all other needs were forgotten.

She felt his gaze upon her, raised her eyes above her needlepoint, and recognized the naked vulnerability in his look. Her exasperation left her and a warm, tender smile crossed her face, before she dropped her gaze back to her sewing.

Daily she could see an improvement in his condition, as his strength gradually returned. Her only concern was that his recuperation would mean his departure again. Could she bear to see him go?

"I feel quite sore. A rubdown would ease my comfort," he announced, breaking into her reverie. Elizabeth put down her sewing and studied him reflectively. Lately he had been making useless demands on her that simply succeeded in winning her attention. It was not that she did not enjoy being able to tend to his needs. It simply annoyed her that he believed she did not see through the obvious ploy.

Robert had already rolled over in anticipation, and Elizabeth's long fingers, curling around the strong muscles of his shoulders, kneaded them firmly. Her hands crept up the cords of his neck and gently rubbed them in smooth, even strokes. Robert's eyes closed in languor when her hands returned to his shoulders and massaged the thick tendons. Each touch revitalized and stimulated, as tiny needles of exquisite rapture darted through his body.

"Roll over," she ordered.

Robert obeyed her command and her hands curled around the muscular biceps of his thigh and slowly worked down the long symmetrical limb to the calf and ankle, bestowing the same treatment to the other leg. Diligently she offered the same care to each of his arms. When her hands finally found the muscular brawn of his chest, he could not conceal a gasp, as her fingers toyed and stroked among the matted hair on his chest.

Elizabeth was not entirely unaffected by the feel of that latent strength at her fingertips.

With a throaty whisper, she asked, "Are you more comfortable now, my lord?"

"What do you think?" he groaned, his eyes clenched shut to conceal his mounting ache.

With an amused smile, she returned to her chair and resumed her needlepoint, satisfied he deserved exactly what he was suffering. Occasionally she raised her eyes to find him studying her, his arms crossed his chest as he sat propped against the pillow. Clearly he was agitated, and Elizabeth wondered what devious scheme was racing through his mind.

It was just a short matter of time before her premonition materialized.

"I need a bath," he declared.

"I just bathed you last night, Robert."

"That was last night," he countered. "I had

a very restless night."

"Very well, my lord. Would you prefer the tub?"

"No, my lady. I will be quite satisfied if you just sponge me."

"As you wish," she replied with a sigh of resignation, then rose from the chair. Crossing to the fireplace Elizabeth ladled some hot water from a pot simmering on the fireplace and returned to his bedside.

She quickly soaped and rinsed each of his arms, before applying the sponge to his chest and neck. The broad shoulders and back next received her attention, before each of the long legs.

Her face was impassive, as she wordlessly applied herself to the task, taking time to thoroughly wipe dry each area.

Robert's eyes never left her face, his expression never altering, as he waited for her to reach the intimate areas of his body.

Elizabeth had already guessed his intent, and rising to her feet, she stood above him. With a sardonic smirk she dropped the sponge between his legs.

"I think you can do the rest."

She had no more than turned away before he grasped her arm and pulled her down, her shoulders flattened against the bed. Robert leaned across her, his eyes glowing devilishly.

"You beautiful bitch," he groaned, before his lips closed over hers.

Elizabeth's arms slipped lovingly around his neck when his lips released hers.

"You are a horny bastard, Robert Kirkland," she sighed breathlessly.

"Aye, love, and you are such an insatiable wench," he murmured, before his lips again lowered to hers.

"I canna believe ye're a' it again!" Artle's shrill voice scolded.

Embarrassed, Elizabeth jumped to her feet and began to nervously adjust her dress.

"I wish you would knock," she stammered.

Robert fell back in frustration. "I swear, old woman, you are devious and scheming."

"An' I swear, m'lord, ye cud be healed a good time sooner if ye wud save yer strengt' and nae drain it awa' by skewerin' the lass."

"Really, Artle, I must insist you cease this talk immediately," Elizabeth ordered. "What we do is our own business."

"No' when I am tryin' to heal him," the old woman declared. "I think 'twoud be wiser to move him to a far room."

"Don't you dare, you old witch, or I personally will cut out your black heart," Robert teased with a wink.

The old crone laughed loudly and bent down to examine his scar.

"Ye' ar' all mended m'lord, an' I rid meself of yer care. I hae much more importan' things to do than care for a lazy Hielander."

Robert grasped the old hag and placed a kiss on the aged cheek.

"I shall always be grateful to you, Artle."

The old woman tried to conceal her pleasure, as she brushed his hands away.

"Och, be off wi' ye. Nex' ye'll hae me in bed and be tryin' to ram me too," she admonished, as she scurried off.

Robert had never felt as alive in the last few months as he did at this moment. The cold air was intoxicating to a man who had been bedridden for so long.

The steed beneath him was a strong one and Robert reveled in the strength he felt, as his legs rested against its girth.

Elizabeth rode beside him, her eyes sparkling and cheeks glowing. She seemed a natural part of the elements, impervious to the wintry blasts. Her laughter tinkled on the frigid air as they prodded their mounts to a canter.

Astride his stallion, Robert now knew he had regained his full strength. His hand felt steady as it gripped the rein, his legs strong. Time had healed his wound and now time was becoming his enemy—for he knew he could not dally much longer at Ballantine.

A rider had been sent to Ashkirk to assure David of his health, and another farther in an attempt to find Montrose, who undoubtedly believed him dead. Daily he expected the return of the courier.

When Elizabeth pulled away from the road, Robert followed her. The ground was covered with deep snow, but the horses trod sure-footed and steadily up the rocky trail.

To his surprise Elizabeth led him to the entrance of a cave; dismounting, he lifted her from the saddle. He failed to release her but continued to keep a grasp around her waist. Laughing gaily, she looked up at him and his heartbeat quickened at the dazzling sight of her.

Her face was radiant with a healthy glow from the frigid air. A green hooded cape covered her, its white fur trim forming a halo around her face, making the dark eyes and long lashes appear lovelier than ever to him.

With the gentleness that is intrinsic to many big men, Robert cupped her face in his hands and stared in awe at her exquisite beauty. Then, slowly, he lowered his mouth to cover her lush red lips in a sweet and lingering kiss—a tender expression of his love.

Elizabeth's eyes misted as she gazed up at him, and in the tongue of his people Robert declared his love for her.

"The gaol agam ort, Ealasaid."

"You are preparing to leave, aren't you, Robert?" she asked intuitively, turning away from him to conceal her tears.

He followed her into the cave and pulled her to him. Elizabeth leaned back against him as his arms enfolded her.

The hood had fallen away and Robert nestled his face against the perfumed softness of her hair. His breath was warm against her ear as he whispered softly, "Don't love. Don't think of goodbyes. Think only of now, this moment."

Elizabeth turned in his arms. Tears glistened in her eyes as she smiled up at him.

"Then love me, Robert," she cried fervently. "Don't let the moment pass. I almost lost you once, my love. If these moments must last a lifetime, then let each one be a precious memory."

"Oh, Beth," he whispered hoarsely, before her searching lips found his mouth.

A short time later, as they prepared to leave the warmth of the cave, Robert pulled her back with a warning gesture to remain silent.

"What is it?" she whispered, alarmed.

"The road is full of Campbells," he said softly.

Elizabeth looked below them, and, as Robert had indicated, an entourage of mounted Campbells was passing by. Elizabeth gasped in surprise when she saw the two figures who rode at its head.

"Good heavens! It's Walter and his uncle!"

"His uncle! You mean that is Argyll?" Robert asked, his hand instinctively slipping toward his sword.

A worried frown creased her brow. "I wonder what they want? We must get back to the castle, but we cannot let them see you."

Cautiously they approached Ballantine. Robert rode slouched in his saddle to conceal his size. As they approached, the postern gate was raised for them to enter, and the Scott sentinel, who had been anxiously watching for their approach, gave them a furtive gesture to come through.

"There are Campbells in the barn, m'lady," he whispered. "Ye can get the young laird in through the gallery." He put up a hand to halt them. "Wait here for my signal."

Robert and Elizabeth clung to the concealing wall as the gateman casually strolled away. In a few seconds they saw him beckoning, and hand in hand they dashed across the courtyard to the kitchen door, that suddenly opened when they approached.

The cook quickly closed the door behind them and cautioned them to silence with a finger to her lips and a gesture toward the other room.

Elizabeth nodded and leaned back against the wall to catch her breath. A narrow stone stairway rose before them, but to reach it they had to cross the open archway that opened onto the kitchen, which at the moment was full of Campbell soldiers being fed an evening meal.

Elizabeth cautiously peered around the corner and saw nothing but Campbell plaids.

"I am going to create a diversion," she whispered to Robert. "When you hear it, get to the top of the stairs."

He nodded, and with a conspiratory wink, Elizabeth walked boldly into the kitchen.

"Oh, Mauddie," she called at the top of her voice, "I need some sugar for my mare."

In apparent surprise she stopped and looked about her in confusion at the roomful of men.

One of the serving maidens carrying trays of freshly baked bread stood before her. Elizabeth seemingly tripped and with a loud cry fell heavily against the young girl. Trays of bread went crashing onto the table, knocking over several pitchers of milk on the men who were sitting at the long trestle table.

All eyes swung in the direction of the disturbance. A great deal of confusion followed, and with an apology and vague references to her own clumsiness, Elizabeth hastily exited and left the men to their dinner.

Giggling, she raced to the top of the stairs where Robert awaited her. The voice of Lord Scott could be heard coming from his library, and quickly they sped across the hall to the stairway leading to the next level. Finally reaching the seclusion of her room, Elizabeth bolted the door and fell across the bed in relief.

Robert remained at the door, his ear pressed against it. Finally convinced they had not been detected, he too fell across the bed.

"What the hell do I do now?" he moaned. "If they discover I am here they have me right where they want me."

"How will they ever discover you?" she protested. "Father will surely bed them in the other wing."

"And what if Walter decides he wants to play Romeo—and picks you to be Juliet?" he grumbled.

"Walter would never do that," she scoffed. "He is too much of a gentleman."

"Oh, is he! I distinctly remember *Walter* with his hand down the front of your gown!"

"I have always been able to handle Walter," she assured him. "Now help me change, Robert. I must make an appearance."

"I do not believe this," Robert grumbled, as he unlaced her frock. "I not only have to suffer your going off to entertain him, but I must help you look presentable in the bargain!"

Within a quarter hour Elizabeth had freshened herself and changed her gown. She quickly brushed her hair, and with a quick kiss on the cheek of a disgruntled Robert Kirkland, she left the room.

Walter Campbell jumped instantly to his feet when Elizabeth entered the library. He took the hand she offered and brought it to his lips. Elizabeth acknowledged his greeting then turned her attention to his uncle.

"My Lord Argyll." She smiled warmly, as Archibald Campbell kissed her hand.

"Come in, Elizabeth, and do sit down," her father invited. "We have just been discussing a matter which deeply concerns you."

"And what is that, Father?" Elizabeth asked lightly, accepting the glass of wine offered her.

"Lord Argyll, in behalf of his nephew, has just petitioned for your hand in marriage."

"What!" Elizabeth gasped, as the glass fell from her fingers. Flustered, she began to wipe up the spilled liquid. "That is impossible, Father, and you know it," she blurted out.

"Impossible, my lady?" Walter declared. "Why is it impossible, Elizabeth? Your handfast marriage to Robert Kirkland is now dissolved."

"I am not ready for marriage at this time. I have no desire to do so," she stammered.

"Come, Lady Elizabeth, what is the purpose of this delaying game you play with my nephew?" Argyll interposed.

"It is not a game, my lord. I am not ready to wed again."

"And just when do you think you will be? Do you expect my nephew to wait indefinitely?" Argyll asked gruffly. "He is a desirable prize, young lady. There are many women who would welcome such a match."

"Then please, my Lord Argyll, I insist you accept whatever offer pleases you, for I have no desire to wed Walter—or any other man."

Archibald Campbell studied Elizabeth coldly. He was a small man in stature with a lean frame. A pair of squinty eyes gave his face the impression of a constant leer, coupled with bloodless lips; red hair was the only color in an almost vacuous appearance. But beneath it all lay a cold and calculating mind. For here was the most hated man in all of Scotland. He was an arrogant, self-serving tyrant obsessed with a need for power, and ruthless enough to stop at nothing to see that purpose served.

"I tire of this pleading," he rasped, incensed. Did this wench think The Campbell would grovel? What woman would not be honored by such an offer? He had indulged Walter in his choice of a wife, but now he, Archibald Campbell, personally would select who his nephew would marry. Perhaps she would not be as comely as this Scott wench, but certainly she would be less thankless!

"Then the issue is passed and will not be raised again," Argyll declared.

Elizabeth expelled her breath in relief, but Walter Campbell's reaction was just the opposite. His face was flushed and his narrow eyes beseeching.

"Please, Uncle, I beg you to reconsider!" he whined.

Alexander Scott could only stand appalled as he witnessed the disgusting scene. Walter Campbell had confirmed every doubt he had ever harbored about him. Rather than appeal to Elizabeth, the woman he wanted to marry, the spineless jackanapes, like a tame monkey on a chain, was attempting to wheedle the man who pulled his strings. What a far cry from that stalwart rogue upstairs! It was no wonder that his daughter, having known one, would never settle for the other.

Elizabeth suffered through dinner, her mind constantly on Robert in the room above. She loathed Archibald Campbell and could barely tolerate Walter's supplicating attitude toward his uncle.

"What is the word on Montrose?" Lord Scott asked later, as they were savoring a creamy custard pudding.

"He is in the West recruiting. The turncoat Seaforth has deserted our cause and has pledged his MacKenzies to him."

"I have heard that the Frasers are also going to join his ranks. And what say you of Lord Douglas's commitment?"

Argyll's face contorted with a grimace of disgust. "I intend to journey to my brother-in-law's, when I leave here, to convince him of his folly."

"Willie Douglas is his own man, my Lord Argyll. It will take a great deal of 'convincing' to alter his thinking," Alexander Scott replied with a placid smile.

"I imagine your former husband will not crow quite as loudly now that we have executed that scurvy friend of his, Nat Gordon," Walter simpered.

"Colonel Gordon has been executed?" Elizabeth asked, stunned. She fought back a choking sob, remembering a pair of mischievous eyes and irresistible grin.

"And you can be sure my uncle will see that Robert Kirkland's head will be the next one to roll," Walter boasted.

Elizabeth paled, as she fought for control, hearing the one fear she lived with daily vaunted before her.

"Father, I fear all this talk of war has made me quite ill. I beg to be excused." Solicitously the men rose to their feet and she left the room.

Robert turned away from the window when Elizabeth entered the room and anxiously crossed to her.

"What is Argyll doing here?"

"He came to get my father's consent for Walter Campbell to marry me," she said hesitantly, meeting his frown.

Robert reached out and slid his hands along the slim column of her neck, resting under her thick auburn mane. His thumbs began to toy lazily with the delicate lines of her cheeks.

"And did he get it?" he asked, his eyes holding hers in a steady gaze.

Elizabeth flushed under his prolonged probe and shifted her eyes downward.

"No," she answered softly.

"There is something else that is troubling you. What is it, Beth?"

She forced her eyes back to his. "Colonel Gordon has been executed, Robert."

Elizabeth felt a stab in her breast at the sight of the naked pain in his eyes. Robert released her and returned to the window, staring out at the starless sky.

Elizabeth went to him and hesitantly reached up to put a hand on his shoulder.

"I am so sorry, Robert."

"I guess I expected it when Andrew told me he was captured," he said with a soft measured tone. "We are all marked for execution."

Then with a balled fist he pounded the wall in frustration.

"But, damn it, Beth! He was one hell of a man!"

The persistent rapping on the chamber door awoke them both simultaneously, and Elizabeth and Robert stared worriedly at one another.

"Who is it?" Elizabeth called out finally in response to the urgent knocking.

"Elizabeth, it is Walter. Will you open the door?"

"What is that spawn-of-a-whore doing here in the middle of the night?" Robert hissed angrily.

"Hush," Elizabeth cautioned. "He will hear you. Go away, Walter," she called out.

"I must talk to you, Elizabeth. I beg you to

open your door and let me in."

"It is too late, Walter. It would be improper," she protested.

Robert had already risen from the bed and had pulled on his breeks.

"If that bastard does not shut up, he will have the whole castle in here," he whispered through gritted teeth.

"Get into the other room, Robert, and I will get rid of him," she whispered, pushing him toward the adjoining chamber.

Elizabeth pulled on her robe and slid the bolt on the door. "What do you want, Walter?"

Walter Campbell forced the door ajar and stepped into the room.

"Elizabeth, you must agree to marry me. I am sure if you apologize to my uncle he will reconsider."

"Apologize to your uncle!" Elizabeth exclaimed. "Are you insane, Walter? For what do I owe him an apology? I think you should leave this room immediately."

Campbell grabbed her and attempted to kiss her, as Elizabeth struggled in his arms. She succeeded in freeing herself and turned to him with scathing disdain.

"You are behaving like a child, Walter. I insist you leave my room immediately or I will scream for help."

"I shall never forgive you for this, Elizabeth. I have waited for you for years, and now you have made a fool of me in front of my uncle. I swear that I will see that you will rue this night."

"Don't threaten me, Walter. Let me remember what we have shared in the past with fondness. Do not make me regret those memories."

"It will not be the past you will regret, my lady. It will be the future! You have not heard the last from me," he said portentously, stalking from the chamber.

Once again Elizabeth bolted the door and leaned against it in relief. Robert was suddenly at her side, staring at the closed portal, an unrelenting, implacable expression in his eyes.

"I swear, as sure as there is a God in heaven, some day I am going to kill that bastard!"

XXIX

Robert reread the letter from Jamie. The winter had passed and the rivers ran swollen with the spring thaw by the time the courier returned.

Jamie was ecstatic to find Robert was alive and expressed his heartrending grief over the massacre at Philliphaugh and the death of such dear friends and comrades as Nat Gordon and Magnus O'Cahan, as well as the many others who had been executed.

He was expecting Robert to join with the Douglas cavalry when it was ready to leave and told him to await word from William Douglas.

Jamie told him the war was going badly for Charles and prayed that by the time his army was ready to move, it would not be too late to go to the aid of his beloved sovereign.

With his usual gracious thoughtfulness, he expressed his gratitude to Alexander Scott for giving Robert sanctuary, while nursing him back to health, and sent a special greeting of love to Elizabeth with the same heartfelt thanks.

As much as Robert regretted leaving Elizabeth, the idleness had become intolerable to him, and he welcomed the prospect of physical action again.

Elizabeth lived each day with mounting apprehension, fearing it would be the one when Robert would leave her. She sensed his restlessness and desire to be underway.

The day dawned, as she had feared it would, when the Douglas banner appeared at the gates of Ballantine, and the affable William Douglas rode into the courtyard.

On leaden feet Elizabeth entered the library, where Robert had already joined her father and Douglas.

All conversations halted when she entered, and William Douglas jumped to his feet at the sight of his favorite niece. Despite the fact that he was the bearer of the news she had been dreading, Elizabeth was unable to disguise the affection she felt for the man.

"Uncle William." She smiled warmly and placed a kiss on the plump cheek.

Douglas stepped back to study her intently. "I have never seen you lovelier," he said fondly.

"Uncle William, you say that every time you see me," she scolded lightly.

His eyes shifted to Robert, standing silently at the fireplace.

"I suspect that tall Highlander is probably to blame. There is nothing like the attention of a young man to paint that extra glow on a lass's cheeks."

"Tut, Uncle, you make yourself sound as

old as Methuselah. Why you are just a young man yourself. Why think you are not the one who has caused such a glow?"

Willie Douglas laughed with pleasure, enjoying the flirting game he shared with his niece.

"I fear the Highlander is better equipped for the role," he said pleasantly, with a pat to his appreciable girth.

"William has just brought us good news, Elizabeth," Lord Scott said exuberantly. "The war has ended. Charles has surrendered."

Elizabeth gaped in astonishment, her eyes immediately swinging to Robert, whose face was inscrutable.

"Under what conditions?" she asked dubiously.

"He turned himself over to the Scots, not Cromwell," Douglas replied. "He felt he would be safer. He has ordered Montrose to disband his army and lay down his arms."

"And what is the fate of the Scot Royalists who aided him?" she asked hesitantly.

"Montrose has been ordered exiled, but any of his officers who wish to do so may return to their homes under complete amnesty."

Elizabeth turned with relief to Robert, who had been completely silent during the whole conversation.

"Does this mean you will be returning to Ashkirk, my lord?"

"I cannot say, my lady. The news has come too unexpectedly," Robert replied with an oblique shrug of his broad shoulders. "I suspect I will try to reach Jamie and see what he intends."

"I am relieved to hear the fighting has ceased, but I fear it will not be the end of Scotland's turmoil. Our beloved country is now left to the mercy of Cromwell and Argyll," Alexander Scott said gravely.

"And both of them will be harboring resentments," Robert declared hotly. "I fear the Highlanders will pay gravely for their support of Charles and Jamie."

"A toast, gentlemen," Lord Scott declared, as he raised his flagon. "To Scotland."

"Here! Here!" Douglas responded energetically, raising his tankard in the air.

"To Scotland," Robert replied, his voice tinged with apprehension.

Later, as Robert stood staring pensively into the fire, Elizabeth approached him and slipped her hand into his. She felt the tightened pressure as he squeezed her hand in response, but he remained silent.

"You do not appear relieved that this war is finally over, Robert."

As though just becoming aware of her presence, Robert brought her hand to his lips and pressed a light kiss to it.

"It is not that, Elizabeth. Of course, I am glad to see an end to the war. What troubles me is Jamie. He was about to raise the largest army Scotland would ever see. Do you realize the significance of such a task? All the clans— excepting those bastardly Campbells, of course—would have been united against a common foe. Frasers, Gordons, Stewarts, Douglasses, MacDonalds! Ah, Beth, what an invincible might! And Jamie Graham would have been the one to have accomplished it!"

Beth smiled fondly at the tall figure beside her.

"You appear almost disappointed, Robert. I fear not seeing the sight of all those colorful tartans, nor hearing the sound of all those skirling pipes is what is causing your regret."

Robert grinned in response to her affectionate teasing.

"Truly, love, can you not see what it would have meant? We were finally growing up as a nation. Our people were willing to cast aside their grievances with one another and put the interest of Scotland foremost. The Highlander and the Sassenach . . ."

"Lowlander, Robert," Elizabeth corrected with a stern frown.

"The Highlander and the Lowlander fighting side by side," he continued zealously. "What a sight it would have been to behold!"

"We will see it one day, Robert. I know we will see it," Elizabeth replied, and slipped her arms around his waist.

"What say you, my lord, we go upstairs and celebrate this night in our own fashion?" Her eyes were warm and inviting.

Robert's smile was wicked as his arms encircled her waist. He felt the first stirring of arousal when he pressed against her warmth.

"You are an insatiable wench, Lady Elizabeth."

Elizabeth could not ignore the hardened

pressure that was beginning to swell against her. Her arms slipped around his neck and she looked up at him with a saucy, mischievous gleam in her brown eyes.

"And you obviously love it, Lord Kirkland."

The following day the morning tea was filled with excited talk of the war's end and the effect it would have on Scotland. All were in complete accord that Cromwell would make Scotland pay dearly for her loyalty to Charles Stuart.

"Well, no Scot will ever recognize him as Scotland's sovereign," Andrew declared.

"How this must be tormenting Jamie," Robert said sadly. "You know how he feels about the Stuarts sitting on the throne of Scotland."

"They will again one day," Lord Scott replied confidently.

That afternoon Robert received a letter from David. Despite the fact that everything was running smoothly at Ashkirk, David Kirkland made it very plain he wanted Robert to return home and accept his duty as laird of Clan Kirkland.

The following week when the Douglas banner again appeared over the hill, Robert stood on the battlements and watched the approach with apprehension. When the rotund figure of William Douglas walked through the door, Robert's suspicions were confirmed.

"I have just received secret word from someone very close to me in Parliament. It appears Argyll has vowed he will not let James Graham get out of Scotland. He has declared he will see him dead.

"Jamie has two weeks before he must leave. If he is not out of the country by that time he can be arrested and executed. It is Argyll's intent to make sure he does not get out."

"Where is Jamie now?" Lord Scott asked solicitously.

"He is with his family. Charles Stuart did manage to get young Jamie Graham released from Edinburgh Castle, so Jamie is savoring these final days with his children," Douglas replied.

"But how can Argyll prevent him from leaving?" Elizabeth asked, puzzled.

William Douglas was clearly perturbed when he replied.

"He is going to close all other ports. When Jamie tries to board the ship on which he is to sail, it is Argyll's intention to seize him. Do you believe that?"

"The man is insane," Lord Scott exclaimed. "James Graham was given licence to leave Scotland. On whose authority does Argyll presume to stop him?"

"On his own power-crazed, maniacal authority," Robert exploded.

"Now, now, Robert, relax," Douglas soothed. "Remember Argyll does not know we are privy to his plans. We will just have to formulate our own scheme and outfox him."

"We all know Jamie will refuse to leave Scotland a moment sooner than he has to. Let Argyll think that Jamie's plans have not been altered," Robert said, a smile erasing the heated frown.

"You know Argyll will prevent any one of us from going to Jamie's aid. It will have to be someone above suspicion."

"I think it should be a woman," Elizabeth suggested. "Argyll would never suspect a woman."

"But what woman?" Andrew Scott pondered.

Simultaneously, all eyes in the room swung toward the suddenly startled and flabbergasted face of Elizabeth.

The carriage rocked through the darkness of the night on creaking wheels, the green and red colors of the Scott crest painted boldly on its doors. The two drivers sat slumped on the high seat, huddling to keep dry against the driving rain that pelted them. Even in May, the rain in Scotland, sweeping across the waters of the North Sea, was a cold, bone-chilling one.

The carriage's passenger sat snug in the careening vehicle, a warm robe tucked around her lap to ward off the chilly dampness.

There was very little traffic this night on the road to Glasgow. All of the citizenry were alerted that Argyll was leaving no stone unturned in his attempt to thwart the efforts of James Graham to reach France. Everyone was content to remain secure behind locked doors, to put themselves above suspicion from the vengeance-seeking eyes of Archibald Campbell.

When the six armed Campbell soldiers appeared on the road, the driver, grumbling, pulled the galloping bays to a halt. With annoyance, Elizabeth leaned out of the window of the conveyance.

"What is the delay, driver?"

"Another inspection, m'lady," the driver responded amicably.

Immediately the coach was surrounded and the harness runners of the bays were seized by one of the soldiers.

"I am late already, my lord," Elizabeth called out to the young officer. "Will this take very long?"

The young Campbell approached the window, recognizing the Scott crest on the side. He was well-acquainted with the prestigious emblem and knew of the relationship between Elizabeth Scott and Walter Campbell.

"May I ask what business brings you out on such a night, my lady?" he asked politely.

Elizabeth's dark eyes flashed flirtatiously, and her face curved into a radiant smile. The young man was devastated at the sight of such incredible beauty.

"I have an appointment with Lord Craver," she answered, smiling teasingly. "He asked that I meet him in Glasgow tonight."

The young man smiled sagaciously. So this was a lovers' rendevouz! How did that swaggering dandy Walter Campbell rate such a playmate in his bed? Surely the mincing fop did not know how to savor such a delectable dish!

"I fear the rain already has overly delayed my arrival." She pouted coquettishly. "Lord Craver will be quite distressed."

I would be too, the young man thought lewdly to himself, his mind racing with erotic thoughts of what a romp with this sensuous beauty would be like. I imagine Craver will have my skin if I dawdle any longer.

"My apologies for the delay," he replied with a polite nod. "Pass them through," he called out loudly.

"Thank you, my lord," Elizabeth responded with a lingering smile. "Perhaps we will meet again," she hinted suggestively.

The young man stood and watched the carriage disappear into the darkness. Soaked and uncomfortable, he hunched his shoulders against the freezing downpour. "Where is the justice?" he grumbled. "While we stand here in this torrent serving Argyll's needs, his nephew lies skewering his doxy!" With a disgruntled shrug he returned to the meager protection of the trees.

A short distance up the road the driver pulled the carriage to a halt and climbed down. Within moments a figure appeared from among the trees and the two men embraced each other emotionally, oblivious to the rain that poured down upon them.

"Let us get into the carriage, Jamie," Robert Kirkland finally suggested.

James Graham stepped into the carriage and smiled gratefully at Elizabeth. He clasped her hand warmly before finally bringing it to his lips.

"You must forgive my state of dress, my lady," he said with an apology. "I fear I am soiling your carriage."

"Nonsense, my lord," Elizabeth assured him warmly. Then, overcome with emotion, she hugged him warmly. This sign of affection surprised him as much as it did her. "Oh, Jamie, it is so good to see you!"

Graham's arms enfolded her and held her pressed against his chest. "Ah, Beth, it's good of you to help me."

They sat thusly for several moments, before he reluctantly pulled away. His eyes were aglow with their usual warmth and he smiled tenderly at her.

"I fear I am getting you all wet, my lady."

"Jamie, you are looking well," Robert said.

"My feathers may be dampened, but I still hope to crow another day," he replied with a grin. "Ah, Robbie, I have missed you, lad."

Once again the two friends clasped hands, unable to restrain their joy at seeing one another.

Elizabeth watched them sadly, knowing how short-lived their reunion would be and how hard it would be for them to part.

"The plans have all been made, Jamie. We can get you through Glasgow in this carriage without rousing suspicion. There is a Kirkland ship awaiting you. Your men have already secretly boarded it. It will carry you to Stonehaver, where you will transfer to a Norweigan freighter that will take you to France. Argyll will never even know you have left the country."

The coach began swaying from side to side when Andrew Scott moved over and took the reins, once again prodding the horses to a slow gallop.

The rain mercifully had stopped by the time the carriage pulled into a tiny hidden cove. A small dory bobbled on the water, waiting for its illustrious passenger.

Andrew remained with the carriage as the three figures walked silently down to the rocky coast, dreading these final moments of farewell.

"You must hurry, Jamie, to avoid detection," Robert cautioned in an effort to disguise the ache he was suffering.

Tears glistened in Elizabeth's eyes when James Graham turned to her. For a few seconds they could only stare painfully at one another, unable to express the depth of their feeling.

"God be with you, Jamie Graham," she finally whispered softly.

With a stifled groan Jamie grasped her to him. He clung to her tenaciously, like a drowning man being pulled into an undertow.

"Oh Lord, Beth, how can I bear it? How can I wake each day without being able to look out at my beloved Scotland?"

"You will be back one day, Jamie," Elizabeth said compassionately. "Charles will be restored to the throne."

Jamie's smile was sad and pensive as he gazed down at her. Elizabeth's heart ached at the sight of the pain in his sad eyes.

"You know, Beth, Mademoiselle du Plessis once called the army my love, but nae, Elizabeth, she was wrong. Scotland is my only mistress—and will be to my dying day."

His eyes glistened with emotion. "My every waking moment is filled with thoughts of her —my sleep with my dreams for her. Her body is the sweet Mother Earth that I sink down upon, and at night I lie against the warmth of her lush curves, as she cradles me to her breast. She pleasures my vision by robing herself in brilliant gowns of green and purple, and caps her glorious mane in snowy peaks that reach to the heavens."

His voice softened wistfully. "The fragrance of her following a rain teases my senses. Oh, Elizabeth, can you not breathe her sweet scent this very moment?

"There are no riches, no treasures, I would not relinquish for her ransom, and I would lay down my life to see her secure."

Elizabeth reached up and pressed a kiss to his lips. "Jamie, you will come back to us." Then, turning, she left the two men to their goodbyes.

Robert and Jamie clasped hands.

"I really fouled it miserably, Robbie. So many have perished—my son Johnnie, Nat, Magnus, George Gordon. Stout-hearted lads all! The list is endless. And all in vain."

Robert placed a comforting hand on Graham's shoulder. "When a man lays down his life for the principal of freedom, his death is never in vain but becomes a commitment of the living.

"You are but one man, Jamie. You could not do it alone. Never lose sight of the fact that you could have restored the Scottish crown to Charles. You were winning that fight! Let England have its own king. Can not we Scots crown our own monarch?"

Graham placed an affectionate hand on Robert's shoulder. "If I live to be a hundred years of age, Robert Kirkland, I will never understand how an intelligent man like myself ever put himself into a position of depending upon a heathen Highlander!"

For a few poignant seconds the two men could only grin affectionately at one another. Then with a final handshake, James Graham turned away and stepped into the dory.

Long after the small boat had been silently swallowed by the somber jaws of the night, Robert Kirkland stood alone, staring across the desolate waters.

XXX

The following morning Elizabeth watched Robert finish packing the saddlebag that was lying on the bed.

"Will you be coming back?" she asked, unable to conceal her scorn.

Robert straightened up in annoyance. "Of course, I will be back, Elizabeth. I am just unable to tell you how long it will take."

"Oh, give it no thought, my lord," Elizabeth declared sarcastically. "Take whatever time you need. Years, if you must! Only do not be surprised if you find me gone when you decide to return. There is a limit to how long I will docilely await one of your infrequent visits."

A nerve began to flex angrily in Robert's cheek.

"Elizabeth, we have been through this same argument time and time again."

"And I fear, my lord, it is an argument that will always lie between us," she retorted angrily.

"I hope to return in two months. Will you go to Ashkirk and wait for me there?"

"I think not, my lord."

"Very well, then I will seek you at Ballantine," he said in placation.

"Do not bother, for I will not be there either."

"Oh, good lord Elizabeth, will you cease this nonsense!" he flared irritably.

"That is exactly what I am going to do, my lord. It is nonsense for me to think there is any hope for a life between us, except an occasional stolen week or month—when you are between battles or flat on your back wounded. First it was James Graham you had pledged your service to. Now it is his cousin who needs your sword. Then it will be a Mac-Donald, or Stewart, or Robertson, and who-knows-what after that! Probably every country on the whole damn continent of Europe!"

Elizabeth's dark eyes flashed angrily as she continued. "I have had enough, Robert, do you understand? Go to fight your battles wherever they take you, but do not expect me to wait for you. If you walk out of this room now, I never want to see you again."

Elizabeth had never meant for the conversation to get entirely out of control, but James Graham had no sooner sailed than Robert had received word that Patrick Graham's home of Inchbrakie was under seige by Campbells. When Robert had informed her he was joining a band of MacDonalds to go to Pate's aid, she had begun arguing the issue, and now she had to vent her frustration by issuing him a foolish ultimatum. Since the words had been spoken, Elizabeth was unable to retract them.

"I weary of this arguing, Elizabeth," he declared in exasperation, and swung the saddlebag across his shoulder. "I will seek you at Ballantine when I return."

Robert paused at the door and turned back to her. Elizabeth's eyes remained downcast, refusing to meet his gaze.

"Goodbye, Beth."

When she finally raised her eyes, Robert had gone.

Robert Kirkland's heart began racing as he entered the gates of Glasgow, and he spurred his horse to a faster gait. Would Beth be waiting for him? It had been six weeks since their grievous parting. The trouble at Pate's had been quickly quelled, and he had immediately sent a message to Ballantine asking her to meet him at her father's house in Glasgow. He prayed she would be there. He had been doing a great deal of thinking since they had parted. It was time to return to Ashkirk and accept his responsibilities. He and Beth would wed properly and they would return home. He was weary of fighting other people's battles. It was time he put aside his sword so he and Beth could begin building a life together. He could hardly wait to see her, to tell her his decision.

Lost in his thoughts of Beth, he was unaware of the two men who began to trail behind him when he turned into a narrow deserted wynd. It must have been the instinct of a seasoned soldier that suddenly alerted him to danger, and he turned in time to see the two men with their drawn dirks.

Robert reacted instantly, as he swung his horse to the side and pulled his sword from his sheath. The attackers were no match for the experienced veteran, who had spent most of his adult life protecting himself, and within moments the two men lay bleeding on the alleyway.

Robert shrugged aside the incident as nothing other than a robbery attempt and climbed back on his horse.

Elizabeth stepped from the bath and toweled herself dry, before slipping on the robe of white lawn that Robert loved so much.

As soon as she had received the letter from Robert, all her indignation was forgotten in her eagerness to pack and join him. Lord Scott had declared she was not to go alone, so Andrew had volunteered to accompany her on the journey, welcoming the opportunity to visit and carouse in the city.

Eagerly Elizabeth awaited Robert's arrival. Surely it would be today! She studied her reflection as she brushed out her hair. Beth, you are a wanton whore, she admonished herself. All he has to do is beckon and you come running! She sighed and laid aside the brush.

"You are the only thing that matters to me, Robert. I love you so much that there is nothing I would not do for you," she said softly.

Below in the library Andrew Scott looked up in surprise when the door suddenly swung open. His startled frown turned to a friendly smile at the sight of Walter Campbell standing in the doorway.

"Walter!" he greeted and rose to his feet. "What a surprise."

Campbell ignored the proffered hand extended to him in greeting and walked arrogantly across the room to pour himself a brandy from a crystal decanter that sat on the oaken desk.

Andrew watched Walter with displeasure. Even as a child, Walter had been vain and overbearing. Andrew had felt complete relief when Elizabeth informed him she was not going to marry Campbell.

"What brings you to Glasgow, Walter?" Andrew asked curiously.

"The same business that brings you," Walter replied uncivilly. "Your sister."

"Elizabeth? What busineess have you with Elizabeth?"

"I have some unfinished business with her," he said scornfully.

"Oh, Walter, why do you persist in pursuing this issue?" Andrew replied exasperated. "Elizabeth is not in love with you. She will not marry you."

"Who speaks of marriage?" Campbell asked lasciviously. "Your sister and I have no need for such a trite arrangement."

"I will bode no insult to Elizabeth's honor," Andrew declared.

"I fear you are in no position to do anything about it," Campbell sneered.

Without warning, he drew his sword and

swung open the door to the library.

"Confound it, Walter, what is going on here?" Andrew demanded, as two other Campbells stepped into the room.

Weaponless, he was helpless against the men, and in a short time they had him trussed and gagged.

"Now go to the city's gates and await Kirkland," Walter Campbell ordered. "When the opportunity presents itself strike him down. I want him dead."

When his clansmen hurried off, Walter Campbell sheathed his sword and mounted the stairway. Without hesitating, he entered the room at the top.

Elizabeth had just finished applying a few drops of lavender on the pulse of each wrist. Her eyes widened in alarm at the sight of Walter Campbell. With an evil, twisted smile Campbell bowed mockingly.

"Good day, Elizabeth."

Elizabeth's face was whitened in anger. "Walter, what are you doing here? How dare you enter my room.'"

"You will find, my charming Elizabeth, before this day is out, there will be a great deal more that I will dare."

"You are a fool, Walter. At this very moment I am awaiting Robert Kirkland. When he finds you here he will kill you."

"Oh, I am aware of the imminent arrival of your lover, Elizabeth. That is the purpose of my being here. I have thought this through carefully and have planned it well."

Campbell laughed maniacally at the evident astonishment on Elizabeth's face.

"You see, dear Elizabeth, I intercepted that missive to you from your ardent lover and had my own courier deliver it to you. I found it a stroke of good fortune, indeed, for now I am able to spend my full vengeance on you, Elizabeth."

"You are insane, Walter. Get out of this room while you still can, or I will call for help."

"You are not listening, my dear." He smirked, as he continued his deranged raving. "There is no one to help you. I have disposed of anyone who can come to your aid. As for your Highlander, at this very moment he is my prisoner—at my mercy."

"What have you done with him?" she cried in alarm.

Campbell lied glibly and convincingly. "Let me say, Elizabeth, he is being detained against his will. Whether he lives or dies, my dear, becomes your decision."

"What do you want of me, Walter?"

"Surely, my dear, you do not have to ask," he replied licentiously.

Elizabeth stared horrified as he removed his sword.

"Are you asking me to submit to you in exchange for Robert's life?"

"Again, you are not paying close attention, Elizabeth. I am not asking you, I am telling you. If you want Robert Kirkland to remain alive, you will see to the gratification of my needs. I have waited a long time for this day. I once offered you the distinction of my name, Elizabeth—even after that Highland swine had used you. But you scorned my offer. Now I will take what is coming to me."

"Robert will kill you for this," Elizabeth said softly, forcing herself to remain calm and not bolt from the room.

"Oh, no, my love. I have planned this well. Seat yourself at your desk, for you have a letter to write. I have no desire to have Kirkland or your father raise their clans against me; therefore, you will tell him you have had a change of heart and your whole scheme in coming to Glasgow was to join me and go away with me. I am sure you are able to make it quite convincing, my dear. You have such a talent when it comes to deceit!"

"What guarantee do I have that you will not harm Robert?"

"I care not what becomes of him," Campbell said deceitfully. "He is but the foil to force your hand, Elizabeth. I seek my vengeance on you, but it pleasures me to think of his anguish when he discovers how you have betrayed him."

"Walter, I beg you to reconsider this scheme before there is more harm done," she pleaded, as she sat down at her writing desk.

"Just write, Elizabeth," he ordered, as he stood over her.

Elizabeth hesitated, wondering if he was bluffing. Should she dare call that bluff? At the sight of the crazed look in his eyes she realized Walter Campbell was capable of following through with his threats without the least compunction. Reluctantly Elizabeth reached for the quill, and slowly began to pen the words he demanded.

With a satisfied smile Walter read Elizabeth's letter to Robert Kirkland. "Perfect, my dear! Absolutely perfect! The love-struck fool will be devasted when he reads this. Truly, I have underestimated your talents!"

His face curled with a lewd smirk, as he pulled Elizabeth to her feet.

"Now it is time to test that talent of yours in other fields. Rid me of my shirt, Elizabeth," he ordered.

With trembling hands Elizabeth pulled the shirt off him, and it fell from her stiffened fingers to the floor.

Walter Campbell reached out and released the tie of her robe. The gown gaped open to expose her nudity. With mesmerized revulsion, she felt his hands at her shoulders, as he slid the robe from her. His eyes gleamed lustfully as they ravished her nakedness.

"I knew you would look like this," he murmured hoarsely.

Elizabeth forced back a scream as his mouth swooped down to seize the peak of a breast. In a frenzy, like a starving babe seeking nourishment, he hungrily attacked her breasts. Elizabeth closed her eyes and bit down on her lip, stifling her sob, praying for blackness to free her of this torture. Campbell's mouth suckled greedily, leaping from one nipple to the other in a carnal gorging.

As though suddenly satiated, he raised his head. "Remove my pants, Elizabeth," he ordered.

Elizabeth recoiled in aversion. "Please, Walter," she entreated.

His look remained unrelenting as he forced her hand to the buttons of his pants. In a nightmare Elizabeth loosened Campbell's pants and they slid down his legs to the floor.

"Now get down on your knees and pleasure me," he ordered lasciviously.

Her eyes widened with increasing horror. "Please, no, I can't," Elizabeth pleaded. "Don't make me do it! I beg of you."

Campbell's eyes were cold and merciless. "Surely, Elizabeth, you realize there is more finesse to sexual pleasure than the vulgar pawings of a Highland barbarian?"

He gripped her arm in an excruciating grasp and slowly forced her to her knees.

"Now pleasure me," he snarled, as he buried his hands in her hair and tried to press her head to his swollen organ.

At that moment the door swung wide and Robert Kirkland burst into the room.

"Beth, I am . . ." The words froze in his throat at the compromising sight of Elizabeth and Walter Campbell. Robert's initial shock began to slowly mount toward a blind rage.

Unaware that Campbell had even released her, Elizabeth remained motionless, staring with a wretched plea for understanding at the furious dark eyes locked with hers.

Walter Campbell could not have been more delighted with this latest twist of events had he planned it himself. The cloutish Highlander, though not dead, had arrived at a most opportune time. The agonized expressions on their faces were all he could hope for! There was no way Elizabeth would convince him of her innocence after what Kirkland had just seen with his own eyes. He pulled up his pants and sidled toward his scabbard lying on the table.

"I am afraid, Lord Kirkland, you have caught us at a most disadvantageous moment," he simpered, feigning embarrassment.

Robert walked over to Elizabeth and picked up her robe.

"Cover yourself, whore," he snarled as he flung it contemptuously at her. Elizabeth's eyes continued to plead with his, as her face flushed with shameful guilt.

"You do not understand, Robert. I . . ."

"Spare me the explanations, Elizabeth. I have no stomach for them."

She rose to her feet and grabbed his arm entreatingly. "It isn't what you think, Robert. You must believe me!"

Robert shrugged aside her arm angrily. With a dramatic flourish Walter Campbell reached for the letter, bearing Robert's name written in Elizabeth's bold script.

"Perhaps, this will clear up some of your doubts, Kirkland," he said smugly.

Robert's eyes quickly scanned the note, his face an impassive, inscrutable mask. When his eyes raised from the paper, Elizabeth was unable to meet his scathing glare.

"I think this explains it quite clearly. I apologize for my untimely intrusion."

Robert turned to depart and Walter Campbell called out jeeringly.

"I am sure Elizabeth will be glad to accommodate you when I have taken my pleasure."

Incensed, Robert turned around and with a curled fist struck out at the supercilious face with a smashing blow. Campbell went crashing against the table, his hand encountering the scabbard. Robert had already turned to leave and was descending the stairway. In a blind rage Campbell lunged at him with drawn sword.

Elizabeth screamed out a warning and Robert turned, his reflexes causing him to immediately step aside avoiding the thrust of Campbell's sword, and the two men tumbled down the remaining steps.

Within seconds they were both on their feet, weapons in hand. Robert held the hilt of a claymore in his right hand, the wide blade of the Highlander that was so effective in the slashing hand-to-hand combat of battle. In his left hand he clutched his dirk, poised and threatening.

Walter Campbell's weapon was the narrow rapier of the court duelist. A lighter blade, it was ideal for long pointed thrusts at one's opponent. He held a tenacious grip on a stiletto in his left hand.

The two antagonists circled one another warily—two masterful duelists, each with an accomplished expertise in the weapon he held. Both men knew it would be a fight to the death, the issue of Elizabeth no longer an excuse. Between them lay a deep-rooted hatred that had spanned generations—Kirkland against Campbell, Campbell meeting Kirkland. Every nefarious incident of the past hundred years had tempered each man for this moment.

Helplessly Elizabeth watched with despair, knowing that her very future rested on the outcome of the duel.

Campbell made the first move with a sudden swift thrust, as he lunged forward. Robert's wider, stronger blade easily parried, and with a quick riposte returned the thrust.

"A skilled move," Campbell said grudgingly, as he adroitly stepped aside to avoid the blade. "You surprise me, Highlander. I did not expect finesse, only brawn."

"I am sure there are a great deal more surprises that await you," Robert challenged. "You forget, Craver, my cunning with a sword was learned on a battlefield, but my skill was taught to me by James Graham."

"More's the pity, Kirkland, for James Graham is not here with you now."

"Jamie Graham is always with me, Campbell, as you will soon discover," Robert declared, and forced a rapid running attack that drove his opponent against the wall.

Campbell successfully counter-parried the thrusts, but was staggered by the strength that was wielding the sword against him.

The hall rang with the sound of clanging

weapons, as time and time again they met one another's thrusts. Campbell's agility was easily met with Robert's swift foot and wrist.

Chairs were overturned as the men fell against them. The aged manservant, attracted by the noise, shuffled from the kitchen to stand gaping at the duelists.

In a series of rapid thrusts Campbell forced Robert against a table and he fell backward across its top. From his semi-prone position Robert succeeded in binding his opponent's blade, as he skillfully controlled it—only to have Walter spring at him in an effort to drive the slender, tapering blade of his stiletto into Robert's heart.

Elizabeth cried out in horror at the sight of the descending blade. Robert swung up his dirk and stopped the descent, but slowly, with their knives crossed, Campbell pressed his advantage as the blade lowered toward Robert's throat. Grunting with the effort and with incredible strength, Robert shoved the lighter man away and rolled over.

Once again the two men faced one another. Robert's shirt clung to him with perspiration, and Walter Campbell's bare chest glistened with sweat. A previous thrust with the pointed blade had nicked Robert's arm. One shirt sleeve was now stained with blood. Robert's claymore had caught Campbell's shoulder in a minor slash, and the blood now mixed with his sweat to trickle down his chest. Neither wound was serious enough to slow the men, as they pursued their gruelling battle.

The two men faced one another, their

chests heaving from the strain of their efforts.

"How much longer will your sword arm hold out?" Campbell taunted, knowing Robert's arm had to be feeling the laden weight of his heavier weapon.

"Long enough to run my claymore through your black heart," Robert countered.

The duel continued relentlessly, as both men sought to find a minor weakness in the opponent's defense. Campbell furiously renewed the attack in an effort to drain the remaining strength from Robert's arm. With a springing lunge he attempted to thrust his weapon into Robert's stomach. With a powerful slash from his wider, heavier sword, Robert parried the thrust—and the point of Campbell's narrow, thin blade broke off and fell to the floor with a clatter.

Absolute shock was etched across Campbell's face before he flung the useless weapon to the floor.

Robert Kirkland was too fair a fighter to use the advantage of his longer weapon and unhesitantly lowered it to the floor.

Again the adversaries faced one another, their knives poised. Campbell's face contained a contemptuous sneer in mockery of Robert's noble gesture.

"You know why you Highlanders lost the war," he scoffed. "You are too full of weak sentiments. War has no place for weak sentiments. It is kill or be killed. The advantage was yours, Kirkland. You had me. But your foolish nobility prevented you from pressing your advantage. You are just like your other weak comrades. Graham and his noble thoughts and causes! They cost him everything he ever owned."

"Except his honor," Robert interjected sarcastically.

"And that foolish Irishman O'Cahan. Mounting his noble sentiments to the end! It gave me great pleasure to be the one that pulled the rope around his bastardly neck."

"O'Cahan? You were the one who hung him?" Robert exclaimed.

"Yes, I hung him—with the same pleasure I will have when I kill you too, Kirkland," Campbell boasted.

Robert had never felt as much hatred toward another human being as he now did toward Walter Campbell. For the first time in his life he suffered a consuming need to kill, to know the satisfaction of plunging his knife into that black heart. In his hatred he wanted to cut out the tongue of the raving, maniacal jackel!

The force of his incensed hatred was transformed into a deadly calm, and Robert advanced on his enemy. Like a braying ass suddenly sensing his death from a stalking panther, Walter Campbell circled away from Robert's manacing advance. Robert's sword lay on the floor near his feet, and with a desperate leap, he lunged for the weapon. Robert sprang at him, and as Campbell raised the sword, Robert's knife sank into the coward's heart.

Campbell's mouth gaped in shock, before he fell to the floor and lay staring up at the ceiling with lifeless eyes. Elizabeth sank her head into her hands, unable to control her trembling body.

When she finally raised her head, Robert had sheathed his weapons. The old servant was bent over Campbell's corpse, shaking his head in a wordless message that Robert already knew.

Robert's mouth curled contemptuously when he turned to her.

"You wanted him, my lady. Now you can have him!"

Elizabeth regained enough of her faculties to cry out a weak protest. "You don't understand, Robert. He told me you were his prisoner. I was doing it to save you."

She cringed under the force of his scornful glare. "If any Campbells come seeking me, I will be at the inn."

Elizabeth could only watch him walk away, the tears streaking her cheeks.

Robert Kirkland drank himself senseless as soon as he had secured a room at the inn. His thoughts were tormented with the memory of Elizabeth with Walter Campbell. How could the conniving, cheating bitch have fooled him so much! It took two steady days of drinking, before he finally passed out and succeeded in sleeping around the clock.

When he awoke, despite the fact that his mouth felt full of cotton, his mind was surprisingly clear. For the first time since his arrival in Glasgow, he found himself thinking rationally.

All he could think of was Elizabeth's pleading eyes. Why did the woman incessantly haunt him! Why was he plagued with such nagging doubts? Had he not seen her with Campbell—naked and on her knees? What better evidence of her guilt? Unwittingly, his thoughts strayed to the tender moments they had shared in the lodge in Kirkmuir, and the sound of her laughter as they frolicked in the snow at Ashkirk. Robert remembered the sight of her beautiful, incredible eyes brimming with love, as she fervently declared her feeling for him. He relived every rapturous moment he had held her in his arms and how she would pull his head down to claim her lips, as her hands roamed his body.

Suddenly the obvious evidence of his own stupidity struck him with full force as he realized Elizabeth had not lied to him. Somehow Campbell had convinced her he was in jeopardy, and she had been willing to sacrifice her honor to save him. He rushed to the stables and within moments was galloping toward her house.

The old servant drew back in fright when he answered Robert's frantic pounding on the door.

"The Lady Elizabeth? Is she home?" he asked wildly.

"Nae, my lord," the frightened man replied.

Robert was unaware when he clutched the old man's shoulders in a desperate grasp.

"Where has she gone?"

"Why she and Sir Andrew departed on

yesterday's morn. They returned to Ballantine Castle," he replied with a shaky voice. The old man quivered in fright at what this wild man's reaction would be to that news.

To his relieved surprise, Robert Kirkland released him and turned away in despair.

A complete picture of dejection and guilt, Robert Kirkland returned to the inn—and daily, throughout the following week, drank himself into brooding, black, alcoholic stupors.

XXXI

The ashes had long cooled in the small fireplace when the door to Robert Kirkland's room was opened slightly and a figure stealthily entered. For several seconds the intruder stood motionless, eyes straining to adjust to the darkness, before finally focusing on the sleeping form in the bed—and then, with silent steps, walked cautiously over to it. Fingers reached down toward the throat of the unsuspecting figure and began to stroke it.

The intoxicating pressure of the soft hand caressing his face began to arouse Robert. He struggled for consciousness through the fuzziness of sleep and an overabundance of ale. When warm lips traced a moist trail to his ear, he felt the heat of a fire ignite in his loins. A hot tongue began to toy with his ear in fiery probes, and the flame that had been kindled flared to an inferno and began a scorching blaze through his body.

In the throes of mounting passion and grogginess of slumber, he pulled the slim figure down to him with a shuddering groan.

"Oh, Beth. Beth love."

A blonde head reared up angrily and the figure rose from the bed.

437

"I fear, *mon ami*, you have made a *faux pas!*"

Robert peered through the darkness in confusion. "Desireé?"

"Mais oui, mon cher."

Reaching out a groping hand Robert succeeded in lighting a candle that stood on the nearby commode. He sank down to sit on the edge of the bed. Propping his arms on his legs, he rested his aching head in his hands.

"Good Lord, Desireé, what are you doing here?"

"I am here because I soon will be sailing for France. When I heard the Earl of Kirkwood was here alone, I came seeking you. But you, Robert, what are you doing here?"

Robert rose from the bed and slipped on his breeks. He walked to the mirror and studied his tousled reflection grimly. His dark hair was rumpled and his eyes appeared red and watery. With a shudder of disgust he turned away.

The soft tinkle of Desireé's laughter rewarded his inspection of himself.

"It appears, *mon ami*, that married life does not agree with you."

"I am no longer married," he snarled. "I am a free man."

"Then I correct my previous statement, Robert. I fear being a free man does not agree with you."

"What does not agree with me is to have to suffer the witless humor of women," he grumbled.

"*Oh, la, la!*" Desireé exclaimed. "The lady has wounded you deeply, Robert."

"What rot! What need have I of her?"

His eyes swept the enticing length of her and a brow was raised suggestively.

"Come here, Desireé."

Her tantalizing green eyes narrowed and a seductive smile curved her mouth. Desireé crossed the few steps to him, and Robert reached out and drew her to him.

"It has been a long time, *bebe*," he whispered hoarsely.

His lips found the hollow behind her ear and with a smothered moan of surrender her arms reached up and encircled his neck.

As though she were a pillow of feathers, Robert picked her up in his arms and carried her to the bed. He lay her down gently and lowered himself to her. Quickly releasing the buttons on the bodice of her gown, he reached in to cup a breast. Eagerly Desireé's lips parted as his mouth closed over hers.

Before the kiss could deepen, Robert dispiritedly pulled away and rolled over on his back to lie staring at the ceiling of the room. Desireé leaned across him and gently caressed his cheek, a sad smile on her face.

"We have lost it, *mon cher*, have we not?"

The stricken look on his face was all the reply she needed. Tears glimmered in her eyes.

"We had many good times—did we not, my love?—but now I fear Elizabeth lies between us."

Arms of gratitude enfolded her and for many minutes they lay silently, each of them aware that this was the final intimate moment they would ever share with one another.

Desireé finally broke the silence between them. "Now tell me about Elizabeth."

Robert's tone was self-accusatory. "I am a bastard, Desireé. I am not worthy of her."

"Does she love you, Robert?"

"I know she once did. I can only pray I have not destroyed that love. I love her and I have hurt her deeply."

"Do you not know, *mon cher*, what you must do? Why do you tarry here? Why have you not gone to her? Are you such a fool, Robert! If she loves you she will forgive you."

Robert's eyes brightened with relief hearing her words of assurance. His face broke into a wide grin as the burden of indecision was lifted from his shoulders.

"You are right, my love. I will leave for Ballantine in the morning. And even if I must bind and gag her, Elizabeth is returning with me to Ashkirk!"

Hugging her warmly, he rolled over and gave Desireé an affectionate kiss. Suddenly the door crashed open and, startled, Robert bolted to his feet. He grabbed his sword from its scabbard and swung back ready to meet his attackers.

Bemusement was clearly etched across his face and he slowly lowered his weapon, recognizing the green and red tartan of the Scott clan on the men who now faced him.

Andrew Scott stepped forward, sword in hand. For a few moments he studied Robert's tousled hair and naked form, clad only in breeks. His gaze shifted to the disheveled figure of Desireé du Plessis sitting on the rumpled bed, adjusting the buttons of her bodice. His expression remained impervious, his voice impersonal.

"You have a choice, Robert, of walking from this room—or being trussed and toted out like a sack of grain."

Robert Kirkland cared neither for the tone nor the command. His smile was cold, and he once again raised his weapon and warily circled Andrew Scott.

"I care not for either option, Andrew. You once saved my life and I do not wish to hurt you."

"I have no intent, Robert, of making this a fair fight. My orders are to bring you back without harming you."

With a nod from Andrew the other men began to approach Robert cautiously. He looked around and found himself entirely circled by Scott clansmen. He could not bring himself to wound any of them, so he lowered his weapon in concession.

"Do I get the opportunity to clothe myself?" he askeed with contempt.

Andrew nodded mockingly.

"I assume you are as accomplished at donning your clothes as swiftly as I am sure you divested yourself of them." Once again his gaze swung to the French woman on the bed.

One of the Scotts quickly gathered up Robert's belongings while he completed his dress. His anger flared when his arms were seized and his hands bound behind his back. He turned glaringly to Andrew, who raised a supplicating hand.

"A necessary precaution, Robert. To insure us you cannot escape."

When they began to force him toward the door, Robert shrugged them away and turned back to Desireé. His anger left him momentarily as his eyes lingered tenderly on his former mistress.

"Take care, little one," he said softly, before he was escorted from the room.

Desireé jumped to her feet and rushed to the side of Andrew Scott. She put a restraining hand on his arm to halt his departure.

"You will not harm him?" she asked worriedly.

Andrew nodded his assurance.

"You are taking him to Elizabeth?"

"That is correct, mademoiselle."

Desireé's soft sigh was a reflection of her relief. Her eyes swept the tall figure of Andrew Scott. She studied the lithe, muscular body and the handsome face appreciatively. Her soft fingers slid slowly up his sleeve and a slight smile tugged the corners of her mouth, eyes narrowing seductively.

"I regret you are not free to tarry longer, my lord."

Andrew Scott recognized the invitation in the tantalizing green eyes. His own wide brown eyes lingered warmly on the lush roundness of her tiny form, and his face curved into an engaging grin.

"Not half as much as I, mademoiselle!"

There was little attempt toward conversation on the trip to Ballantine. Robert's hands were kept tied, unbound only at mealtimes. This treatment, combined with Andrew's hostility and reticence, only increased Robert's anger, which continued mounting with every mile. Andrew's only response to Robert's demand for an explanation for his abduction was a curt, "My father wishes it thus."

They rode a full two days and a night, stopping only to rest their mounts or for an occasional meal. When the gates of Ballantine finally appeared before them, Robert was relieved as any to ease his cramped position on the horse.

Andrew Scott paused to untie his prisoner's wrists, and Robert gratefully flexed his aching arms and legs, seeking to restore circulation to the stiffened limbs.

"You know the way," Andrew ordered brusquely.

Robert's lips curled into a derisive smirk. "To Elizabeth's room?"

At this arrogant implication, Andrew's eyes flashed angrily and his hands curled into fists, as the young man fought to control himself from striking out in defense of his sister's honor.

"The library," he replied grimly through gritted teeth.

Despite the late hour, the hall was still lit. The men's footsteps echoed loudly through the quiet castle as they approached the closed door of the library.

With a light tap, Andrew opened the door. "Father, I have returned."

The Earl of Ballantine rose to his feet from behind a huge oaken desk. There was no welcoming smile on the aged but handsome face.

"Thank you, son," he acknowledged. Then with a short nod of dismissal Andrew stepped from the room and quietly closed the heavy door behind him.

Robert stood silent and watched the imposing figure cross to the fireplace. The man appeared burdened as he wrestled with the wisdom of his decision. Lord Scott placed both hands on the mantel and lowered his brow to rest against it, staring reflectively into the glowing logs. For a few moments Robert thought the man had completely forgotten his presence and was about to speak when the tormented figure finally turned and faced him.

"I thank God for His divine mercy that your father is not alive to have to suffer the dishonor his son has brought to his name."

A muscle began a warning twitch in Robert's jaw and the dark eyes deepened in anger.

"I have never dishonored my father's name, Lord Scott, nor do I wish to bring insult to the house that offered me refuge when I had need for it. But as my father's son, I can no longer stand here and permit my name, or my father's name, to be blackened without even the benefit of explanation."

For a fleeting moment Alexander Scott felt a grudging respect for this young man. His impression of Robert Kirkland had always been most favorable, but recent actions had destroyed any admiration he had ever harbored.

"Your treatment of my daughter, Lord Kirkland, is unchivalrous. I will not tolerate it."

"I see no offense in my treatment of your daughter, my lord."

Alexander Scott's contained anger now erupted and Robert met glaring contempt.

"It is a sorry day for Scotland when our nobles' weaknesses can be blatantly flaunted. My daughter is not some doxy you can skewer for an evening's pleasure!"

"I have never thought her thus, Lord Scott, nor have I treated her in a like manner."

"Did you not take her virginity, use her at your will, and then discard her as you would a cast aside garment! I sent you my daughter as a chaste, young maiden, believing you to be a man of honor. You abused her, my lord, in a most ignoble fashion!"

Anger now blazed from his dark eyes, and he adamantly declared, "My grandchild will not be born a bastard, Robert Kirkland! You have done my daughter foul and I will see the proper end to it!"

Robert gaped in astonishment at this announcement. Why hadn't Elizabeth told him she was carrying his child? Was it her intent to let him return to Ashkirk unaware of her condition? Would she have notified him when the child was born? One question after another flooded his thoughts.

A slow rage began to creep through him. God's truth, he was a Highland laird! Why had he permitted himself to be trussed like a chicken? Why hadn't he been properly informed that Elizabeth was with child? Damn the woman! Love her or not, he had his dignity, too!

Alexander Scott, enmeshed in his own feeling of righteous indignation, continued his tirade.

"You and Elizabeth will wed immediately —this night! I have summoned a minister and he awaits us in the chapel."

As he spoke he walked to the door and flung it open. A retinue of Scott soldiers stood waiting. Lord Scott turned back to Robert, his bearing proclaiming the conversation at an end and the outcome a foregone conclusion.

"Your escort, my lord."

Robert squared his shoulders and faced the enraged earl.

"Since I have already been tried and sentence passed, the condemned man is entitled to a few words."

Alexander Scott closed the door and turned back to Robert, his manner hesitant, eyes wary.

"Because of Elizabeth's condition I will wed your daughter, Lord Scott. But bode this well. A child bearing my name will be raised in my house!"

"And what of the child's mother?" the earl asked with circumspection.

"The child's mother remains with the child," Robert announced obdurately.

Lord Scott flung his hands in the air in rejection. "I will not permit such an arrangement. My daughter has been abused enough at your hands. Do you believe I would subject her, or her child, to the same ill treatment?"

"Need I remind you, my lord, that once I am her legal husband you have nothing to say in the matter. I then have the ultimate authority over her and everything she posseses. She then becomes subject to the whimsy of my mercy—or delectation," Robert said ominously.

The earl flushed with mounting rage at the threatening implication. "I would see you dead, you blackguard, before I would become a party to such a pact."

Robert's manner remained confident. "Then your grandchild would still be born a bastard, would he not?"

The earl saw the truth to this logic. He sighed compliantly. "The advantage appears to be yours. Then we must strike a bargain to . . ."

"Bargain you say! I seek no bargain—no terms," Robert shouted in intense fury at this latest affront. "It is you who insists on this union. I seek only to remind you of the possible ramifications of this act."

"Your vision is short-sighted, Lord Kirkland. What would prevent me from seeing you dead once your vows are spoken."

"Elizabeth," Robert answered with calm assurance.

"Have you no honor?" Alexander Scott asked scornfully.

"It is because I do that I will see this through. I knew not of Elizabeth's condition. I am not a cad, my lord. I would have willingly met my obligation to her and my unborn child. I, too, have no desire to hear my child tagged 'bastard.'

"I am also a man of reason, my lord. Had you requested my presence at Ballantine I would not have ignored that petition. The manner you chose to deliver that *invitation* was a debasement to you, as well as myself. I can assure you, were it not that I felt an obligation toward the house of Scott, it would not have been a simple task to bring me here. Some of your clansmen would have fallen in the effort.

"So do not speak to me of honor, my lord, for I have rendered you more than your due."

The two antagonist's eyes met and locked—Robert's unrelenting, Alexander Scott's beginning to glimmer with admiration. The earl realized that this young man had completely reversed their roles and was now in the position of dictator. He sensed that there was not a power on earth that could force Robert Kirkland to do anything he actually did not wish to do. The young man desired this marriage as much as he did. There was no conflict—no cross purpose. Nothing would be gained by a power struggle between them. Elizabeth would be the only loser in such a ploy.

With a nod of concession, Alexander Scott turned to leave the room, and Robert followed.

Elizabeth sat in the chapel, her fingers nervously twisting a tiny linen square clutched in her hand. She waited with trepidation for the appearance of her father and Robert.

From the time Andrew returned and informed her of Robert's abduction, Elizabeth had struggled with her conscience. What was the wisest solution to this unbearable situation? She loved Robert and was willing to fight to keep him. In time would he not forgive her? Time—that benevolent healer!

She glanced toward Andrew, who was silently pacing at the rear of the chapel. She sensed he too was torn with guilt over his treatment of Robert. Perhaps, she could discuss the situation with him.

Elizabeth's heart leapt to her throat when the doors of the chapel swung wide. The Earl of Ballantine was the first to enter, and Robert Kirkland stepped in a few paces behind him.

Elizabeth felt a stabbing pain in her chest at the sight of the familiar tall figure. He looked very weary from the arduous trip. His raven-black hair was rumpled and his chin was covered with the stubble of several day's growth. Elizabeth knew by his stance that he was still seething with anger. Her eyes shifted guiltily downward when his stormy eyes sought hers.

"Father, I would have a few moments alone with Lord Kirkland."

Alexander Scott hesitated, as though fearing for her safety if she were left alone with the Highlander. Then, with a compliant nod, he gestured to the others and they departed.

Once alone with Robert, Elizabeth's courage faltered. He stood stiffly, his contained anger seemingly overpowering as he loomed above her. The room seemed to vibrate with the force of his fury.

"My compliments, my lady. Your courage is remarkable," he snarled. "Pray thee, what is to prevent me from wringing your treacherous neck this very moment?"

Elizabeth faced the full force of his wrath unflinchingly. Her wide round eyes met his cold angry glare.

"You once put a dirk in my hands and bade me follow my wont. I now offer you the same. If it is your desire to kill me, Robert, then do so, for I have no intent of trying to halt our marriage."

"Better you would have used *that* dirk, than the one you later plunged into my heart," he said bitterly.

Her eyes clouded pleadingly. "I seek only to try to explain that night at Glasgow."

"Madam, I am trying to rid my mind of the events of that perfidious evening. Would your father be so insistent we wed were he to know the truth of that night?"

"The truth! How speak you of truth when you know naught of it! Walter Campbell said he was going to kill you, Robert. He promised your release if I remained with him."

His hands seized her shoulders in a savage grip, his eyes piercing in their contempt.

"Madam, I have been escaping from Campbells my whole lifetime! Did you believe I wanted my freedom purchased at the price of your honor! Did you not know that the purity of your love was more precious to me than life itself?"

"Fault me if you must, Robert, but I did it for you."

"Did it for me!" Robert exploded. "Madam, you Scotts have tried my patience and endurance with your noble deeds committed for one another. For the last two days your brother *for the sake of your father* has had me trussed like a fowl, pushed and prodded like a cow and jostled like a sack of oats in a complete assault upon my dignity as well as my body.

"Your father *for the sake of you and our unborn child* has blackened my name, insulted my honor, threatened my life, and coerced me into a marriage.

"While you, my devoted wife, have scorned my love, betrayed my trust, shattered my manhood, and doubted my courage. Now you

451

cry sacrifice! And all *for the sake of my life!*
Nae, wife, I will neither hear nor suffer any
more of it!"

At his scathing declaration of ingratitude,
Elizabeth's temper flared, and, as in the past,
whenever their wills clashed, her resolve dissipated. Her head raised defiantly.

"I am not your wife! I was not your wife
then! I am not your wife now, and I care not
to be your wife ever!"

She began to turn away and her arm was
grasped roughly as he pulled her back to face
his seething rage.

"You are my wife, Elizabeth! You were
then, you are now, and you will always be.
You carry my child and for that reason we will
see this evening through!"

How long they stood glaring at one another,
neither could say, for each was completely
enfused with individual indignation. They
were totally unaware when the others re-
entered the chapel.

"Let us be on with it," Lord Scott ordered,
and the minister quickly stepped to the small
altar. Elizabeth felt her father's hand on her
arm and let him direct her to the altar steps.
Should she stop this farce now? She began to
open her mouth to speak when suddenly she
was standing beside Robert. Her legs began
trembling and she stole a glance at the angry
profile. Sensing her stare, Robert turned and
Elizabeth wanted to bolt from the room at the
sight of the dark eyes glaring down at her. Oh,
Lord, he hates me, she thought in anguish.

Her fingers were frigid when Robert's warm hand closed around them, and she lost awareness of everything except his presence next to her.

Her ears were deaf to all except the thumping of her heart, but miraculously she must have succeeded in speaking her vows, for suddenly the ceremony was ended and Robert released her hand.

Elizabeth raised timorous round eyes to him, and for a brief moment his anger faded, replaced by a glimmer of sadness as his knuckles lightly traced the delicate line of her jaw.

"It appears, my lady, once again you have been denied your maiden's dream of a felicitous wedding day."

"I fear that foolish maiden no longer exists," she retorted. "She vanished as swiftly as my innocence."

Robert's gaze on her was sad and pensive. "More's the pity, my lady, for she had a precious charm, and willingly I would have pleaded, 'Linger, fair maiden, how sweet thou art.' "

Then shrugging aside the moment building between them, he turned quickly to Alexander Scott.

"It has been a long and tiring trip, my lord. I trust your hospitality includes a hot bath and warm bed."

"It is always a pleasure to service the needs of my guests," he replied graciously.

Robert turned back to Elizabeth and raised

her hand to his lips.

"I will say goodnight, my lady, until tomorrow."

Confused and hurt, Elizabeth watched the broad shoulders recede from the room.

Elizabeth returned to the privacy of her own room, thankful to be free of the sympathetic glances of her father and brother. She knew not whether to burst into tears or scream in anger at the top of her voice.

So the chess game between us continues, she thought anxiously. I have made a bold move with my bishop, but you would not play the pawn and have cleverly countered with your rook. A thoughtful frown crossed her brow as she dwelled on the strategy of her next move. Suddenly the brown eyes gleamed brightly and the lovely face broke into a self-complacent smile that could only mean trouble for the unsuspecting Earl of Kirkwood.

"I think 'tis time the queen be put in jeopardy," she murmured aloud. "But be wary, thou wily king, for this time you will find yourself in *checkmate!*"

After a hot bath that had eased the ache from his limbs, Robert Kirkland donned a pair of breeks and a white shirt tied loosely at the neck. He now stood deep in reflection staring out of the small window. He was aware of Elizabeth's movements in the next room and was tempted to go to her.

Lord, how he loved her! How his body ached for the warmth of hers! Again I have seen to hurt her. Why do I do it to her? he bitterly chastised himself. Why do I allow my anger at the actions of others to affect my treatment of her? She is but the innocent victim of it all. 'Tis only my pride and vanity that has been pricked by these Scotts. But were they not trying to service Elizabeth's interests? How can I fault them for their intentions because of the manner they used to implement them? Did I not plan for this marriage myself?

But still, he thought cautiously, I have been sorely used at their hands, and I am not about to let the wench think I will take the indignity lightly!

He heard the sound of a sliding bolt and swung around as the door between their chambers was opened. Elizabeth stepped into the room holding a delicate crystal glass of wine in each hand.

At the sight of her, Robert fought for control. Her long dark hair flowed luxuriantly across the smooth satin of her bare shoulders. The gossamer transparency of the white lawn night dress clung to the lush fullness of her breasts and hugged the undulating slim hips, as she moved toward him with feline grace. For an instant her glance flickered down to the revealing bulge in his breeks, before her eyes swung back to his face. A slight smile of satisfaction tugged at the corners of her mouth at this blatant evidence of her effect on him.

As if her body were not enough of an assault on his senses, her eyes continued their assault on his will, when they met his—boldly, challengingly, seductively.

" 'Tis good vintage, my lord," she said huskily, as she offered him one of the glasses. Robert reached for it eagerly and quaffed it in a single swallow.

Twin pools of pure enticement studied him from above the rim of her glass, as she slowly sipped from it.

"Shame, my lord, 'tis better appreciated if just sipped," she admonished lightly. "Here, drink mine, 'twill help to relax you."

Unprotesting Robert accepted the extended glass and once again quickly gulped its contents as she set aside the other empty crystal.

"Just what the hell do you think you are doing, Elizabeth?" he snarled angrily.

"This night can be as pleasant or as unpleasant as you choose to make it, Robert," she said softly, as she took the empty glass from him.

Her long fingers entwined around his hand and she lifted it to press the palm to her mouth. At the touch of her warm, moist lips, a stabbing pain pierced his already tortured loins. Her eyes did a tantalizing dance as she released the button on each of his sleeve cuffs, halting just long enough to press a lingering kiss on each wrist.

Warm fingers reached up to release the tie at his throat, before sliding a hand into his shirt to toy caressingly with the matted hair on his chest.

Through the agonizing pain that gripped him came a dawning memory of a long ago wedding night at Ashkirk, and an uncontrollable grin of remembrance captured his eyes and face.

Elizabeth witnessed this sudden awareness, and her eyes sparkled merrily. She pressed her warmth against him, and raised up on the bare tips of her toes, she slid her arms around his neck.

"Would you force yourself on a man who is not willing?" he asked in amused response to the game.

"You horny Highland knave," she whispered affectionately, " 'twas such a night you boasted of your prowess in the saddle. It would appear, my lord, this is one mare you lack the mettle to mount."

The tantalizing brush of lips and breath in his ear was the final enticement, and he grasped her to him, his lips claiming hers in a searing endless kiss that rendered them both breathless and gasping.

"Sweet bitch. Sweet, sweet bitch," he groaned with rasping breaths, as he covered her face and neck with quick, fervid kisses.

Elizabeth reveled in the throes of rapture at the feel of his arms around her and his warm lips on hers.

"Oh, Robert," she half-sobbed, "I love you so much. Can you ever forgive me."

His hands cupped her face as he gazed

down in wonderment at her glowing love.

"Forgive you? It is I who begs your forgiveness," he whispered fervently.

Her lips were on his and when finally they were forced to part, Elizabeth clung to him. Her arms encircled his neck and she buried her head against the broad chest.

"I have no shame—no pride, where you are concerned. There is nothing I would not do to be with you, my love. Had you not married me I would willingly have followed you anywhere, had you but asked."

Robert's arms tightened around her and he pressed a kiss on the top of her head before smothering a soft chuckle in the perfumed thickness of her hair.

"I was coming to get you, love, when Andrew found me. There was no force that could have prevented me from taking you home to Ashkirk."

Elizabeth leaned back in his arms and smiled up lovingly at him, tears glistening in her eyes.

"Home. Home to Ashkirk," she sighed contentedly. "I swear, my love, I will never leave those hallowed hills again. No matter where your sword takes you. I will wait for your return without complaint."

"Nae, love, never change. It is the Elizabeth you are now that I love—that indomitable, unpredictable, spirited wench that I wed. I seek no vapid, submissive surrogate in your stead. I want to watch the promising bud blossom into the full flower of womanhood, to watch my seed grow within you to bear the fruit of our love. There will always be quarrels between us, but there will always be our love to temper them. Oh, Beth, there is so much ahead for us."

"Robert, there is something I must confess," Elizabeth said contritely.

Robert put his fingers against her lips to halt her words.

"I have not been completely honest with you, love. There is one thing I have not told you. I am returning to Ashkirk to remain. I am laird of my clan, and long remiss in that responsibility. I never hope to raise a sword again except in the defense of Kirkmuir and the people who dwell there.

"David and Anne have a desire to sail to the Colonies, so I will free them to do so. You will wake each morn, Elizabeth, with your husband at your side, and our child growing within you need never wonder of his father away on some foreign battlefield."

Elizabeth's lovely brow creased in a frown.

"What is it, love? Does my news distress you? I thought you would be pleased."

"Nae, Robert," she declared fervently, "you have answered my nightly prayers—to know you are safe, to have you always beside me."

"Then what troubles you, lass?" he asked tenderly.

Her eyes rounded in beguiling innocence. Never had she seemed more adoringly appealing to him. She lowered her eyes and hung her head shamefully.

"I told a dreadful lie, Robert." Elizabeth faltered and he prodded her gently.

"Go on, love. What was it?"

"I am not carrying your child, Robert. I lied to my father, knowing he would have you wed me. I told you I had no shame where you are concerned."

For a few seconds Robert maintained an astonished silence. Then he reached out a hand and placed a firm finger beneath her chin, forcing her gaze to meet his. A slight twinkle of amusement was in the dark blue of his eyes as he grinned lovingly at her.

"You are a conniving, impossible wench, Elizabeth Kirkland, and I know not what I am going to do with you."

Elizabeth returned a smile that had become more impish than sheepish. Robert could not resist taking the adorable sprite into his arms. Elizabeth giggled gaily as he held her to him in a loving hug. Once again his lips began a play on hers, and breathlessly she pulled away and placed a restraining hand against his chest.

"What of father, Robert? How can I tell him it was all a lie—that I am not carrying your child?"

"You will have no need, my lady," Robert declared, his face alight with devilishness. "I promise before either of us leaves this room you will be carrying my child."

Elizabeth backed away from him, a hand extended entreatingly. Robert began to stalk her slowly across the room.

"Robert!" Elizabeth gasped, shocked and

entirely flustered, clearly indicating she would be no party to such an audacious scheme.

"Elizabeth!" he retorted mirthfully, entirely undaunted, clearly indicating he meant exactly what he said.

Reaching her, he pulled her to him, and with a roguish grin on his handsome face, the Earl of Kirkwood swept his Lady up into his arms.

EPILOGUE

June 1650

Jamie Kirkland squealed with delight as he sat astride the velvet-black stallion, secured in the strong arms of his father. The three-year-old's face was aglow with happiness when his father goaded the stallion to a run as they approached the barrier. The mighty steed, in a flawless exhibition of muscle and coordination, lifted its long legs and cleared the obstacle in a smooth and rhythmic leap.

"Please, Father, again?" he begged, as Robert Kirkland stepped down from the saddle, then lifted his young son into his arms.

The small lad's arms encircled his father's neck lovingly and the lad pressed a kiss on the bronzed cheek before Robert lowered him to the ground, reaching out a hand to slightly tousle the mane of dark curly hair.

"Now, off with you, lad. Go find your mother and sister," he ordered lightly, and fondly watched the youngster race down the hillside.

Robert Kirkland's eyes brightened with sudden pleasure at the sight of the man who stopped to pass a few words with the boy, before climbing the hills to his side.

"Pate Graham!" Robert exclaimed, and the two friends hugged each other with repeated pats to one another's backs.

Robert's smile was warm as he studied his old comrade in arms.

"I swear, Pate, you are getting older. Your step looked heavier to me."

The smile slowly left Robert's face when he observed the sorrow in Graham's dark eyes.

"What is it, Pate?"

Patrick Graham raised his head sadly and this time the pain was naked across his swarthy countenance.

"Jamie is dead, Robbie."

The initial shock of Patrick Graham's announcement was staggering to Robert Kirkland, and he leaned back against a tree groping for words.

"When, Pate? How?"

"The young fool came back to help raise an army to restore the young Prince to the throne. You know how badly Jamie took the death of the King. When they beheaded Charles, he vowed he would give his life to see that Charles' son would sit on the throne of Scotland. The whole scheme became a disaster. Jamie was betrayed and captured. Since there was a price on his head, Argyll and his puppets rushed through his execution."

"Who betrayed him?" Robert asked, his voice deadly and ominous.

"Neil Macleod of Assynth. Turned him over

to the Estates for thousands of pounds."

"That pathetic, quaking bastard!" Robert cursed as he buried his head in his hands. "Go on, Pate, let me hear it all."

" 'Twas not just Macleod that betrayed him. The young Prince withdrew his support at the last minute or the Estates might have been forced to show mercy. They would have turned down a personal request from the young Charles Stuart. As always, Jamie gave the Stuarts more than they warranted. His loyalty to them never wavered, even when the vultures were putting the noose around his neck.

"He might have done it this time, Robbie. Scotland has had all they can swallow of Cromwell. William Douglas had promised Jamie complete support, but everything went wrong from the beginning. Ships of mercenaries were wrecked or landed in wrong positions. Jamie needed Highlanders, and before he could rally any, he was forced to meet a superior force at Carbisdale and was defeated. From then on he was pursued."

Robert was astonished. "I didn't even know he had returned. Why didn't he come here?"

"He tried to get messages to you, but there was no way he could have come this far West; he was ill with fever himself. In desperation he sought help from Macleod and the bastard turned him over to the Estates."

"When was he executed, Pate?"

"On the twenty-first day of May in Edinburgh at Mercat Cross."

Patrick Graham looked up at Robert, eyes misting. "They didn't even give him the execution his rank warranted." Pate could no longer keep his composure and began sobbing with shuddering rasps. "They hung him, Robbie. They hung him like he was just a common criminal! Then they cut off his head and stuck it on a spike of the Tolbooth."

Graham's whole body became wracked with sobs. Robert went over and placed a comforting hand on his shoulder. Pate looked up, tears now flowing freely down his cheeks.

"That's not the end of the foul deed, Robert. They quartered him. They sent his precious limbs to be hung on a town gate at Glasgow, Stirling, Perth and Aberdeen."

Robert steeled himself not to break as Patrick Graham continued.

"The foul scurvy wouldn't even give us his torso to bury. This lad, who loved every grain of Scotland's soil, was denied the privilege of even being buried in it! Archie Napier's young wife was able to bribe one of the soldiers to get his heart. She vowed that it was the heart of the man that really was *The Graham*, and said she would die before she would see it become food to be thrown to the dogs."

Robert stood silently and let the Highlander vent his tears. When he felt Graham had finally composed himself, he asked him softly, "Were you able to speak to him before he died?"

"No, Robbie. They wouldn't let him speak to any of his relatives or friends."

Pate looked up with a proud smile. "He

died the way you would expect—dignified, composed, forgiving to the end. The whole crowd was in tears—even the hangman was crying. Jamie looked over them, calm as usual, completely unvindictive, and said, *I leave my soul to God, my service to my Prince, my goodwill to my friends, and my love and charity to you all.*"

Robert's hand pressed Pate's shoulder in compassion, two anguished souls trying to cope with the despair of their mutual grief.

"Jamie will never die, Pate," Robert said softly. "His memory will be an inspiration to any Scot whose heart swells with pride each time he holds his native earth in his hand. We will mourn the passing of Jamie because each of us will lose the benevolence he brought into our lives."

Robert studied the dejected figure of Patrick Graham and realized the poor man was completely drained, physically as well as emotionally.

"Pate, why don't you return to the castle to rest. You have had a long journey."

"Aye, Robbie, I fear the years are gaining on me much too swiftly." Without a show of haste he turned and made his way down the hillside.

After Patrick Graham had told her of Jamie's death, Elizabeth Kirkland had gone to the chapel to say a prayer and spend a few moments alone with her memories of James Graham. After servicing the needs of her guest, she had gone seeking her husband to offer him comfort. Upon seeing the beloved figure on the crest of the hill, Elizabeth let him remain undisturbed, knowing he had to have this time alone to say his own farewell to James Graham.

When the sun began to sink in the sky Elizabeth took a hand of each of her children and began to climb the hillside. Robert turned and studied the approach of his family. For a few brief seconds his mind freed itself from the torment of his grief and he found himself marveling at the beauty of his wife. Motherhood had only enhanced what had already been perfected by nature.

In the years since their return to Ashkirk, he had never known such complete happiness and contentment that he now shared with this exquisite and incredible woman.

Elizabeth paused at the top of the hill and the children scampered away. Robert opened his arms and wordlessly she walked into them. Her softness molded to him and her arms encircled his waist, transmitting all her love and compassion. At the feel of her in his arms, all the ache he was suffering began to drain from his body and he clung desperately to her, savoring the moment.

Elizabeth agonized in her need to comfort him. She knew the anguish he was suffering, the depth of his despair. She wanted to absorb his pain, to be able to take him in her arms and rid him of his torment.

"Oh Lord, Beth, he had so much to offer. Why did he sacrifice it all on the altar of Charles Stuart?"

Elizabeth's eyes glistened with tears as she remembered the passionate dedication and beautiful sensitivity of James Graham.

"He did what he thought he must, Robert. Are we to judge the wisdom of his act? I felt Jamie was a man that seemed to be driving himself toward his own destruction."

"Perhaps you are right, Beth. I have oft thought that he might have served Scotland more by directing his remarkable and sensitive mind toward the quill and not the sword. In this land of ours—afflicted with strife and turmoil—was there not the need for statesman as well as soldier? Would not Scotland have profited had Jamie's exploits been parliamentary rather than military? Ah, Beth, would he not have wanted to linger longer if he could have seen his beloved land with the people standing free?"

Elizabeth looked at her husband in wonder at this amazing declaration.

"I have always thought you believed in the merit of living by the sword, Robert?"

"Those of us without the gifted genuis that was James Graham are forced to do so. His needless death gives merit to that philosophy."

Elizabeth took his hand and brought it to her lips, pressing a kiss into the palm. "In the beginning I resented him so much, Robert. In my vanity I cast him in the role of rival and was jealous of the demands he put on you— demands which I myself wanted to inflict. I had to grow up, my love, to learn the nobility of the man I married, and in doing so I came to realize you could never have committed your trust and devotion to Jamie were he not worthy of it."

Elizabeth raised her eyes to his. Her face shone with a glowing radiance, her eyes mirroring the depth of her love.

"I love you, Robert Kirkland. Your existence gives me my life's breath, your needs my intent. Without your touch I would wither, denied your love I would die. I ask for no greater blessing than to spend the rest of my days at your side."

Robert's gaze worshipped her. He would mourn the passing of James Graham. He knew the pain of Jamie's loss would be slow in healing. But Elizabeth was here to help him; there was nothing he could not endure as long as there was Elizabeth.

He hugged her more tightly to him, his lips descending to claim hers in a tender kiss.

"Beth, love, I know not what I have ever done to be worthy of your love. But worthy or not, I will never relinquish it."

With a contented sigh Elizabeth turned and leaned back against him, his arms encircling hers, and they stood thus, watching their children cavort among the heather.

The stallion Olympus snorted loudly, drawing their attention to him. Robert's mouth nuzzled her ear as he whispered softly, "Do you remember the night he was born, love?"

A whimsical smile teased the corners of her mouth. "I remember every moment of that night."

Robert's arms tightened, drawing her

nearer. The tugging at his breeches interrupted any further pursuit of those thoughts. He looked down at his impatient son.

"Father, let me feed Olympus?" the lad pleaded.

Reluctantly, Robert released Elizabeth and reached down to pick up his son in his arms. He carried him over to the stallion and Jamie reached into a pouch on the saddle and withdrew some pieces of bread. Another tug at his leg caused Robert to peer down to find his two-year-old daughter reaching her little arms up to him.

Robert adored this tiny cherub, whose wide brown eyes were a constant reminder of Elizabeth.

"All right, little love," he crooned, as he picked her up with a fond smile and kissed her soft cheek.

"Now be careful and hold the bread the way I showed you," he cautioned.

Giggling, the two youngsters held out their hands, pieces of the dark bread in their palms. Olympus's large head swooped down and his huge jaws plucked his morsels from their outstretched hands in a repitition of an oft-played game.

"Oh, Father, it is silly to feed a horse bread," young Jamie protested.

"Now, now, youngster, don't scoff. It works! He hasn't lost a race yet!"

The words were like a poignant echo of the past, and for a few stricken seconds Robert halted his speech, forcing back the painful lump that threatened to choke him. Then, composing himself he turned and, carrying a child in each arm, started down the hill.

"Remind me someday, Jamie, to tell you about this dear friend of mine. He always fed his horse bread and ale."

The smile of relief on Elizabeth's face was coupled with love as she walked over and patted the horse. Nestling her head against the velvet mane she pressed her lips to its ear with a whispered sigh.

"He's going to be all right, Olympus. He's going to be all right!"

Author's Note

When my sister Liz and I began our collaboration on this novel, it was difficult for us to contrive a fictional hero when confronted by the reality of such factual ones as Colonel Magnus O'Cahan, General Alistair MacDonald, Colonel Nathaniel Gordon, and, of course, the remarkable James Graham, the King's General of Scotland. His brilliant and incredible achievements have made military annals. We have merely touched upon a few to give you an insight into his character.

For the reader, whose curiosity always extends beyond the final page of a book, the story of James Graham has a happy ending in its own ironic fashion. After Charles II was restored to the throne, Montrose was given the honor and recognition that his loyalty and dedication to his king had warranted, and all of his titles and estates were returned to his children.

Archibald Campbell, the First Marquis of Argyll, was beheaded for his acts of treason to Scotland.

Eleven years after his death, James Graham

was given a full military funeral and his remains are entombed in St. Giles Cathedral in Edinburgh.

Ana Leigh

BE SWEPT AWAY
ON A TIDE OF PASSION
BY LEISURE'S THRILLING
HISTORICAL ROMANCES!

UNDER CRIMSON SAILS

Lynna Lawton

Beautiful, spirited Janielle Patterson had heard of the reckless way pirate Ryan Deverel treated his women. He seduced them with the same abandon with which he plundered ships. To the handsome pirate, women were prizes to be won, used, and tossed away.

Ryan intrigued and repelled Janielle—and when they finally met, she was shocked to discover that her own nature was as passionate as the pirate's!

But while he was driven by desire, she was driven by a fierce hatred. Yet she knew neither of them would rest until she had surrendered to him fully.

LEISURE BOOKS   2002-5/$3.50

Thrilling
Historical Romance
by
CATHERINE HART
Leisure's
LEADING LADY OF
LOVE

Make the Most of Your Leisure Time with
LEISURE BOOKS

Please send me the following titles:

Quantity	Book Number	Price

If out of stock on any of the above titles, please send me the alternate title(s) listed below:

Postage & Handling _____

Total Enclosed $ _____

☐ Please send me a free catalog.

NAME _____
(please print)

ADDRESS _____

CITY _____ STATE _____ ZIP _____

Please include $1.00 shipping and handling for the first book ordered and 25¢ for each book thereafter in the same order. All orders are shipped within approximately 4 weeks via postal service book rate. PAYMENT MUST ACCOMPANY ALL ORDERS.*

*Canadian orders must be paid in US dollars payable through a New York banking facility.

Mail coupon to: **Dorchester Publishing Co., Inc.**
6 East 39 Street, Suite 900
New York, NY 10016
Att: ORDER DEPT.